I0574121

The only path out of destruction is through a nightmare.

WHEN THE SMOKE CLEARS

KAT EDWARDS

When the Smoke Clears
Copyright © 2023 Kat Edwards

All rights reserved.

No part of this publication in print or in electronic format may be reproduced, stored in a retrieval system, or transmitted in any form or by any means, electronic, mechanical, photocopying, recording, or otherwise, without the prior written permission of the publisher.

This is a work of fiction. Names, characters, organizations, places, events, and incidents are either the products of the author's imagination or are used fictitiously. Any resemblance to actual persons, living or dead, or actual events is purely coincidental.

Editing, design, and distribution by Bublish

ISBN: 978-1-647047-28-3 (paperback)
ISBN: 978-1-647047-27-6 (eBook)

This book is dedicated to all of us who have loved and lost
and to those who have been our butterflies in winter.

PROLOGUE

The runner's shadow, swift and agile as the wind, slipped along the sandstone cliffs beside her, spurring her on like a ghostly driver, over rocky ridges; under archways of massive oaks; and along the rim of steep, sheer ledges. *One, two, three, four; one, two, three, four; one* . . . She metered out her pace with the silent mantra that had always accompanied escape.

But there would be no retreat this time. She would face it now. While every fiber of her being cried out for her to turn around—to head back down the mountain trail, back to the warmth of her bed—she pushed on, her heart in her throat, her lips dry with fear.

As she summited the final plateau, the hills on either side of the trail fell away into the predawn darkness of the Santa Monica Mountains. In the distance, she could see the faint outline of the corral fencing, newly replaced, its freshly painted posts milky in the soft moonlight. The horses had not yet returned to Sycamore Ridge. They would still fear this place—this hallowed ground—where her world had ended. The smell of charred oak, heavy in the damp night air, even after all these months, still shrouded the pasture. She slowed then, stopping in the ankle-deep ashes—her breath in the cold night air floating up like a phantasmic cloud into the endless inky abyss.

And now she could feel it had been waiting for her. Something so unspeakably dark, more mournful and soul-crushing than she had dreamed. It seeped out of the shadows from every direction like a giant inkblot—like ashes spreading on the surface of still water—unfolding from the hollowed-out tree stumps that dotted the pasture, out from the void where the old barn had once stood, wrapping itself around her, holding her fast. She opened her mouth to cry out, but it was too late; the breath had already left her body, and her limbs were floating away like smoke in the wind . . .

CHAPTER 1

GRIEF IS A GHOST

Talia's eyes flew open to see the bright-red numbers of the bedside clock, glowing like embers in the darkness. Her heart pounded as if trying to free itself from her chest.

It was 4:15 a.m. *Oh no. Is it happening again?*

She threw the covers back and sat on the edge of the bed, gasping for breath. In the next second, she was on her feet, her shadow darting across the hallway into her five-year-old daughter Riley's room. Had the child called out in her sleep? It was expected now, the night terrors, the crying—ever since their world had been turned upside down.

The girl's room was cool and silent. The window was slightly ajar, and the dankness of fall seeped in like an unwelcome guest. Toby, the family's yellow lab, was lying at the foot of Riley's bed. He rolled his heavy head backward, giving a lazy groan as Talia leaned over him, trying not to step on him in the darkness. Balancing on one leg, she strained to drag the window closed with her outstretched fingertips.

Like most things in the house, the windows probably needed replacing.

She peered out of the shutters into the moonless night. A pair of tail-lights flashed on the street below, accompanied by the soft thwacking of rolled newspapers as they collided with neighborhood driveways. Of course.

It was just the paper delivery. That's what had woken her, saving her from the clutches of another nightmare. Would they ever end?

Talia tried to silence the thoughts, but the voices in her head had already started their maddening debate, and she knew there was no point trying to go back to bed now.

What had Russ been thinking? *Why take such a senseless risk?* Seven hundred and ten days had passed since the fire, and Talia was no closer to finding any reprieve. How could anyone expect to get a good night's sleep without answers, without closure? Whatever *closure* was.

In Talia's view, the term was just one of those senseless euphemisms that the untouched tossed about carelessly. It was a word meant to neatly file away unthinkable tragedies. An expression used by the same folks who thoughtlessly cast about labels like "next of kin" or "surviving family" without knowing just how deeply those terms cut. Surviving family. *Barely.*

Talia stood over Riley's bed, looking down at her sleeping daughter. She was curled into a tight ball, wedged up against her headboard, clutching a stuffed toy horse below her chin. She pulled the covers over her and kissed the child's silky dark hair. At least she was sleeping in her own bed now.

The dog stood out in the hallway, wagging his tail as she drew the bedroom door closed behind them. Then Toby led the way downstairs, heading toward the front door at a pace belying his robust girth. Talia made a mental note to supervise Riley's generosity with the "good-boy treats" a little more closely in the future and reached over him to let him outside. This took a while; there were three locks now, and somehow that still didn't quite feel like enough. The extra locks had not been a wise decision, though. *Think of the fire escape hazard,* she told herself, ripping the final lock open.

Talia and Toby walked side by side, striding past the towering oaks that stood like stalwart sentinels lined in formation along her driveway. Toby retrieved the morning newspaper and delivered it to her, every inch of his body wagging with self-adulation.

"Why, thank you, kind sir," she said quietly, taking the paper from him before he waddled off in search of the perfect spot to relieve himself.

Talia sat on the front steps of the house, facing the deserted street, basking in the predawn silence of her secluded neighborhood, Oak Ridge, composed of a dozen single-family homes, nestled in the foothills of the Santa

Monica Mountains just a few miles east of the Pacific Ocean in Southern California. The residents—her neighbors—were mostly working families and a few retired folks.

The front lawn was a canvas of glistening dew shimmering between patches of fallen oak leaves. She studied the contrast in the tapestry of light and shadow as if examining a Rorschach test, looking for meaning, a spark of promise in the pit of despair that still called to her. She pulled the collar of Russ's old robe up around her neck and tucked her feet in underneath her, as if wrapping herself in a comforting blanket. *A blanket of Russ.* She wished it still held his scent. She would have to let that foolish desire go; it was too heavy to carry now.

She drew in a deep breath and sighed, reminding herself that there was a certain ease in having no expectations. A liberty from wanting or wishing. A freedom from the ache of shattered hope. The crisp, cool silence of dawn made for a comforting sort of purgatory after all. By now she was accustomed to floating in that void between night and day, sleeplessness and nightmares, stillness and turmoil. Even now, she could feel the darkness, crouched like a beast behind her back. Waiting.

Toby explored the shadowy recesses of shrubbery alongside the house— far beyond the reach of the porch light—no doubt scouting for rabbits again. The clear night sky overhead was a kaleidoscope of bright stars—each one a tiny candle in the boundless cathedral of Talia's grief.

After a while, the heavens began to glow in the east, as if a giant brushfire loomed just over the horizon. Talia sat with her arms wrapped around her knees and her head thrown back, watching the tiny stars fade one by one as the inky darkness retreated.

And then the silence broke, and the birds began their morning salutations, as if all were well again in the world. And for some people, Talia supposed—other people—perhaps all was well.

Talia turned on the automatic coffee pot and made her way to the bathroom, where she listened to the pot's dripping and spluttering as she tied up her hair.

Her ponytail was almost the length of Riley's now. It had grown faster than she had expected. She leaned over the sink, cupping handfuls of warm water over her face.

She gripped the porcelain rim for balance, thinking back on the night after Russ's funeral—almost two years ago—when friends and family had vacated the house and left her there alone. In retrospect, she never should have been by herself that night. She was not of clear mind in those hours when she took a pair of scissors and stood in front of the vanity, chopping off her long chestnut curls as close to her scalp as she could manage. She remembered the locks of hair falling to her feet softly, like petals peeling away from a dying rose.

And why not? Some cultures shaved their heads as a sign of mourning. Perhaps the ritual would be cathartic in some way. Maybe while growing her hair back, her heart might also mend. Perhaps the act had been more about guilt than about grief. When she thought about it now, she couldn't quite remember which she'd felt more.

Her bald head had solicited glances of consternation in the following weeks from strangers and loved ones alike. But she'd never felt compelled to explain herself, the decision she'd made to chop it all off in one fell swoop. She owed no one that much of herself. She was entitled to grieve—and more, to express her rage over losing Russ—in any way she chose. As it was, at the funeral earlier that day, her bitter, unchecked emotions had been laid bare for everyone to examine. Hadn't she sobbed like a child? Hadn't Russ's colleagues had to hold her upright when her own legs refused to obey? There was nothing left to hide now. There was no need to pretend anything at all was normal. *She* was certainly not normal.

The chime on the coffee pot in the kitchen signaled that her morning brew was ready. Talia finished washing her face and patted it dry with a slightly crunchy hand towel. It smelled suspiciously as if Riley had used it to mop up an apple cider spill somewhere on the kitchen floor. Life was full of sticky surprises these days when no one was really keeping house. Her priorities were different now. There were too many things to take care of.

Talia headed down the hallway to appease Toby, who was pacing energetically in hopes she hadn't forgotten it was time to feed him. She filled his bowl with dog kibble, the pellets ringing out like hail on a tin roof while he swayed from side to side in anticipation.

Then she poured herself a mug of coffee and pulled a chair up to the kitchen counter, where she unfolded the morning newspaper, dated October 8, 1997. She scanned the headlines absently, doing her best to block out her growing doubts about having scheduled an appointment with a grief counselor that morning at 10:00 a.m.

Russ's chief had been the one to refer Talia to Dr. Cohn. The fire department's insurance policy would cover eighteen sessions, he had told her.

"There's no sense in letting all that free advice go to waste," he had prodded. Talia had wondered what was so miraculous about the number eighteen. Could simply talking about losing Russ eighteen times make it all better?

"Take the card, Talia. You need it."

Talia doubted that Chief Graham knew what she needed, though she couldn't blame him for trying to help in whatever way he could. After all, in those days, her shaved head must have looked like a desperate cry for help, despite her intent being just the opposite. She had hoped to isolate herself. No, not just isolate. More than that. She had wanted to *ostracize* herself.

"Thanks," Talia said, forcing a smile, but as soon as the chief had turned his back, she folded the business card in half and stuffed it into the coin pocket of her blue jeans. It surfaced again, weeks later, when Riley was frisking her impatiently for a stick of gum. She'd tossed it then into a drawer at home where she kept receipts and other loose paperwork.

That's where she found it, on that morning, the morning when she finally had to admit things had gone too far. Seeking help was no longer an option; it was a requirement—if she didn't want to lose Riley too.

Dr. Cohn's business card had been sitting in the drawer next to the receipt for Talia's new running shoes. She had frantically searched for that receipt to prove to herself that it had been only a day previously that she'd purchased those shoes. She *needed* that proof. Even though it would ultimately confirm what she most wanted to deny—that *yes*, she posed a danger to both herself and Riley.

She'd been terrified that day—only a week ago—truly shaken to the core.

She had just come home from dropping Riley off at kindergarten. She sat on the garage floor to slip on her new running shoes for a quick trail run. She'd purchased the shoes just the day before. She was hoping they would prove to be as comfortable as the last pair of the same model—she'd put countless miles on those. They had held up well, but it was time for a fresh pair. Talia opened the new shoebox and peeled back the tissue paper, expecting to see a clean pair of white and green running shoes, but instead she pulled out a pair covered in ash, their scarred and rutted underbellies black with charcoal. She sat in confusion for a moment, staring at the soiled shoes and their dusty laces, trying to make sense of what she was seeing. Weren't these her new shoes? The ones she hadn't worn yet? *What was going on here?*

She'd rushed into the house then, throwing the box of shoes onto the counter. She ripped open the kitchen drawer. The receipt was there, right on top of the pile of other papers—takeout menus and appliance warrantees. And yes, the date of purchase was clearly marked—it *had* been only yesterday. How was that possible? Had the salesgirl at the store inadvertently put a pair of old shoes into the box instead of Talia's purchase?

And then it all came flooding back, crashing in on her. Her nightmare, her terrifying ordeal, running up to the horse corrals at Sycamore Ridge the night before. It *had* been a dream, hadn't it? Her stomach dropped. She felt sick with fear. Surely, she would have remembered leaving the house in the dead of night. She would never have left Riley alone at home. *Oh God, it is happening again,* she'd thought. Her hands were shaking when she fished Dr. Cohn's card out of the drawer and dialed the number.

The golden rays of dawn flickered like flames between the swaying birch trees in the backyard, bringing a soft glow to the kitchen window where Talia sat sipping her coffee. Next to her, Riley's kindergarten artwork hung from the window latch by a piece of braided yarn. It was a small picture of Russ in his firefighter's uniform she had framed with cardboard and decorated with rainbow glitter. Most of the glitter was gone now. They had both kissed it away over the months.

Angel dust, Riley had called it.

"We need more angel dust, Momma," she'd said one morning, standing barefoot on a kitchen chair in her Snoopy pajamas, holding Russ's picture by its frayed string. It struck Talia then that her daughter—a five-year-old child—was telling her what they both needed to feel better. In moments like that, she felt so inadequate as a parent, so lost, so incapable of filling the void in their lives. But then again, she'd never dared believe that she would become a single parent—that she'd do this, one day, without Russ.

It seemed now that her worst fears had come true.

Talia sipped her coffee, exhaling through her nose. *Things are not going well without you, Russ. Look at me now. I've finally gone over the edge.*

She glanced at the clock on the oven range. The second hand ticked over rhythmically, in perfect synchrony with the dripping tap in the kitchen sink that she hadn't bothered to have fixed. As she sat at the counter—the bitterness of coffee on her palate, a jumble of dread and hesitation percolating relentlessly at her core—Talia had to be honest with herself. Was she *really* going to make that therapy session at ten o'clock? Why would she want to invite the light to shine on those dark places of pain? And could she even risk letting it slip that she was sleepwalking again—inadvertently leaving her five-year-old daughter alone in the middle of the night? As someone who had spent the last ten years of her life as a social worker, Talia already knew the answer to that question. And as a victim of her own traumatic upbringing, she would be the first to agree: crazy women don't make good mothers.

It was clear she was in over her head. It had all just become too much—even for her. She was broken now—officially broken. She would keep the appointment, but she would have to be careful. There were things that could never be shared, truths that should never see the light of day.

CHAPTER 2

THE DEVIL'S BREATH

Talia stood before the offices of Drs. Saul and Eleanor Cohn, located on the edge of town, at the end of a string of single-story brick buildings in an industrial park that she hadn't even known existed. Despite her abysmal navigational skills, she'd arrived with ample time before her ten o'clock appointment. Ironically, this was an instance in which she would've welcomed getting lost and showing up late—or better yet, not showing up at all.

And yet here she was. Miracle of miracles, she hadn't lost her way.

Russ had always been so good with maps and directions. Like all firefighters and first responders, he had possessed that enviable skill and knew the approximate location of any given address in town. She felt that pang in her belly, the feeling that seemed to say, *Yes, he's really gone forever.* She tried to choke it back and down and away. It was always the little things she missed about him that stung the most.

The flagstone walkway before her meandered through the belly of a perfectly manicured lawn. Nearby, Talia spotted the patient work of a maintenance man raking away the golden fall leaves, as bright as lit matches, cast off nearby birch trees. It'd be a few weeks yet before the trees would rest for winter, embracing the cycle of life. They were a reminder that there was a time for everything.

How brave they were, casting off their leaves and trusting the process like that. If only she could be that trusting. Talia coached herself along the walkway, emerged before the brick building's wisteria-shrouded entryway, and finally ventured in. *Best to rip off this Band-Aid.*

"How may I help you?" An entirely too-chipper redhead beamed from behind the front desk. The waiting room's decor felt pretentious and forcefully optimistic, with expensive faux leather sofas, too-bright windows, and an enormous vase of fresh flowers from the most exclusive florist in town.

"I . . . " Talia looked over her shoulder again at the empty waiting room.

"Are you Ms. Brighton?" the young woman asked, flashing a perfect white smile. "If so, Dr. Cohn is able to see you a few minutes early. It's her policy to give new patients a little more time than what's on the schedule."

"How charitable," Talia managed flatly.

"Her office is just that way." The receptionist gestured to the door to the right of the front desk—a pricey fashionable walnut. "I've been in touch with your insurance provider and am aware this session is covered, so feel free to exit through the back door and call us for a follow-up appointment when you're ready."

Oh, that's funny. They expect me to be crying when I leave, hence the back-door exit. Clearly, they don't know they're dealing with Talia "No Cry" Brighton.

"Thanks," Talia said almost breathlessly, edging toward the door to the right, which opened to an office that was as quiet as a tomb. *A fitting place for the internment of grief,* she told herself, trying to explain her growing unease. The stillness of the office was finally broken by Dr. Cohn's self-introduction as she swiveled around in her armchair. Talia did her best to look comfortable and not at all like a canary in a coal mine as she made her way to an oversize recliner. The French doors behind Dr. Cohn's cluttered desk faced a shady courtyard with a cobblestone patio surrounding a small pond. Talia caught the vivid flash of golden koi as the fish darted between the lily pads. The sky between the oak trees shading the patio was bright and clear, testimony that the maddening Santa Ana winds had already begun to usher in the fall as they did each year in California.

Dr. Cohn sat across from her in a high-back chair, her legs crossed at the ankles. She was armed with a notebook and pen, which Talia thought the woman held rather like a sword and shield. She reminded Talia of someone, but she couldn't make the connection.

Dr. Cohn was slight in build—hardly more than a hundred pounds. Talia suspected that she was a woman of discipline, both professionally and personally, considering the fact that she was not only a doctor but also undeniably very well put together. Too well put together, perhaps. She couldn't help but wonder if Dr. Cohn was compensating for something. After all, wasn't everybody?

The woman was dressed in a knee-length gray pleated skirt and a crisp white blouse with tiny, square mother-of-pearl buttons. They were almost exactly the color of her silver hair, which she wore as straight as a pin and neatly cropped above her collar. She was poised on her padded perch with impeccable posture and the laser focus of a bird of prey.

"Welcome," Dr. Cohn said at last. The small woman looked up from the notepad, where she'd been jotting something down. *God knows what. Surely there wasn't anything to report just yet.* "Before we begin our session, I'd like to cover a few things . . ."

For the life of her, Talia couldn't focus on what Dr. Cohn was saying. Every detail of the office seemed to scream artificiality. The lack of family photographs on Dr. Cohn's desk and the deliberate color choice of pastel-yellow paint. *Wasn't that shade scientifically proven to make people feel happier?* And worst of all, Dr. Cohn's glasses, which kept slipping farther down the slope of her nose with every mumbled word. Talia's hand itched to reach forward and shove them back into place, and she practically had to white-knuckle the armrest of her chair in order to avoid acting on the impulse.

"Do you have any questions, Ms. Brighton . . . or may I call you Natalia?"

Talia's focus snapped back into place like a rubber band. "Oh, I . . . just plain Talia is fine, actually."

The resigned neutrality of Dr. Cohn's expression suggested she realized that Talia hadn't heard a single word she'd just said. "Tell me a little about yourself."

She cleared her throat, which was growing tighter by the second. "Well, I have experience as a social worker, but I'm not really working right now." It hadn't been Talia's plan to go into any detail about her prior work life in Los Angeles, but for some reason, she'd started the description of her current situation there. Perhaps to delay getting too personal, or perhaps to portray her-self as a professional peer, she'd opened that door first. True, her past career had taken an emotional toll, one that could have justified intense therapy all on its own, but clearly, there was more to her than her professional past, and there were certainly far more reasons for seeking counseling now. Like addressing her insufferable lack of sleep, for a start. The distant traumas sur-rounding her role in social work were pretty much irrelevant these days, but she'd set the stage, and now it appeared Dr. Cohn was expecting her to elabo-rate. After an awkward moment of silence, Talia added, "I'm currently doing a little volunteering, twice a week for a women's shelter in Ventura . . ."

Dr. Cohn didn't look up. Talia wasn't sure if she should go on. Apparently, she'd started on the wrong foot altogether. Her time in counseling was going to be limited. She had finally made the appointment, and kept it, and sud-denly she realized, even though she was stalling in order to avoid more risky subjects—like the growing doubt in her own sanity—she did want to get something useful out of the endeavor.

"And before that? You were working where?"

"I worked full-time in Los Angeles," Talia offered. "Before . . . before . . ." To her surprise, the rest of the sentence caught in her throat, and she thought her voice might crack. "Before the fire. Before my husband's death."

Dr. Cohn peered at Talia over her silver-rimmed spectacles but said noth-ing. Her clear eyes were inscrutable. Something seemed out of place. The oppressive silence in the office seemed to collapse in on Talia like a muf-fling avalanche. Perhaps she'd become so accustomed to the condolences and reflexive sympathies of strangers regarding her loss that the doctor's cur-rent lack of response to her revelation seemed completely shocking. Not that she'd come in search of sympathy—that would not have been a productive venture. Still, *any* reaction after taking that leap might have been more reas-suring than the poker face gazing back at her now.

The doctor sat silently, staring at the notepad resting in her lap, as though she wasn't sure what to write down. "I am very sorry to hear about your husband's death," she said at last, and again, Talia felt herself struck by the doctor's reaction—specifically, her blunt usage of the word *death*. Everybody else seemed inclined to sugarcoat things by saying, *I'm sorry for your loss*, or *I'm sorry for Russ's passing*.

Death felt final. Death *was* final.

And after such a long pause before speaking, she knew Dr. Cohn had to have chosen that word deliberately. Strategically, even. Talia wasn't sure if she should be wounded or outraged or thankful—thankful that somebody else finally acknowledged the gravity of it all. Someone who knew euphemisms were inadequate—insulting, really.

Talia impulsively twirled a lock of hair that had escaped her ponytail. Working with Dr. Cohn would be heavy, even brutal.

Of course, Dr. Cohn wouldn't feed her the fluffy, sentimental approach her friends had over the last two years. She'd take a pickax and start plumbing the depths of Talia's despair like a miner in search of coal. What unsettled Talia now was that her notion about grief—that once buried, it should not be exhumed—was clearly at odds with Dr. Cohn's intent.

Talia began to realize just how much she'd buried—starting with the guilt she felt about Russ's tragic last minutes and ending with the fact that she sometimes heard his voice in the house at night. Or that twice now, she'd been sure she had caught a glimpse of him standing in the shadows near the woods where she went for her morning runs. And now, most concerning of all, proof that she was sleepwalking again.

Dr. Cohn tapped her notepad softly with her pen, bringing Talia back.

Again, distant memories stirred, like the broken threads of a half-remembered dream. Who was it that Dr. Cohn resembled?

The woman's brows furrowed in a way that struck Talia as unreadable. "I know this may be hard to talk about, Talia, but could you tell me more about how not working in your chosen profession has affected you?"

About how not working in my chosen profession has affected me? What about the senseless, tragic death of my husband I just mentioned? Where are the questions about Russ and the fire? What about how Riley is coping or how I'm barely holding it together as a single parent?

Talia stared back at Dr. Cohn, openly puzzled. Annoyed, if she was honest. Yes, she'd clumsily led with a disclosure about her past career—wanting to establish herself foremost as a professional peer rather than as a raving lunatic—but she wasn't in a hurry to explore that aspect of her life any further. There was no need to educate anyone, let alone a practicing psychiatrist, on the horrors of social work in the big city.

But then again, maybe Dr. Cohn's methods were beyond Talia's understanding. Maybe she was skilled at seeing through well-built emotional walls.
Wasn't it worth her time to at least try Dr. Cohn's way? Talia considered the
question earnestly. How did she feel about not working? Well, what choice
did she have? She was a single parent now, and she wasn't about to put Riley
in day care.

"I have other obligations now. Being a good parent is obviously
my focus."

Again, Dr. Cohn did not respond, not even to Talia's slightly affronted
tone, nor did she look up from her notes. The silence pervaded in an odd adul-
teration of civility. After a while, it became irritating. Talia wondered if she
was failing some sort of test. Was she obliged to break the silence?

"To be honest," she finally blurted, "I couldn't possibly handle the stress
of full-time social work right now. I have more than enough on my plate." The
words tumbled out carelessly, making her look weak and perhaps betraying
the fact that she wasn't coping as a parent. For the first time since the session
had started, Talia thought she saw a flicker of curiosity in Dr. Cohn's eyes.

"Tell me more. I'm listening," she said. Talia's stomach dropped. If she
was honest, she was barely keeping her chin above water when it came to
raising Riley. "You must have some feelings about walking away from your
professional life. Do you intend to return to work?"

Talia almost laughed out loud with relief. Dr. Cohn seemed to have
entirely missed her self-indictment in the parenting department. Now she was
completely flummoxed.

"I don't understand why it matters," she retorted, flushing with frustration. Dr. Cohn's eyebrows elevated in surprise. "Why does my career *matter*,
Dr. Cohn? Before losing Russ and before becoming a single parent and struggling with that trauma on a daily basis, sure, my career was a priority for me,
but I'm not that person anymore. I'm not the same. *Nothing* is the same!"

Dr. Cohn nodded in a way that said, *Now we're getting somewhere.* "This
is going to be a process, Talia. We will be examining more than just the loss
of your husband if we are going to get you back on track."

This was the most telling remark Dr. Cohn had made during the visit
so far.

What did she mean about getting Talia back on track? Had she already given the impression she'd been derailed?

The room seemed to be shrinking, closing in. Again, Talia thought of her bedside clock that morning, those bright-red numbers screaming 4:15 a.m. Another night of fragmented sleep and nightmares. Another night of fearing she might leave the house while sleepwalking, abandoning Riley. All those locks on the front door. What good had they been?

"With all due respect, Dr. Cohn, the only process I'm currently interested in is getting my insomnia under control. My lack of sleep . . ." Her throat tightened, but the words slipped out anyway. "It's driving me insane. Sleep is really all I need help with today."

"Driving you insane?" Dr. Cohn inquired neutrally. "Are you being hyperbolic?"

"Doesn't sleep deprivation drive people crazy? Isn't it used as a form of torture?" Talia asked, trying to distract from her confession and move on. "As I've said, my priority is parenting my daughter—and I can't do that effectively without sleep."

It was more than just a lack of sleep, and Talia suspected they both knew it, but something held her back from exploring her biggest fears outright: What if she *was* losing her mind? What if that put her daughter in jeopardy? Riley was the only thing in the world that still mattered to her.

Dr. Cohn lapsed into silence. Talia busied herself surveying the office as she waited uncomfortably for Dr. Cohn to go on, knowing that the woman was no doubt deftly calculating her next line of inquiry. It was very quiet. Too quiet. Where was the other Dr. Cohn? Saul, was it? The partner who shared the office space, according to the plaque on the front door. Maybe he was chattier than Eleanor. Maybe he was somewhere on the green, swinging a golf club on a day of truancy with his colleagues, leaving his wife to the cold business of staring at her patients in silence.

"What I'm getting at, Talia," Dr. Cohn finally broke in, and when she did, it suddenly dawned on Talia who the woman resembled—Sister Mary Ignatius, a particularly villainous character from her early childhood—"is how your identity might have hinged on your professional role."

Now that Talia saw Sister Mary Ignatius in Dr. Cohn, the resemblance was too uncanny to ignore. "And?"

"And losing that sense of life purpose may be affecting your self-image and the belief in your own ability to cope with your reshaped circumstances. Does that seem possible, Talia? Do you feel that you might have also lost yourself since your husband's death?"

"Yes." Her words tumbled out without permission. "I haven't just lost myself—I have effectively lost everything."

"And how does that make you feel?"

"Well, that's a no-brainer, isn't it?" Talia snapped, voice shaking. After a few breaths, she realized there were more respectful ways she might have responded. She could have said she was predictably grief-stricken, numb, perhaps even despairing and hopeless. But in truth, none of those labels described how she felt anymore. "Resentful."

Dr. Cohn nodded in a way that suggested Talia had given the right answer—an honest answer.

And it *was* honest. Talia resented the metamorphosis she had undergone since losing Russ. Instead of being a respected, trusted professional in her department and a member of an intact, loving family, she had been reduced to a part-time volunteer, an insecure single parent, and a questionably sane widow.

And the sad truth—the glaring truth—was that she felt entirely powerless to change any of it. In the past, she'd managed the stressors of her profession with well-honed expertise. The more chaotic things became at work, the better she could manage them. She'd had the reputation of someone who always looked after everybody else. Except when it came to Russ, that was. Russ had been such a great partner, a perfect match for her. He was the one person she deferred to in her personal life, and the only person she would lean on when it came to raising Riley.

Dr. Cohn committed another note to the pad. "Resentment for unforeseen and tragic life circumstances is perfectly normal. From what I understand, however, it's been almost two years since your husband's death. Were you resentful from the beginning? Or has the sense of resentment grown along with the passage of time?"

"I'm not sure," Talia admitted. "In the beginning, I think I was focused only on maintaining some semblance of normalcy for our daughter."

It sounded so responsible when she put it that way. But in reality, her behavior in the first few months after Russ's death hadn't been healthy at all. There had been the head-shaving incident, for one, and to be honest, she'd often found herself counting the hours each day until she could put Riley to bed. Mainly to find a little peace and quiet for herself. She'd been desperate for a reprieve from her grief. No, from her guilt.

And Riley hadn't made things easy. Perhaps she had been picking up on Talia's angst. Her bedtime became a nightly struggle for both of them. And then there were the everyday insults that cut to the bone—the ones that made Talia's heart race and her mouth dry up. Seeing a couple strolling hand in hand through the mall, or even a TV commercial featuring an intact family, could set her off. She'd made some progress since those early days, but the gains had seemed to plateau, and now . . . well, now she was at a loss.

"So," Dr. Cohn went on, reeling Talia into the present moment, "it was your dedication to your daughter, Riley, that kept you going. What did Riley's life look like before the death of her father?"

"After Riley was born, Russ and I worked opposite days, so one of us was always at home to look after her. Often this meant working extra-long hours, but the schedule allowed us to have two days off together every couple of weeks."

"And since your husband's death, you've taken to volunteering part-time?"

"Yes, volunteering provides a little bit of a distraction for me, and I don't have to commit to anything permanent—or suffer the commute to LA. Fortunately, Russ's life insurance policy paid off the house," Talia added quietly, feeling as if using the word *fortunately* in that context was atrociously disloyal. "I refuse to put Riley in full-time day care. She's in kindergarten now for a few hours a day. It's a private school, so the fees are quite high, and I've taken out a small loan to help cushion the financial blow." She couldn't bring herself to mention that the modest income she received from the city as a part of her survivor benefits wasn't nearly enough, making the loan itself unavoidable.

"So finances aren't my biggest worry." Talia's voice trailed off as her mind swirled with the chaos of her daily life. Since Russ's death, she'd lost the ability to be objective. The smallest of her concerns seemed on par with her biggest worries—and there was so much to fret about.

Russ would have told her not to worry about things she had no control over. "If it's out of your hands, Tal, it should be out of your head," he would say. But it wasn't out of her hands, was it? *Everything* was in her hands now. How often should she set the lawn sprinklers to go off? Five minutes twice a day or ten minutes once a day? Did the house need a new roof or a new coat of paint first? Had she put aside enough for property taxes this year? The list was endless, but above all else, Talia's biggest fears involved her ability to be present for Riley.

What if something happened to her and Riley was orphaned? This wasn't an irrational fear, as Talia herself had been orphaned as a small girl. And now that Riley had been unlucky enough to lose one parent, she could just as easily lose another.

Dr. Cohn quietly eyed Talia over her notepad. "What does your daily routine consist of?"

A harmless question, Talia mused, realizing she would be able to run out the remainder of the session without the risk of self-indicting blunders. But before she could launch into a summary of a regular day in her life, Dr. Cohn added, "Do you have any regimen to alleviate your anxiety?"

"Running has been a lifesaver for me," she offered casually. "After Russ's death, my daily routine used to include a good run through the foothills of the Santa Monica Mountains, between home and the beach. I find that when I run regularly, I'm less likely to suffer from migraines, which is a bonus. I suppose it's an effective means of alleviating anxiety, too, though that wasn't always at the forefront of my mind in those days."

"Is it at the forefront of your mind now? Do you still run?"

"I do still enjoy running," she replied, dodging the first question and the implication that she was battling anxiety. Despite her chronic lack of sleep, a cup of coffee and a brisk morning run fueled Talia for a day's challenges like nothing else could. After an hour or so out on the mountain trails, she would usually return home feeling renewed and relaxed. Talia couldn't help but notice Dr. Cohn's puzzled expression. She realized, of course, that most people would not understand a love of running. Some would even think it masochistic. Only another long-distance runner could appreciate the benefits gained from floating along for miles at a time, feeling weightless and worry-free.

Dr. Cohn's next inquiry brought Talia back abruptly. "So what is it, Talia? What have you been running away from all these years?"

Talia's eyes jumped to the clock on the wall. She was relieved to see that Dr. Cohn had posed the question at the very end of their session. "Well, that's an interesting question." Talia forced a smile, pushing back at the insinuation. In case Dr. Cohn had missed her first cue, she pulled back the sleeve of her sweater and consulted her watch.

"Shall we schedule your next appointment, then?" the doctor finally suggested.

On her way out of the office—taking the back door, the way the receptionist had offered—Talia said she would call and schedule after referencing her calendar. Dr. Cohn, seemingly unconvinced, replied only by eyeing her over the rims of her precariously perched spectacles, which set Talia on edge. She could still feel the woman's gaze on her as she crossed the courtyard and headed toward the parking lot. The wind was picking up. It was a hot, dry wind—the kind that cruelly whipped loose strands of hair around her face, threatening to make her eyes spill over. She hated the Santa Ana winds— the devil's breath—the winds that had, in a raging wildfire up on Sycamore Ridge, swept away her world and robbed her of Russel.

CHAPTER 3

A SISTERHOOD OF TEARS

Talia drove her old pickup truck across Westway Street and turned onto the two-lane overpass just as the booms were lowering and the flashing red lights signaled the approach of a cargo train. She cursed softly, checking her watch. For once, it would be her turn to be late for a lunch date with her sister. Normally, that was Naomi's privilege. The multi-engine train rumbled past her. *Clickety-clack, clickety-clack, clickety-clack.*

Well, no sense in fretting. There was nothing she could do to speed up her commute now. Besides, she'd probably end up arriving just as Naomi was pulling into the parking lot of the Rising Sun, her favorite lunchtime haunt.

Talia suspected their conversation would revolve around either Naomi's latest failing romance or her other favorite obsession, the dating sagas of her sixteen-year-old daughter, Tory. Talia didn't mind which. Either would be a welcome change of topic. For once, they wouldn't be focused on her own issues. Perhaps she could even avoid disclosing that she'd finally broken down and gone to counseling that morning. If she made that admission, Naomi would no doubt want to know what had changed her mind, why she had finally budged on the topic. She wasn't about to get into any details on what had finally cracked her. That would only worry Naomi, and Talia knew her sister was well past due for some intense therapy of her own. As children, they had shared a lifetime of trauma. As adults, they consequently held the same perspective on seeking outside help: it was to be avoided at all costs.

In front of Talia the cargo train sped by. *Clickety-clack, clickety-clack, clickety-clack.* Her mind raced back through time.

She was three years old, looking out the window as the train snaked its way through the Australian countryside on a winter morning. She knelt on the padded wooden bench while five-year-old Naomi sat across from her. Their aunt was seated beside them in the small private cabin, and Talia could still recall the scent of her pungent perfume. The floral print of her skirt, her stockinged legs crossed at her thick ankles. They say children don't remember that far back, but that's not true. Some things are never forgotten.

Talia gazed out the window, trying to distract herself from her older sister's sobbing by studying the green meadows and rolling hills of eastern Australia. As an adult, she realized that they must have been on their way from Brisbane to Melbourne, but as a child, she didn't really grasp where they were going. Naomi's crying finally subsided, though she still huffed in sharp gasps of breath, and her nose and eyes still oozed with grief.

Aunt Miriam looked up from her knitting. "Blow your nose and stop that sniveling, Naomi, unless you want to upset your little sister again."

Naomi broke her gaze from the window, looking with renewed concern at Talia. She untucked her hankie from the sleeve of her white cardigan and, with a clenched fist, wiped the sticky remnants of sorrow from her face. Talia, who hadn't uttered a word in days, fixed her gaze on her older sister with curious uncertainty. Naomi did her best to smile, though her quivering lips refused to cooperate.

Talia's gaze shifted slowly between her sister and her aunt. *Where is Mommy?*

Try as she might, she couldn't recall an image of her mother's face. She could only summon the soft, warm scent of her—the scent that would wash over her when her mother cradled her on her lap, singing her a lullaby. The soft clicking of Aunt Miriam's knitting needles conjured the gentle noise of the long pearl strands Talia's mother would wear around her neck. The same strands that Talia used to wrap her fingers in as she was rocked to sleep.

"Where's Mommy?" Talia finally asked. Aunt Miriam looked up from her knitting, mouth forming an *O* that suggested she might speak but then saying nothing. Naomi crossed her forearms on the tabletop in front of her and lowered her head to them, trying hard to bury the sobs that were rising again, despite her best efforts.

Having received no response to her question, Talia perched on her knees and shifted her attention to the passing landscape beyond the confines of the cabin. The green meadows gave way to hillsides of long yellow grass and rocky ledges that whipped by as the train sped along its tracks. An old gum tree standing alone in a field like a scarecrow waved its arms about in the wind, as if to warn of some danger ahead on the tracks.

Talia told herself that it didn't matter if Mommy was gone; Naomi would look after her.

Earlier that day, in fact, Naomi had done so by holding Talia's hand when they got on the train so that she didn't fall onto the tracks and get cut in half by the wheels—which Aunt Miriam had said might happen if they didn't pay attention. Talia remembered Naomi's warning: "Train wheels are as sharp as knives, especially when they're going fast."

Now it was Talia's turn to cry—not because she missed her mother, or because she and Naomi were being taken away from Grandad, but because her stomach ached with hunger. Aunt Miriam had told her earlier she couldn't have anything to eat because she might vomit on her best dress again—which wasn't fair, she thought. She didn't do that on purpose; it was an accident.

At the sound of Talia's soft whimpering, Naomi raised her head from the tabletop and did her best to distract her little sister before Aunt Miriam noticed she, too, was now crying. She cupped her hands against the window, fogging up the pane of glass with her breath. With her finger, she drew heart shapes and daisies on the misty surface. Talia watched quietly as Naomi cleared the windowpane with her sleeve, fogged it up again, and drew a new picture of the two of them. They were small stick figures with big heads, wearing triangle-shaped dresses. Between them stood a larger figure, holding their hands. *Mommy.* Her face was as happy as the sun, and she was smiling like a daisy.

Suddenly Naomi stopped drawing and jumped to her feet. She pointed wildly at the train window, tapping the glass excitedly. "Look, Talli! Look at all the horses!" She laughed with delight. "They're beautiful, just like Grandad's herd. There are so many of them!"

Talia stood up on the seat and put her hands on the window, straining to see the animals. She loved horses, more than the cattle dogs on Grandad's farm or even the fluffy baby chicks. A herd of horses surged over the hilltop above the tracks as the train approached a wide bend. They were beautiful creatures, and they were running very fast. There were more horses than Talia could count, and for a moment, she wondered if Grandad had sent them to fetch her. Had he come to stop the train and take her back home?

"They're just brumbies," Aunt Miriam said with a snort, only bothering to glance out the window for a moment before returning to her knitting. "Sit down, Talia. Little ladies don't put their shoes on seat cushions, especially when the cabin floor is so filthy."

"But she can't see if she sits down," Naomi replied softly.

"Wild horses aren't much good for anything but dog food and the glue factory. Nothing but a nuisance to the farmers," Aunt Miriam replied curtly.

Talia didn't know what a nuisance was, but she was sure she would like it. Sometimes Aunt Miriam called her a nuisance too.

As predicted, when she sat down, she couldn't see the horses—but Naomi offered to let Talia sit on her lap for a better view. After she scrambled onto her sister's legs, the two of them watched four men on horseback rise over the hillside, behind the "brumbies," in aggressive pursuit. The herd swerved this way and that, trying to break away from the men and the rifles they held. A big gray mare led the way. Her mane and long tail were white; her belly was as round as the full moon. The girls knew this meant she was carrying a foal. She pounded at the earth with her hooves as she veered to the left and then again to the right, tearing up the tall grass as she hurtled past boulders, skirting the steep drop-offs, only to find herself hemmed in by the approaching train.

Even from afar, Talia and Naomi could see the mare was spooked and didn't know which way to run. The men on horseback pointed their rifles into the air, and the noise they made was so loud it could be heard above the train's rumble. Aunt Miriam looked up again. Her expression had changed from contempt to attention.

The big gray mare tossed her head furiously and darted away from the men with their rifles. Her eyes were wild with fear as she hurtled blindly toward the train. The herd followed. Talia could only think of the danger of the train's wheels and how fast they were moving and what they might do to the beautiful horses—what they might do to the mare, with her big belly, and the foal she carried.

"Stop! Go back!" Naomi yelled as she jumped up, rolling Talia off her lap, and stood on the seat.

This time, Aunt Miriam offered no objection to shoes on seat cushions, and Talia scrambled back into her original place, kneeling on the cushions for a better view. Naomi pounded the window with her fists, screaming at the horses to turn away from the train, but the herd kept coming, faster and faster, their mouths frothing with panic, their eyes peeled in terror.

Aunt Miriam rose quickly to her feet, joining the girls at the window. The cabin rocked back and forth, and she tried to hold herself steady by grasping the overhead wooden rail with both hands. Her knitting fell to the dusty, filthy floor.

Suddenly everything went pitch black.

The terrible wail of the train whistle pierced Talia's ears. She was going to be sick again.

Above the noise, Naomi was screaming in the darkness, and Talia braced herself for the impact of the train slicing through the herd. Her mind filled with thoughts of dog food and glue and what that stunning gray mare might look like in the wake of the train.

She squeezed her eyes shut against the darkness and cried out with Naomi, "Stop the train! We've got to stop the train!"

It was then that Aunt Miriam shouted over the din, her wavering voice betraying her own panic. "Girls! Girls! It's only a tunnel. For goodness' sake, it's only a tunnel."

Talia's gaze snapped back, and suddenly she wasn't on the train anymore.

A semitruck behind her honked wildly. The red lights had stopped flashing, the boom gates now elevated and out of the way. Reflexively, she punched the gas pedal, tires shrieking, and zipped ahead in the direction of the Rising Sun.

Her heart hammered against her ribs—from both the memory and the semitruck's rude awakening but also from something more. Though she couldn't quite pinpoint what.

Talia followed her sister as Naomi brusquely directed the hostess at the Rising Sun to seat them in a specific booth in the back of the restaurant. Normally they would have sat at the east-facing counter, which had the best view of the lake and didn't get too hot in the afternoons, but today, apparently, Naomi needed privacy above all else. A quick glance at Naomi's out-of-control hair and uncharacteristic dress suggested that today, she wasn't at all the glamorous woman who usually outshone the rest of the Westlake socialites at lunch. Today Naomi King was not the woman who turned heads as she strode by with the fluid grace of a supermodel.

Today her head hung low, veiled by a hood of dark curls. When Naomi reached the back of the restaurant, she surveyed the room over the top of her sunglasses before removing them.

They took their seats in a booth and remained quiet for the first few minutes while waiting for their drinks to arrive. Talia watched curiously as her sister poured several packs of sugar into her iced tea and then stirred it noisily with her chopsticks, refusing to meet her eyes. There was clearly a storm brewing.

The best move was to remain quiet. This was something Talia had gleaned from years spent in social work—and with a pang of comprehension, she realized she was doing exactly what Dr. Cohn had done during their session earlier that day.

Sitting patiently and silently, waiting for information. And Talia had hated it.

She cleared her throat. "Well, how bad is it this time?" Talia ventured, doing her very best to sound respectfully concerned and not the slightest bit patronizing.

"Oh, I'm sure you'll think I'm blowing it all out of proportion." Naomi's voice betrayed a flicker of sarcasm, a warning for her sister to proceed with caution.

Naomi locked her dark eyes on Talia. They were almost as black as the mass of thick curls that cascaded over her slender shoulders. Like the night sky, like deep space, they embodied a captivating sort of mutual exclusivity—the sense of being so full and so empty, all at once.

They aptly represented Naomi's personality, Talia decided right then, reflecting on how Naomi had never had trouble establishing relationships but somehow always struggled to keep them. She could be charming until you crossed her, and when that happened, she was not one to soon forget a grudge. Naomi couldn't really be blamed, though—not after everything she had been through. When she was angry or upset, her entire demeanor changed, as if she lived with two totally different people inside of her.

Talia's early memories of Naomi were of a carefree child with a big smile and an easy laugh. Things had changed over the years, however. Time and troubles had cast their patina on Naomi's once-shiny countenance, leaving indelible stains that clouded the lives of those in her orbit. Talia had watched helplessly as Naomi morphed from a gentle, sweet girl into a jaded and cynical woman. She didn't know all the facts about Naomi's personal life, but some of her sister's adult decisions had made little sense to her. On occasion, they seemed nothing short of masochistic. In her most self-destructive phase, Naomi had walked away from her husband, John King—the only man who had ever treated her with any respect—and proceeded to invite a cadre of toxic men into her life. These choices had further enforced her sister's cryptic and pessimistic worldviews, much like a self-fulfilling prophecy.

The waitress arrived, took their lunch orders, and departed again, leaving the pair in an extended silence that Talia had little patience for.

"Okay, sis, what's going on?"

Almost at once, Naomi's demeanor shifted in a way that conveyed a sense of total resignation. She leaned back in her seat, blinked the threat of tears out of her eyes, and cupped her mouth with both hands.

"What is it?" Talia added gently. "Tell me what's going on."

"Tory is a good kid," Naomi began, starting with the necessary disclaimers. "She's so responsible, and I don't think she would keep anything from me, but John is giving her too much freedom. Ever since the divorce, he's given the girls everything they want. He never says no, which, of course, means that I'm the one who gets to play bad cop."

Naomi's marriage to John had lasted twelve years, far longer than Talia ever would have imagined possible. Before John, Naomi had been engaged four times to a string of controlling and abusive men. In some ways, it had been the same relationship played out four times. They had all been such similar men: wealthy, cocky, and selfish. Somehow, though, Naomi had always come to her senses and broken off the engagement at the last minute. For some reason, John had been different. She had been comfortable with him—for a while, anyway. Inevitably, though, Naomi had called it quits. That was what she did. Apparently, the love and satisfaction had slowly receded from her marriage after two children and a series of affairs with a few of her colleagues and clients in real estate.

As far as Talia could tell, John still adored Naomi. The couple had remained friendly—close, even—over the years since their split. John treated Naomi with the same respect and tenderness he showed their two daughters, Tory and Elizabeth. If Naomi ever needed anything, John was there for her in a heartbeat. He was a patient man, a good man—slightly boring but a good man. Talia was glad that John was still peripherally in her life too. Riley was crazy about her uncle John-John.

Neither Naomi nor John had remarried. They still spent holiday gatherings together so that their girls didn't feel they needed to choose one home over the other. Only time could tell how things would turn out for them, but Talia secretly hoped they would reconcile. John was good for Naomi. She was not sure her sister realized this, nor was she sure that Naomi was any good for John.

Naomi ran her fingers over the tabletop absently, as if erasing a defect in the varnish. She looked up just as tears began to brim in her eyes. Her chin quivered a little.

"Tory wants to live with her dad," she said, picking up her napkin and pressing it firmly under her eyes, catching the mascara that had already begun to free itself from her long lashes. "And that's not all," she added, the tears now flowing freely. "I'm pretty sure Elizabeth does too."

Talia found herself holding her breath. She was at a loss for words. She couldn't think of anything that wouldn't poke the proverbial bear, triggering the land mine that was her sister's temper—or worse, reveal that she'd been expecting this news for some time now. It had always been clear that the girls were much closer to John than they were to their mother. Nevertheless, Talia knew the realization would be painful for Naomi. She reached across the table, resting a hand on her sister's arm in an effort at consolation, but almost as quickly as Naomi's tears had started, they stopped. She recoiled from Talia's touch and did her best to smile.

"Fine by me, I guess. Hey, if my home's not good enough, let them have at it! We'll see how long it takes before John needs to start playing bad cop. Ha! Maybe I ought to say, 'Sure, go ahead, but you can't come back home once you leave.'"

Talia sat back. Things were getting dark. How did Naomi expect her to respond to that? Did she expect Talia to cheer alongside her, rooting for her daughters to regret their choices? She did her best to steer the conversation in another direction. "I wonder what Tory's thinking. What could have sparked this decision?"

The ploy backfired almost instantly. Naomi's mood seemed to plummet as she tossed the crumpled napkin she'd used to dab her eyes moments ago onto the tabletop. "Oh, I know exactly what it is. She wants to go to the homecoming dance with that kid, Taylor—the one from the wrestling team. I told her in no uncertain terms that she was not going, and I will not permit her to date a senior. She's only a sophomore; it's out of the question!"

Talia tried to hide a sigh. Her niece's request was a reasonable one. It was a totally normal expectation for a sixteen-year-old to start dating. Of course, she didn't mention this to Naomi. She could see her sister wasn't ready to hear it, even though the dance was just around the corner. Talia knew Tory had designs on attending. The girl had already begged her to broach the subject with her mother. Talia couldn't let Naomi know that, of course. She was sure Naomi would find it disloyal that her daughter had felt more comfortable talking about it with her aunt than with her mother.

"Ah, she'll come around, sis," Talia said optimistically. "I think she's probably just feeling pressure from her friends, who are all most likely dating already. Right?"

Naomi shot Talia a look—a look that suggested she'd already said too much.

Talia grasped at options to lighten the mood. "Seriously, though, Tory's so tall. And that Taylor kid is—what? Like, maybe five foot two." She threw in a giggle for effect. Sixteen-year-old Tory was almost her dad's height of six feet. The wrestling star would have made a comical match for her, but apparently Naomi saw nothing humorous in the scenario, leaving Talia scrambling, but she was coming up empty.

Thankfully, the waitress arrived, depositing the salad she'd ordered before her. Talia stared down at the plate of radishes, sprouts, and cabbage. Naomi broke her silence as she pulled out her compact mirror to check her makeup and reapply her lipstick. She clearly had no intention of touching her lunch.

"How's Riley enjoying school?" To Talia's relief, Naomi seemed to want to change the subject—or maybe she was just working at being less self-centered for once.

"Great!" Talia said enthusiastically as she washed down a bite of her salad with a mouthful of tea. "She's digging it. She loves the activities and all the other kids. She's very much a social creature, and being an only child has been hard on her. She seems to be thriving in all the commotion that is kindergarten. I think it's been good for her."

At this, Talia discreetly checked her watch. Forty-five minutes before school let out.

Naomi had given her an opening to move on to another topic, but she could tell her sister was still mulling over the prospect that her daughters would be less supervised under John's rules, and Talia knew this would cause Naomi angst.

"I wouldn't worry too much about Tory," Talia added, carefully choosing her words. "She's such a sensible kid. It will all sort itself out. You'll see." Naomi seemed to soften at this, and Talia seized the moment. "Honestly, you and John have provided beautifully for your girls. They have had wonderful role models, lots of love, a good focus on the importance of education . . .

nothing but the best. I don't think you need to be concerned that Tory will get herself into boy trouble. She doesn't know what you've been through personally. I know that must weigh on you. History can't repeat itself if your girls don't know your past." At this point, Talia knew she was on thin ice, but she also knew that if she didn't say it now, while Naomi seemed open to feedback, she might not get the opportunity to ever vocalize it.

Naomi leaned her elbows on the table and rested her chin in her hands. The light had gone out of her eyes. She was staring straight through Talia, as if she wasn't there. It was ominous, a sign pointing to the likelihood of everything falling apart if Talia didn't get straight to damage control.

"Look, you and I made plenty of mistakes as youngsters," Talia added, trying to engage her sister again. "Who could blame us? We didn't have a chance. We had no one to guide us, to protect us from ourselves. Your girls are not like we were. They're loved."

If Naomi heard her sister's words, they didn't register on her face. Her mind was a continent away, as though revisiting an episode from a lifetime ago.

Talia's brows furrowed. "What are you thinking?"

"Remember that train ride when we were girls?" Naomi began. Talia's blood ran cold. "When we thought the horses, spooked by ranchers, were going to get hit?"

"I . . . " For some reason, she couldn't bring herself to admit she'd thought of just that memory on the way to lunch. "Vaguely."

"And do you remember where Aunt Miriam took us after that?"

"The orphanage," Talia replied quietly. Naomi's eyes blazed in the way only hers could, and Talia was sure she wasn't there anymore—no longer in the restaurant or sitting with Talia or ignoring the plate of now cold tempura sitting before her—but back in time.

Back at Saint Mary's.

Talia's first recollection of the orphanage involved her and Naomi holding hands, cast in the shade of an awning. They stood beside a stone-and-plaster building encircled by a cobblestone walkway.

Talia and Naomi had been dressed in matching peach-and-white floral dresses that were wrinkled from the long train ride. The front of Talia's outfit—to her horror—still bore the dried remnants of her regurgitated breakfast.

Naomi held on tight to her younger sister's hand. A tiny old woman, eyes enormous behind a pair of thick spectacles, emerged from the building in a long white dress. "You girls, wait there," she directed, pointing to a nearby bench. The old woman's voice was commanding for such a small person. Talia glanced up at Naomi and gave her sister's hand a tug.

Naomi leaned over, and Talia whispered, "She looks like a kookaburra."

The girls giggled but obediently took their seats on the bench. There, they had a better view of the building, which had a large sign on the front that Talia couldn't read. "What does that say?" she asked Naomi, who then looked up, squinting against the midmorning sun.

"It says 'Saint Mary's Orphanage for Girls,'" she replied pensively.

"What's an orphanage?"

Talia could hear her aunt talking with the old woman through the open door; they spoke freely at first. Talia was sure she heard Aunt Miriam mention her mother's name and then something about her grandad.

The chatter paused for a moment while Aunt Miriam poked her head out of the office door to remind the girls to remain on the bench. She pulled the door partially closed then, making it difficult for Talia to follow the rest of the muted conversation. She wrestled her hand free from her sister's and tugged at the growing hole in her white tights, where her scraped knee poked through bloodied threads. Earlier in the day, she had stumbled when getting off the bus from the train station, and her bruised kneecap still throbbed.

Talia thought she heard Aunt Miriam say something about the family's "trus fun." She didn't know what a "trus fun" was, but it was clear that it had nothing to do with fun. It was something Aunt Miriam and Grandad argued over regularly. At the thought of Grandad, Talia's eyes welled up with tears. When would she see him again? When was the next time he might read her a bedtime story or push her on the swing he had made for her near the barn?

It was then that she started getting restless on the bench.

Naomi seemed to fear that she couldn't convince her little sister to remain obedient to the old woman, so she began singing nursery rhymes. Somewhere close by, church bells tolled. Their deep tone resonated across the cobbled courtyard and then faded away as the distant sound of children laughing and shouting rose over the surrounding walls.

After a while, the kookaburra lady and Aunt Miriam came out of the office together. Aunt Miriam walked past the girls without saying a word. Her knitting bag swung rhythmically at her side, like a metronome keeping time to a march. Her low heels clicked loudly on the cobbled walkway as she passed under a row of jacaranda trees alongside the far wall of the compound. She did not turn to look back at the girls.

A quiet resignation settled over Talia as she watched her aunt's stout form disappear through the courtyard gate and out into the busy street. Next to Talia on the wooden bench, Naomi began to wail loudly—not in the same way she had cried when they had lost their mother. Not with helplessness or crushing sorrow but with the raw, unchecked fury of a wild animal caught in a steel trap.

"More iced tea?" The waitress seemed to appear out of nowhere, jarring Talia and Naomi back to the present moment.

Naomi blinked, swallowing hard. She used her napkin as a tissue and asked for a to-go box for her untouched meal. Talia leaned over and placed a hand on Naomi's forearm. She could see her time to break the spell of Naomi's despair was running out.

"As I've said," she reiterated quietly, keeping her tone even, "our kids have had something we never did: a safe, loving home. Tory will grow up one day to be grateful for your vigilant guidance, even if she's too young to recognize that now—and the same goes for Elizabeth. Don't hold your daughters' immature whims against them."

Naomi sighed. "If that Taylor—"

"If he does anything to Tory, there will be hell to pay," Talia interjected with a smile, afraid of her sister setting off on another tangent. "And most importantly, Tory will learn her lesson. Sometimes in order to learn, we've got to learn the hard way, right?"

Talia watched her sister's lips purse, blocking out a smile. "Like mother, like daughter."

It was too dangerous to agree with that statement, so Talia resisted the urge. Instead, she lowered her voice a little more and added, "I'm sure they'll miss their time with you if they move in with John—and that's a hard *if* because there's still a chance they won't. Either way, treasure every moment with them in the interim. Time with those we love is priceless."

Talia's final sentence dropped like a bomb, so charged and heartbreaking that Naomi would never dare argue against it. With a deep breath, Talia sat a little straighter, knowing she had, for once, said all the right things in exactly the right order. And now they were free to explore far less turbulent topics of conversation.

The rest of lunch was spent talking about how the real estate market in town was doing, and when Naomi finally got around to asking Talia how she'd spent her morning, she offered a premeditated lie. "The same as always, really. Took care of Toby. Read the paper. Took Riley to school . . ."

At that, Talia's heart nearly skipped a beat. Again, she checked her watch.

"Everything all right?" Naomi asked, brows raised.

"Yes—I've just gotta run," Talia said, standing suddenly. "Riley gets out in ten minutes."

"Oh, that's right. You better get going. Traffic . . ." Naomi said, glancing out the window, as if to forecast the status of the roads.

"Hey, I have a favor to ask," Talia added, trying to make her request sound like a passing fancy rather than a desperate plea, a ploy to ensure that should she leave the house again while sleepwalking—at least until she had another safeguard in place—Riley would not be left alone. "Do you think Elizabeth would mind visiting this weekend? Maybe she could spend the night? You know, it would be good practice for her. She could learn some babysitting skills while I'm supervising. Riley would absolutely love that. Someone to play tic-tac-toe with and someone besides me to read to her."

"Sure, I'll ask her today after school," Naomi agreed. "She's old enough now, and with Tory always out on the weekends, I'm sure she'd jump at the chance."

Talia pulled her wallet from her back pocket, took out a couple of bills, and put them on the table, only for Naomi to shove them back into Talia's hand. "Thank you for meeting me," she said, standing to hug her sister good-bye. Naomi had been making a killing in real estate over the past few years and usually insisted on picking up the tabs for their shared lunches. But today, the gesture felt like something more.

"Of course. Anytime." Talia managed a one-armed hug, more of a pat on the back than anything else. An image of Naomi at the orphanage as a little girl rose up, still so fresh in her mind's eye as to feel real. Talia missed that sweet little girl. The girl Grandad had always called their butterfly in winter. But that Naomi had disappeared years ago.

CHAPTER 4

A CALL FROM AFAR

Riley sat next to a potted orchid on the bench seat of the family's old pickup truck, swinging her legs and singing along with a *Sesame Street* tune as Talia drove her to a late-afternoon karate lesson. Ballet hadn't exactly worked out for her, but she seemed to be thriving in her new martial arts practice. Talia was happy to have found an outlet for her daughter's seemingly boundless energy.

"How was your shaved ice?" Talia asked, glancing over at Riley's blue-stained lips. It was Wednesday, which meant after-school shaved ice. The pair had a tradition for most days of the week: Thursday was their library day, and on Fridays, they would go to the lake to feed the ducks. Talia tried to keep her daughter's days full. Sometimes it helped them both forget how much they missed Russ.

Riley nodded with a grin, and Talia returned her focus to driving. Yesterday—Tuesday—used to have a tradition as well, back before the fire. As a family, they would go up to Sycamore Ridge to pet the horses boarded there. They didn't venture over that way anymore. Talia didn't trust herself to walk on that hallowed ground for fear it would break what was left of her. For fear there would be some telltale sign of the hell it had been for Russ.

She pulled into the parking lot and escorted Riley into the dojo—a room as loud as a carnival and steeped in the pungent odor of bare feet. "I've got an errand to run, kiddo," she said, kneeling down and gazing into her daughter's eyes. "I'll be back by the time your lesson is over, all right?"

Riley nodded. Talia leaned over to kiss the top of her head but missed completely as Riley bounced away, barefoot, across the mats in the direction of her classmates, her ponytail swinging energetically behind her.

Hilltop Manor was only a few short blocks away from the dojo. Talia pulled into the nearly empty parking lot of the nursing home—another Wednesday tradition—just after four o'clock, easily securing a spot at the very front of the building.

Five years earlier, Aunt Miriam had joined the residents there after a stroke left her paralyzed and unable to speak. At the time of her stroke, she had been in her late sixties—a relatively young woman to have had such a catastrophic blow to her health. She had been living in Seattle, just a few blocks from Talia's paternal grandparents, when she collapsed in the garden one Sunday morning.

Russel had insisted at the time that Talia owed her aunt nothing. Naomi had agreed. She hadn't seen Miriam in years, and she was adamant that she wanted nothing to do with the woman. But Talia had felt obligated—on two fronts—to take care of her mother's sister. First, she hadn't wanted her paternal grandparents up in Seattle, who were kind to a fault, to feel they had any obligation to oversee her care or check on her, as they no doubt would have. Second, Talia was a social worker, and it was her job to take care of people— even people who might not have appeared deserving. In the end, Russ had agreed to help Talia transfer her aunt from a rehabilitation hospital in Seattle down to California and to a nearby nursing home.

Talia sat in her truck for a few minutes, engine turned off, staring at the asylum-white double-story building confronting her. There were only three occupied parking spots outside of hers, and she thought those likely had been taken by staff, not visitors. Was it that some families lacked the patience to witness the cruel tricks time played on their loved ones?

Here we go again. As the commercial says, "Just do it." Talia took the potted orchid from the seat, got out of her truck, meandered up the cracked sidewalk to the front of the building, and pushed through the swinging glass doors of Hilltop Manor. She tried to hold her breath for as long as she could— her record for doing so was to the end of the hall, where only a hint of cafeteria food and the stale scent of the elderly still hung in the air. Eventually, she'd have to breathe, of course, but she put it off for as long as humanly possible. This time, she made it all the way into the elevator.

Talia punched the button for the second floor, hitting it two or three times before it registered. The ascent was slow and jolting, the jawlike doors grinding open at last. Old people in various stages of undress were secured in wheelchairs in the hallway.

Senility and dementia had taken many hostages on the second floor. Some folks cried out to Talia as she passed along the corridor, as though she might somehow free them from the confines of the place. Others shuffled along, using their walkers or canes, as if on a conveyor belt heading toward the ends of their lives. Where they were going, it was impossible to say.

Some of the residents were trapped in bodies with failing vision or hearing—and others, like Aunt Miriam, were unable ever to give voice to their thoughts or needs. As she made her way to Miriam's room, Talia spotted a shriveled-up old woman with a bent spine and gnarled fingers fumbling with the top button of her sweater. She stopped briefly to help, and the woman smiled back at her as if recognizing a long-lost friend, resting her clawlike hand on Talia's in an expression of open gratitude.

Talia walked faster down the hall toward her aunt's room, suppressing the urge, as she always did, to turn and head for the exit. This place affected her similarly to the prisons and children's hospitals she'd visited as a social worker—places devoid of joy and filled with dread. How many times had Hilltop Manor conjured memories for Talia of Saint Mary's Orphanage for Girls?

She turned the corner and found Aunt Miriam's room. The door was open, as though her aunt were soliciting visitors. She felt a wave of guilt. Miriam's door was always open like this, and yet she only visited once a week on Wednesdays. Six days out of the week, that door sat open in futile hope.

She peeked inside, knocking on the open door to be polite.

"Hello?" she asked, even though Miriam wasn't able to answer. "It's me, Talia . . ."

She entered to find Aunt Miriam propped up in her bed by a pile of pillows with a pink shawl over her shoulders. The woman's hands were drawn up under her chin, the rest of her body bent into a crooked question mark.

She looked closer to a hundred years old than someone in her seventies. Her mouth was slightly agape, pale-gray eyes staring at nothing. She stirred when her niece entered the room, her slow gaze tracking Talia from the doorway. Dr. Frankel had said Aunt Miriam was aware of what was going on around her but that she was imprisoned in a body that could not serve her with self-expression or communication. At first, Talia had felt that her aunt's preserved consciousness, and the fact that she could still see and hear, was at least some good news.

But at every visit since, including now, Talia realized that her aunt's condition must be torture for her. A living hell. Perhaps it would've been a mercy for Aunt Miriam to have lost her mind too.

"I brought you another beautiful orchid for the window. I thought it might brighten the place a bit since the last one has lost all its blooms."

The old woman grunted something inaudible in response. She looked paler and more exhausted than usual—if that was even possible. Talia had no real way of knowing if her aunt's utterance was a sign of appreciation or ire or even one of confusion. *Do you even know who I am anymore?*

Talia placed the ceramic planter of mature white orchids, their blossoms hanging like heavy bells, on the windowsill. She did her best to smile as she pulled up a chair to the side of the bed. The woman made no effort to look at her.

"It's a nice day out there. They say we'll get another wave of warmer temperatures over the weekend," Talia said, leaning over and straightening the collar on her aunt's bedjacket. "Riley's really enjoying her new karate lessons. She'll be up for testing for her yellow belt soon."

Miriam coughed. It was a deep, rattling cough—the kind that deserved concern. Talia rose to her feet, looking down at the frail woman, and reached for the bedside pitcher of water, then gently raised a glass to her aunt's lips. *Even death after her stroke might have been a kinder outcome. What a terrible life.* But Aunt Miriam had always lived a terrible life.

Talia found herself holding her breath as she recalled Saint Mary's Orphanage for Girls—specifically, the memory Naomi had triggered at lunch just that afternoon, when she'd overheard Aunt Miriam talking about a "trus fun." Of course, she'd grown up to realize that it was a trust fund of which they spoke, and she suspected it would have been sufficient to have improved

Naomi's and her life greatly if they'd ever received the gift that Grandad had intended for them.

But they later realized it was likely that Miriam had misappropriated those funds. Talia suspected, though, that her aunt had never imagined she'd spend the remainder of the family fortune on her own convalescent care.

Only last week, Naomi had pointed out how ironic it all was that Aunt Miriam had ended up alone and confined in the prison of her own body after she had been the perpetrator of the girls' institutionalization at Saint Mary's all those years ago. Naomi was still obsessed to no end with Aunt Miriam's moral inventory, it seemed.

Talia took her seat again, staring at her aunt's vacant eyes, listening to the rattling of her breath. *Yeah, to be honest, I can't say I really blame Naomi. I want to scream sometimes too.* Talia regretted not being more persistent when her aunt had still been capable of providing answers. It was all too clear now that if Miriam had been waiting until the twilight years of her life to come clean about what had happened all those years ago—to Talia and Naomi's parents—it seemed she had been robbed of that opportunity by her stroke. They had all been robbed. As Talia saw it, Aunt Miriam was a vanishing bridge to the family mysteries. Nevertheless, she was now a vulnerable old woman and still family. That left only one option—compassion. There was nothing Talia could do now but make sure the woman was cared for, despite there being no chance of a deathbed confession and regardless of where the funds for her care had come from.

The old woman's body shook violently as she coughed again and then drew in a long, slow breath—as though it might be her very last. Talia sprang to her feet once more, leaning over her aunt, concern clouding her face. Finally, the rattling in the old woman's chest subsided. Talia guessed that Miriam was probably facing the last months of her life. Looking down at her frail, crumpled form, she realized that somewhere in there was a person she had never really understood or been able to love.

Miriam stared past her niece as though looking into another dimension, one that the cognizant cannot enter. As Talia gently raised the drinking glass to her aunt's lips a second time, the woman placed her shaking hand over Talia's. Her eyes drifted toward her niece's face. Her lips closed in a crooked grimace as she swallowed awkwardly, her chin bobbing back and forth in an attempt to stem the inevitable stream that dripped from the corners of her mouth. For a second, she locked her gaze on her niece. If Talia hadn't known better, she would have sworn there were tears welling up in the old woman's eyes.

There was a quick knock on the door then, and one of the nurses poked her head into the room.

"Ms. Altman? Natalia Altman?"

"Yes, that's me," Talia answered, though she was a little puzzled. Altman was her mother's family name; she hadn't heard it used in years. "I'm Talia, but it's Brighton now. Who's asking?"

She hadn't seen the nurse before. The young woman offered an enthusiastic handshake, and Talia could immediately see that she fit the mold for the institution. The staff at Hilltop Manner was the highlight of her visits to see Aunt Miriam. She admired their unyielding devotion to the elderly in their care. Perhaps their dedication assuaged her own feelings of guilt, to some degree as they offered more of themselves to her aunt than Talia ever could.

"Lynn Banning, RN." The young woman beamed. "I'm a new graduate, just started here on Monday. Pleased to meet you!" She then motioned energetically for Talia to follow her into the hallway. She didn't speak again until they were both outside of Miriam's room and the door had been pulled closed behind them. "There's a phone call for you from Australia, a Mr. Bergelsohn—I just love his accent. He called yesterday and on Monday, too, looking for you. The desk staff told him you usually visit on Wednesday afternoons. They were reluctant to give out your home number. You understand, of course. Mr. Bergelsohn says he's an attorney and has some urgent business to discuss with you. They're eighteen hours ahead of us in Australia."

"Would it be possible to have the call transferred to my aunt's bedside phone?" Talia asked.

"Well, I did think of that, but your aunt got so agitated yesterday when I mentioned Mr. Bergelsohn had called, I really didn't want to risk it again today. The nurse on the night shift said she refused to be fed dinner and didn't sleep a wink. She was still so upset this morning that the day nurse had to call Dr. Frankel and get him to order a tranquilizer for her."

"Oh, all right," Talia replied, brows furrowed. *Is this man someone Miriam knows?* "Where can I take the call instead, then? Downstairs?"

"The nurses' station," Lynn clarified, already waving her down the hall-way. "Follow me."

The nurses' station was a busy glass-walled hub where the chatter of the staff was so loud Talia had to put a finger in one ear while holding the phone receiver to her other. Mr. Bergelsohn sounded very old. He also sounded quite excited to have finally reached her. Talia could almost hear his smile as she reassured him that he had indeed reached the granddaughter of Josif and Esther Altman of Brisbane, Australia.

"Are you in touch with your sister, Naomi, my dear?" Mr. Bergelsohn queried. Talia found the question odd, but she confirmed that she and her sister were close.

"You're probably wondering why I've been trying to contact you. Let me first reassure you that I was both legal counsel and a very close friend to your grandfather, Josif." The man on the other end of the line cleared his throat and then added, "For many, many years. He was like a brother to me."

"Is that so?" Talia asked, intrigued.

"The law firm that Miriam—your aunt Miriam, that is—hired in Seattle years ago, when she first emigrated to the US from Australia, has recently contacted us. They have been taking care of her legal issues, and it's their understanding that your aunt is in a declining state of health and that you are currently seeking guardianship over her affairs."

There was an awkward voice delay on the long-distance line, so Talia listened patiently, not wanting to interrupt Mr. Bergelsohn with any ques-tions until she knew where all this was going. It was true—she'd taken care of her aunt's health and personal business ever since her stroke but had only recently sought to gain legal guardianship.

"There shouldn't be any problem," he explained hurriedly. "There will be some routine paperwork and that sort of thing." The man then went on to clarify that the guardianship issue wasn't why he was calling. He wanted Talia to know that he was in possession of some legal documents from her grandfather's estate that she would need to see soon, given the current cir-cumstances. He sounded almost breathless as he added, "I believe these doc-uments will be of great interest to you and your sister."

His tone took a serious turn, and Talia found herself waving her hand at the nurses who were at the station, indicating she needed them to quiet down a little so that she could hear the man on the other end of the line. She didn't know exactly what Mr. Bergelsohn meant by the current circumstances, but she trusted he was referring to her aunt's failing health. When he spoke again, his voice cracked a little, surprising Talia. Was it regret she heard?

"I'm afraid I'm not long for this world myself, dear girl . . . cancer of the pancreas. My time is quite limited." His voice was heavy with resignation. "Not long now, they say. It's spread to the lungs, you see. I've already outlived the prognosis."

Mr. Bergelsohn went on to tell her that his grandson, Ari, was a full partner in the law firm and would be contacting her soon. For reasons she couldn't explain, Talia felt she could trust Mr. Bergelsohn. Something in his voice had been reassuring, even familiar. Perhaps it was the Australian accent or the way he called her *my dear* that kindled a memory of Grandad.

Finally, Talia found her voice again. "My condolences for your condition, Mr. Bergelsohn. I'm glad you tracked me down. I look forward to hearing from your grandson, Ari."

"He'll be in touch as soon as confirmation of legal guardianship comes through. You can have full confidence that Ari will take care of whatever is necessary to get your affairs in order. I've briefed him on everything that needs to be handled."

My affairs in order? What affairs?

"If you were a friend of my grandfather's, I know I can trust you, Mr. Bergelsohn. Thank you. Let me give you my home phone number and address so that you can reach me more easily."

Talia hung up the phone, more curious now and feeling something else too. Deep inside her, a tiny flicker of hope had been sparked. The rediscovered memory of what it felt like to have a vaguely familiar voice call her *my dear* was somehow comforting. Talia made her way back to her aunt's room, her mind racing with questions.

Aunt Miriam was asleep when she peered in. Had she finally exhausted herself? The woman's pale face, etched with the deep creases of a lifetime of discontent, seemed to underscore her labored breathing. Talia found it impossible not to feel some concern. Miriam was in limbo, anchored somewhere between a tortured past and the final release from her earthly bondage. Talia stood at the bedside watching her aunt, noting the jarring rise and fall of her bony chest, knowing that she was in another realm and wondering what secrets she guarded there. Why would Mr. Bergelsohn's call have unsettled her so?

"God knows," Talia whispered. "For your own sake, old woman, I hope you find some peace before you leave this world." She reached down and lifted her jacket from the chair next to her aunt's bed. She needed to get back to Riley at the dojo.

CHAPTER 5

THE BELLS OF SAINT SORROW

Momma! Look at the cute baby ducks! They're so fluffy. I hope the nasty goose, the one that pecks, isn't here today!"

Riley squatted next to the lakeshore, pulling handfuls of defrosted green peas from a bag in her lap and scattering them into the shallow muddy water at the shoreline. The ducks nearby eagerly snapped up her offerings. Riley seemed unbothered by the mud sucking at the heels of her boots or the briskness of the October air.

She was a rough-and-tumble kind of kid. She would have been just as happy digging earthworms out of the soft bank of the lake and examining them as she was feeding the ducks. To Talia's dismay, she regularly discovered dried bugs and snail shells in Riley's pockets when she did the laundry.

As if reading her mind, Riley sat down on a patch of moist dirt, tugged off her rubber boots, and sank her toes joyfully into the cold mud. Talia thought briefly about cautioning her daughter to stay dry and, better yet, clean, but she knew if Russ had been with them, he would have permitted Riley her curious pleasures.

"That's what dads are for, Tal," he would say, laughing. "To pierce the bubbles that moms wrap their kids in." And it was true. Talia knew she had to make an effort not to be too overprotective, too limiting.

The afternoon sun was low in the west, and Talia found herself missing the long, lazy days that summer afforded. A silver light danced over the surface of the lake as a small catamaran slipped along the opposing shoreline. A couple pushed a double stroller on the north side of the water's edge, where the long afternoon shadows had already staked their claim. Talia's heart ached with envy.

She closed her eyes and turned her face to the fading autumn sun, drinking in its soft warmth.

The bells of Saint Thomas's chapel across the parkway rang in the four o'clock hour. Their solemn tolling reverberated through every cell in her body, reviving the apprehension she had so often felt as a child, hiding in the bell tower at Saint Mary's. It was amazing how that sound affected her, how quickly it brought her back to those wretched days—flashes of being locked in the stairwell for some minor transgression that Sister Mary Ignatius had found so egregious. *What would that woman have made of a child like Riley?* Talia's blood ran cold at the thought.

The bells pealed out their tone boldly, *one . . . two . . . three . . . four . . .* But today they struck a different chord with Talia. They seemed to bellow out an admonition for her two-year absence from the church.

Her head swam momentarily. She couldn't imagine crossing the parkway and passing through the huge oak doors of Saint Thomas's ever again— not after so much time spent foolishly believing that a relationship with God might undo all the losses she had suffered. All she'd found at Saint Thomas's were broken promises and unanswered prayers.

Saint Thomas's had been the location of Russ's funeral.

Talia's eyes swept over the rolling hills of the park, settling on the towering silhouette of the chapel's bell tower, the memory springing to mind so clearly, as though she were reliving it now. She could see the blue light slipping through the stained-glass windows and vast stretches of austere marble floors, their polished surfaces echoing sharply with the footsteps of uniformed pallbearers carrying a flag-draped casket containing Russel's remains.

Russel.

"Ashes to ashes, dust to dust." She could hear Father McCoy's words as if he were speaking them right now. They rang out above the oppressive silence of that somber space. That space that cried out to be filled with her anguish instead of the inadequate and muted condolences of the mourners who believed they had come to share the burden of her grief. She could see the countless faces now, trained on her and Riley as Naomi and John steered the two of them to their seats in the front pew, next to Chief Graham. So many faces she recognized and so many she had never seen before. They were like a sea of curious masks, feigning comprehension of how her world had collapsed.

It wasn't that Talia had discounted the sincerity of their intent but rather the depth of their ability to understand the gravity of her loss. She shouldn't have resented them. They were to be thanked, if anything, but that was hard to see at the time. Each of them had come to take their designated place in the formal pantomime of grief that must be played out. They had all diligently executed their roles in recording the dreadful loss. Their collective farewell to a loved man, a trusted friend, and a brave hero had confirmed the realities of the day.

Ashes to ashes, dust to dust. Once completed, the funeral ceremony had signaled, if only for the onlookers, that such a terrible truth had slipped irrevocably into the past. What the members of the congregation didn't know, though—what they *couldn't* know—was that those truths, and others they would never understand, were taking Talia with them into that void, into that place of immeasurable grief and regret. *Ashes to ashes, dust to . . .*

It was Ash Wednesday, 1966. Talia and Naomi had just been lectured by Sister Mary Ignatius to think on matters of life and death. But five-year-old Talia did not know what the old kookaburra lady had meant by this. She dragged her feet next to Naomi as they made their way down the long aisle of Saint Mary's chapel. Today the girls had each been allowed to light the first candle of Lent. Like the string of dormitory mates in front of them, Talia and Naomi were dressed in their best frocks and carried small white candles with cardboard circles around their bases. The cardboard was to stop the hot wax from dripping on their hands, they had been told. This was the part that had most upset Talia, as she was the only girl in the whole parade who had not been allowed to light her candle. Sister Mary Ignatius said that she was too young and could not be trusted to safely carry a lit candle.

"But Yvonne is only five years old. How come she got to light a candle? That's not fair!" Talia stomped her feet and let out a wail.

"Quiet, Talli, unless you want to get into trouble again," Naomi whispered. Some of the members of the congregation turned their heads to see what the commotion in the back of the chapel was about. Fortunately, Sister Louise, seated at the organ, began to play just then, and all eyes turned back toward the altar. The girls all placed their candles in the racks at the base of the stairs, in front of the chapel crowd, and quietly made their way onto the stage.

The organ music boomed and hummed loudly above the congregation, as if Sister Louise had just released a host of dragons from their prison of tall brass pipes. Talia imagined their wings carrying them out of the open windows and into the skies above, off and far away.

As she and Naomi took their positions with the other girls in the choir box, Sister Louise shot them a look of concern. Mother Superior was in attendance for Mass, and everyone had been warned to be on their very best behavior for her visit.

Talia smiled broadly at Sister Louise, revealing her missing front teeth. It was a comical sight that almost unseated the musician. When she was sure Sister Mary Ignatius wasn't looking, Sister Louise smiled back and winked at Talia. Sister Louise was Talia's favorite. She never once called her a larrikin or a nuisance, as the other nuns at Saint Mary's did. Talia knew her real name was safe with Sister Louise; she was sure she had even heard it in the woman's mumbled prayers at bedtime.

On the way home from the lake, Talia and Riley stopped at the local farmers market and picked up some fresh apples, homemade noodles, and pasta sauce for dinner. It'd been a long day, and Talia was exhausted. By the time they had taken Toby for his walk, finished dinner, and cleaned up the kitchen, it was pushing Riley's bedtime. Talia sent her to her room to pick out a book for her bedtime story while she called Naomi. She needed to let her sister know about the most recent development since her intriguing call from Australia with Mr. Bergelsohn the previous day.

"Hey, sis, I might have to call on you to pick Riley up from school one day next week if I can't get after-school care arranged. Do you mind? I'm a little worried about getting caught in traffic coming back from LA." Before Naomi could object—Talia knew how busy her sister was at the office—she hurried to explain herself. "It's just that I had a message this evening on the answering machine from a legal assistant in LA working with Aunt Miriam's attorney in Seattle. I need to get down to the city soon to sign those guardian-ship papers. I'll call tomorrow when the office is open and see how quickly I can get an appointment."

There was an uncomfortable pause before Naomi responded, "Ah . . . yeah, I guess I could probably figure something out if need be. Just give me as much notice as possible, okay?"

"Sorry for the inconvenience. It's just that I'd rather get things taken care of as soon as possible, if you get my drift."

There was another pause on the other end of the line. Talia was sure she heard Naomi sigh. She knew her sister would not want to make any conces-sions in her busy life to accommodate Aunt Miriam's affairs in any way. Why did Naomi have to make things more difficult than they needed to be?

"I'm dying to hear what Mr. Bergelsohn has for us, and you know you are too," Talia nudged. "The sooner I gain guardianship, the sooner he can enlighten us about these cryptic legal documents."

"Well, yes, I have to say, I'm intrigued on that front. Especially if it means there's a chance one of us might have to go back there . . . to Australia, I mean."

"Really?" Talia asked, taken aback. Neither of them had returned to Australia since they had left more than twenty years earlier. Talia had been only fifteen and Naomi seventeen when they'd immigrated to the States—to Seattle with Aunt Miriam.

"So many bad memories there, I don't ever want to go back," Talia added, her voice drifting off.

"Well, I'd go," Naomi said. "I'd want to visit Saint Mary's and bust some chops, get to the bottom of just how we ended up there, captive—literally imprisoned for all those years—when it has since become clear there were other options for our care after Mommy died. Why would we have ended up in an orphanage when we still had an extended family around? I want answers, and someone is going to be accountable!" Her words stirred Talia's angst. *Jesus*, Naomi could be a riptide.

"That's all water under the bridge now, Naomi," Talia added gingerly, not wanting to spark a disagreement with her sister. "It's true we never *belonged* at Saint Mary's, but really, did we ever feel like we belonged anywhere?"

The line fell silent, both of them thinking, both of them remembering.

Aunt Miriam had come back to the orphanage in 1969 to finally claim them. Naomi was ten years old by that point, and Talia just eight. A full five years had passed since they'd seen their aunt; she was a total stranger to them. The gruff man accompanying her was a stranger, too, though the girls were instructed to call him Uncle Gus.

"You've got to admit, it's highly suspicious that shortly after Grandad's death, Aunt Miriam showed up to claim us." Naomi practically hissed the words. "I know you're not that naive, Talia."

Talia weighed her options for a response but settled on silence.

It was well past bedtime that night when Talia read Riley her story. As usual, this was followed by Riley's nightly prayers, which, on her insistence, included thanks to Mother Nature and Father Time for all their blessings. Perhaps it was Riley's way of keeping things in balance, of affording her some sense of control over the aspects of life that were largely out of control. This was the way of most adults, Talia had noticed during her years in social work. So many people, especially those who were avid churchgoers seeking God's wisdom, refuge, forgiveness, and strength, invented their own customized realities. While most children expressed some interest in the *why* of things in life, they rarely possessed the enthusiasm or imagination Riley did—which had, Talia assumed, to be the result of her father's untimely death.

There was no question Russ's death had affected Riley. Both of them had felt a tremendous impact. But to see her daughter lose the blissful sense of invincibility of other kids her age so early on, in favor of acute awareness of her own mortality and that of those around her, was devastating in a way that was almost too painful to acknowledge directly. And so Talia didn't. She focused instead on respecting Riley's whimsical prayers to Mother Nature and Father Time and whomever else she thought of in between.

As though on cue, Riley looked up from her pillow with questioning eyes. "Momma, do angels get thirsty and hungry?"

Sometimes her innocent questions cut to the bone. Talia leaned over and kissed her daughter's forehead. The child's cheeks were a perfect pink. They matched the scent of peach bubble bath emanating from her.

"I don't know, sweetie. I don't think so. In heaven, there is no hunger or thirst. There are only happy things," she replied with more conviction than she felt.

"Well, when I'm an angel, I'm gonna get hungry and thirsty," Riley professed, pulling on a strand of dark hair that had escaped her ponytail. "Especially for rainbow shaved ice. I bet sometimes Daddy gets hungry and thirsty. He's an angel, isn't he, Momma?"

Talia leaned down and kissed her daughter's forehead again. "Yes, honey, he is an angel. I think Daddy was always an angel. Go to sleep now." She turned off the light and headed down the hallway, holding her breath until the tightness in her throat had passed.

How could she possibly fill the void Russ had left in their lives? Had that been the right thing to say to Riley? Shouldn't she have been more practical? More honest? Russ had been only human, with faults and imperfections, just like everyone else. Was she wrong not to discourage Riley from lionizing him? Would that prove more painful later in life when Riley came to find that no one was superhuman, that Russ had been just a regular guy? That he had been flawed and at times even silly—impractically fearless, foolishly fearless. No, *recklessly* fearless.

It was the middle of the night when the landline at Talia's bedside started ringing. Panicked, she groped through the post-midnight darkness, searching her nightstand for the handset.

"Hello?" she demanded breathlessly, the receiver pressed to her mouth. Her eyes struggled to focus on the bright-red numbers glaring back at her from the clock on her bedside table—they read 2:03 a.m.

No response.

There was rustling on the other end of the line, though. It sounded something like static, suggesting the call was long distance, the connection tenuous. *Perhaps another call from Australia. What time would it be there now?*

"Hello?" she said again, more urgently this time, hoping the ringing hadn't woken Riley. "If you don't answer, I'm going to hang—"

"Tal," a voice replied at last. "It's me."

Talia's breath caught in her throat, her heart thumping wildly. *But it can't be you. That's impossible—because . . .*

"You're dead," Talia sobbed, the words blurting out uncontrolled. "No, this isn't happening. You're gone, Russ. You're dead. You left us! *You goddamned left us!*"

"You've got to listen to me, Tal," Russ replied, his voice calm and commanding. "You can't leave Riley to be here with me."

"This isn't real," Talia whispered to herself. If only she could click on the light, draw herself out of this darkness, break free from whatever was paralyzing her limbs. "This isn't real, Russ, because you're dead, and I *am* here. I'm at home with Riley. She's asleep in her room right now!"

"I just wanted to warn you to keep Riley close," Russ said, his voice softening in the way one's might after delivering sobering news. "She needs you more than ever. She needs you to pull yourself back into the world of the living, Tal."

"What do you mean?" Talia protested, her voice finding itself. The darkness of her room began to fade. A soft light was bleeding through the closed drapes over her bedroom window—the full moon peering in. What was Russ trying to say?

"The truth is, Russ," Talia insisted, "Riley needs you more than ever. *Not me*. I'm a wreck without you, Russ!"

At first, there was no response—only broken static buzzing on the line. And then, just before the line went dead, she thought she heard him say, "Tal, you *are* Riley."

Click.

CHAPTER 6

NEW NEIGHBORS, OLD HAUNTS

Talia jolted awake, heart pounding. After a few frantic breaths, she realized it had only been a dream. Riley was safe at home with her, the phone hadn't rung, and Russ most certainly wasn't on the line, issuing cryptic warnings or philosophical doublespeak. *You are Riley? What the hell does that mean?*

Talia rolled over in exhausted resignation, staring at the clock on her bedside table. It read 2:03 a.m. *Two o'clock again.* She regularly woke up at that hour. It seemed this was a new habit in a string of other oddities determined to destroy her peace of mind. She would do her best to go back to sleep—but not before checking on Riley.

The house was still and oddly quiet. A milk-white glow bathed the walls of Talia's bedroom, the full moon at its zenith. The drapes of her bedroom window billowed softly in the night breeze like the gossamer sails of a dream galleon. She clicked on the bedside lamp, casting an orange hue over the room, and ventured down the hallway toward Riley's bedroom.

Riley's room was peacefully dark and still, her breathing slow and sweeping. Talia knew it had only been a dream, but she felt compelled to whisper, "Don't worry, Russ. She's safe with me. She will always be safe with me."

With that, she closed her daughter's bedroom door and tiptoed back to her bedroom. Toby, panting eagerly, followed on her ankles, seemingly aware of her distress. In the wash of orange light, things felt dreamlike, and for a moment, Talia wondered if she really was awake. Toby trotted over to the corner of the room, curling up like a furry accordion, nose covered by the fluff of his tail, and his calm—the calm of a dog with heightened senses— was just enough to settle Talia's nerves.

She climbed back into bed, heaving her bedcovers over her legs, and clicked off the light. Head resting on her pillow, she stared at the moonlit ceiling. The dream had been a strange gift, an opportunity to remember what Russ had sounded like, even if only through a long-distance call with poor service. "Maybe you can call me again sometime," she added, half laughing. Tears welled in her eyes, burning with protest, as though to say, *No, stop. No tears. We've cried enough about this. It's over.*

But something told Talia it would never be over, and she'd never stop asking for glimpses and dregs of whatever was left of Russ—even if it meant digging into the dark recesses of her subconscious and dragging them out through her nightmares.

"We're going to visit your mom tomorrow," she whispered, rolling over, envisioning what it might feel like to have him lying beside her the way he used to. The heat of him. The presence. The sense of calm and being cared for. "Riley's really excited, even though it's a long drive. I love you. I . . . " The next line was harder to say. "I know you didn't mean to leave us, Russ. I'm sorry I said that."

Talia closed her eyes, blinking back the tears. She would fight them off. She would stay strong. But a minute later, she drifted off to sleep—the best sleep she'd had in months, without nightmares or sleepwalking or disruptions brought on by the 4:15 a.m. paper delivery.

You are Riley. You are Riley?

Talia slept soundly until her alarm clock went off at seven. The buttery sunlight of an autumn day filtered in through the curtains of her bedroom window, and she almost expected to roll over and find Russ lying there, half-asleep. She'd give anything to lean over and kiss him good morning.

Instead, she heaved herself out of bed, threw on Russ's robe, and walked down the hallway with Toby trailing at her ankles, trying all the while to ignore the gaping hole Russ had left in her life. The hole that she couldn't get rid of, no matter what she did or how hard she tried. It all felt so unfair.

But life wasn't fair, was it?

While waiting for Toby to collect the newspaper, Talia stared out over the dew-cloaked lawn, now peppered with multicolored fall leaves. It was nice doing this part of her routine after it was light outside rather than in the two-dimensional plane of early-morning darkness—and in that light, she noticed details that she'd apparently missed.

For one thing, there was a green jeep with a utility rack on its roof parked in the driveway across the street from her house. It looked out of place in front of Bob and Cindy Reed's old home. The Jeep's California license plate read "C KAYAK." A large moving van blocked most of the road, leaving Talia just enough room to inch her pickup truck out of her driveway later that morning, when she and Riley were scheduled to head out for a long weekend in Pismo Beach to visit Russ's mom.

The Reeds had moved back to Ohio after Bob had been transferred to his company's corporate offices in Cincinnati, and their house had been vacant for several months. Talia felt her mouth slope into a frown. There was something sad about an empty house, especially one that had been almost a second home for her and her daughter. She was glad to see someone was finally moving in, even though she missed the Reeds terribly. In times gone by, Bob Reed and Russel had been surfing buddies, but the two had had far more than hobbies in common. They had often helped each other with projects around their respective homes and enjoyed watching the same baseball teams. Cindy, Bob's wife of twenty-five years, had been not only a dear friend to Talia but also a doting figure in Riley's life. She'd never had children of her own and had showered Riley with her pent-up maternal love. Cindy had a green thumb and a spectacular vegetable garden and orchard that proved it. She'd kept her neighbors' kitchens full of fresh produce in the summer and their hearts full of love all year round.

No one in the neighborhood had been happy to see the Reeds leave—least of all Talia. Bob and Cindy had been there for her on the morning the chief and fire department chaplain had shown up at her door, after all. They'd been there for her at her very lowest—and to this day, she wasn't sure if she'd ever properly thanked them for that.

Talia suddenly felt something wet nudging her shin and looked down to see Toby, who'd dropped the newspaper at her feet. "Thanks, buddy," she said, patting him on the head. "Now go potty before we run out of time. We've still gotta wake up Riley."

Toby trotted back off into the yard in search of the perfect spot, allowing Talia to drift back in time once again, eyes fixed on Cindy and Bob's old house. Perhaps it was hearing Russ's voice last night, or her therapy session earlier that week, but the events of two years ago felt so present this morning—so palpable.

"What are you running from?" Dr. Cohn had asked her, and for the first time in a while, Talia realized that she hadn't been running away from anything. For all these years, she'd been running from one point to the next, trying to get by. It hadn't felt like an effort at escaping reality as much as it'd felt like keeping her head above water. But Dr. Cohn's message, perhaps, was still applicable because no matter what direction she'd been running in, she'd still been running, and that inherently meant avoiding something. *Something painful.*

And so, instead of turning away from the memory, Talia forced herself to tumble into it. After all, hadn't Russ told her in her dream last night to move into the land of the living? Maybe consciously embracing it was the best way to move through it—and surface on the other side. Well then, here she was, ready to face that terrible day all over again. No running from the memory—*just attack it head-on.*

Talia was still in her pajamas. She had just put on a pot of coffee and turned on the TV, waiting for the morning news—specifically, an update on the

brushfire to the southeast, where Russ was hard at work as a firefighter. He'd
been there for two days and didn't have service, so the only way for her to get
an update was through the local news. The wind had been blowing out to sea,
as the Santa Anas always did at that time of year, and the blaze had quickly
gained ground between the 101 Freeway and the coastline. Fortunately, Talia
and Russel's neighborhood was in a safe zone.

As was common practice with big brushfires, fire departments from
counties across the state had put together strike teams and sent them to help
in hot zones. There were plenty of evacuations to the east of town and lots of
standby help on hand. If the winds shifted again and threatened more homes
to the north, additional resources could make all the difference in saving
property and lives.

Russel was typically stationed in Los Angeles, but by chance—or perhaps as a result of his enthusiastic entreaties—his engine company had been
deployed to help in the vicinity of his hometown. Talia felt safer knowing
that Russ was part of the response team looking out for their area. The previous evening, he had called home from a pay phone at a campground near
Sycamore Ridge, where his unit was temporarily stationed and awaiting
assignment. Talia knew the campground well. She and Riley often passed
through it on Tuesday afternoons, en route to the park on the eastern ridge of
the mountain, where they'd pet the horses boarded there. This tradition was
often the highlight of Riley's week.

Russel had assured her that the canyon wasn't under direct threat—but
the abundance of dry fuel was making fire containment difficult, and multi-
ple structures to the south of the canyon were at risk. Because of the strong
winds, dispatchers at the fire command center were worried about new spot
fires popping up. Russ had sounded energized and happy to be involved in the
response, which made Talia swell with a sense of pride. He was always glad
to be a part of the solution to any problem. Sometimes that *was* the problem,
though. Russ never set boundaries. People took advantage of his generosity
all the time. He was too soft-hearted when it came to helping out, no matter
the size of the task. And now, when Talia reflected on that horrible day, she
felt herself fill with an upsurge of bitter resentment and frantic hate for those
people who'd made it so easy for him to volunteer.

But he *had* volunteered. There was no changing that. And thus Talia had been left waiting for the morning news to come on for a status update. She'd missed a phone call from him the evening prior, right around Riley's bedtime, and she was eager to learn about how the fire had progressed.

She was just about to call Riley down for her breakfast when a live update on the morning news caught her attention. A news affiliate in Los Angeles stood before the screen, face pale and expression grave as she pressed a finger against her earpiece and said, "Two city firemen have been airlifted to the LA County Burn Center at General Hospital in critical condition early this morning after the Santa Ana winds kicked up last night, spreading the conflagration to the coastline . . ."

Talia stopped what she was doing and returned to the TV, cupping her mouth with a hand.

The news affiliate went on, "We've just received reports that a third firefighter is missing, though fire crews from both Los Angeles and Ventura County Fire Departments continue to battle for control of this blaze and search for the missing firefighter. The names of those in critical condition and that of the missing engineer are being withheld, pending notification of their families—"

The doorbell rang.

Talia was jolted, startled by the sound. Desperate for more critical news on the wildfire, she ignored the doorbell, turning up the TV, only to see the affiliate shuffle her notes and say, "More live updates on this after a break. Stay with us."

"Come on," Talia said, the words barely a breath, watching helplessly as a Mr. Clean commercial clicked into view. "*Come on*, I've got—"

The doorbell rang again.

Frustrated, Talia abandoned the TV and marched to the front door. Who would dare ring the doorbell twice so early on a Sunday morning? She softened then. Perhaps it was just the Reeds coming over to check on her, to see if she had heard an update from Russ. She glanced through the window in the living room to view her front porch. The fire department's red Suburban was parked outside, and she was pretty sure she saw somebody in uniform move just out of sight.

Talia exhaled, breathing a sigh of relief. *It's just Russel stopping in to assure me that he's fine. He can fill me in on the injured firemen I've just heard about on the news. He must have forgotten his key again. Why else ring the doorbell?*

With a yank, she pulled the front door open. The smile on her face wilted almost immediately at the sight of the fire department's chaplain and Chief Graham standing on her porch, their faces grim to the point of being almost unrecognizable.

"Can I . . . ?" Talia noticed the chief was holding his hat in his hand. Her heart practically stopped dead in her chest. "What's wrong? What's going on?" she demanded. The chief's hat-holding was somehow more telling than the grave look in his eyes.

The men staring back at her seemed to freeze in place, eyes tearing up, and that's when it hit her.

Instantly, like a train.

Her legs could barely hold her up. The floor seemed to shift beneath her in a blur. It had finally come to pass—what she had feared every time Russ left for duty. And all at once she felt as though she were floating somewhere outside of herself and watching hell unfold.

"No," she choked out, falling. Her knees broke against the concrete porch, but she barely felt it. The world tilted on its axis, reality slowing to a dull, muted crawl. "No, no, no . . . "

Chief Graham, whom she'd known for years, knelt down beside her, eyes brimming with tears. "I'm so sorry," he said with a shaking voice, placing a hand on her shoulder. The world blacked out, and all she could hear was the terrifying and involuntary raw sound of her grief echoing through the neighborhood, ripping through her throat.

It was unstoppable—dreadful and as loud as a train whistle.

Through the haze of her hysteria, she was informed that two firefighters from Russel's engine company were in the burn unit at LA County's General Hospital, just as the reporter had announced moments earlier on the news, but that Russel had been lost at the scene.

"So he's not dead—he's just missing," she said desperately, though her body already knew the truth. The men only looked at each other as though searching for strength and then back at her with despair in their tear-filled eyes. Talia would later find out that the expression was just a euphemism. It was kinder to say that Russel had been lost at the scene instead of that Russel had been incinerated alive in an entirely preventable and senseless tragedy.

It would be more than a year before Talia could bring herself to read the official transcripts of the inquiry into her husband's death. She suspected it would take a lifetime to process the guilt she felt over the role Russel's love for his family had played in his untimely and cruel death. He'd only wanted to do the right thing by Talia and Riley — he'd only wanted to save the horses up on Sycamore Ridge from an unthinkable fate that night.

Talia spent the rest of the morning with her head in the toilet, vomiting. A migraine had set in, which was the hallmark of stress for her. It was her body's way of giving up and shutting down when everything around her became too much to bear. She'd suffered them since puberty. Sometimes they were crippling. They were more crippling than ever then, after losing Russ.

Cindy Reed and Mrs. Kravitz from up the road stayed with Riley while Bob made phone calls to Russ's mom and Naomi. Talia's chest ached, either from the weight of her grief or from her constant retching. Almost a full day passed before she was able to compose herself enough to explain to Riley that her father had gone on a long journey and wouldn't be coming back. She didn't expect her to grasp what was happening at the young age of three. She could barely grasp it herself, as an adult.

As predicted, Riley didn't seem to understand, a reality that became clearer in the days, weeks, and months that passed. Whenever the house phone rang, she was convinced it was her father calling to talk to her, to tell her he missed her, that he'd be home soon. For weeks after the accident, whenever Riley saw a fire engine on the road, she would wave frantically and yell, "Dadda!"

Each time this happened, Talia felt a piece of her soul being torn away. On some nights, Riley refused to go to bed without a good night call from her father. Their evenings became sleepless battles against Riley's tears and Talia's frayed nerves, and neither of them had a restful night for months. Not until kindergarten started and Talia put Riley into karate lessons did she settle into a regular sleep routine. Before that, Talia had done her best to keep her daughter's days full and stimulating.

They joined every library within a twenty-mile radius of the house. There was always a pile of children's books in the living room. They began new traditions to distract from the absence of the old ones that had included Russ, and rather than trail hikes from the house in the late afternoons, Talia started the tradition of sharing a good book, hot apple cider, and homemade oatmeal-raisin cookies with her daughter. She began reading to Riley every afternoon and at bedtime, doing her best to keep evenings enjoyable and relaxing, hoping that they would both sleep well. Typically, a warm lavender bath was followed by a good bedtime story and evening prayers Riley herself scripted—often quite comically. In the first year after Russ's death, Riley slept with Talia every single night. This only changed when Talia adopted Toby from the pound.

They spotted him on one of their weekly trips to the shelter to pet the dogs and cats there. This activity had replaced their visits to the horses on Sycamore Ridge.

Toby had been an instant fit in their family, bonding strongly with Riley. In some ways, he'd taken on Russ's role as the man of the house, forever watching over them with the vigilance and enthusiasm of a guardian angel. Once Toby had settled into his new home, Riley insisted he sleep in her room at night. His presence was a big comfort for her and a sanity saver for Talia, who finally got her bed back to herself—which was, at first, a relief. But later, her daughter's nightly absence only amplified Talia's sense of loss, which hadn't been as obvious with Riley wiggling beside her every night.

And shortly after that, the battle with insomnia began.

Talia swallowed hard, returning her focus to her driving—the Pacific Coast Highway unfurling itself like a scroll before her, a newly paved ribbon of asphalt, and the sunlight reflecting off the vast expanse of the ocean over her left shoulder.

"How much longer until we're at Grammie's house?" Riley asked.

"We'll be there soon enough, sweets." Talia lowered her sun visor and glanced over at Toby, impressed by how well he was doing on such a long road trip. "Grammie's all the way at the Central Coast, but we're more than halfway already."

"That's okay, Momma. I've got Toby to play with."

"Yes, you do," Talia answered, raising her eyebrows and casting Toby an expression of sympathy. He'd settled on the bench seat, his head in Riley's lap, embodying all the patience of a monk as Riley played with his ears and combed her fingers through his pale coat.

Talia glanced at the dashboard's clock, realizing she'd been daydreaming for nearly an hour. With a deep breath, she cracked the window, allowing the brine-scented breeze to rush into the cabin of the truck and wash away the pang of grief in her chest. *I faced that memory well,* she told herself, despite how it had left her feeling. She always feared a setback with every tiny advance she attempted. *Okay, now just let it go.* She did her best to conjure the sound of soft wind chimes in a gentle breeze.

Riley giggled, drawing a smile from Talia's lips. "Look, Momma," she said with a grin. "Do you like Toby's new hairdo?"

Talia snorted a laugh at the sight of poor Toby, whose ears had been swept back by his collar, which Riley had used as a headband. The dog was a saint. "I love it," she said, "but I think we should put Toby's collar back where it belongs. He can't hear when his ears are back like that."

"Yes, he can!" Riley challenged with a giggle as she bent down and kissed the top of Toby's head and gave her mother a smile. Talia felt herself melt at the sight of those bright-blue eyes and that lopsided grin.

She looked just like Russ, especially when she was happy. Russ's colleagues at the fire department hadn't called him Baby Blues Brighton for nothing.

It was Russ's eyes and that smile that first caught Talia's attention on the day they'd met.

She would later tell her friends that he was too handsome to be trusted. Very few people *that* good-looking went through life without inevitably becoming self-centered or one-dimensional. Being as attractive as Russ was a near guarantee that he'd turn out conceited and shallow. Talia argued that tall, attractive, affable white men had easy lives because everyone gave them the benefit of the doubt. They seldom had to earn respect and simply felt entitled to it all too often. She was dead serious when she said she didn't even want to know his name. That smile, though—it was hard to ignore.

Looks aside, Russ's character was what made him the sort of guy who never let you down—and after the life Talia had had, someone who wouldn't let her down was a godsend. What she could never fully comprehend about him, though, was his adoration of her. It never seemed to waver. Even at her worst, when she surely didn't deserve it—even when she had tried to push him away, to keep him from getting too close—Russ had adored her.

Talia felt her shoulders tighten. She shrugged, trying to relax. Distantly, she could hear Riley reading one of her storybooks to Toby, but that reality felt strangely far away. Did she regret falling for Russ? What would life look like if she'd just trusted her instincts and refused to go anywhere near Baby Blues Brighton? It was a question she'd grappled with often. Was loving Russ for the time they had together worth the destructive gravity of his loss? Would it have been easier if she'd never loved him at all? *Not if it had meant there would be no Riley.*

Life was like that, wasn't it? Full of double-edged swords.

The city's investigation had gone on for ten months after Russel's death.

Throughout that span—which often felt like purgatory, like an impossible blend of time holding still and passing far too quickly all at once—Talia was deliberately uninformed of the brutal discoveries regarding Russ's final hours. For a while, she was sure she didn't want to know those details, anyway. The most important man in her life was dead—that was all she needed to know, and no report could change that fact. After a year had slipped by, however, she began to wonder if her imagination wasn't worse than reality. The brain is a self-destructive force like that. If it doesn't have a clear answer, it will speculate unconsciously until it arrives at a conclusion, and Talia's brain's speculations were horrific. Her nightmares alone were proof of that. Knowing the *facts*, even if they were grotesque and painful, started to feel essential to reaching a sense of closure regarding the tragedy. And so, eventually, she requested a formal summary of the findings.

The two injured firefighters had been badly burned but had been back to work within the year. Neither of them had attempted to contact Talia to discuss the incident. At first, she thought they might be suffering from survivor's guilt, and she wondered if she should be the one to make contact. Maybe they expected her to reach out. As the months passed, she lost her nerve. She wasn't sure what she could offer them, anyway. It was pointless, throwing someone else a life preserver when she herself was drowning. Russel had been the supervisor, the one who had made the decision that had put the engine company in danger that night. The responsibility rested on his shoulders. Yes, he had paid the ultimate price, but this did not seem enough to undo the months of suffering his two subordinates had endured. And Talia—as his wife, the one person who knew what he'd been thinking that night—could not help feeling a sense of culpability for the decision Russel had made.

By the time the first anniversary of his death rolled around, Talia had made up her mind to keep her distance from Russ's firefighter colleagues. After a while, she had no desire to hear from anyone in the department ever again. Aside from the occasional call or note from one of the other firefighters' families, she felt disconnected from that part of Russel's life, which had once been so important to her. It seemed that the time had come for all of them to move on. On occasion, Chief Graham still made a point of phoning to see how she and Riley were managing, but Talia usually let the answering machine pick up his calls.

The drive to Rose's place in Pismo Beach was long. As usual, traffic on the highway was slow going through the small tourist towns dotting the coastline. Riley napped a good deal during the second leg of the journey, as she often did on road trips, and Toby had finally curled up on the floorboard below her feet.

It was late afternoon by the time they pulled into a driveway lined with blooming Chinese flame trees and foot-long margins of blue-gray gravel. A spot had been left open at the front of the 1950s-style bungalow, which was part of a well-kept network of beachside homes for seniors. The front yard comprised the same blue-gray gravel along the driveway and was peppered with gorgeous clematis that would bloom blue-violet flowers in the spring.

Rose was a lovely, level-headed woman who was remarkably social despite being in her eighties. She truly seemed to cherish the times Talia brought Riley up for a visit—and Bixby, Rose's gray-snouted poodle, seemed just as excited to play with Toby.

Only seconds after they'd pulled up to the bungalow, the front door opened, and Bixby sprinted out, his tail wagging like a propeller. Rose was soon to follow. Talia, Riley, and Toby hopped out of the car, distributing hugs—and in the dogs' case, lots of sniffs and bouncing—before making their way inside.

"It's been five months since I've seen your sunny little face," Rose lamented, more to Talia than to Riley, as she bent down to hug her grand-daughter again. "You're as tall as a sunflower now."

There were tears in Rose's eyes when she stood up and reached over to squeeze Talia's shoulder in warm welcome. Rose's tears had become a nor-mal part of their greetings after Russ's death—Talia always felt regret for the mixed blessing her visits posed in both rehashing Rose's grief and allowing her time with her only granddaughter.

"We'll come out over Christmas," Talia said, forcing a smile. "We really need to visit more often, don't we?"

"I couldn't agree more," Rose replied with a weathered smile. "Family is important."

Talia knew how important family time was—but in truth, she'd been purposefully distant. Not only because Rose's home was practically a shrine to Russ but also because Talia didn't feel that she could offer the solace Rose probably needed and deserved from a daughter-in-law. The myriad of pic-tures and newspaper clippings related to Russ, which were plastered through-out Rose's home, was more than Talia could bear. But she had to admit, it felt good to see Riley and her grandmother together again.

Later that evening, Rose treated them to homemade pizza—Riley had requested it over the phone before they'd even left home—and then they played checkers and tic-tac-toe until well past Riley's bedtime, as they usu-ally did on visits.

"You're beating your ol' grammie mercilessly, my little sunflower." Rose laughed. "But it's time for bed now. Go and hop under the covers, and I'll be in to read you a story in a minute." Riley always shared Rose's bed on visits—there would be no bedtime arguments tonight. Riley bounced over to Talia, gave her mother a good-night kiss, and headed for the bedroom at full speed.

"Don't forget to brush your teeth," Talia called after her.

Less than five minutes later, Rose returned from her bedroom, chuckling. "She's out like a light already."

"Must be all the excitement and the fresh ocean air," Talia added, finishing her last sip of wine.

"She's the spitting image of Russel, isn't she?"

Here we go, Talia thought, bracing herself for the tears.

"I see it, too, the older she gets," Talia agreed, smiling wanly.

"Just like Rob. Those eyes!" Rose curled up in her recliner, and Bixby was quick to join her. Talia shot Rose a look of concern. Rob had been Russ's father; he'd died of colon cancer when Russ was only a four-year-old boy.

"Is it true you never dated . . . I mean, after Rob?" Talia ventured, hoping she wasn't overstepping or that her motive for the question wasn't too transparent.

"Oh." Rose chuckled. "It's not that there weren't plenty of suitors. They seemed to come out of the woodwork. Lordy, the things I had to do to dodge the offers, even from the married ones." Rose laughed, but the humor was short-lived. She ran her fingers through Bixby's graying curls. "But no, I was really never interested, to be honest. Rob and I had Russ when I was already quite old—by the standards of the day, anyway—and I certainly was not looking to have more children."

"And he did fine?" Talia's voice was barely a whisper, as if she was talking only to herself. "Russ, I mean," she added, shifting her gaze from Russ's portrait on the wall above the fireplace to Rose.

"He turned out to be such a balanced, lovely man," Rose answered with a slow nod.

"You did a great job, Rose. Thank you for that. Russ was one in a million." Talia thought about how easy it had been to trust Russ and how impossible it was not to have loved him.

"Russ always had a mind of his own. He was so mature, even as a small boy—an old soul, some would say." Rose reached for a tissue on the coffee table next to her. She dabbed her nose and then crushed the tissue in her closed fist. "There was no talking him out of something once he set his mind to it. College was the perfect example." Rose chuckled then, sighing in resignation. "There was no way I was going to get him to change his major to something more practical. Philosophy. I ask you?"

Talia was quick to jump in. "I loved that he was so well read and such a source of wisdom and peace, Rose. I miss so many things about him, but his sage advice—his wise words—was most definitely on the top five of my list of favorites." Talia sat for a moment as if lost in the past. "And he was never afraid to take a stand. I loved that he stood up for what he believed in, even when it was unpopular." She rubbed her eyes with her thumb and forefinger, doing her best to stifle a yawn that eventually escaped. "Like the time he was the only man in the department who supported hiring women firefighters."

"Well, he was always that way, Talia. He never minded being controversial."

Talia wondered for a moment if Rose was referring to Russ's decision to marry her, despite all her obvious baggage.

"And oddly, it seemed to make him more popular, his willingness to face pushback when he felt he was right," Talia went on, steering the dialogue. "I know he was well respected and loved in the department." Over the years, she had heard stories about Russ from his colleagues at the annual picnic or holiday parties. "He had a reputation on the street and within the department as a man with a kind heart and exceptional patience." Talia realized she was perhaps endorsing the idea that Russ had been the only man in the world who could have put up with her. She'd heard the firsthand accounts of his empathy and understanding when the department's emergency calls took his engine company to the most poverty-stricken and crime-infested neighborhoods in Los Angeles.

"He was a good man, Talia," Rose said, standing to open the sliding door and let the dogs out into her small, fenced backyard before they all called it a night. "But he wasn't the only good man. You're a lot younger than I was when I lost Rob. You, as beautiful and smart as you are, are not resigned to the fate of a lonely widow. And while it's not impossible, it is hard to raise a child alone—and as an only child. I often wondered if I did the right thing by Russ."

Talia realized Rose had understood her question about dating all too well. It seemed she was giving the green light for Talia to move on, if not outright encouraging her to do so.

After Rose went to bed, Talia settled herself on the sleeper sofa. It was just as uncomfortable as she remembered. She wasn't likely to sleep, anyway. Her insomnia was bad enough as it was, but it was significantly worse with Russ's childhood photographs and baseball memorabilia surrounding her. Everything she fought hard to put out of her mind at home was now staring, almost literally, back at her from every direction. The images seemed to pull her back, out of the world of the living and into the world of the past—the world of the dead.

She rose and opened a nearby window, turned out the light, and tried to free her mind from the long day of driving and the angst of seeing Russ's face everywhere. She lay awake for hours thinking about him, thinking about her dream and the call from him last night, and listening to the distant crashing of waves on the sea cliffs and the soft snoring of the dogs, which had decided to join her on the sofa.

Rose had organized a visit to see the migrating western monarch butterflies in the eucalyptus grove the following morning. The grove was part of a nearby nature reserve where she volunteered as a docent, and so they all got in free of charge.

Talia was fascinated by the vibrantly colorful creatures and the sheer volume of their masses clinging to the sagging branches of the eucalyptus trees. The reserve was one of a few safe harbors in California for tens of thousands of the beautiful orange-and-black butterflies as they made their annual migration from the Pacific Northwest to central Mexico. Talia had expected Riley to be full of questions, but the child seemed strangely passive, a little mystified. She stayed close most of the morning, holding on to her grandmother's hand, her eyes wide in awe, scanning the masses of insects.

Talia had never seen Riley so subdued. She reached down and felt her daughter's forehead, wondering if she was warm. Maybe she was coming down with the same cold that had struck some of her kindergarten classmates earlier in the week.

"Grammie," Riley finally ventured, looking up at her grandmother pensively, "my friend Trisha at school says butterflies are little angels. Is that true?"

Rose shot a concerned look at Talia and did her best to compose a reasonable response, stumbling slightly before settling on what to say. "Well, that's an interesting idea, isn't it?"

"She says that after her grandpa died, he became a butterfly," Riley went on, taking the conversation on an oblique trajectory. Talia braced herself. "She says he always comes back to visit her."

Rose made eye contact with Talia again, as though to solicit assistance in navigating the innocence of the question. But Talia quickly turned her head, her fingers twirling a few loose strands of her hair, as she often did when she was at a loss for words.

"I'll have a talk with some of these butterflies when they wake up. Shall I?" Rose went on. "And then I'll let you know what they have to say for themselves." She winked and smiled lightheartedly, but Riley's expression remained troubled. Rose bent down and held Riley's face in both of her hands. "I'm sorry about your friend's grandpa, sweetie, but I'm glad she had a visit from him. If you're thinking that maybe I'll be a butterfly, too, one day, there's no need for you to worry about that just yet. Okay? I have a feeling that I'll have to wait a very long time before I become a butterfly. You'll be as big as your mama by then. So no need to think about it just yet."

"Okay, Grammie, but if you do become a butterfly, can you please be a blue one? That way, I'll know it's you. Blue is my favorite color—you know that, right?"

They spent the afternoon on the beach. Bixby and Toby kept Riley entertained for hours, playing along the water's edge. In the evening, Rose prepared one of her wonderful spicy pasta dishes for Talia and went out of her way to make a separate meal that Riley would enjoy—her famous baked macaroni. It was obvious she loved having someone to cook for and share a glass of wine with again. After dinner, Rose read Riley her bedtime story while Talia sat on the sofa between the dogs and watched a romantic comedy. It cheered her a little, keeping at bay the familiar darkness that usually settled over her in the evenings.

The following morning, she was up early for a run on her favorite route along a nearby cliff while Rose and Riley slept in before their planned walk on the beach with the dogs. Perhaps it was time to start allowing Riley to spend an occasional weekend with her grandmother—for both their sakes. Now that Riley was a little older and was sleeping better at night, it was a feasible option and maybe even a necessary one. Riley should have a close connection to each of her loved ones.

By the time she'd made it to the trail, the sun was doing its best to show itself through the dawn haze. The heavy scent of the ocean hung in the morning air, rekindling memories from past visits to the beach with Russ. Talia's eyes roved the early-morning shoreline, empty of tourists or visitors, and found a particularly pale stretch of beach beneath a rocky outcropping. The view from the cliffs was perfect. It'd been a favorite spot of Russ's. How many times had they hiked that very stretch of coast together, gazing out at the water, listening to the call of the seabirds?

Running usually lightened her mood, but she couldn't seem to shake the fog of grief hanging over her that morning. There was no bounce in her step, no sense of peace, no mesmerizing pull from the winding trail ahead, calling her on. Here it was, Talia realized, the setback she had been expecting since her attempt to move back into the land of the living—to do as Russ had begged in her dream two nights ago. This was the inevitable payback, the effect of facing memories head-on. Such attempts were always rebuffed with a vengeance. And it hadn't helped her angst to see the pictures of Russ all over Rose's bungalow. Even so, the thought of heading home to an empty house . . . She felt the slice of the double-edged sword. In some ways, the visit had awoken things that she was trying to keep at bay, but now that she was here, she realized that she really didn't want to go home.

The fogbank hanging over the Pacific was advancing quickly, threatening to swallow the coastline, casting off a breeze that was colder than Talia had expected. She stopped at an outcropping and stood for a while, staring at the waves crashing into the jagged rocks a dozen feet below the trail, keeping her hands tucked into her long sleeves. Arms crossed tight over her chest, she watched the water roil and churn ominously beneath her. The turquoise swells, laced heavily with sea-foam, moved violently over and through the rocks, hissing at every impact. The Pacific Ocean seemed foreign here, hostile—not like the calm waters she and Riley enjoyed in Southern California. Here, there was no soothing cadence metered out by the waves, no steady predictability, no rhythm. Rather, it felt as though she stood before an angry god, every whip and thrash an extension of his fury and disappointment. Talia found herself watching the bold display of raw emotion the ocean seemed to relish. But she held tight to her own anguish, refusing to relinquish, refusing to break—her bottled-up tears boiling like a red-hot fury in her chest.

She leaned down and picked up a fist-size rock—its surface pitted like the craters of a moon—and heaved it up, hand cold and damp and numb. She'd had enough of watching her life derail over and over again, like a mute conductor watching the chaotic symphony of her despair run wild, as frantic as that gray mare barreling toward the railroad, the oncoming train.

A curtain of darkness crushed in on her, quashing the light that did its best to shine through her perpetual darkness—and suddenly, she felt Russel standing beside her the way he used to, right there, in that very spot.

"Throw it," he urged, his voice barely a breath. "Throw it as hard as you can, Tal."

And so she did, channeling every ounce of fury and despair and heartbreak into the gesture. For a few silent breaths, the rock flew skyward, only to free-fall against a backdrop of froth-filled seawater as the angry god's maw gaped wide, receiving it.

"Attagirl," Talia thought she heard Russ whisper—but she didn't dare turn around, didn't dare reveal to herself that he wasn't behind her. That she was still *alone*.

"This will pass," Talia tried to reassure herself out loud, shaking out her numb hand. But the raw upsurge of emotion had rattled her. It was different this time. It was sinking in that Russ would never, ever come back—and yet here, somehow, he felt so close, just beyond the veil, within reach.

And that rock . . .

It had fallen so effortlessly and then was swallowed up. Vanished.

She couldn't break her gaze from the hypnotizing dance of the cold, hostile water beneath her. Was Russ on the other side of that? Was freedom, release, and the absence of torment waiting patiently beneath that roiling surface?

"Breathe, Talia. Just breathe." But the ocean's call was louder, the waves beckoning, taunting her.

Just take the leap, Talia, they goaded. *Riley will be fine with her grandmother. You can be Riley's blue butterfly if you just take the leap—which is so much better than being a sleep-deprived wreck of a woman who's so lost in grief, she can't even trust in her own sanity. All the despair you're feeling, it could end. Right here, right now.*

Talia took a step closer to the edge of the cliff, peering over, swallowing hard. One leap, one brave hurdle, and it could all be over.

Before she could take that step, she heard him again. "Come on, Tal, what did I just tell you?" Talia paused, lips quivering. Russ's presence, like the weak rays of the muted sunrise, pierced the fog and bathed her in a gentle glow. "Riley needs you more than ever."

But Talia still couldn't break her gaze from the rocks. "That was just a dream."

"And if it was?" Russ challenged. "It's still true. Our daughter needs you. It's one thing to lose a parent. It's quite another thing to lose both. You should know that better than anyone."

Those final words hit hard. Suddenly she was filled with shame. How could she be so selfish? So self-absorbed and senseless? *What the hell has happened to me?* How had she let her grief change who she was? She had always been a fighter, not a victim.

Russ's voice softened. "Come on, sweets. You gave me your hand once. Let me take it again." And she took a step backward. "That's right. You've got this, Tal. You are so much stronger than you remember. I need you to love yourself just as much as you love Riley."

Always the philosopher. So that's what Russ meant by "you are Riley." Talia nodded in resolve, taking a deep, heavy breath. Then she turned around. As expected, she was standing there alone. Russ wasn't behind her, of course, and yet it'd felt real enough to talk some sense into her, and for that, she was grateful. She looked up as a flock of birds flew overhead. Had it only been their calls that had broken the spell the waves had cast? She turned then, away from the edge of the cliff—her feet heavy—and slowly headed north.

In a few minutes, her running shoes seemed to take over, as they usually did. They would ensure her safe passage out of the darkness again. In no time, they were metering out their comforting rhythm. *One, two, three, four; one, two, three, four.* She relaxed her shoulders and tried to release the lump in her throat and shake off the fog that seemed to linger in her eyes. Breathing deeply, she lengthened her stride until she was safely away from the cliff and heading toward the mountains.

Near a stand of coast live oaks, between the trail and the rolling green hills, a deer and her fawn grazed peacefully in a green pasture. They looked up at Talia, undisturbed by her passing, as if she were simply one of them.

She ran five miles along the rocky trails in the foothills of the coastal range before turning to head back to Rose's place. It was warmer now, and the morning fog had finally burned off. As she neared the beach, the sun glistened on the moving water, and she stopped to take in its magic. Finally, a sense of peace settled over her. She headed back to join Rose and Riley for brunch before the long drive home. She had beaten it again, though it had been a close call this time.

She was here. She was still here.

CHAPTER 7

LAST WORDS

The sun dipped behind the western hills as Talia and Riley made their way down the steep trail that wound its way through the foothills of the Santa Monica Mountains from the coast to their neighborhood. Talia had decided it would be good to get back to their evening hikes, to return to some of the activities they had both enjoyed with Russ. Besides, an occasional evening hike had to be better for Riley than the apple cider and homemade cookies that had become an all-too-frequent option.

"Momma, my legs hurt. Carry me."

"Okay, sweets. Grab on and pull yourself up."

After securing Toby's leash to the belt loop of her jeans, Talia hoisted Riley onto her back. *Russ would have put Riley on his shoulders right about here.* The child had always folded at this point on their family hike. Riley's chin rested in the crook of Talia's neck as she wrapped her small arms tightly around her mother's shoulders.

In the distant pink hills, the coyotes began their evening song, as if issuing the last rites of the day. Talia forged on toward the twinkling lights of their little neighborhood below. She tried not to think of what lay ahead. The darkened windows of the house and the cool, hollow silence within when she cracked the front door.

"What will we make for dinner tonight, sweets?" she asked, doing her best to sound upbeat. Not to show that she wished someone was waiting at home for them, having already prepared dinner. Waiting to hug them and ask them how the hike had gone, how their day had been.

"Mac and cheese," Riley yelped with sudden renewed energy.

"Um, I think you had enough of that at Grammie's yesterday." Talia laughed. "Let's shoot for something really healthy for us. Let's take good care of our bodies, shall we? Something yummy *and* good for us."

"All right, Momma. You choose."

And Talia did choose. After a meal of stuffed sweet potatoes and sautéed green beans, she tucked Riley, who appeared thoroughly exhausted for once, into bed for the night. There was something she had been wanting to do ever since Russ had called her on the phone in her dream last week. She'd almost forgotten what his voice sounded like. She couldn't let that happen. She didn't want to forget anything about Russ.

She sat on the edge of her bed after having quietly closed her bedroom door behind her. She pulled the old answering machine out of the top drawer of her nightstand and plugged its cord in next to the night-light. Her mouth was suddenly dry, her heart quickening more than she had anticipated. She opened the silver metal flap on top of the device and peered in. The recording tape was fully rewound, ready to go. Ready to play for her. She snapped the cover closed again, feeling her throat tighten as she hit the little black button with the silver arrow on it. She'd played the tape so many times in the first year. But there had come a time when she was afraid to play it again, in case the tape stretched beyond repair or suddenly snapped or, worse, wore out completely.

"Hi, Tal. Just checking in to say good night to my girls." Talia's jaw tightened. She held her breath. In the background, she could hear the howling wind, the chatter of emergency radio traffic, and the wail of distant sirens almost drowning out Russ's voice. "You must be over at the Reeds. I'm up here with my engine company. We're staying at the campground near Sycamore Ridge. It's blowing like hell out here. Really can't talk now, anyway. Looks like we're gonna be up all night."

Tears welled in Talia's eyes. Her nose tingled. She swallowed hard, pushing the pain away. Russ had called that night—*his last night*. But she had missed that call. She must have been running Riley's bath at the time. Neither of them had heard the phone ringing. Riley was only three then, but on nights when Russ was at work, she would shriek with joy when the phone rang. She'd loved saying good night to Dadda.

How many times had Talia regretted missing that call? More times than she'd been brave enough to play the message, she guessed.

"Just wanted to say I love you, Tal." His voice faded for a second, and then he went on, "There's a pay phone here. If we don't change locations tonight, I'll try calling again in the morning. Otherwise, I'll check in from the station when we get back to the city tomorrow. Sleep tight. I love you, Tal."

Those were the last words Talia ever heard from Russ. *The last real words.* A few hours after leaving that message, he would be lost to her forever. She sat for a moment, reflecting on whether it had been a good idea to play the tape again, to take the risk of ruining the only recording she had of him instead of saving it for when Riley was old enough to hear it for herself. Was she moving in the right direction? Back in the direction of the living? *Yes,* she thought so. Hadn't she just reinitiated the family hike? But then again, was this a case of one step forward, two steps back? Listening to the recording of Russ's voice always made it more difficult for her to believe he was really gone. And it made her angry more than sad. Like a mirage, he seemed so close yet so frustratingly unreachable, so maddeningly obscure.

What a waste of a beautiful human being. What a senseless, absurd, and pointless waste.

CHAPTER 8

THE SWAN AND
THE MONKEY

That Wednesday, Talia wouldn't be pursuing her usual tradition of rainbow shaved ice, karate classes, and an obligatory weekly visit to Hilltop Manor, because she had an altogether different tradition. One worthy of celebration—a joint celebration: it was her thirty-seventh birthday and Naomi's thirty-ninth. They were born on the same day, two years apart and, like twins, had always celebrated their birthdays together.

Talia leaned forward, getting a closer look at herself in her bathroom mirror. She'd already walked Riley over to Mrs. Kravitz down the street, who had been kind enough to offer to babysit anytime Talia needed her. Now Talia was busying herself with the tall order of making herself presentable for a night on the town. This year, it was Naomi's turn to be surprised. That meant it was Talia's turn to plan and pay for the event. They had been taking turns for years as adults. The day was to be a true sacrifice on Talia's part, but she knew Naomi would be wild for the idea. She would take her sister to see the Bolshoi Ballet, which was on tour in the US.

A few weeks ago, when she'd found out they were performing *Swan Lake* at the Shrine Auditorium in Los Angeles, it seemed like the perfect choice for their birthday adventure—that was, until she saw the price of the tickets. But she knew Naomi, who had aspired to be a ballerina herself as a young girl, would be overjoyed by the gesture, and given how hard things had been for her sister in the past few weeks, with Tory threatening to move in with her father, Talia felt it was a kind thing to do.

The only issue for Talia now was that it was a formal event—and she wasn't a formal sort of person.

Gussying up for the theater would take a fair bit of work. And so she'd borrowed some of her niece's secret makeup stash that she'd brought with her when she'd spent the weekend recently. Talia fished through the bag filled with overly bright lipsticks, shattered eye shadows, and clumpy mascaras. Thankfully, with a bit of work, she was able to resuscitate the necessities: a blue nail polish to match her dress, a baby-pink blush to bring a little life into her cheeks. She also found an old tube of tinted lip balm in the kitchen drawer of receipts—even if it did smell a little on the rancid side after sitting idle for the past two years.

The truth was, she'd never been a girly girl, and any inspiration for making herself pretty had been extinguished on the day she'd shaved her head after Russ's funeral. Yes, her hair had grown back fully, and her chestnut curls hung below her shoulders now. But the desire to look attractive was something that didn't cross her mind these days. *What was the point?*

Talia paused, standing straighter. Was that true? Was she choosing to let herself go?

Well, no, not consciously, anyway. But she would rather have been pulling on a pair of jeans and a sweatshirt and heading out to a baseball game instead of the theater for the evening.

"What do you think?" she asked Toby, who was watching her curiously from the doorway as she leaned over to check her eye makeup one last time in the mirror. "How's this for a resurrection?" As if on cue, the dog stood and headed for his bed. Talia couldn't help but chuckle. "Jeez, it can't be that bad," she called after him.

Just then, blaring through the silence of the empty house, the landline rang. Talia practically skipped over to the phone beside her bed. Maybe she was happier to be getting out on the town for the night than she had realized.

"Hello?"

"Hey, sis," Naomi said. "I'm still picking you up tonight, right?"

"Well, I could drive, if you'd like. This year it's my turn—"

"No, thanks," Naomi cut in, chuckling. "I insist. That wasn't really a question."

"You're that afraid of being seen in my old pickup truck?" Talia teased. They both laughed for a few seconds before she added, "Hey, I was just thinking about our birthday surprises. Do you remember how when we were younger, when we were living in Brisbane with Aunt Miriam—"

"That we'd get those mysterious birthday presents?" Naomi interjected. "Yeah, of course I do. Why do you bring that up now?"

"I dunno. I was just thinking about it—now, as an adult, how creepy that was. How freaked out I'd be if some mysterious person was sending Riley gifts on her birthday. Whoever was sending them had to be someone who knew us but who didn't want to go through Aunt Miriam to get to us. Someone who knew where we were after we'd left Saint Mary's. Maybe someone from the family. I say that because the gifts were always age-appropriate. You know, think about it. Books and coloring pencils early on, and then, when we were old enough, the bottles of nail polish and cards full of pocket money. That was so weird. Bizarre, actually. Never a return address on the packages, always a cryptic note, signed only with the initial *M*."

"*M* for mystery," Naomi added, her voice amplifying as she hummed the tune from the TV show *The Twilight Zone*. They both laughed.

"Where's my age-appropriate gift now?" Talia joked.

"I know," Naomi replied with a scoff. "I'd like my mortgage paid for the month—thank you very much, M!"

Talia took the phone into the bathroom, the receiver on speaker mode, returning to the job of adding some color to her eyelids when a casual thought crossed her mind. "Do you remember my eleventh birthday? Your thirteenth? The year I got the bike and you got the skates."

"Ohhh, that was the best year ever. Great gifts," Naomi affirmed.

"Well, something came to mind last week when I was talking to the attorney from Australia, Mr. Bergelsohn. Something he said jogged my memory, and I thought of it again today. During the call, he had referred to me as *my dear*, and I remember the card that came with our gifts that year. It was signed, 'Many happy returns, my dears.'"

"Jeez, how can you remember shit like that?" Naomi laughed. "That was friggin' twenty-six years ago."

"I dunno. It's always stuck with me, though. I still would love to know who the mysterious M was. Or if M is still alive after all these years and if they lost track of us when we moved to the States."

"No idea, sis, but you're right. The mystery gifts definitely stopped once we left Australia. Anyway, I'm going to finish getting ready. I still haven't decided what dress I'm wearing, Versace or Prada. I'm beside myself. See you soon. I'll be at your place in half an hour. Give or take."

"Okay, thanks for checking in," Talia said, eyeing herself in the mirror again—this time with horror—as she took in the very plain, off-the-rack department store dress hanging loosely from her slight form. The conversation got her thinking, though. Back then, if it hadn't been for the mysterious M sending them gifts all those years, she and Naomi wouldn't have received anything at all on their birthday—certainly not from Aunt Miriam or Uncle Gus. In fact, the kindness of M's gestures had always left Talia feeling hopeful that someone out there still cared about her. When they were younger, she and Naomi had imagined that they must have a fairy godmother. As they grew, they came to see these thoughtful acts of generosity as proof there were good and kind people in the world.

Talia redirected her attention to brushing her thick curls, throwing on the only long jacket she owned—a pretty violet faux suede that Russ had always said was the same color as her eyes. It covered the loose dress quite well, she thought. There was little more she could do to improve her appearance. She threw on a pair of comfortable walking shoes and went downstairs to let Toby out one more time before Naomi arrived.

An hour later, Naomi was driving Talia in her black BMW toward the city just in time to catch the Wednesday-evening rush-hour traffic.

Both Naomi and Talia despised the traffic jams characteristic of Los Angeles, but sunny Southern California had been appealing following their dreary years in Seattle, where they had first lived with their aunt upon immigrating from Australia. They both loved the beach and sunshine, so California was a natural choice. By the time Talia had finished her undergraduate studies at UCLA, both she and Naomi had considered themselves true Californians.

The sisters enjoyed a harried but satisfying birthday dinner at a tiny, famed Italian restaurant in Burbank before continuing another thirty minutes along Interstate 5 to downtown Los Angeles.

"I'm surprised to see you in a dress tonight," Naomi said, nodding at Talia as they made their way from the overflow parking lot a full four blocks away from the theater's grand entry.

Talia sighed. "I'm just as surprised as you are, but the occasion mandated it." She pulled her coat flaps closed and wrapped her arms around her waist as she walked. Naomi's smoky-pink satin gown with a chiffon overlay was spectacular, but Talia had already complimented her at dinner. Once would have to be enough, she decided. If the chiffon had been tarlatan, it might've passed as an offshoot of a ballerina's tutu, but Talia chose not to mention this.

They walked for a few strides before Naomi added, "How did we turn out so differently? It's pretty crazy, isn't it? That I'd be a girly girl and you such a tomboy." Talia tried not to let her face register any offense as she glanced around uncomfortably, surveying the beautifully adorned women in their long, flowing gowns and their tuxedo-clad partners gliding along the sidewalks in the direction of the Shrine Auditorium. *Just like butterflies and penguins,* she told herself.

"Yeah, pretty crazy," she said, letting it go. But her mind jumped to how uncomfortable she'd been in dresses in her earlier years. And to Aunt Miriam's awful husband, Uncle Gus, or Pumpkin Head, as she and Naomi called him in private—the man who, during Talia's adolescence, had made her blood run cold. How Aunt Miriam had forced her as a young girl to wear dresses in order to look feminine for her bridge club guests even when doing so made Talia so uneasy, so terrified she'd solicit the same looks from Uncle Gus that Naomi was regularly subjected to—and sometimes she did, despite the benefits of her boyish figure.

Talia shook off the thought, wiping sweaty palms on her faux-suede jacket. She looked at the tall-standing buildings and traffic and throngs of people around her, all the activity and life. Los Angeles seemed to be powered by it, if not warmed by it, year-round, as though the city itself was attached to the battery of the people who lived within it. They strolled through another intersection, walking alongside a stream of cars jamming up in front of parking lot entrances dotted between a series of shopwindows decorated for Halloween.

Beside the front door of one shop was a large scarecrow with a pumpkin head. Talia's shoulders tightened at the sight of the thing.

"Look who it is," she quipped, trying to make light of it as she nodded at the scarecrow.

"Are we supposed to know that fellow?" Naomi asked with a laugh. "Is he your date?"

"It's Uncle Gus, the Pumpkin Head."

"Oh God," Naomi replied, sighing. They took a few steps, memories of that wretched man funneling into their minds. "Have you ever thought about what you'd do to Pumpkin Head now that you're an adult? What you'd say to him?"

"Say to him? It's what I would do to him that he would need to worry about. But seriously, I haven't given that horrid little man any thought in years," Talia lied.

"Yeah, I gotta say I'd punch him in his pumpkin-size nose or kick him in the—"

"Okay, okay, well, he's probably dead by now. So maybe we should let it go. All that drink and those smelly cigars likely did him in years ago," Talia said, leading Naomi around another corner, grateful to have worn a pair of sneakers beneath her long dress.

"I can't decide what I'd do or say," Naomi went on, clip-clopping over the sidewalk. "He was the only person in our lives who terrified me more than Aunt Miriam did."

"Well, he was sure scary enough to look at," Talia said, and then, to lighten the mood, added, "and for sure, his temper was shorter than he was."

They both laughed then, but truth be told, they'd never get over the emotional scars Pumpkin Head had left on them. And as far as his looks went, those had not been easily forgotten either. Cold blue eyes—so light they were almost translucent—sat deep in his wide face, below a furrowed brow and a shiny balding head marked by a large, unsightly scar that ran the length of his scalp. The girls' school friends had been so afraid of him, they seldom visited, and those who did often told unsettling stories about what he had said to them in private. Perhaps Uncle Gus had been aware of how his looks affected people, because he wore a bowtie and jacket on most days, even when he was at home. And he was at home a great deal of the time. He didn't seem to be employed, though he was always well stocked with cigars and spirits.

"God knows where Miriam found that creep," Naomi added.

"You know what was most weird about him?" Talia asked absently. "The fact that he and Aunt Miriam never, ever argued. I guess they were just happy to have found such good company in each other. You know? Misery loves company."

Talia recalled then that, on occasion, Uncle Gus even mustered displays of affection toward their aunt, particularly when he was planning to spend the afternoon at the horseraces and needed a loan. On those days, he could be downright charming, showering her with praise for her buxom shape and her culinary creations and coaxing her to muster one of her elaborately decorated tea cakes.

"The audacity of Aunt Miriam, bringing that little cretin into our lives. I can't *believe* you still visit that witch."

"She doesn't have anybody else," Talia muttered, hoping to drop the subject, but Naomi kept going.

"After all the hell the two of them put us through, she deserves to die alone in that miserable nursing home." Naomi was clearly unafraid to vocalize this loudly, drawing curious and offended stares from the people nearby, but that was her sister for you. Naomi simply didn't have a filter.

Talia decided it was likely best to end the downward spiral now and walk on in silence. After a deep breath, she said, "You're probably right, and I can assure you, she's quite miserable." She allowed Naomi to lead her the rest of the way while her mind strayed back to the first day they had ever met Gus.

He had been with their aunt when she showed up out of the blue at Saint Mary's. It was a curious sight—Miriam and Gus arriving at the orphanage. No one had been to visit them since they had been abandoned there five years previously. Some of the girls were lucky enough to have regular visitors on Sundays. Relatives and prospective adoptive families would come to spend the day, bringing coloring books, paper dolls, and sweets.

While no one had paid Talia and Naomi visits, regular or otherwise, for all those years, there was one memorable occasion on which a visit of sorts had occurred. During a Palm Sunday Mass at Saint Mary's, a certain woman and her husband had noticed how "angelic" Talia's violet eyes were and thought they might want to adopt her. The couple had been dressed in their Sunday best, she in a pale-blue frock with a yellow scarf around her long dark hair and her husband in a jacket and tie. He held his hat in his hand, the way their grandad had whenever he greeted anyone.

The couple had been chatting in the shade of the courtyard with Sister Mary Ignatius when the girls exited the chapel after the service. Talia overheard part of their conversation as she hurried by to join Naomi, who had raced ahead with the older girls to the playground, where they often gathered after Mass. Before long, Sister Mary Ignatius and the couple made their way to where Naomi and Talia were skipping rope and singing songs as they dodged the undulating twines held by two of the older girls. It was Naomi's turn to skip, and she slipped quickly between the double ropes, her graceful knees flying high as they always did. The rest of the girls, standing on the sidelines, sang in unison.

> *Charlie Chaplin went to France,*
> *To teach the ladies how to dance.*
> *First the heel, then the toe,*
> *Then the splits, and around you go!*

Then it was Talia's turn. She jumped in as Naomi skipped out. The song changed to her favorite tune. It started slowly and quickly became faster. "Applesauce . . . mustard . . . cider . . . how many legs has a spider? One, two, three, four, five, six, seven, eight."

Talia jumped on one foot at a time and then with both feet at the same time, going faster and faster as the rhyme was hastily repeated. She wasn't as graceful as her big sister, but with her speed and agility, Talia made up for what she lacked in poise. The older girls swinging the ropes never could stump her, even when they were going at full speed.

When her turn was over, Talia sprang out from between the ropes and kneeled on the grass next to Naomi, catching her breath and waiting impatiently until she could go again. She noticed that the woman with the yellow scarf seemed to be staring at her. Though she pretended not to pay attention, Talia could feel the woman's eyes on her and strained her ears to hear above the other girls' chanting so that she could eavesdrop on what Sister Mary

Ignatius was saying to the couple. The nun shook her head in disapproval, indicating something along the lines of Talia not being a wise choice. She steered the couple toward Yvonne, who was sitting in the shade of a giant tree with a book on her lap. Yvonne generally avoided skipping rope with the other girls. Talia supposed Yvonne was afraid her glasses might fly off her face, but it also could have been because some of the older girls often called her Fatty. The adults were closer now, and Talia could hear their conversation clearly.

"Yvonne," Sister Mary Ignatius offered boldly, "is well behaved, a good student, and of agreeable temperament. She is a much safer choice than a girl who refuses to wear shoes and disobeys rules about climbing trees."

Talia froze. Her suspicions had been confirmed: Sister Mary Ignatius was talking about her—and not just that but talking a couple out of adopting her.

The couple had looked a little doubtful, like they didn't care at all about adopting a wild child, as long as she had the eyes of an angel. They'd kept staring at her, and to this day, Talia could remember exactly how strange and alarming that attention had felt. Something wasn't right about the way they were smiling excessively. The man was bald and was missing both of his front teeth, making him a curious vision, not unlike an overgrown baby.

Talia's bigger source of concern then, however, had been Sister Mary Ignatius. The old nun wasn't even trying to hide how troubled she was by their persistence. Talia remembered wondering briefly if the grumpy old woman would miss her if she were adopted. She didn't think so, and she was right to have doubted it. Only years later would Talia deduce the real reason for Sister Mary Ignatius's refusal to release her from captivity.

"Honestly," Sister Mary had said with a snort, "that one belongs on the other side of the compound wall, with the Aboriginal children, if you ask me." Again, the couple stared back at Talia, as though trying to decide for themselves if the nun's assessment was to be trusted. But it wasn't their attention, this time, that Talia observed.

She'd kept her eyes locked on Sister Mary Ignatius only. At the time, she felt confused. How could she call herself a woman of God and yet clearly be discouraging the adoption of an orphan? Did Sister Mary really hate her that much? Was she right?

But it hadn't been hatred in Sister Mary's eyes that day. It'd been something else, something far more nefarious.

Either way, the nun's comment had caught Talia's attention. She'd always wondered what was on the other side of the compound wall, where she often heard squeals of laughter and the echoes of balls bouncing off cement. How difficult would it be to scale the wall? Was it possible?

Talia had looked to the courtyard's perimeter. The thick brick walls were so tall, with shards of broken glass poking up from their cemented tops. The Aboriginal children must have been quite precious; it seemed they were very well guarded.

It looked like the couple was asking more questions, but Talia couldn't hear them over the songs of the skipping girls. She hoped Sister Mary Ignatius would be convincing. She wasn't keen to go with the strange-looking man. For one thing, she knew the couple would not adopt Naomi too. She had overheard the woman telling her husband she only wanted the little girl with the beautiful violet eyes. It was plain to see, even at a distance, that Naomi had eyes almost as black as her long eyelashes and the two thick braids that hung down to her waist.

The woman seemed to be considering her options. She and her husband eyed Yvonne carefully but made no move to approach her. Again, they turned toward Talia, staring as if they'd stumbled upon a prized treasure. Behind her white glove, the woman had whispered something into the man's ear, to which he offered an enthusiastic nod of agreement. Sister Mary Ignatius did her best to lead the couple back in the direction of the chapel, but they seemed not to hear or see her. Unlike most orphans, the last thing in the world Talia wanted was to be adopted. She had spent night after night fantasizing about her mother, somehow resurrected from the dead, just like Lazarus, returning to Saint Mary's to reclaim her, and now that a couple had set their sights on her, she felt a wild sense of panic take flight in her chest.

Her eyes flashed between the grotesque baby-man's smile and Naomi, who played within sight across the playground. She'd rather never be adopted at all than be permanently separated from her sister, but that was what appeared to be unfolding at that very moment.

Talia looked to Sister Mary Ignatius next, who gave her a stiff-lipped, deadpan stare.

And somehow, that spoke volumes. It was time for Talia to take matters into her own hands.

She kicked off her shoes and scampered over to the closest tree. It was one of her favorites, a huge elm. She knew every branch and foothold by heart. She launched herself at the trunk and quickly scrambled up to a height that was well out of any adult's reach. She believed this would be a clear demonstration of her ineligibility to be anyone's daughter. The stunt seemed to work like a charm.

"This way," Naomi said, guiding Talia toward the grand entry of the Shrine Auditorium at last. "What are you grinning about back there? You've been spacing out for the last five minutes."

"Oh, nothing," Talia replied, clutching her coat around her waist as they made their way to their seats. If only her younger self knew how far they'd eventually go. To this day, she could still remember the look on the woman's face when she'd climbed up that tree. She had grasped her husband's arm with both of her white gloves, her mouth forming a perfect circle. If it were necessary, Talia had been prepared to demonstrate her terrifying monkey calls, show her teeth, and maybe even bite someone. But thankfully, it never came to that. The couple had hastily disappeared into the rectory. Sister Mary Ignatius was on their heels, dragging a baffled Yvonne behind her.

Talia's punishment for the display of wanton defiance, as Sister Mary Ignatius had put it, was to be locked in the stairwell under the bell tower during Sunday dinner that evening. At the time, Talia had simply accepted her punishment, as she always did. In her view, not being separated from Naomi forever had been well worth missing a Sunday dinner. Besides, she enjoyed climbing the stairs of the bell tower in the dark. She would practice taking them one by one and then two by two until she could manage all three flights at full speed without tripping once. This was a particularly good way, she had discovered, to tire herself out enough to be able to fall asleep on the landing without a pillow or a blanket. She had been so confused, though, at the time—she'd thought she'd helped Sister Mary Ignatius's cause, discouraging the would-be adoptive parents so effectively. She had almost expected to be praised for her quick thinking.

But now that Talia was an adult, she and Naomi realized that someone at Saint Mary's had been colluding with Aunt Miriam—someone had helped to conceal their true identities and keep them hidden for all those years. Someone in that house of God had been willing to enter into a bargain with the devil—to help Miriam get her hands on Talia and Naomi's trust funds. Talia still wondered if that someone had been the small woman in the long white dress, the one with the huge eyes behind thick glasses, the kooka-burra lady whom they'd met on the day Aunt Miriam had taken them to Saint Mary's—Sister Mary Ignatius.

The lights faded in the Shrine Auditorium, and the curtains rose before the audience. Talia and Naomi had made it comfortably to their seats with time to spare, and if it weren't for the matter of a tall man sitting in front of Naomi, everything would've been perfect.

Talia offered to trade seats with Naomi. She knew how much the event would mean to her, and her sister agreed. At least that way, one of them would get her money's worth.

Talia scanned the auditorium for celebrities but came up short, spying only a local TV sportscaster. With a little effort, she admonished herself to return her attention to the stage, where the flowing white dresses and long pink legs of the dancers had now been set in motion. She braced herself for a performance that wasn't going to be nearly as much fun as a Dodgers game would have been—they were playing the Giants tonight—but she did her best to find some joy in the moment, knowing that Naomi would be enthralled.

And it seemed Naomi was captivated from the moment the curtains rose. She might as well have been on the stage performing alongside the dancers. She tilted her head sympathetically when the music took on a melancholy tone and straightened her back when the music flared again dramatically. She seemed bewitched by what Talia would later sum up in her review of the evening as bad romance, trickery, and an overly tragic ending. It was not lost on Talia that this review could just as easily sum up her sister's love life as it had the ballet.

The ballet went on. The musical arrangement, heavy on the timpani, softly brought in the long, lilting notes of clarinets. *Music fit for dying swans,* Talia thought. Just past the right ear on the giant head in front of her, she could see the lead ballerina, center stage, spinning interminably, her flowing white gown encircling her like a pastry doily. Talia was dizzy just watching her.

She could tell by the dramatic change in music, and by the stillness that settled over the audience, that a somber act must have been coming up next. Naomi dabbed her cheeks with a tissue. Talia closed her eyes and leaned her head against the back of her seat, the music of the orchestra carrying her far, far away, back to a memory of a music box with a dancing ballerina.

Talia and Naomi sat on the ends of their beds in the dormitory of Saint Mary's, along with all the other girls at the orphanage. It was bedtime and Naomi's turn to carry the music box. Talia sat beside her sister, staring at the box with adoration, loving every detail of its floral wooden engravings.

Inside the box was a dancing ballerina and an assortment of toffees and sweets.

Each night at bedtime, after their baths, the girls were required to apply to their chapped hands and faces a thick, sticky goop that smelled like dead fish. They hated the stench of the balm, but Sister Louise insisted that it kept the cracks in their skin from bleeding and that it was good for them. The girls didn't have a say in the matter, regardless, and so they did as they were instructed. But even after the balm vanished into their skin, they could still smell it. Even then, while reflecting on the memory in the Shrine Auditorium, Talia felt a gag prodding the back of her throat at the very thought of that smell. It'd been so bad once that it'd made her vomit on her bedcovers. The matron had made her sleep without sheets or a blanket that night.

But on special nights—when all the girls had been good and no one had vomited on their bed or accidentally peed in the bathtub—Sister Louise let each of the girls take a sweet out of the music box before they brushed their teeth and said their prayers. Since they had all been very well behaved on the night it was Naomi's turn with the music box, Sister Louise agreed to read them a story—a bonus. The tale was one of Talia's favorites: a story about a poorly behaved boy named Oliver, who was an orphan, just like she was.

Just then, the audience in the auditorium broke into applause, startling Talia back into the present moment.

Had she drifted off to sleep? If only she could sleep that well at home in her bed. The velvet curtains lowered for intermission. *Final inning,* Talia rejoiced, wondering what was going on at Dodger Stadium, just a few miles away. Naomi dabbed her nose with a tissue and wiped away the mascara running under her eyes. Talia sneaked another look at her watch as they stood to stretch their legs before battling the crowd headed for the ladies' room.

CHAPTER 9

COLD COMFORT

Two days after her birthday night at the ballet with Naomi—who was still raving about the Bolshoi's rendition of *Swan Lake*—Talia flipped on the evening news while cooking dinner. A federal jury had just convicted Ramzi Yousef in the 1993 Trade Center bombing, according to Dan Rather. *Well, that only took four years, didn't it?* Talia skipped channels, settling on a sports broadcast. The Florida Marlins would be up against the Cleveland Indians in the upcoming World Series. *Now that ought to be interesting.*

"Toby's eating Nay-Nay, Momma!" Riley called out, running in from the living room, in hot pursuit of the dog, Riley's stuffed toy horse in his mouth. Then they were gone again, back down the hallway at full speed. *"Momma!"*

"I'm coming. *I'm coming!*" Talia yelled over the TV while trying to avoid reducing the stir-fry she was preparing for dinner to charcoal. Toby returned then, now in the lead, bolting for the back door that, to his dismay, Talia had just closed, the toy whipping around in his mouth like a flag. Riley shrieking.

To top it all off, the phone rang.

Talia snatched the toy from Toby on his harried U-turn from his obstructed escape route, threw it at Riley like a star quarterback, and muted the TV before finally making it to the phone on the kitchen wall.

"Hello?" she asked, trying not to sound at her wit's end.

It was Dr. Frankel. She recognized his voice immediately. "I'm afraid we've had to move your aunt to West Oaks Regional Medical Center, Talia. Unfortunately, it looks like she may have had another stroke. She's not doing well. Can you come?"

Talia's silence embarrassed her. She flushed with guilt. She'd missed her usual Hilltop Manor visit this week to attend the ballet with Naomi. And any bad news like this stunned her, flooding her with memories of other bad news. She wasn't ready for this turn of events. It was too sudden—not entirely unexpected but too sudden.

"Things are looking quite serious, Talia," he added. "In cases like this, it's nice to know what the patient and family would want, what measures they might want us to take to prolong life, should such actions become necessary."

Talia figured he was trying to ask whether Aunt Miriam had ever shared her feelings about life-support measures. She realized how dire the situation was. And though Dr. Frankel's question was posed in a serious tone, it almost made Talia laugh out loud. Her aunt would *never* have discussed so personal an issue with her. And ever since her stroke five years ago, she hadn't been able to discuss anything with anyone.

She hesitated before answering. "I'll have to consult with my sister," Talia finally said in her calmest voice, trying to buy herself time. "We're the only relatives she has, and of course we'll want to do the right thing."

The right thing, she thought to herself. *Whatever that is.*

Talia hung up the phone and called Naomi. There was no answer, so she tried Naomi's office and then her mobile number, where she was then prompted—after Naomi's detailed and lengthy voice-mail greeting—to leave a message.

This meant she'd be going to see Aunt Miriam at the hospital by herself.

She picked up the phone once more, dialing Mrs. Kravitz down the street. "Hey there, Mrs. Kravitz. It's Talia *again*. Sorry to ask, but are you available to watch Riley this evening? There's been a bit of a family emergency."

"Oy, of course, my *bubbale*. You know you can call on me anytime," she said in her heavy Ukrainian accent. "I hope everything's okay?" But before Talia could elaborate, the woman hastily added, "Have you met the new neighbors yet? Quite the story there!"

"Ah, not yet, Mrs. Kravitz. But if it's okay with you, I'll drop Riley off in a few minutes. You're a lifesaver. I just need to get her fed." It was then that Talia realized she'd completely forgotten about dinner on the stovetop. She threw her free hand up in the air in desperation as though grasping for help from above.

Dinner was beyond salvage.

Cold pizza leftovers would have to suffice. Riley would be happy, at least.

Talia nursed a lukewarm cup of coffee as she paced back and forth in the West Oaks Regional Medical Center front lobby. She'd been waiting for over an hour for Naomi—whom she had finally reached from the pay phone next to the elevator bank by the hospital gift shop.

Upon arrival at the medical center, Talia had learned Aunt Miriam was in the intensive care unit on a ventilator. Her brain scan showed she had experienced a massive intracerebral hemorrhage, according to Dr. Frankel, who explained that the brain damage was catastrophic. The mechanical breathing provided by the ventilator was the only thing keeping Miriam alive. She would be reevaluated in the morning, but it was almost certain they would have to decide whether to remove her from life support. If not, Miriam faced the prospect of spending the remainder of her days in a vegetative state, with nursing care around the clock. Dr. Frankel's words stuck with Talia. She knew she could trust his advice, but she couldn't imagine being the one to decide to pull the plug. *What the hell is taking Naomi so long?*

Dr. Frankel had rested his hand on her arm soothingly. "Take a little time," he'd advised. "Discuss this with Naomi. I'm just about to start my evening rounds. I'll meet you upstairs when your sister gets here. Just have the ICU desk staff page me. Then we'll discuss the next steps."

After that, she'd called Naomi repeatedly until she'd finally gotten a response on her mobile line.

A moonless night had fallen, giving the illusion that the hospital lobby, with its floor-to-ceiling windows, had been transformed into a giant shiny black box. The walls pressed in on Talia as she counted out her steps across the black-and-white tiled lobby. The overhead lighting was harsh and clinical. She felt like a rat in a laboratory experiment, not knowing which way to turn in the maze to avoid the electric shock that would follow any erroneous decision. And there were decisions to be made.

Just then, Naomi's high heels clicked loudly on the tile floor as she crossed the hospital's main lobby. Her designer purse swung below the black cashmere shawl draped over her shoulder. The oversize lenses of her Fendi sunglasses obscured most of her face, despite the fact that the sun had set hours ago.

"Well, here I am," she said, clearly annoyed. "I was showing a home in Westlake. What's the latest?"

"Showing a home?" Talia inquired skeptically, noting Naomi's evening attire and bright-red lipstick, which looked freshly applied. She couldn't help but think her sister had perhaps been at a cocktail party rather than at a property showing.

"What's happening?" Naomi reiterated, her voice flat.

"As I said on the phone, Miriam's had another stroke. It's worse than that, though. I just spoke with Dr. Frankel an hour ago. The damage appears irreversible. It seems our next step will be deciding whether to keep her on life support. He'll be meeting us upstairs to discuss options, but he'll need an answer by the morning."

The cold coffee Talia had been sipping wasn't sitting well with her. A wave of nausea swept over her as she crushed the cup, tipping the remaining contents into a nearby trash can. The back of her head throbbed. Maybe a migraine was about to add to the turmoil of the day.

Naomi raised her brows until they showed over her sunglasses, seemingly unmoved by the news. Talia suspected her sister was about to say something along the lines of, *Let's pull the plug tonight and get it over with; I've got places to be.*

Thankfully, she didn't say that. Instead, she said, "What do you think should be done?" But before Talia could muster a response, Naomi continued on. "Essentially, the bottom line is that she has no chance of making it. Right?" It was clear Naomi did not care to know the details, but Talia was surprised at the venom in her voice. "Christ, just take care of it, Talia. I don't want any part of this mess! You should have known better than to call me. You know I don't give a damn about what happens to her."

Talia stared back at her sister, speechless. "Jeez, I only did what I thought was right."

Naomi tilted her head condescendingly, stopping Talia in her tracks. "If it were up to me, I would have left the sorry witch in Seattle years ago and washed my hands of her. You're the one who decided to take on this charity case—and now it's *your* responsibility to see this through to the end."

"Someone had to take over her health decisions—"

"That isn't true. Nobody had to do anything. You chose to insert yourself into this situation."

"I don't want to be the one to decide when she takes her last breath," Talia said, trying to keep her voice down. People in the lobby had begun to stare.

"Then you should've thought of that before—"

"Don't make me do this alone, Naomi!"

Talia's plea rang through the air, and time seemed to slow in the wake of it. And there it was—the heart of the matter. Talia was asking for help, and Naomi should have known that Talia *never* asked for help.

Talia took a deep breath through flared nostrils and let it out slowly, trying to reset the tone between them. "I wish more than ever that she would've sorted this out when she had her wits about her, but then again, she was only in her sixties when she had the first stroke. It probably never occurred to her she would need to. I understand your stance," she added. "You're right about her, and you're right that I agreed to take on her care alone, but it's not fair to ask me to now be the sole decision maker when it comes to essentially ending her life."

Naomi sighed, falling into a petulant silence. Talia noted that she looked thinner than usual. And the way Naomi crossed her arms was less like a testy child and more like somebody trying to physically block an oncoming assault—an effort at self-defense.

Naomi finally removed her sunglasses, and Talia realized that her sister was not being petulant but that she was utterly furious. She raced to stave off the assault. "This isn't the time, Naomi. Not here!"

"What do you mean, this isn't the time?" Naomi's tone was cutting, her voice loud enough to now draw looks of concern from people in the hospital lobby who had been watching them since Naomi's arrival. "Jesus, Talia!

Haven't you been seeking legal guardianship over her health care for the last few months?" Naomi's nostrils flared, and her lips raised into a snarl.

Talia felt her knees buckle slightly. *Where is all this rage coming from?* It had been a colossal mistake to call Naomi.

The situation would only worsen if Talia admitted she still hadn't attained legal guardianship over their aunt's affairs. She thought about the phone call she'd received a week earlier, from the legal assistant in Los Angeles, and how, despite saying she would do so, she hadn't firmed up an appointment yet. How she'd had second thoughts about imposing on Naomi to pick Riley up from school when she knew she was so busy in the office. Naomi had not exactly been overly eager to play taxi service for Talia. But in truth, Talia knew she alone was to blame for not having made it to the law firm in Los Angeles.

"I . . . " Talia was lost for words. Why *hadn't* she gone to sign those papers? Maybe she was more worried than curious about what Mr. Bergelsohn in Australia had for them. Whatever he had unearthed from their past could not have been good news. It never was. Something even darker than Naomi's anger occurred to Talia. What if Aunt Miriam died before she could get down to Los Angeles? She couldn't have legal guardianship over someone already dead, could she? It dawned on her then that she was between a rock and a hard place. She couldn't agree to ending life-support measures for her aunt, even if she had wanted to. If that happened, she'd probably never get any information from Mr. Bergelsohn in Australia.

Talia's chest tightened, anxiety knifing through her body in spikes. Now she might have to deal with the legalities of probate, which could take *years* to sort out. She was in a situation that could have been avoided if she'd followed through with the attorneys, as she should have.

Naomi was still talking, her voice agitated and escalating, but Talia heard none of her sister's words.

Her temples throbbed. The pain in her head had finally grown to an unmanageable level. If she were honest with herself, the history of strokes among the women in her family, combined with her migraines, was scary. Her maternal grandmother had succumbed to a stroke at an early age, and Aunt Miriam had now had two significant incidents. Would she be next?

"*Stop*, Naomi!" Talia broke in, her tone surprising even herself, her right hand clasping her forehead. "Aunt Miriam is in a bed up there, circling the drain, and here we are arguing morosely about who is going to give the order to pull the plug. I'm telling you, I don't have the heart for that right now."

She had wanted to add that she thought Naomi was behaving like a spoiled princess and that she was sick of handling Aunt Miriam's affairs all alone, but she knew this would only pour gasoline on the fire. Though her heart was pounding in concert with the throbbing of her temples, she was able to remain silent and headed straight for the elevators, leaving Naomi in her wake.

Talia pressed the elevator's up button, only for it not to register. Frustrated, she pressed it again and again and again, until she felt somebody's hand on her shoulder. She turned around to see her older sister there—sunglasses pushed up on the top of her head but clearly not angry anymore.

"Let's take the stairs," Naomi said quietly, piloting Talia toward the stairwell.

It wasn't even remotely close to an apology, but Talia recognized this for the olive branch that it truly was, at least when Naomi was involved. And for now, that would have to do.

The rhythmic hissing of Aunt Miriam's ventilator dominated the small ICU room, creating the sense of all four walls closing in on them, getting smaller and smaller. As Talia and Naomi stood at the foot of the bed, numbly watching their aunt, Talia whispered, "I feel like we're standing in the middle of a giant pressure cooker."

"I promise not to turn off the ventilator while you're gone." Naomi winked. "Do you need to step outside for some air?"

"Probably, but I'm not going to," Talia replied, tucking her hands into the pockets of the long sweater that draped over her faded blue jeans. Fresh air wouldn't help. Their aunt was entirely helpless, and it was strange to see her that way—more so for Naomi, probably, who hadn't seen her in years. Miriam was a frail old woman, clinging to her last days of life. But for Talia, Aunt Miriam was more than that. She was a vanishing bridge to their past.

When she was gone, she would take with her critical details of their family history, the truths that had been kept from her and Naomi for so many years. *Well, unless Mr. Bergelsohn was in the know.* If he had been as close to Grandad, as close as a brother—as he'd told Talia he was—he might have intimate knowledge of the family he would be willing to share.

Naomi seemed to be thinking along the same lines about Miriam. "We should've interrogated her harder before she lost her mind. God, I hope she kept a journal or a diary," she muttered, referring to the grim reality that perhaps nobody outside of Miriam knew the details of their mother's death, their father's disappearance, or their abandonment at Saint Mary's when they'd still had extended family capable of caring for them.

Talia held the solid heart-shaped pendant on the long chain around her neck up to her lips, thinking deeply. Naomi was partly right. "Well, she didn't actually lose her mind, Naomi. She was in there, conscious, but just not able to express herself. I always thought maybe she'd get better," she said a few machine hisses later.

"Well, better as far as her functional state, maybe. She was never going to improve her character," Naomi added without bothering to whisper. "There will never be an excuse or an explanation for how she treated us as kids."

Talia took the cue to stay silent.

"She looks dead already," Naomi said coldly.

"I think she died years ago," Talia acknowledged, knowing she was right. A familiar tightness in her throat was growing. She found herself wondering what Aunt Miriam's hopes and dreams had been and if they had ever been realized. The woman had been an enigma to her for as long as she and Naomi could recall, going all the way back to 1969, when they'd been transferred from Saint Mary's to Miriam and Gus's care. When the couple had suddenly shown up, out of the blue, to claim the girls as Miriam's wards.

Talia took a seat beside Aunt Miriam's bed, reaching for her hand. Naomi scoffed quietly, shaking her head as she walked to the hospital room's window, staring out at a parking lot.

"What are you thinking?" Naomi asked. Talia pretended to miss the insulting tone in her sister's voice—to ignore the fact that Naomi was calling her out for showing their aunt any human kindness. And who could blame her? When they had been living with their aunt and uncle after leaving Saint

Mary's, they had both overheard Miriam telling someone on the phone one evening that she had been able to locate Talia and Naomi at the orphanage with the help of a private detective. But at the time, this had made no sense to them. Because both she and Naomi—even though they had been so young when they arrived at Saint Mary's—clearly remembered that it was Aunt Miriam who had dropped them off there in the first place.

"Nothing, really," Talia lied. Their minds were everywhere at once: there in the room with a slowly dying woman and, in Talia's case, nearly thirty years earlier, when Aunt Miriam had arrived at Saint Mary's to take over her custody.

That morning, Sister Louise—who had always shown the girls kindness—came to the office to say goodbye to Talia and Naomi. She was overjoyed that the girls, who had been at Saint Mary's for five years by that point, had finally been found by family. The story had even made the papers. The nun attributed the apparent miracle to her prayers to Saint Thomas and the Virgin Mother. She had fallen to her knees in front of the girls, wrapped her arms around them, and proclaimed, "In the dark night of the soul, bright flows the river of God." She had cried with joy then and promised to hold the girls forever in her prayers to Saint Mary, whom she would ask to watch over them in their new lives. Then she'd reached into the pockets of her pinafore and handed them both small boxes with a mother-of-pearl rosary neatly nestled inside soft tissue paper.

Talia glanced at her sister across the hospital room—Naomi in her black cocktail dress and spiked heels. Back then, all those years ago, she'd cried as Sister Louise had hugged her goodbye, completely torn apart by it. Talia, conversely, had fallen into a state of silence that would last for a week. It was strange how the two of them had changed so much in their adult years and how their preferences for coping had morphed. How life's traumas had altered the very essence of who they were.

Sister Mary Ignatius hadn't even come to the office to say goodbye that day. But no one had seemed surprised.

As a small child, Talia had thought all the answers to her prayers lay outside of the orphanage. But once they were free, she didn't experience the sense of relief she'd thought she would. How was it that there was as little joy in the outside world as there had been when she was trapped within the confines of Saint Mary's?

The answer to that question, of course, was right in front of her.

Talia stared at her dying aunt, whose mouth was taped to a breathing apparatus pumping oxygen into her lungs. Everything around her seemed clean and white and sterile. Cold. In their new home outside of Saint Mary's, Aunt Miriam had decided that Naomi and Talia—being ten and eight years old, respectively—were grown-up enough to take on laundry, wash dishes, and do other general housekeeping tasks. The household rules were as rigid as the orphanage's: the girls' homework was to be done after their daily housekeeping duties and before bed. This was often more difficult than it sounded, as their guardians' standards fluctuated depending on their mood. Talia's only escape had been going to school—though she had been slow to make new friends.

Aspley Elementary was a public coeducational school, so she and Naomi were in class with boys for the first time in their lives. Talia knew very little about boys beyond what Sister Louise had read to them about characters, like Peter Pan. At Aspley, she learned the boys' uniforms were usually dirty by the end of the morning break. They teased girls, especially when they liked them. Some ate with their mouths open, and none used handkerchiefs. She had watched them from a distance, with interest. They seemed not to care what anyone thought of them, even when they were doing stupid things, like getting muddy catching toads in the gully next to the playground after a rainstorm. Boys were strange, carefree creatures—a quality Talia admired but could not imagine for herself.

Something she knew now, as an adult and as a social worker, was that children learned to wear masks, and unwanted children favored masks of indifference. She glanced up at the pale face of her aunt in front of her, hoping that the dying woman would not hear what she was about to say. Knowing that she probably should have heard it years before.

"I think the hardest thing I had to grasp after we left Saint Mary's," Talia said softly, staring down at the shiny polished floor of the ICU, "was that when Miriam and Gus came to collect us, that moment signaled a bitter finality. We were then forced to accept the truth that our mother was really gone—that she was never coming back for us."

Naomi turned from her post, surveying the lamplit parking lot below from the window. She leaned against the sill, arms crossed over her chest, watching Talia's slight form bent over in the bedside chair, her head bowed under the weight of her words.

"That finality really destroyed me . . ." Talia added, her voice trailing off.

"I know what you mean. Our hopes died that day. Even though we knew that she was gone, I can still remember going to Mass, praying for a miracle, hoping that Mommy would somehow still be alive somewhere."

"And that she would come for us," Talia added. "Not that I would have recognized her if I ever saw her," she said tersely, pulling her hand from her aunt's. Naomi returned to her post, gazing out the window. Talia tried to conjure a vision of what their mother might have looked like, but for as far back as she could remember, she had no recollection of her features. Though she had always imagined she would have a big smile and a long string of pearls around her neck, and that her voice would rise in joy whenever she called her daughters' names. Talia had locked that vision of her mother into the little place where she kept all the things that she dared not speak of. And there were so many things that she didn't speak of.

A profound sadness had settled over her in the days after she left Saint Mary's as an eight-year-old. A pervasive darkness had seeped into her thoughts until there was no part of herself she still recognized. The cold disdain her new guardians had shown for her tears had been deeply unnerving. She remembered thinking that if only she could cry tears of blood, they might realize the depth of her despair. But Aunt Miriam ignored tears, and Uncle Gus punished them. To make matters worse, Naomi, at the time, seemed to have settled into their new school environment well. She made friends easily—a skill Talia had always struggled with. Talia had felt entirely alone and shocked by the vastness and severity of the world outside the confines of Saint Mary's walls.

She tried to pull herself out of those painful memories, taking a deep breath. Her head still throbbed, and she found herself wondering if Riley was behaving herself for Mrs. Kravitz and how late she would be for her bedtime. Her hand itched to reach for Aunt Miriam's again, just a few inches away, but she didn't want to provoke Naomi. The last thing she wanted was to trigger another tangent.

Instead, she just stared at the woman's pale face. She looked exactly as Naomi had said—already dead.

Talia had cultivated a strange relationship with death over the years. It'd been something that had followed her seemingly from birth until now, starting with the loss of her mother, then Russ, and now her aunt. Death was a funny thing. One's perspective of it could either be empowering or make one feel utterly powerless—it was all in the angle.

She reflected on her recent visit to Rose's house—her run along the beach, specifically, and those dark feelings that crept in while she was standing on that outcropping overlooking the sea. The itch to simply get it over with. To dive into the darkness. To be free.

That had felt empowering, even then.

Somehow, as macabre as it was, Talia had always quietly considered death an option. The thought took hold of her when she left Saint Mary's and was in Aunt Miriam's care—when she started to struggle while Naomi thrived.

Once, in second grade during swimming practice, she had the notion to drown herself. Not until much later in life did Talia realize these were not the normal thoughts of an eight-year-old girl. She had gone to the deep end of the pool, slipped quietly under the pink-and-blue lane ropes, and sunk to the bottom of the pool, where she'd blown all the air out of her lungs. Sprawling out on her back with her limbs extended like a starfish, she'd opened her eyes and stared up at the water's surface. It was so peaceful—the way the sound dulled and the light was refracted by the silent splashing of the other children at the surface. Everything seemed delightfully far away, and she felt safe. All she had to do was inhale—but that was proving more challenging than she had imagined, and so Talia waited patiently for death to come to her. Perhaps it would arrive in the form of her mother, and then she might recall just how she looked. Talia kept floating, just an inch or so off the bottom of the pool, her arms and legs swaying gently in the current of her own effort to remain submerged.

And as she drifted, she came to realize there were more barriers to drowning herself than she had anticipated. First, she'd recently learned to swim so well that she couldn't imagine she would simply now be able to forget that skill. And tying her own wrists behind her back before jumping in had been entirely too difficult to contemplate. Perhaps a more practical approach, she conceded, would have been to put on her school blazer, fill the pockets with heavy rocks, and try again. But while she was down there, waiting for death to remember her, Talia had focused on the sunlight dancing over the surface of the water like a river of light above her. It was so brilliant, so otherworldly, and somewhere deep inside her, she'd heard Sister Louise's words again: "In the dark night of the soul, bright flows the river of God." Those words had prodded her then, and it occurred to her in that instant that what she was doing might be at odds with the prayers Sister Louise was no doubt still offering to Mother Mary on Talia and her sister's behalf.

Prayers not only for Talia but also for Naomi.

Naomi.

Talia saw Naomi's smiling face flash before her eyes then, and for the first time, she realized that maybe it was enough that only one of them was happy. And if she died—especially by choice—she'd perhaps ease her own suffering but at the cost of her sister's happiness, which had only just been regained.

She couldn't do that to Naomi. She *wouldn't* do that.

And so she'd jilted death and risen to the surface, gasping for life.

"...journal." Talia flinched, brought back to the present moment. Naomi tapped a freshly painted fingernail on the windowsill to get Talia's attention. "Are you listening?"

"I—"

"I was saying," Naomi went on, "that maybe we'll find that Miriam's kept a journal over all these years, and maybe . . . " Naomi dropped her gaze to the floor. "Maybe it'll shed some light on what happened to our mother."

Their mother. Miriam's younger sister. Shira.

Talia sighed, rubbing sweaty palms on her jeans. Her headache seemed to be ebbing slightly. "Maybe," she said. Her eyes found a clock ticking above Miriam's bed. "Dr. Frankel should be here soon," she added, keeping her voice low and even. "Thanks for staying."

Naomi shrugged and returned to her vigil at the window.

Maybe they *would* find a journal. Though after all these years, Talia wasn't sure where it'd be or how Aunt Miriam would've kept it hidden. Her mind riffled through all of Aunt Miriam's properties and houses over the years, wondering whether one might've been hidden beneath a loose floorboard. Once control of the girls' trust funds had been transferred to Miriam, she'd purchased a small two-story house in a middle-class neighborhood just outside of Brisbane, and it had plenty of excellent journal-hiding potential.

That had been so long ago. Naomi had just started high school while Talia continued to take the bus, alone, to Aspley, their old elementary school. Two years later, she would join Naomi at the exclusive Saint Augustine's Catholic High School for Girls. Nothing less would've been acceptable to Aunt Miriam, who lived to keep up appearances.

Talia thought she saw a flicker of movement in her aunt's closed eyes.

"You don't think there's any way she could be hearing us now, do you?" Talia asked, tilting her head toward her aunt. "They say hearing is the last thing to go."

"I don't care if she can," Naomi replied. "But from what you've told me of Dr. Frankel's report, I'd say you have nothing to worry about." Naomi raised her eyebrows and looked askance at Miriam. "And if I recall correctly, that's just how she liked us—out of sight and out of earshot. Remember?"

When Uncle Gus was off to the horseraces, Miriam would have the ladies from her bridge club over for afternoon tea. She had always made it clear to Naomi and Talia that they were to be seen and not heard during these visits. They were to greet her guests respectfully—with pleasant smiles, of course—and then they were to promptly disappear, preferably to their rooms, where they could finish folding laundry or doing their homework.

"How could I forget?" Talia acknowledged. "But still easier to take those slights than the overt threats and Pumpkin Head's wrath."

On the days when Uncle Gus was home and he wasn't too drunk to aim his pellet gun, he would sit on the back porch, amid swarms of black flies, and shoot sparrows out of trees where he'd hung baskets of birdseed. Apparently, in Queensland, there was a bounty on sparrows, and Uncle Gus intended to cash in. He'd said the overpopulation of the little birds posed some ecological threat—though to whom or what, Talia couldn't say. It seemed to her that the population of flies should have been of greater concern, but she was only a child and not brave enough to object to the slaughter of little birds. Besides, she was smart enough not to openly question Uncle Gus, especially when he held a weapon of any sort.

Aunt Miriam had never been much of a communicator and was not inclined to answer the girls' questions about their mother. She told them only that Shira had made poor choices in her youth. Over years of persistent questioning, they learned snippets about her life. She had reportedly become pregnant out of wedlock while she was a first-year university student in New South Wales. A sense of propriety and a desire to spare her family from embarrassment must have forced her to marry the young man, though no one ever confirmed these details to Talia and Naomi. The girls simply believed them to be true, given the tone with which Aunt Miriam described the events.

They also learned their father had been an American serviceman, fresh out of an assignment in Vietnam and stationed in Sydney when he and their mother married. It seemed their union had been ill-fated from the beginning. Supposedly their father had been a violent man—a monster, according to Aunt Miriam. This part of the story she was always eager to share, though she never expounded on his monstrous behavior. Talia and Naomi had always been left to imagine his cruelty, which sparked wild and terrifying ideas, especially in the dark of night when Talia was unable to sleep. She and her sister both suspected, based on the various scars on their own bodies, that the monster had been abusive not only to their mother but also to them. No one confirmed or denied these beliefs, and so they grew to be unchallenged facts.

Talia could not have been much more than three years old when her mother died. She had almost no memory of her and none whatsoever of the monster. Naomi surely could've remembered a bit more about their mother— though she claimed she'd told Talia everything she knew already—but she said that try as she might, she couldn't recall a single detail of their father. Who he'd been and what his relationship with Shira had been fragmented over time, until Naomi and Talia were not sure what to believe. They came to think their father, damaged by what he might have experienced in Vietnam, was responsible for whatever had gone wrong in their lives.

Though Aunt Miriam's contempt for their father was understandable, they could make no sense of her distaste for their mother. Their aunt placed the blame squarely on Shira for the tragic way her life had ended. They had gathered as much, anyway, from the tone she used whenever she spoke of her younger sister. Perhaps they had never been close siblings; Aunt Miriam was fifteen years old when Shira was born, after all. As an adult, Talia could acknowledge that the birth of her mother had to have been a surprise for the aging Altmans—and a rude adjustment for Miriam, who'd grown up as an only child. And yet it just didn't make sense that she felt so disrupted by Shira's birth that she'd come to despise her younger sister so much—even after her tragic death.

"What haven't you told us?" Talia whispered to Aunt Miriam's gray-faced form, her body frail and roped in tubes and tape. "What really happened to your little sister?"

Talia's eyes roved across Aunt Miriam's face, somehow expecting something. Perhaps a twitch or a moan—a sign of some kind. Nothing. And it seemed likely that she'd forever be left with nothing. Well, at least nothing more than the vague hints she'd collected over the years through Aunt Miriam's snide comments and Uncle Gus's drunken rambling—that it was their father, Jacob Emerson, who was responsible for the death of their mother, but neither of them ever elaborated on what had become of him.

Talia was left to assume he had returned to America to face sentencing, perhaps for murder or manslaughter. She hoped his penalty was harsher there than it would have been in Australia. She had heard on a radio program that the death penalty for murder had been abolished in Queensland in the 1920s, and she knew their mother had died in 1964. At least Americans still believed in killing monsters. But for all she and Naomi knew, he could still be alive, perhaps even walking the streets. This thought had terrified her as a child, plaguing her with late-night dreams of a shadowy man banging on the front door in the middle of the night, calling her name and demanding she come out into the darkness with him.

Just then, a nurse knocked on the door to Aunt Miriam's room. "Excuse me, are you Talia?"

Talia rubbed her hands on her jeans. "Yes," she said, standing as she gestured to Naomi. "And this is my sister."

The nurse nodded a greeting, then got down to business. "Dr. Frankel asked me to apologize to you. He has emergency matters to attend to tonight. I know you were hoping to speak more with him, but I'm afraid that will have to wait until tomorrow."

Naomi sighed, not bothering to hide her annoyance, and gathered her things hastily.

Talia cleared her throat. "That's all right. I should be getting home to my daughter. But I plan to be back here early tomorrow morning. Just keep me posted, if you would? I've left my number at the nurses' desk."

"Absolutely," the nurse said, ushering them out of Aunt Miriam's room. And just as she crossed the threshold, Talia turned to give her aunt one last glance. She could have sworn she saw the woman's mouth moving.

Naomi stomped her foot. "Talia, we've already spent hours—"

"*I know*. I'm coming," she retorted, still peering over her shoulder.

CHAPTER 10

DNR

Talia dozed in the recliner next to her aunt's ICU bed, lulled by the rhythmic hiss of the ventilator, as the warm midday sun streamed through the open drapes of the hospital room's large window, where Naomi had staked her claim the previous evening. The claustrophobia Talia had experienced the night before had vanished with the sunlight, replaced by the dull throb of anxiety in her chest. Today was the day she would be pressed to make the decision.

It was only just fully dawning on her now. She'd been in a near stupor when she'd dropped Riley off at Mrs. Kravitz's earlier. It didn't help that the three cups of coffee she'd had that morning had yet to counter her fatigue.

Had Dr. Frankel come by to discuss next steps with her already, only to find her fast asleep?

And where was Naomi? Wasn't she on her way hours ago?

Before returning to the hospital that morning, Talia had braved the freeways and gone into Los Angeles to see Darla O'Malley, the legal assistant dealing with the Seattle law firm handling Aunt Miriam's affairs, who'd graciously agreed to come in on a Saturday, given the direness of Miriam's situation. With a few signatures, legal guardianship had finally been transferred to her. She now had full legal authority over her aunt's health-care and financial matters—not that there was much to oversee in the way of finances.

As far as Talia and Naomi knew, Aunt Miriam had spent the bulk of their trust funds before her first stroke. The money from the sale of her home in Seattle was all but gone after five years of full-time care in a nursing home. After the initial stroke, Aunt Miriam's attorney had handled her affairs in Seattle. The transfer of authority was something Talia was glad to have put to rest.

As though he'd read her mind, Dr. Frankel entered the ICU, beelining her way.

The intensive care unit was at capacity—filled with young trauma victims, heart attack patients, and people who had undergone lengthy or complicated surgeries. In his kind, reasonable way, Talia was sure that in just a few moments, Dr. Frankel would tell her what she already knew: Aunt Miriam didn't belong there. The need for space in a hospital's ICU was always an issue. In her capacity as a social worker, Talia had been familiar with this sort of thing, but now it would affect her personally.

"Talia," Dr. Frankel said, hand outstretched, as though they were close friends. She took his hand in hers briefly, accepting the greeting. "How are you?"

"I'm fine," she replied, realizing she hadn't brushed her teeth that morning. "What's the news? I'm sure you're going to at least suggest moving Aunt Miriam from the ICU—this isn't where patients in her condition belong, after all, and—"

"Talia," the doctor said softly, prompting her to just listen for once. "You let me do all the worrying. This was the right place for Miriam to be last night. Where we relocate her in the future, however, depends on those next steps we've yet to discuss."

"Oh," Talia muttered. "Right."

"We performed an EEG this morning." His face softened, and Talia already knew, based on that alone, what was to come. "The results suggest she's on the very trajectory we discussed last night—which leaves us with a few decisions to make."

Despite Talia's physical and mental exhaustion, she did her best to focus on his words. His voice faded away like a train entering a tunnel. She caught snippets of what the doctor was saying about the importance of being realistic and the limitations of Aunt Miriam's age and prognosis.

Talia could see a man and a woman in the glass cubicle across from her aunt's. They seemed to be having a disagreement while standing over a teenage boy who lay motionless in the bed. She supposed the man and woman were the boy's parents. The boy's head was wrapped in white bandages, a stark contrast to the deep-purple patches that surrounded both of his eyes. A tube protruded from his mouth. He was hooked to the same sort of machine that was hissing breath into Aunt Miriam. Through the glass doors, Talia watched the couple perform a pantomime of blame and recrimination. The woman was crying, as much in anger as in sorrow. The man stood frozen, his head bowed, arms crossed tight over his chest. Talia could not determine whether it was a gesture of defiance or self-defense or even total resignation, but she recognized the expression he wore. It was the same mask of disbelief she had worn after Russel's death. Her throat grew tight. She felt like she was suffocating.

"I've heard that you've received power of attorney," Dr. Frankel went on, drawing Talia's focus back to Aunt Miriam's frail body, the four walls closing in around her. "That's great. Does your sister plan to play a role in your aunt's care?"

"I—it doesn't look like it, Dr. Frankel," Talia replied. Naomi was smarter than that. The room's sunlight suddenly wasn't enough to keep her from feeling boxed in, trapped.

Dr. Frankel's brows furrowed over his glasses. "Are you all right?"

"I've just . . . " Talia's eyes darted to the door, and her legs followed. "I need some air. I'll be right back, Doctor. I'm sorry."

And with that, she bolted out of Aunt Miriam's hospital room, blurring past the parents arguing in a state of grief over their motionless son—and countless others, all facing terrible prospects, prognoses, and perhaps even their greatest fears.

A moment later, she exploded through the ICU's fire exit and plunged into the sun, suddenly sobered by the fresh air and warmth of midday. The claustrophobia had felt familiar somehow. It was a beast that'd been awoken, lying dormant in her bones. And as she looked at the sunlit day around her, it started to fade away, but she knew where it had come from, as a memory flooded in.

Twelve-year-old Talia—her heart thumping wildly—dragged herself, belly down, over the hard, cobweb-strewn soil of the crawl space under Aunt Miriam's house in the suburbs of Brisbane. She struggled to catch her breath, trying not to cough in the dust kicked up by her frantic crawling. Through the cracks between the boards of the porch above her, she could hear the roar of Uncle Gus's voice at the front door. He ran his words together in a breathless tirade of Germanized English that might have been comical under other circumstances.

"Zis lazy bitch is runnink off again!"

Talia pulled her blouse over her mouth and nose, sucking in fabric-filtered air while she waited for the dust to settle and her eyes to adjust. Her temple throbbed from Uncle Gus's blow, ears still ringing, and she knew that if he found her now, after she'd run off, she'd pay for it dearly in ways far worse than being struck in the head.

Above her, the front door slammed shut.

Uncle Gus's heavy footfalls shivered the floorboards of the porch. Talia heard the jingling of keys—or perhaps it was the buckle of his long brown belt, the one he often used to get his point across. It was early evening. He was either headed out to look for her, or he was going to the pub to calm himself with a few more drinks. Talia held her breath, her eyes frantically sweeping the perimeter of her secret lair until she heard the rumble of the old Hudson starting up.

It was getting dark. In her haste to escape, she'd forgotten that there were no more matches in the box she kept under the house. An arm's length away from her was a half-burned candle in a pewter stand, left over from the last time she had taken refuge in the darkness. She shimmied forward on her elbows, feeling the earth etch itself into the soft skin of her belly where her blouse had bunched up.

She knew Uncle Gus would kill her if he found out she'd ever been under the house with matches, and she doubted Aunt Miriam would make any effort to stop him.

As a rule, any infraction by the girls was swiftly met with the back of Uncle Gus's hand. To Talia's relief, her older sister often devised clandestine retaliations as a way of settling the score. Naomi occasionally deposited a surprisingly small but effective quantity of castor oil into the beaten eggs during Aunt Miriam's omelet preparation for her husband's Sunday brunch. The concoction would send Uncle Gus scrambling for the toilet within the hour, which would keep him from dropping the girls off at Mass—a weekly ritual of sheer boredom that Naomi despised—on more than one occasion. An added benefit to this routine was that—for the remainder of Sundays, at least—Uncle Gus would have less energy to be disagreeable.

Naomi had used her culinary surprises to defend Talia from more than just Uncle Gus's brutality. She'd once added a fair dose of chili powder to the strawberry jam intended for the inner layer of a tea cake Aunt Miriam was baking for her bridge club.

Naomi told Talia she had overheard one of the ladies in the club telling another that she thought Talia looked like a half-breed. The woman had said the girl's skin was far too bronze in contrast to her deep-violet eyes and that she suspected Talia was some sort of savage or half-Abo. The intended slur had not been surprising to Talia. She'd often heard the ladies in Aunt Miriam's bridge club make unkind remarks about people who did not look like them. And so, when the opportunity had presented itself that afternoon, Talia had distracted her aunt by dropping a bottle of milk—which shattered like a bomb on the kitchen tile floor—while Naomi covertly added her spicy surprise to the afternoon's recipe. Talia was only sorry that she and Naomi, banished to their rooms for the rest of the day, could not witness how the fare had been received. She and Naomi had been left to their imaginings, picturing the puckering faces of those stuffy old ladies, who had no doubt drained their teacups with savage haste that afternoon.

Talia and Naomi never got caught in these covert escapades, but there were plenty of times when they were subject to Uncle Gus's rage without any provocation—and that afternoon had been just such an occasion, leading to why Talia was hiding under the porch.

Uncle Gus had flown into a rage when he discovered that she had not yet washed and ironed the shirt he intended to wear to the racetrack on Saturday afternoon. Before she could even explain that she had just returned from school and that it was only Thursday, he'd struck her on the side of the head with his open hand. Talia knew there would be more blows to follow if she didn't make a hasty escape. She'd darted toward the stairwell in the far corner of the kitchen. If she could make it to her bedroom, she could lock the door behind herself, but the angry drunk had anticipated this move and lunged in her direction, almost knocking her off her feet midway across the room. He grabbed her shoulder, but Talia was fast, ducking quickly and breaking free—but not without the blouse of her school uniform being torn around one of its sleeves.

She changed direction and darted through the screen door to the back porch, vaulting over the waist-high railing like a wild animal. Fortunately, the grass was thick where she landed, cushioning the blow to her ankles. She was able to scamper out of sight before Uncle Gus's short legs could make it down the stairs.

Now she waited in the growing darkness under the house, trying to calm her fears about what would happen when Uncle Gus eventually caught up with her. Her eyes filled with tears at the thought of her school uniform being torn. It was also doubtlessly filthy now as she lay in the thick dirt under the house. She would have to mend and wash it before the following morning.

Uncle Gus's acts of brutality made no sense to her. But then again, not much he did made sense in general, even when he wasn't being cruel. The man's mercurial whims, from Talia's adult perspective, were likely due to his level of drunkenness, but as a young girl, she'd interpreted his capriciousness as predictably unpredictable. The man was a walking time bomb—and sometimes Talia worried she hadn't yet seen the limits of his temper.

When she was sure Uncle Gus was not likely to return anytime soon, she scooted herself backward until she reached an area where there was enough space overhead to allow progress on her hands and knees. If she could get to her room and lock the door before he came home, she would be safe for the night, at least, and Naomi could wash her uniform for her.

As she made her way toward the dense hedges abutting the front porch, which hid the entry to her secret retreat under the house, she caught sight of something she had not noticed on her previous excursions: rows and rows of Aunt Miriam's tall preserve jars were lined up along the underside of the porch. There were dozens of glass containers stacked neatly, one atop another, and Talia wondered what purpose they served. She reached over and picked one up carefully. It was filled with something white, and when she shook the jar, it gave a soft rattling sound, like broken eggshells in a glass. It was a sound she would never be able to erase from her memory. She strained her eyes in the half light to see what the jars held, but her mind would not acknowledge what was coming into focus. She only remembered the crushing horror of recognition that followed. Uncle Gus's trophies. As an adult, she sometimes still dreamed of those rows and rows of glass jars and the hundreds of tiny sparrow skulls they held.

The lighthearted tinkling of birdsong brought Talia back to the hospital's second-story fire escape, where she stood with her back against a brick wall, collecting herself. Below her, in a small rose garden, somebody was smoking, watching her suspiciously through the metal grate of the stairwell. "You all right?" the woman croaked as Talia pushed off the wall, blinking the light of day out of her eyes.

"Not really," Talia answered bluntly, leaning over the rail, looking down at her.

"Few people here are." The woman took a drag of her cigarette before nodding at a bird's nest on the lip of a stone pillar above Talia's head. "Watch out. Babies just hatched—and they're sparrows. You know about sparrows, right?"

Talia blinked back at the woman, speechless.

After coughing into her arm, the woman added, "Sparrows fiercely protect their young."

Talia gave her a silent nod and took a wide berth around the pillar, scooting back in through the open fire exit. It had felt like she'd been outside for an hour, but she was surprised to see she'd been there for under ten minutes, and Dr. Frankel was seated at the ICU desk, reviewing Aunt Miriam's records, waiting for her return.

Unfortunately, he wasted no time getting back to business as he ushered Talia into her aunt's room. "There is nothing more we can do for your aunt, except to make her comfortable. I suggest we transfer her to an intermediate level of care this afternoon. The nursing staff and respiratory therapists will check on her frequently, but she will not benefit from being in the ICU any longer."

"Agreed," Talia said quietly.

"The other matter we must consider has to do with the reality that Miriam's heart could stop all on its own," Dr. Frankel went on. He leaned against the table in Miriam's room, glancing at the open door in a way that suggested he wished he'd closed it for privacy. "In situations like these, in which a patient is in the process of dying, there's something called a DNR—"

"A do-not-resuscitate order," Talia filled in, and Dr. Frankel nodded.

"The process of resuscitating a dying patient can be rigorous and traumatizing," Dr. Frankel said, though the explanation wasn't necessary, "which is why a DNR is often the choice families opt for instead. Can I ask if you've formed a stance on this yet?"

"Yes, we have discussed options," Talia said numbly, mentally distancing herself from her own treacherous words—words that would separate her aunt from this life, words that would forever sever the bridge to any hope she had of learning her mother's story. Her mind, somehow, refused to look at that stark reality, focusing instead on the memory of those jars filled with sparrow skulls and all the times Aunt Miriam hadn't stopped Gus from taking his belt to her. "We've decided to let nature run its course."

Dr. Frankel was quick to endorse Talia's decision. But it seemed he wanted more than a DNR agreement from her. He was pushing her to give the word to discontinue the ventilator. He would give her a little more time, he agreed, perhaps a day or so. In the interim, he would arrange for Aunt Miriam to be transferred out of the ICU as soon as possible.

Talia called Naomi at work from the ICU to tell her about Dr. Frankel's recommendations and the DNR. Naomi said nothing at first. When she finally spoke, Talia thought her sister sounded like a different person. She was perfectly calm.

"Let's be realistic, Talli. She'll pass soon," Naomi said softly—in a tone that Talia read more as coercive than one intended to simply soften the harsh realities of the inevitable. Talia resented her sister's ability to speak so frankly about death when she intended to play no part in it—just as she had played no part in caring for their aunt after her first stroke.

She saw what was happening—what she had seen so many times before in her role as a social worker: that it was always the least involved family members who held the strongest views on what should be done when it came to making difficult end-of-life decisions. She knew then that she was truly alone. As far as Dr. Frankel and Naomi were concerned, Talia was just delaying the natural order of things, and perhaps she was. But she also felt the natural order of things was allowing Miriam to die at her own pace rather than as the result of denying her oxygen. If Aunt Miriam were dying of cancer instead of a stroke, would she and Naomi have been justified in withholding lifesaving antibiotics if she also had a treatable pneumonia? No, they wouldn't. It was one thing to be practical; it was entirely another to be opportunistic.

There was another long silence before Naomi said, "I don't understand you, Talia. Miriam . . . she was wretched to us as girls—abusive, socio-pathic—and she never stopped that awful man from brutalizing us. The things he would say still turn my stomach."

Talia fell silent for a moment. They didn't talk about the things Gus would say to them. Not even to each other. That type of shame should never see the light of day.

"I'm no one's puppet, Naomi," Talia said calmly, taking the sting out of her sister's words. "I'm not reacting because Aunt Miriam or anyone else has pulled my strings. I'm making decisions based on what I feel is the ethical thing to do in this situation, not in retaliation for unforgivable past cruelty." Perhaps it was the lack of sleep, or the usual fog that clouded her mind on the day after a migraine, but Talia wasn't buckling to her sister today. "I'm not interfering with the order of things. Legal guardianship is not a license to play God."

"We are playing God already—by pumping oxygen into a corpse!"

Talia was at a loss for words. "Goodbye, Naomi," she said and hung up the phone, feeling like she'd just dodged a bullet—like she'd narrowly escaped making a mistake. She had put herself in the position of choosing life or death once before, when she was a nineteen-year-old college student. She'd always thought she was pro-choice. And she was, but that stance had been more complicated than she had imagined at the time. Matters of life and death were not frivolously dispensed. They were complicated and complex and emotionally scarring. The stuff of nightmares and of lifelong guilt that could prey on a young woman's psyche. She had been alone then, at that time in her life. Just as she was alone now. Naomi had chosen not to show up at the hospital as promised that morning, and so Talia had decided to take matters fully into her own hands. Abandonment had a way of doing that to her—provoking her.

She paused for a moment, drawing a deep, cathartic breath, knowing she had done the right thing. Yes, she had agreed to withhold heroic measures if Aunt Miriam's heart stopped beating, but she was not turning off the ventilator. If Aunt Miriam wanted to make a dramatic exit, she was going to have to do so without making a victim of Talia again. That afternoon, as Talia was leaving the hospital to pick up Riley from Mrs. Kravitz's care, Aunt Miriam was moved out of the ICU.

It was the last time Talia would ever see her.

CHAPTER 11

IN ABSENTIA

The call came at 11:04 p.m.

Talia had just drifted into that curious dimension between consciousness and sleep—where nothing is in order but everything makes perfect sense—when the shrill tone of the landline next to her bed jolted her awake.

"Hello," she rasped.

It was Dr. Frankel. His voice was slow and sober. Talia kept the phone to her ear, but nothing he said seemed to stay with her. Above the pounding in her chest, she heard a few of his words but was incapable of stringing them together in a logical sequence: "cardiac arrest . . . house doctor . . . life support discontinued."

After she'd hung up with Dr. Frankel, she lay in bed waiting for the pounding in her ears to stop. She was both saddened and strangely relieved by the finality of her aunt's departure. She hadn't had to pull the plug after all. The woman had gone on her own. That was how she would have wanted it. Things were always best for Aunt Miriam on her own terms.

So why feel sad at all? Talia had to acknowledge that this wasn't about Miriam but perhaps more about her relationship with death in general. It was impossible not to be reminded of Russel's untimely passing and her mother's tragically short life at a time like this. The whole experience felt weirdly and inexplicably interconnected, like a bug getting stuck on one strand of a web and wiggling enough for the whole thing to vibrate. And then, out of nowhere, the spider would arrive—and for Talia, it wasn't a spider but a daunting wave of traumatic memories.

Though they occurred decades apart, the deaths of her mother and her husband had both torn pieces from her soul. They left wounds that would never heal. Thinking of her aunt's death, Talia's field of vision filled suddenly with a flood of tears.

Sitting up quickly, she pressed her clenched fists into her eye sockets, ordering herself to stop.

A mixture of rage and grief, perhaps best described as a deep sense of injustice, rose in her. Aunt Miriam wasn't worth Talia's tears. *Not a single tear,* she told herself. The woman had been both an accomplice to and an active participant in her misery over the years. She deserved nothing now. Yet a nagging frustration, a sense of what could have been, grew rapidly, replacing Talia's anger. Even in death, her aunt was tormenting her. Why had Miriam been so difficult over the years? Why had she made it impossible for Talia to be more understanding of her? It was hard not to feel robbed of the opportunity to ever make amends—or to have ever shared a sense of family or belonging together.

Eventually, Talia calmed herself enough to realize it was now past midnight. The odds of getting back to sleep felt increasingly slim, but she was running on fumes and had to shuffle Riley around to several sports activities and playdates the following day. In a fit of desperation, she drew herself a bath, allowing the gentle rumbling of hot water to soothe her senses.

She lifted a bottle of sleeping pills from the top shelf of the medicine cabinet. Dr. Frankel had prescribed them to her after Russel's death. The label said they were two years old but still good for another month. She would break her own rules and take one tonight. There was no need for her to keep a clear head right now; Riley was deeply asleep.

Without any further reason to listen for a phone call from the hospital that might come in the middle of the night, she uncapped the bottle and took one pill. For now, just for tonight, she'd block it all out and find some reprieve. The hot bath would relax her and help the pill work faster. Tomorrow she would call Naomi and give her the news. There was no point in waking up anyone else tonight.

A single large candle flickered on the sink, keeping the darkness at bay. Curtains of steam rose off the water as Talia lowered herself into the soothing heat. Her head felt heavy, proof that the sleeping pill had already begun its magic. She tried to put all thoughts of Aunt Miriam out of her mind, to forget the hiss of the ventilator and the shape of her unmoving form under the hospital's white linens. She closed her eyes and leaned back in the tub, soaking up the comforting warmth. A vision of her sister as a young girl floated up before her.

Naomi's face was pale and expressionless as she followed Aunt Miriam into the house on the evening of her return. Talia hadn't seen her sister in over five months, and Aunt Miriam hadn't provided any meaningful explanation for Naomi's extended absence. Naomi had even been missing on her sixteenth birthday—the day coming and going without Aunt Miriam acknowledging it as anything other than a regular day.

Talia had opened her mouth to speak but was at a loss for words. Her sister trailed inside, following their aunt silently, head bowed and arms wrapped around a soft duffel bag that she held in front of her like a giant pillow. Oddly, she was wearing pajama bottoms under her coat. Naomi climbed the stairs, dragging her bag like a soft anchor behind her. She passed by Talia without so much as a glance or a single word, but there was a darkness in her eyes that Talia had never seen before—a shadow of grief that would haunt them both in the years to come.

For the first few weeks of her absence, Talia had thought Naomi had been sent back to Saint Mary's. Strangely, this had been a relief, as Talia wanted to go back to the orphanage too. Anything would have been better than staying with Aunt Miriam and Uncle Gus. In an effort to speed things along, Talia had done her best to break every house rule and cause as much trouble at home as she could, but not even shrinking Aunt Miriam's favorite silk blouse in the washing machine had done the trick. The sum of her efforts had earned her only an occasional open-handed slap on the ear and the customary litany of insults.

In the end, Talia was never sent back to the orphanage—and she later pieced together that Naomi hadn't been sent back either. Her sister's location, however, remained a mystery. Talia began sifting through the details of the months prior to Naomi's departure, recalling the way her sister had begun to act differently toward her around the same time Naomi's teachers started sending notes home to Aunt Miriam. Apparently, Naomi was daydreaming in class too often, as well as falling behind on her homework.

When Talia had eventually braved asking her aunt, almost four months into Naomi's absence, if her sister's grades had been the reason she'd been banished from the house, Aunt Miriam cracked.

"That little liar is paying the price for boy trouble," she had said, staring Talia straight in the face. "And if you don't mind your manners, you'll follow right behind her."

This had left Talia utterly flabbergasted. Boy trouble? They hadn't had the time or the opportunity to even interact with a boy, let alone somehow establish trouble with one. Aunt Miriam, Naomi, and Talia were usually in bed by nine o'clock most nights while Uncle Gus was parked on the couch in the flickering light of the black-and-white TV with a glass in one hand and a smoldering cigar in the other. Talia had finally figured that Naomi must have been sneaking out of the house at night after everyone else was asleep. It would have been the only opportunity she could have had to start seeing a boy. It was the first time in their lives the closeness of their sisterhood was replaced by secrecy and a deep sense of distrust.

Upon reflection, Talia also recalled how right before Naomi's five-month absence, her clothes and hair had begun smelling like cigarette smoke — particularly on the days she was late returning home from choir practice. She'd tried chewing gum often and dowsing herself in cheap perfume to mask the smell of it, but that wasn't fooling anybody, especially Aunt Miriam.

Naomi had become quite popular at school among a group of girls with strange nicknames like Pinky, Fizz Pop, and Dee-Dee. At lunch, their endless chatter about boys would leave Talia bored. She'd often doodle in her notebooks, pretending to be lost in her own world, when really, she couldn't help but eavesdrop on the girls' conversations. Naomi and her friends were constantly plotting schemes by which to attend weekend cricket or rugby matches at the boys' school. Pinky, a heavyset blonde girl who rolled up the waist of her school uniform skirt until it was the length of a miniskirt, had suggested that Naomi lie to Aunt Miriam about attending extra choir practices on Saturday afternoons, as that would allow her time to join her friends at the boys' school and to ride the bus into Brisbane to the picture shows when there was a new attraction.

It had only been a matter of time until Aunt Miriam caught Naomi in her lies. It all started shortly after Naomi kept returning home reeking of cigarette smoke. She'd often blame other students, saying they'd smoke while waiting for the bus like she was, but Aunt Miriam wasn't falling for it. And one afternoon, she decided to snoop through Naomi's jacket pockets. Even as an adult, Talia couldn't forget the blazing look of fury in her aunt's eyes when she'd found a pack of cigarettes in her sister's pocket. Naomi was instantly banned from choir practice—or any other extracurricular activities. Aunt Miriam stopped providing funds for school lunches, which meant that Naomi and Talia were tasked with the additional duty of making their own lunches each morning.

Talia had resented the shared punishment almost as much as Naomi had resented the loss of her Saturday excursions. When Aunt Miriam announced that it had been Talia who had clued her into Naomi's after-school misadventures—which was a lie—the girls' relationship started to crumble. Talia had begged Naomi to believe her, but her sister wasn't hearing it. The whole incident eventually blew over, but by then, the damage was done.

Naomi had always been a stable presence in Talia's existence—and so Talia had to acknowledge that perhaps her growing sense of resentment toward her sister was because she saw Naomi's friendships with other girls and her fascination with boys as an abandonment of their closeness.

Following Aunt Miriam's newly imposed restrictions, Naomi had become even more distant and had begun spending long hours sequestered in her bedroom, which was adjacent to Talia's. Even in those days, Talia was a light sleeper, and she would often be awakened at night by the soft squeaking of the hand crank on Naomi's bedroom window, followed by the rustling of tree branches. Talia found herself distrusting her sister as much as she did the adults in their home.

As an adult, Talia looked back on these happenings and pieced it all together easily. Her sister was a teenager and, as such, was pushing boundaries—and somehow, despite Aunt Miriam's tight restrictions, fell pregnant at only fifteen. Aunt Miriam's decision was to send Naomi away to the Young

Women's Crisis Center in Brisbane. Well into adulthood, they still couldn't
bring themselves to revisit those turbulent days, and they would rarely discuss that time in their lives. It created a strange gap in their life portrait
together, a glaring hole in which Naomi was never fully honest about how
the pregnancy and adoption of her first child had affected her, and Talia was
equally enigmatic about how life had changed for her without Naomi around.
For one thing, she'd had to spend an agonizing five months alone with Aunt
Miriam and Uncle Gus.

If there had ever been any reason to be grateful that Uncle Gus was a
drunk, it was during their teenage years. When he had been drinking for several hours, he would hardly notice that the girls existed, unless Aunt Miriam
directly pointed out their offenses. But when he was sober, his abusive language toward the girls had become too much for even Aunt Miriam to bear on
a regular basis, and she had started to curtail her complaints in his presence.

When Aunt Miriam went to a bridge game for the evening, Uncle Gus
took to following Naomi around the house, teasing her about her changing
body and trying to grab her bra strap. Naomi hated his overtures and began to
lock her bedroom door at night. She took to calling him Uncle Dis-Gus-ting
when he was out of earshot. The name quickly stuck.

But during the five months of Naomi's absence, everything changed,
and Talia began to worry that perhaps Uncle Gus might turn his attention to
her. Even with her bedroom door locked at night, she had trouble sleeping.
Shadows in the room transformed into Uncle Gus, closing in on her. The only
way she could think to deter him was by making her body as different from
Naomi's as possible. More than once, Uncle Gus had called her skinny and
boyish, and he'd said it in a condescending and repugnant way—like a judge
for Miss America. "Only dogs want bones," he'd said, glaring at the cask of
her ribs, the sharp dip of her hips. "Not real men."

That's when it occurred to her—she'd keep herself as skinny and boyish
as possible.

Remaining thin had not taken much effort on Talia's part. Her appetite
had disappeared along with her sister. After three weeks of Naomi's absence,
Talia's smallest clothes hung loosely on her slight frame. Aunt Miriam began
calling her a scarecrow, which Talia felt aided her objective to keep Uncle

Gus away from her. She did not mind the would-be insults. Others, however, were concerned about these changes in Talia.

Her French teacher, a kind woman Talia adored, took to adopting a concerned expression each time Talia entered her classroom. One afternoon, she asked Talia to stay after the lesson, and when they were alone, the woman asked if she was feeling all right and if she was getting enough sleep. She had noticed, she said, the dark circles under her eyes. Talia enjoyed hearing her teacher's lovely accent and took comfort in the woman's concern. Her French teacher had made no mention of Talia's physical transformation, unlike her swimming coach, Miss Tornay, who had very impolitely pointed out, in front of the rest of the swim team, she was afraid Talia would sink like a bag of bones during practice.

If any of Talia's teachers had mentioned their concerns to Aunt Miriam, Talia heard nothing of it.

At night, she would lie awake in bed, worrying about Naomi's fate. She berated herself for not having been kinder to her sister before her banishment. The void in Talia's world had been made wider by the converging sense of a double loss: Naomi's absence itself and the fact that she and her sister had become strangers to each other in the months before Naomi's disappearance.

Talia wanted to convey all this to Naomi the second she walked back into Aunt Miriam and Uncle Gus's house—when she'd slinked up the stairs, barely looking at Talia as she went, her face as red as a sunburn. But despite her best efforts, she couldn't find the words, and it seemed that Naomi wasn't ready or willing to hear them, anyway.

For the rest of the weekend, Naomi kept herself locked in her bedroom, venturing out only for a sip of water now and again from the bathroom sink. By the time Monday morning rolled around, Aunt Miriam had had enough of Naomi's moping. She ushered her out of bed and into her school uniform— which was tighter on her than it had been before her absence—and sent her straight off to school. Before long, it was as if nothing at all had changed since Naomi's mysterious absence.

CHAPTER 12

AN ORDEAL

For the first night in weeks, Talia slept soundly for several hours—thanks to taking that almost-expired sleeping pill Dr. Frankel had prescribed her. However, despite the welcome rest, she still woke with a start the following morning, heart hammering in her chest. *What was it that had me so upset last night? What happened?*

And then she remembered. *Aunt Miriam died.*

Sleep is wonderful and cruel in that way. It blocks out the things that plague us during our waking hours. But as soon as that sleep slips away, we're tossed mercilessly back into the reality we've sought to escape.

Perhaps that was why Talia struggled to sleep. On a subconscious level, she preferred not to, after one too many times of waking up the following morning to remember, once more, that she'd never see Russ again. It was like being dealt unnecessary blows. Why put herself through that when she could just avoid sleeping and never forget he'd died in the first place?

After waking up to remember Aunt Miriam's death, Talia had gone through the motions of her regular daily routine—taking Toby outside; collecting the newspaper; making breakfast; and dropping Riley, who was none the wiser to her great-aunt's demise, off at a friend's house to play.

Talia figured she should've called first, but she didn't. Instead, she drove almost mindlessly all the way across town to Naomi's house. And now she found herself sitting in a large plush chair in her sister's family room, with her legs draped casually over the cushioned arm.

Naomi sat across from her with her hands wrapped around a coffee mug. She had always been a late riser—Talia had found her still in her robe when she'd rung the doorbell at 9:30 a.m. Naomi's girls were at John's, so they had the house to themselves.

"So what's the news?" Naomi asked, sipping her coffee. "Are you going back to the hospital today?"

"Aunt Miriam died just before midnight." Talia hadn't meant for her delivery of this news to be so cut-and-dried, but she found there wasn't really any other way to say it.

Naomi's eyes widened, her hand slowly lowering her mug to the nearest coffee table. "No way."

Talia balked, taken aback. "What do you mean? Did you expect her to pull through?"

"No, no. I just . . . " Naomi's expression glazed over, as if she were stepping out to check on an alternate reality—as if she weren't there at all anymore.

A pensive, quiet mood hung in the air between the sisters as Naomi sat nursing her cup of coffee.

Talia knew her sister needed time to process her thoughts. They had both understood that Aunt Miriam couldn't last long in her compromised state. Her passing was not a surprise, yet it had created a sudden void they had not anticipated. Perhaps it was the finality of her departure they couldn't process. Things like that take time. Talia knew this all too well.

"I still hate her," Naomi croaked, breaking her long silence. For a moment, Talia couldn't help but see past her older sister's fully grown face, the mask of maturity, and instead see the sixteen-year-old teenager she'd once been—her red-faced shame upon returning after a five-month-long absence, during which she had surely faced a tremendous amount of trauma, only to be told to never speak of it again and to go straight back to school. "I'm happy she's gone. She made our lives pure hell."

Talia said nothing. But she did nod because she could understand Naomi's perspective, and if she were being honest, part of her hated Aunt Miriam too. But it was more complicated than that. Why else did she feel so empty? Talia was reminded suddenly of something Russ had once said to her when she had asked him about how losing his father at such a young age had affected him. He'd said, "Tal, I was too young to even remember him. You can't mourn what you never had."

And there it was. She'd never had love or support from her aunt, so that wasn't what she was mourning. The fact that she would never receive an apology or an explanation from her, some acknowledgment—any acknowledgment—that she'd regretted the way she'd treated them all those years. That was what Talia was grieving.

Had she ever really thought she'd get that from Aunt Miriam?

It didn't matter anymore. The woman was dead, and the hope of that apology had died with her.

She leaned her head back on the soft, rounded arm of the chair and closed her eyes, hoping for Naomi to fall silent again. The grandfather clock in the hallway ticked loudly, measuring out the awkward minutes that followed.

Ladybug, Tory's calico cat, sprang into Talia's lap and nestled there. Talia stroked her soft fur. The cat's loud purring reminded her of her first kitten, Rainbow. She'd found him when she was fourteen, on the way home from Saint Augustine's during a torrential rainstorm.

She was about a kilometer from home when she sat on a park bench, removed her rain-soaked shoes and socks, stuffed them into her book bag, and trudged in the ankle-deep waters that surged through the storm drains with bare feet, going up the hill toward Aunt Miriam's house. Flocks of green parakeets chattered loudly in the trees overhead—but not loudly enough to drown out the persistent meowing of a kitten.

Her eyes followed the cries to a small brown box on the stairs of a church on Seventh Street. The box was only half-soaked; it couldn't have been there very long. When she peered inside, a small gray-and-white creature looked up at her. The tiny kitten was soaked to the bone. He struggled to stand on wobbly legs as Talia reached for him. He was as light as a feather when she tucked him into the front of her sweater.

She knocked on the door of the church, hoping to ask if the kitten belonged to anyone. No one answered. The doors were locked and chained. It struck young Talia as odd that a church would ever lock its doors. *What would someone do if they needed to speak to God urgently?*

She had always longed for a pet and settled on the idea that the kitten was the divine answer to her prayers.

She had named him Rainbow before she even reached home. The little creature snuggled close to her chest, purring softly. Talia already loved him and planned to care for him faithfully. She knew Rainbow would love her too. He would grow to be strong and agile under her care, and he would wait patiently for her to return from school each afternoon. He would keep her company while she did her homework and when she read her books on rainy days. At night, he would sleep on her pillow, purring softly. She couldn't wait to get him home so that she could warm him up and dry him off, but there was just one problem Talia could foresee.

Aunt Miriam despised the idea of having pets indoors. She said all animals carried filth and belonged outside, so Talia knew better than to ask permission to keep him. She sneaked him upstairs to her room and brought him a saucer of milk and some canned tuna from the pantry. He had no appetite and was interested only in sleeping. She made him a soft bed in an old shoebox lined with two small hand towels, which she'd used to dry him off, and then covered him gently with a third. When she went downstairs to do her chores and have dinner, she locked her bedroom door behind her and put the key in her pocket. Later that night, she brought Rainbow onto her pillow, where he purred himself to sleep.

By dawn, the warmth had left his little body, and Rainbow's tiny form lay lifeless.

He was still where she had placed him on her pillow.

As the sun was rising through a heavy bank of clouds, Talia buried him in the shoebox. She had located a quiet spot in the backyard, away from the house, between the green ferns that grew alongside a wooden fence. The earth was damp from the previous day's rain, and it gave itself willingly as a resting place for the little creature.

Naomi, still in her pajamas, stood barefoot next to Talia, reciting the Lord's Prayer. It was the first time Naomi had spoken to Talia since her return from her five-month absence. "Talli, he was probably sick before you found him. That's why he was abandoned."

Talia paid no attention to her sister, continuing to pat down the earth over Rainbow's little shoebox coffin. Tears ran down her cheeks like rain. When

she was finally able to speak again, she turned to Naomi and said, "He probably died of a broken heart. He was way too young to have been taken away
from his mama."

And for some reason—one that Talia could not discern at the time—this
observation left Naomi sobbing.

Talia was yanked out of the memory by the grandfather clock in Naomi's
hallway striking 10:00 a.m.

Its heavy chimes were strong and lengthy, reverberating through both the
house and Talia's bones—every peal chasing away her thoughts of Rainbow
and Naomi's sobbing and the small box in deep, wet soil.

"I suppose you've got some housekeeping to do," Naomi commented,
making it clear she was excluding herself. "You know, as far as her estate."

Talia nodded, though there wasn't a lot to go through. Miriam was effectively bankrupt by the time she'd died and didn't have any remaining assets
that Talia knew of. "I'll have to collect her things from Hilltop Manor soon."
She knew Naomi would never make the trip with her, and she dreaded going
alone. "Dr. Frankel said I could call his office assistant on Monday morning
for the name of a funeral home. What do you think? Should we just plan
a cremation?"

Naomi sat silently, staring into her coffee mug.

Finally, she looked up at Talia and cleared her throat. "Yeah," she said
lightly, as though they were merely discussing a place to go to brunch. She
stood to pour herself another mug of coffee, and as she went, Talia heard her
add, "Burn the witch."

It was only after Naomi had given birth to Tory that she told Talia what she'd
gone through before she was sent away all those years ago.

During a routine school-mandated checkup, Aunt Miriam had been
informed that Naomi appeared to be pregnant. Before the facts had been confirmed, or any questions could be asked, the girls' aunt had flown into a rage.

"She was completely out of control—it was as if she blew a mental
fuse. I've never seen her so angry," Naomi said. Her face still reflected the
trauma of that day, even after so many years. Talia swallowed hard at this

news Naomi had kept from her for so long. But she was not surprised by their aunt's reaction to Naomi's condition. As was usually the case with Aunt Miriam, her rebuke for any misdeed, perceived or real, had been immediate and vicious. And Talia couldn't think of anything that would have made Aunt Miriam crazier than a teen pregnancy. After all, that had been the undoing of Shira's life.

"She slapped my face in front of everyone in the doctor's office. It was so humiliating. I could have died from shame. And of course, the news was devastating to me too. I was terrified. Jesus, truly terrified," Naomi said before her voice trailed off and a vacant gaze returned to her eyes. "And nobody did anything to help me, even when Aunt Miriam dragged me out of the office by my braids. Nobody did a thing. No one lifted a finger or spoke up or tried to intervene."

Talia could only imagine the scene, as well as the shock of the news for Naomi, who was fifteen years old at the time. Learning what had happened all those years ago, events and memories from around that time in their lives started to come into clearer focus for Talia. Still, she refrained from asking Naomi any questions. The subject was a painful one for everyone involved; Talia would let it be in the past, where it belonged.

"I'll admit," Talia agreed, "she was always out of control, Naomi. I don't know how someone could have such a short fuse. I remember walking on eggshells around her day in and day out." She glanced over at Naomi, leaning back on the couch, bare feet on the coffee table, looking like she had every intention of spending the entire day in her silk robe.

"The craziest thing was, she would accuse us of doing what she was doing herself, right in front of our eyes. Or worse, she would tell us we did something offensive and that even Uncle Gus noticed it." Naomi laughed cynically. "Talk about gaslighting." Then, as if it had only just occurred to her, Naomi finally offered, "Oh, sorry, sis. Do you want a cup of coffee?"

Talia shook her head. She sat quietly stroking Ladybug's soft fur, remembering how often Aunt Miriam would threaten to return them to Saint Mary's if they didn't entertain her every whim and meet her every need. Her eyes ached to close. The ticking of the hall clock was hypnotizing.

". . . biggest insult," Naomi was saying when Talia's attention returned.

"Say again? Sorry, I dozed off, I guess. Bad night."

"Maybe you do need a cup of coffee, Talia. You know where the cups are," she said, clearly not making any move to wait on her sister. "I was saying the biggest insult Miriam could levy my way was to tell me I was just as dumb as Shira. Can you believe it? Talking about your little sister—your dead little sister—that way?"

Shocking, Talia had wanted to say, but she held her tongue. Naomi's unbridled hatred for Miriam was difficult to take, given that the woman's body probably wasn't even cold yet.

She tried to put her sister's animosity in context. Miriam's insults of their mother must have been particularly painful for Naomi, who remembered her as a kind and loving woman.

"What was clear was we were nothing but an aggravation to her. She wasted no time in telling me how my teen pregnancy compromised her good name in the community."

In retrospect, Talia had learned that abortion was not legal under most circumstances in Australia in 1976, but Naomi had told her that this inconvenient detail didn't stop Miriam from seeking a way to achieve her aim. She was a persuasive woman and had tried her best to have the family doctor certify that Naomi was emotionally unstable and thus eligible for a medically necessary abortion. Her attempt had failed, however, and the doctor had simply referred Aunt Miriam and Naomi to a care center for unwed teen mothers.

During the time she was away, Naomi escaped Aunt Miriam's constant berating and Uncle Gus's biting insults. This reprieve in absentia was short-lived, though, and soon replaced by misery of another nature. Five months after being sent to Brisbane's Young Women's Crisis Center, Naomi had given birth to a baby boy.

"I wasn't even allowed to hold him," she told Talia, unable to meet her sister's eyes. Whether or not she had wanted to be a mother, Naomi couldn't help but love the boy she would never see again. The midwife had quickly removed him from her sight and placed him in the nursery, where he was to await the arrival of his adoptive parents. Naomi had stood in the hallway, looking through the glass windows of the nursery, peering in on the rows of bassinets, wondering which one of them held her infant son. Two days later, the child would be released to his new family, who had traveled all the way from Cairns to claim him.

Following her pregnancy and the subsequent relinquishing of her son, Naomi's fragile state worsened. She had been given no choice at all in the matter of his adoption. She was young and incapable of caring for a baby, Aunt Miriam had decided. Not to mention that their aunt had wanted no part in shouldering the obligations brought on by Naomi's shameful actions. More importantly, Aunt Miriam was adamant that children were nothing but a burden.

The events following the delivery of Naomi's baby boy were not entirely clear to Talia, even years later. She did learn that her sister had almost died in the aftermath. The self-inflicted scars on Naomi's wrists were barely visible these days, but she still carried deep wounds from that time in her life. Naomi's physical recovery had been complicated and protracted after the delivery, but it was her mental anguish and grief that posed the greatest threat to her survival. And so in the end, Aunt Miriam's assertion that Naomi was emotionally unstable became a self-fulfilling prophecy.

Ironically, only a few short months after their aunt had forced Naomi to give up her baby, Miriam herself would suffer a devastating loss. It all started one afternoon when Talia had returned home from school to find Uncle Gus's car missing and Aunt Miriam sitting on the kitchen floor, surrounded by a pile of broken glass. Her favorite tea service was in pieces in a corner of the kitchen, where even the glass cabinet doors were not spared. The woman's face was red, and though she had turned her head away from Talia, it was clear her cheeks were wet with tears.

Talia had never seen her aunt cry—not ever.

She stood frozen in the doorway, her schoolbag hanging from her shoulder, not saying a word, calculating the odds that her aunt was crying and not just terribly angry. After a moment, Aunt Miriam picked herself up and retreated to her bedroom, loudly locking the door behind her.

Talia ventured from room to room in stunned disbelief. Almost every piece of glass in the house had been broken. In the living room, torn drapes flapped softly in the afternoon breeze that passed through a shattered window. She wondered if the house had been burgled.

It was only when Aunt Miriam had cracked her bedroom door that Talia understood who the perpetrator of the destruction had been.

"Clean it all up!" she commanded, though Talia thought her aunt's voice wavered just a little. "If there's one shard of glass left on the floor when I come out, there will be hell to pay when Gus learns what you've done." Talia froze at the prospect of Uncle Gus blaming her for the almost unbelievable mess surrounding her. She glanced again around the living room in silent disbelief, wondering how many hours it might take to undo such destruction.

In the next minute, she had a broom and dustpan in her hands.

But when Uncle Gus did not return home that night—much to Talia's relief—or the next, she and Naomi began to puzzle out together what had transpired. Over the coming weeks, they eavesdropped on their aunt's phone conversations with the local bank manager and learned more about what had caused her undoing.

The drunkard, Uncle Gus, had apparently emptied Aunt Miriam's bank accounts before absconding. The only clue their aunt had to his whereabouts was a receipt for a one-way flight from Brisbane to Poland. Why Aunt Miriam hadn't contacted the police about these events at the time was not clear to the girls and would not become clear for many years to come.

The stigma of Miriam's embarrassing change in social circumstances was of more concern to her than her sudden financial jeopardy. After the incident, as Uncle Gus's crime became known, Miriam did not leave the house, except to visit a real estate agency in town. The girls were charged with grocery shopping and taking the bus to and from school and Sunday Mass at Saint Augustine's. Aunt Miriam avoided her bridge club friends altogether and refused to take phone calls unless they were from the agent she had engaged to advertise her house for rent.

Within a month, their home—which the girls would later discover Aunt Miriam had owned outright—was leased to an Italian family, newly immigrated to Australia. The new tenants expressed an interest in purchasing the house, should Aunt Miriam be pressed to sell it—and this possibility had distressed Talia and Naomi greatly. As much as they hated living with Aunt Miriam, they had grown accustomed to the certainty of their surroundings and their friends at Saint Augustine's. Moving to an entirely new area would effectively erase the small amount of comfort and joy they had in life, leaving them alone with Aunt Miriam, whose bitterness and shame would only sour her temper, they imagined. It was hard enough moving out temporarily, but to sell the house altogether would make their relocating permanent.

That reality, however, seemed more and more inevitable by the day. Only a few weeks after the incident with Gus, Aunt Miriam moved them into a tiny two-bedroom apartment in the heart of Brisbane. Miriam sought employment and worked as a librarian to make ends meet, as she refused to spend a single cent of the income she earned from renting the house. That money, she had asserted, was destined for a special purpose in the distant future. They would all just have to learn to live modestly.

As they'd feared, Talia and Naomi were forced to leave Saint Augustine's in favor of enrolling in a public school within walking distance of the apartment, which was located in a less-than-desirable part of the city. They deeply resented the disruption the midyear transfer inflicted, not to mention the loss of their friends and extracurricular activities. There were no more French lessons and no choir or swim team for Talia. To her further distress, there was no room in the small apartment for her bicycle, and she was forced to sell it at the local flea market and use the meager proceeds to augment her school lunch fund.

Their new coed high school was not a hospitable place for Talia. Naomi, on the other hand, made friends easily and seemed happy at the chance for a fresh start in a place where no one knew of her painful past or her recent pregnancy. Before long, she smelled of cigarette smoke again and began disappearing from campus during lunchtime with a group of boys who sported long, greasy hair and loose-hanging jeans, frayed over their heels where their loafers had worn them down.

The rift between Talia and her sister had widened once more. Talia was struggling with loneliness at home and a sense of isolation at her new school. Her appetite soon flagged, and so did her zeal for most things. The girls in her class, for a reason she could not determine, avoided her completely. She could hear them whispering behind her back. Aside from the boys in her class harassing her with childish and rude questions about her weight, Talia felt unseen—though it turned out she was anything but. She soon learned she had earned the nicknames Twigs and Snake Hips.

Ironically, the taunting further dissuaded her from eating well or taking care of herself. To add to her misery, there was no quarter for her—no comfort—in her new surroundings. Even her teachers seemed aloof and unforgiving when she was slow to catch on to school routines, and their reprimands for her failures were often swift and shamefully public. Talia braced herself each morning for the onslaught of whatever hostility her new environment might deliver that day. The weekends could not come soon enough. In time, though, she began dreading Sundays almost as much as she hated Mondays—as they foreshadowed another week of public isolation or, worse, public humiliation.

Aunt Miriam stopped insisting the girls attend Sunday Mass. She had never joined them in the ritual, but it had been required of Talia and Naomi in the years they attended Saint Augustine's. Talia missed the routine and comfort of Sunday Mass and the fellowship of her peers in the choir. Without the joys of music and song or the comfort of her weekly meditation during Mass, she soon forgot the importance of faith. This development undermined her hope in all things. Her heart felt empty on most days, but she learned to tolerate that feeling just as she had learned to accept the aching of an empty stomach. Her weight continued to drop—now to dangerous levels.

Within a month of their move to the city, she became ill, with a terrible cough and fever. It was the first time she could recall feeling truly sick. Her nose ran constantly—thick yellow mucus that seemed to have no limit. During the day, she coughed wildly, as if she were drowning in her own fluids, and at night, her chest rattled and whistled, making a sound like wind howling through dry branches. At school, she couldn't carry enough tissues to stay ahead of the flow of mucus. This drew additional ire from her classmates, who either avoided her completely or stared at her in utter disgust. She had never been such a pariah, in any setting, and the situation did little to boost her confidence in navigating her new environment.

At lunchtime, Talia had taken to sitting under a tree next to the ball field, alone, watching the other students mill about, carefree in their small cliques.

She hated her new life.

She hated the dubious company Naomi was keeping at school and the way her sister effortlessly lied to Aunt Miriam. But more than all these things, Talia hated herself. At some point, she'd stopped feeling shocked by the sharp, judgmental glares of her peers and instead began expecting them— and worse, understanding them. Of course she'd deserved to be called Twigs and Snake Hips. She was nothing but a walking bag of bones, and without the substance of personality or charisma, she didn't stand a chance at establishing friendships. At first, the solitude forced upon her by her classmates had felt like unwanted isolation, a public sort of solitary confinement. But eventually, she took comfort in the fact that she was largely left alone.

She didn't want to be seen at all. In fact, she wanted to disappear altogether. It seemed she had been invisible to the people who mattered to her from the time she was a small child. Why would she need to be visible to those who cared nothing for her? She had always been invisible.

Aunt Miriam was too busy to notice Talia's mucus-filled sickness, and even if she had, she wouldn't have taken the time off work for a doctor's visit. The illness lasted for more than two weeks and then disappeared almost as quickly as it had emerged. By then, Talia had earned a few more epithets at school and had been completely ostracized by her peers. It'd become a strange comfort, however, to simply accept that she wouldn't ever make any progress with them. Instead, she began embracing the alienation by spending her lunch hour in the library, where she studied hard for her tests and final exams. Her grades began to reflect her renewed academic efforts, but the only joy it gave Talia was that her teachers ceased pointing out her deficiencies. By the end of the term, she was able to fade into obscurity—which, again, had begun to feel more and more like a luxury than a punishment.

Aunt Miriam ended up getting a second job at a local bakery. She was allowed to take home the day-old bread, and she often smuggled it back home under her raincoat like a drug mule hiding illicit cargo from the police. It was clear to Talia that Aunt Miriam despised poverty less out of her dislike for the inconveniences it presented and more due to the social stigma of it all. From her perspective, her jobs were painfully beneath her social station, and the constraints and disgrace of poverty did little to improve her demeanor.

Miriam suffered frequent crippling headaches that would send her to bed for days at a time, leaving the girls to supervise themselves. Over the months that followed, her thick chestnut hair began to gray prematurely, and her typically plump form seemed to shrivel, giving her the appearance of a far older woman.

She had not mentioned the girls' father in many years, and so when, one evening, Aunt Miriam announced she had located his parents—Talia and Naomi's paternal grandparents—in the United States, Talia was nothing short of shocked. It was the first time her aunt had not referred to her father as "the monster."

The Americans, as Aunt Miriam had called Talia and Naomi's newfound family, were pleased to have news of their long-lost granddaughters. More importantly, they seemed anxious to help them in any way possible. Aunt Miriam had filled them in on the girls' recent change in circumstances—and had no doubt portrayed herself as their devoted, yet financially constrained, guardian.

The Americans faithfully replied to Aunt Miriam's letters and expressed an interest in righting their son's wrongs. They wanted to pay the girls' way to the US and help with their financial support through their remaining school years.

The news of their generous offer seemed to brighten Aunt Miriam's mood. Naomi was curious about the prospect of a move to the US, but Talia had her concerns. She was reluctant to have any contact with the family of the man Aunt Miriam had long portrayed as abusive, and she was dubious about Aunt Miriam's sudden change of heart regarding them. It occurred to her that Miriam's plan may have included passing the responsibility of raising her and Naomi off to their paternal grandparents. She knew nothing of her father's family—none of them did, really. What if they were monsters just like him?

In 1977, during one of the coldest winters in modern US history, and with the help of a generous donation from their American family, the Emersons, Talia and her sister immigrated, along with Aunt Miriam, to the state of Washington. It had been a thrilling and terrifying experience to leave what they knew in Australia, but by this point, the girls were accustomed to big changes.

Within a few months of arriving in Seattle, Talia and Naomi transformed from curious immigrants to typical American teenagers. Everyone loved their Australian accents, and they immediately became popular at their new high school.

To her surprise, Talia made friends almost immediately, which did much to renew her interest in and excitement for her new country and her new high school. She was thrilled to find there were plenty of extracurricular activities, including an excellent cross-country running team and French lessons. She was even invited to a sock hop, which she learned was a fifties-style dance, the first week of school.

Later, as an adult, Talia often reflected on how her zeal for life had returned in those months. She felt welcomed and supported for the first time she could remember. She wasn't sure of it—she didn't have much experience in the area—but she thought she might even have been truly loved by her newfound family and high school friends.

Marie and Joe Emerson—the Americans—opened their home to the girls and their aunt until Miriam could find something permanent for the three of them. They embraced Naomi and Talia as if they were their own children, returned from afar. The aging couple, who struck Talia as authentic and kind, overwhelmed the girls with their generosity, showering praise and love on each of them from the moment they met. No matter how hard Talia looked, she could find nothing monstrous about them. Even Aunt Miriam seemed to soften in their presence.

Gran Marie, as the girls called their grandmother, was a masterful cook and kept everyone well fed every day, from breakfast until dinner. She even saw to it, without making a fuss, that Talia gradually gained a little weight with each passing week. She took Naomi under her wing, and the two spent many hours laughing together in the kitchen after dinner, sharing the task of cleaning up and planning novel menus for upcoming meals.

Naomi seemed to bond with her in a way that never would have been possible with Aunt Miriam. The two prepared a wonderful holiday meal for everyone that Easter. Gran Marie also had other skills the girls had never seen. She patched Naomi's torn blue jeans with a detailed needlepoint full of colorful flowers and butterflies, and she sewed a beautiful dress for her for the school dance that spring.

Aunt Miriam watched all this without uttering any objection in front of the Americans. She seemed relaxed—relieved, even—to have the girls so accepted. She began smiling again, especially when Gran Marie and Naomi prepared for her a special afternoon tea with some of her favorite cakes. But in private, she scolded the girls for being too trusting and admonished them not to get too close to the Emersons. She never gave a reason for these warnings, which made them all the more ominous. Although Miriam largely ignored Grandpa Joe, she often "helped" Gran Marie cook dinner by giving her advice and directions in the kitchen. Gran Marie, in her humble way, did what was necessary to please everyone. She even introduced Miriam to a friend of hers, who gave her a temporary position at the local library.

Grandpa Joe and Talia hit it off from the start. That spring, he introduced her to American League baseball, and she instantly fell in love with it. In the following years, they regularly enjoyed Seattle Mariners games together and even made it to Los Angeles to see the New York Yankees beat the Dodgers in the World Series.

It was a wonderful time in Talia's life, full of joy and the excitement of meeting cousins and aunts and uncles she hadn't known existed. The experience of looking into the face of a newly acquainted relative and seeing how much it resembled her own was nothing short of astounding.

It became clear early on that the Emersons were reluctant to discuss their son, Jacob, the girls' father, in any real detail. Aunt Miriam had warned Naomi and Talia never to raise the subject of their father, lest they upset their grandparents, who were grieving his past actions toward his own young family and his apparent unexplained disappearance. Talia obeyed this rule dutifully, not wishing to upset anyone, least of all the kindest people she had ever encountered. What were they going to tell her, anyway?

On occasion, Talia heard Jacob's name raised, but it was always in hushed tones, in the way that folks spoke of the dead. What she did learn through an occasional opportunity to eavesdrop was that Jacob had always been a bright and cheery boy but that he had seemed a different person when he returned from a special diplomatic mission in Vietnam under President Eisenhower in 1957—before his assignment in Australia, where he had met their mother.

The girls went on with their lives in their new surroundings and soon stopped thinking about the part of their past that wasn't up for discussion. On their shared birthday that October, Talia and Naomi were so distracted by their new milieu that they didn't miss the usual gifts from the mysterious M. Instead, they enjoyed the generosity of their grandparents. The Emersons paid for driving lessons for Naomi, and Talia received a Yankees baseball cap and a pair of new running shoes, which delighted her to no end. Her grandparents had made it to almost every one of her cross-country meets that year to cheer her on, and this kindness alone had been more than she could have hoped for.

Despite the gratitude she felt toward the Emersons, Talia was never quite free of questions about the past. She and Naomi had both seen the large framed photograph of a young man in a US military uniform that hung above the fireplace in their living room. His telltale violet eyes gave him away as a member of their clan, and his hair—short cropped as it was—appeared to be of the same unruly nature that Naomi struggled to tame. When Talia saw the resemblance between her sister and the soldier in the picture, it became clear why Gran Marie had become so close to Naomi so quickly.

In the following year, 1978, Aunt Miriam engaged an attorney to begin the process of securing permanent residency in the US, claiming that she intended to remain Talia and Naomi's long-term legal guardian. Once this was accomplished, she purchased a two-bedroom cottage for the three of them, just a few blocks from the Emersons' home. She used the proceeds from the sale of her house in Australia, which she had recently sold to the Italian immigrants who had been renting it. If there were any funds remaining, the girls assumed Aunt Miriam had used them over the following years to supplement the modest income she earned as a librarian.

By the time Naomi graduated from high school in Seattle, both she and Talia were as American as baseball and Gran Marie's delicious apple pie.

CHAPTER 13

IN THE VALLEY
OF SHADOWS

After Talia dropped Riley at kindergarten that Monday, she drove to Hilltop Manor. Lynn, the new nurse, had been kind enough to box up Aunt Miriam's possessions for her, and so the trip to the nursing home felt quick and emotionless. There had been only two boxes anyway, so Talia was on her way home before she could even acknowledge that she would never need to return to Hilltop Manor again. Wednesday afternoons while Riley was in karate would be forever changed.

One of the boxes she'd loaded into her truck contained Aunt Miriam's personal items. The other was unmarked and had been sitting, undisturbed and sealed, in her aunt's closet at the nursing home ever since she had been transferred there from Seattle. When Talia got home, she cleared a corner in the garage and stacked the boxes on top of each other, planning to go through them later. Though she was certain she would find no use for her aunt's old nightgowns and other personal items, there were probably a few things that could be donated to local charities. She was in no hurry, though. She would go through them when she was ready.

She slipped back into the house from the garage that now felt like a place that held all that remained of Aunt Miriam. She couldn't help but feel another wave of emotion overtake her—not necessarily sadness or grief but pity.

Pity that Aunt Miriam had alienated herself from Talia and Naomi when they were just small girls. The three of them could've truly felt like a family, if only their aunt had facilitated it. If only she'd kicked Gus to the curb, advocated for them as a mother would have, and bothered to care about anybody but herself. The best thing Miriam ever did was unite them with the Emersons, but even that contact had diminished over the five years since she had moved Aunt Miriam to Southern California.

Talia was itching to get out for a run before the morning was over, but first, she needed to make a call.

"Gran Marie? Hi, Gran, it's me, Talia. How are things with you and Grandpa Joe?"

"Oh, Talia, so good to hear from you. I was just saying to Joe last night I should have called for your birthdays. How is Naomi? And the girls?" The woman's voice was frail, but it still rang with the same kindness that always lifted Talia's spirits. She felt a pang of guilt. She should call more often. The Emersons were in their mideighties now. How long would they be around?

"Listen, Gran," Talia cut in, "I'm calling with some sad news." To her surprise, her throat tightened, and her eyes began to fill. She choked back her emotions, shocked at how she was reacting. "It's Aunt Miriam," she said, swallowing hard. "She had another big stroke, and I'm sorry to report she passed away this weekend."

There was a long silence on the line before Gran Marie responded. But then they talked for over an hour, and as always, Gran said all the right things, and as always, Talia promised to check in more frequently.

By the time Talia got out for her run, it was almost midday. The sun was already high and unforgiving. Offshore winds were keeping the tail end of October warmer than usual, but the gold and crimson leaves clinging to the maple and sycamore trees in the forest declared autumn's full force could not be held off much longer. She had missed the earlier start with her friends Kim and Pamela and the other women they usually ran with on Monday mornings. On any other day, she might have been disappointed, but today she was happy for the solitude.

Sometimes a solitary escape was ideal to clear her mind. And there *was* something quite unsettling on her mind.

Last night, at around 2:00 a.m., she'd woken up—startled and confused—to find herself standing at the back door in her pajamas, with her running shoes on, no less.

That marked the second time in a month that she'd awoken during a sleepwalking episode. How many more had there been that she did not recall? The reality was that sleepwalking had become a part of her life ever since Russel's death. The first time it had happened, she had found herself standing in front of a framed picture of Russ in the living room when she'd woken up. That had also been around 2:00 a.m.

This coincidence was baffling. Why two o'clock in the morning? Was there significance to that? Or was she hitting a particularly influential time frame in her sleep cycle? Was it something she'd had for dinner that triggered these sleepwalking instances?

When she'd found her new running shoes inexplicably covered in ash and charcoal, she'd had the additional locks installed on the front door, and when that hadn't been enough, she'd hung a string of Christmas ornament sleigh bells on the door handles for extra precaution. The noise the bells would generate if disturbed would be loud enough to wake her, she reasoned. She'd also placed a wooden rod in the rails of the sliding glass door that led to the backyard. And that's where she found herself when she woke up last night—struggling to budge the unyielding sliding back door, with Toby right next to her, wagging his tail wildly at the prospect of a 2:00 a.m. rabbit-scouting adventure.

Why she had begun the disturbing habit of sleepwalking—and now, to her horror, exiting the house at 2:00 a.m., leaving Riley unattended—was beyond Talia's comprehension. She could only imagine it was a bizarre manifestation of stress. It had to be. The only other explanation was that she was losing her mind, and that possibility was not something she could stomach entertaining. The implications were just too disturbing.

Okay, there were also times she'd heard unexplained noises in the house at night, as well as times she'd thought she'd seen Russ in the yard from her bedroom window, only to rush downstairs and outside to prove to herself that no one was there. But that was to be anticipated, wasn't it? Wasn't that normal after a tragic and unexpected death? Really, was sleepwalking any less expected? Perhaps her aunt's death, the migraine she'd recently suffered, and the argument she'd had with Naomi last week had affected her more than she'd realized. Her threshold for stress was almost nonexistent these days.

Stress was surely the explanation. Just too much stress over too much time.

And what better way to de-stress than to get out for a solo run that morning? As Talia began her descent into the partially shaded valley, on a trail that looped between the towering oaks, she did her best to put her mind at ease by letting go of these questions. She lengthened her stride, made a conscious effort to relax her shoulders, and settled into a comfortable tempo. Her feet moved effortlessly over the earth. She concentrated on the sounds of nature around her, on the rhythm of her breathing, and on counting her steps in fours, as she always had. *One, two, three, four; one, two, three, four; one . . .*

When running rocky trails, keeping her eyes trained on the ground directly ahead was critical for avoiding an unexpected tumble. All trail runners learned this rule, and some had the scars to prove they'd learned it the hard way.

Talia followed the trail down alongside a streambed into a little valley—her favorite part of the whole route—and realized she hadn't seen a single soul since leaving home. That was a surprisingly refreshing development. It was peaceful to run alone but even nicer to run the entire five-mile trail loop without bumping into anybody else along the way. The natural beauty of the Santa Monica Mountains, the singing birds, and the tranquility of the forest—all gifts, just for her alone.

As she approached another fork in the trail, she slowed her pace and checked her watch reluctantly, knowing it was probably time to turn around and head home. She still had to grab lunch, shower, and pick up Riley from school before her appointment at the dentist.

She pushed the pace on the last big hill out of the canyon, enjoying the effort that kept her totally focused on the present, on the burning in her legs and the rhythmic sound of her breath. As she approached the last rise in the trail, she slowed to a jog and then to a relaxed walk, catching her breath.

At the far end of the road, looking down toward the trailhead, she saw the figure of a tall man. He was standing at the foot of one of the giant sycamore trees, in the shadows, and he seemed to be watching her. She pulled the bottom of her T-shirt up to her face and mopped the still-streaming sweat from her eyes. When she looked again, the man was gone. He had simply vanished. She stopped in her tracks, scanning the tree line warily, trying to make sense of what had just happened.

CHAPTER 14

RAMBLING ON

The following morning, Talia sat at her kitchen counter, hands cupping a ceramic mug of coffee that had long since gone cold. Her fingertips tapped the side of it repeatedly, measuring her building anxiety.

Was that Russel she had seen yesterday at the end of her run? Was she starting to see things again? Might it have something to do with her recent increasing bouts of sleepwalking? The more pressing question rose into view, so unnerving as to silence her finger tapping and prompt her to squirm restlessly. Was she a safe guardian for Riley? It had been alarming enough to realize that she had once left the house while sleepwalking. And yes, she had handled that immediately. She'd put safeguards in place to prevent that from ever happening again. The extra locks on the doors, the noisy sleigh bells on the door handles, the barricaded back door. She'd even invited her niece to spend the night on weekends. She'd gotten away with that, making it look like she was just being a good aunt and wanting Riley to have company. But now she was seeing things again. There was no safeguard to put in place for that.

At her core, she knew the answer about whether she was a safe guardian for Riley. But handing Riley over to someone else was never going to be an option. And so she was left with the one and only alternative she'd been avoiding from the start: continuing therapy with Dr. Cohn and getting to the bottom of all this.

It didn't help that the second anniversary of Russ's death was closing in on her, and the thought of facing such sadness again made her feel physically ill. With that date looming—it was tomorrow, in fact—along with all the memories Aunt Miriam's death had dredged up recently, she had to face the reality that she needed support. She needed to talk to someone capable of helping her—someone who had no emotional investment in her and could be impartial. Naomi, of course, was out of the question. And Talia's friends had been so understanding over the past two years, she was hesitant to share such personal pain with any of them again.

There comes a time when grief is a burden best borne in silence. There comes a time when people don't have anything else to say, when they can't console you without repeating what they've already offered.

Besides, talking about her pain felt futile. The same way shedding tears in front of her aunt and uncle had felt when she'd first left Saint Mary's. *Futile*. Words, just like tears, could not reveal what she was feeling. Words were like discordant notes played on a piano: they broke the silence but failed to bring satisfaction to the player or resonate with the audience.

She grabbed the phone book and started flipping through the yellow pages, searching for a therapist who might be a little more charismatic than Dr. Cohn—a therapist with more energy, who was prone to say more than, "Go on, I'm listening."

She sat back, groaning. Her shoulders sagged. Seeing a new therapist would mean rehashing all the most destructive aspects of her past—reliving every moment, even. Was she up for that? It all sounded exhausting. She reached for her address book on the countertop and flipped through it until she arrived at the page where she'd paper-clipped Dr. Cohn's card.

Like it or not, she was the only logical choice.

After tipping the remains of her cold coffee into the kitchen sink, she picked up the phone and dialed Dr. Cohn's number. To her surprise, the receptionist didn't answer—Dr. Cohn did.

"Good morning, Dr. Cohn. This is Talia Brighton calling. We had our first session a while—"

"It's good to hear from you, Talia. When would you like to come in?"

"Could we meet soon?" Talia detested the way her throat tightened around those words, as though trying desperately to hold them back. *Accept the help, Talia, for God's sake.* "My aunt passed away over the weekend, quite unexpectedly, and the second anniversary of my husband's death is tomorrow. I think it would do me well to talk to somebody."

"Sounds like you have a lot on your plate," Dr. Cohn offered, sounding slightly warmer, and Talia's chest tightened, as though bracing against the sudden impact of such vulnerability. "I've actually had a cancellation this morning. Would you like to come in at ten?"

This caught Talia off guard, but she decided to rip the Band-Aid off again.

"I'll be there. Thank you."

As Talia sat in Dr. Cohn's office, she noticed a box of tissues had been placed on the table next to her chair, which she was sure hadn't been there on her first visit. Would her no-cry streak last through the session? She was pretty proud of that streak. Almost two years now since the night she had shaved her head and vowed never to shed another tear. But she was feeling particularly worn down today. Her lack of sleep and the fear she was seeing things again had given her a sense of being in free fall, of spiraling well outside of her own control.

She couldn't help but recall the run she'd taken when she and Riley had visited Rose on the coast—standing on the edge of a dizzyingly high cliff and looking at the rocks below, wanting to jump. To just get it over with.

When the office door closed, Talia didn't know where to begin. She just started talking, the way she used to when she visited Aunt Miriam in the nursing home and wasn't sure anyone was listening. She prattled on, without direction—purging, feeling numb. At times saying more than she wanted to and at others, failing to connect the dots in her train of thought.

"My biggest concerns revolve around my daughter," she heard herself saying, her own voice drifting into her awareness as if from some remote source. Raising the topic of Riley had put her suddenly on alert, to tread carefully, not to inadvertently disclose just how her own unconscious actions were putting Riley at risk.

And before she knew it, she had moved on to the safer topic of Naomi. "My sister and I grew up without a father, and Naomi, that's my older sister, well, she just doesn't seem to be able to live without men constantly in her life. Even toxic and controlling men. I don't want that for Riley. I don't want her to be so needy, so dependent on men for a sense of self-worth."

Dr. Cohn tipped her head slightly, ever so slightly, but said nothing. Talia didn't mind the silences on this visit. They didn't feel as uncomfortable as they had on her first go-around. She cast her eyes to the bright-red-and-gold rug between her chair and Dr. Cohn's, staring at the woman's shiny black pumps and rambling on as though in a trance, channeling someone far more verbose, just letting her thoughts tumble out of her mouth like a load of laundry when the dryer door is opened midcycle.

And Dr. Cohn just listened. Her glasses perched precariously on the tip of her nose, as Talia had come to expect. Dr. Cohn was not pressing for any details. Perhaps Talia was providing all that was necessary. Was she sharing a little too much? Well, what if she was? She could only keep so much bottled up, it seemed.

As she went on, Talia realized that Riley hadn't known many men at all in her short life besides Russ. Well, except for Bob Reed, their neighbor who had recently moved away. Riley had been close to him as well as his wife, Cindy. And then there was her uncle John, Naomi's former husband. Riley adored him, and with good reason. John was a sweetheart. Sure, there were plenty of male strangers and acquaintances, fathers of other children at kindergarten, but Riley wasn't close to any of them. Before Dr. Cohn could question it, Talia found herself wondering if she had perhaps designed it that way. Had she subconsciously avoided men? Well, *maybe*.

"We really don't have any men to speak of in our life right now, so of course, Riley being dependent on the approval of one isn't really an issue just yet," Talia said, realizing just how silly that sounded. Then, before she could think about how it might come across, she was practically betraying herself outright. "The girls I run with have tried to set me up on a couple of dates in the last few months. Even some of my neighbors—well, just Mrs. Kravitz, really—have been bold enough to ask if I'm seeing anyone yet. I'm not in the least bit interested, you see," Talia said firmly in an attempt to undo the impression she must have already inadvertently given. "I'm still very much in love with Russ, and I take my responsibilities as Riley's mom seriously."

Dr. Cohn's eyes settled on Talia as she tugged on her necklace, her voice trailing off softly. Russ had given her the necklace when Riley was born. It had a long, delicate chain and a solid-gold, heart-shaped pendant that rested on the middle of her chest. She brought the heart to her lips, as she often did when she was deep in thought.

"Despite growing up without a father, my husband, Russel, came out of the experience as a caring, intelligent, contributing member of society. There's no need to think two parents are a requirement for a good childhood, is there?" Talia asked, not looking up. She had decided long ago that what had been good enough for Russ would also have to be good enough for his daughter. The experience of growing up without a father was something all three of them shared now. Like Rose, Talia would manage alone. It would all work out. Riley would be fine. *Wouldn't she?*

After a minute or so, Dr. Cohn finally spoke up. "What do you find so threatening about having a new partner, Talia? Someone to help you raise your daughter."

The question itself was threatening. *My God, this woman is blunt.*

Talia stammered, trying to sort out a response. "Did I say I found men threatening?" she asked in a neutral tone, not knowing how to proceed. "Do you think that a man in my life right now would help me sleep any better? That *would* be helpful."

She knew she was skirting civility and also playing with fire if she didn't watch herself closely. She had almost added: *And do you think a man might keep me from sleepwalking and abandoning my daughter in the middle of the night?*

Dr. Cohn's lips curled ever so slightly in what was only a hint of a smile. "I think everybody could use help with raising a child, don't you?"

Talia didn't know where to go with the question. What was Dr. Cohn getting at?

Maybe her consternation was evident, because a few moments later, Dr. Cohn quickly changed her approach. "Tell me about the relationships among the adults in your own family, Talia. How would you characterize them?"

Talia froze. Thankfully, the session was almost up. She'd run the clock out talking about Riley, filling almost fifty minutes with seemingly aimless rambling. She brought her pendant to her lips again, stealing an oblique glance at the clock above Dr. Cohn's desk. All she had to do now was fill a few more minutes. She would talk slowly, if necessary.

"My sister and I were raised by a single aunt, the one I mentioned on the phone. She passed away over the weekend. It was a massive stroke. She'd had one once before, so she had really been in a bad way for several years already—"

"But on the phone, you said her death was unexpected," Dr. Cohn added abruptly. It wasn't a question.

"Yes," Talia clarified. "She was relatively young, though. She was in her sixties when she had the first stroke, five years ago. She was not chronologically old, but she had always been pretty old-school, if you know what I mean—more interested in appearances than relationships. I'm not saying we had it hard; our basic needs were met. We had a roof over our heads, food on the table, and an education. Relationships weren't a big focus for folks in her generation, I guess."

Talia wondered if she had gotten away with it again—not really answering Dr. Cohn's question. She had no intention of revealing the misery she and Naomi had experienced living with their aunt, nor the years of Uncle Gus's horrific abuse. It just wasn't worth it to go there, to rehash the immutable realities of the past. There was no sense in agitating the sword of Damocles above her head. It wasn't as though Aunt Miriam were sitting here with her, eager to make amends. And besides, Talia was sick of rehashing that ugly past.

With that, Dr. Cohn nodded. "Well, Talia, our time is up for today."

She sighed with relief. *Thank God!* And yet Talia found herself disappointed again by the lack of progress she'd made. She'd only briefly—and tersely, at that—mentioned her issues with sleep deprivation. But discussing her concerns about Riley growing up without her father was cathartic to some extent. Perhaps the simple act of vocalizing her worries to somebody outside of herself would be enough to facilitate a little peace of mind. Maybe that was all she'd needed all along.

"Thank you," she said, standing up. "I feel . . . there's just a lot to process . . ."

"Of course there is," Dr. Cohn said evenly. "We're all the sum of our own experiences, Talia, and when we're decades into life, there's a lot to total up and reflect on. Most people never even consider the impact their early experiences have on their adult lives." Dr. Cohn's expression changed. Talia had not seen her that pensive before. A darkness seemed to settle on her as she added, "And then there's the burden of generational trauma that seems to sneak quietly into our children's lives, seeking to mend old wounds, finding its way to the light. In good time, we'll sort through all the most impactful events—but it will take *time*."

This was the first instance in which Talia felt understood by Dr. Cohn, though she had a nagging feeling the woman understood more than she had wanted her to. More than Talia had shared. Nevertheless, she thought it best to leave it there—end the session on a positive note. "Agreed," she said, turning toward the exit.

"Would you like to schedule another session now?" Dr. Cohn asked, staring at Talia from over the rims of her glasses.

Talia had felt more comfortable during the session than she had on her first visit. And if she was honest, she *did* want to schedule another appointment. Partly because not doing so might imply she had something to hide. Something like being a deeply damaged individual who wasn't quite sure she hadn't lost her mind altogether.

CHAPTER 15
APPLES AND ORANGES

Talia didn't know the first thing about sewing. That was the sort of skill she'd just never picked up or felt drawn to, and yet here she was, grappling with an old sewing machine Russ had purchased at one of their neighbors' garage sales years ago, giving it a try.

Riley sat on the kitchen counter beside her, swinging her legs and watching her mother's every move. "Do you really know how to make an angel costume, Momma?"

"Of course I do, sweets." She grimaced, trying not to drop the straight pins she was holding between her lips while she wrestled with a scrap of white fabric. If she could just make sense of the instructions on the sewing pattern, she could get a handle on this project. Patterns were sort of like maps, and she was hopeless with maps. Riley had asked to be an angel for Halloween, and Talia had ten days to get it right. It would be a lot easier than Riley's alternate request, which had been a hammerhead shark. Ten days should be plenty of time to construct an angel costume, even for Talia—provided there were no wrong turns with the scissors. This challenging task had come at the right time, as it kept her mind from straying to the fact that tomorrow was the second-year anniversary of Russ's death.

Just then, the doorbell rang, and Riley launched herself off the counter. Before Talia could untangle herself from the bolt of fabric in her lap, Riley and Toby—barking madly—were racing each other to see who was at the door. A moment later, Talia heard the sleigh bells on the front door handle jingle loudly and Riley shout, "There's a stranger at the door, Momma."

Talia—now on alert—sprinted to the front door to see for herself. Holding the door ajar, she peeked through the gap while preventing Toby from escaping with a strategically placed knee and said to the tall man standing before her, "Yes? Can I help you?"

"Hi, we're your new neighbors," a small redheaded boy said, peeping around the man's hip and gesturing to the Reeds' old house across the street. Talia forced herself to adopt a happy smile and relaxed her grip on the door handle.

"We just figured we'd stop by and introduce ourselves," the man said.

The redheaded boy then pushed past his father and energetically introduced himself as Brandon, asking if he could come over to play sometime. At that moment, Toby burst through the gap in the door that Talia had let widen and began licking the child wildly and thrashing his tail—apparently signaling his approval of the request.

"Nice to meet you, Brandon," Talia said to the boy without taking her eyes off the tall man. "And you are . . . ?"

"Oh, silly of me," he said with a laugh—the kind of laugh that warmed Talia to the bones. "I'm Sam." He held out a bag of oranges from the tree in their backyard—the same tree, Talia knew, that Cindy used to pick from. At first, she wasn't sure if Sam intended to offer her the bag of oranges or if he was trying to shake her hand.

Talia went for the handshake. But of course, he'd been handing her the bag, which would've fallen to her feet if Sam hadn't caught it in time.

"Oh my God," Talia remarked, mortified by the social mishap and suddenly acutely aware of the fact that she was barefoot and wearing a pair of very short, tattered denim trunks under a baggy sweatshirt. "I'm sorry. I have no idea what I was thinking."

"Oh no, that was all my fault. I think midway through handing over the oranges, I randomly decided to go in for a handshake, and . . . " Sam trailed off, bowing his head. Talia realized she was grinning from ear to ear. "Sorry," he added, tousling Brandon's hair. "It's been a while since I've interacted with an adult."

"I understand completely," Talia replied, tilting her head toward Riley. "This is my daughter, Riley."

While they all got acquainted, Talia couldn't help but reflect on how Mrs. Kravitz's observations of their new neighbor were spot on. He was tall, that was for sure, and his little boy did seem to be adorable. Mrs. Kravitz had also said the man was a real mensch, and Talia was sure that was a compliment because Mrs. Kravitz had been practically purring when she said it.

She noticed more than just the man's height as he knelt down to pet Toby and give him a bear hug, allowing the animal to cover him in wild licks. He was quite attractive—striking, really—with salt-and-pepper hair; dark eyes; and a healthy, natural tan that indicated he was an outdoorsman.

"Why don't you two come in?" she said suddenly, slowly getting ahold of herself. But little Brandon was already three steps ahead of her, well on his way through the living room. He and Riley began chattering as they all headed to the kitchen. Talia placed the oranges in a wooden bowl sitting on the counter, which contained the remains of a single apple that Riley had sampled and apparently returned as a reject. Toby was doing laps around the kitchen.

"I'm going to be an angel for Halloween!" Riley beamed, holding the palm of her hand up in the direction of the old sewing machine on the counter. "Just like my daddy. He's in heaven, you know. With a princess. Momma, what's the name of that princess that's with Daddy?"

Talia felt her stomach drop. *What an introduction!* Riley had a way of bringing her back to the brink with the most innocent comments. After having smiled so effortlessly only moments ago, she struggled to force one into place now.

"Princess Diana, sweetie," Talia said. "Now do you and Toby want to show Brandon some of your race cars? I bet he'd love your new Corvette."

After the minute of silence that followed Toby and the children's exit, Sam spoke up. "I ran into two of your friends this morning on the beach. They said that you often run with their group. I can't say I remember their names, but when they heard I was the new guy in the neighborhood, they suggested I drop by and introduce myself. I hope you don't mind. One of the ladies said our kids are about the same age and would probably get along great."

"Oh sure. I bet that was Pamela or Kim," Talia said. Things suddenly made sense. When her friends suggested Sam drop by, they had undoubtedly had more in mind than Brandon and Riley becoming playmates, and she was sure of it. The ruse was not lost on Sam either. He had a smile that could stop traffic, and now he was the one who was grinning from ear to ear. Imagining exactly how the scene had played out, Talia couldn't help but laugh out loud. She was sure her friends had carefully sized up Sam before making their recommendation.

Sam pulled out a stool from under the kitchen counter and straddled it. Talia flushed. Had she forgotten all her manners? She tried to atone by offering a glass of iced tea, but Sam waved his hand in polite protest.

"We really don't want to intrude, and besides, Brandon has a school project that needs to be completed. First grade has its challenges, you know," he said, winking. "The little guy has had a long day already. We went out this morning before school in one of the kayaks."

Of course. Talia suddenly remembered seeing the green Jeep with the C KAYAK license plate in Sam's driveway a couple of weeks ago. "We put in at Sycamore Cove before the surf was up, just after dawn. It was beautiful out there this morning," he was saying when Talia's attention returned. She knew the spot. It was a small beach on the other side of the canyon, just a few miles from home.

"Yes, it's a beautiful little cove," she said. "I often see kayakers out there when I run to the beach and back from home, and it always looks like they're having so much fun."

"Well, maybe you can find out for yourself one day. I'm happy to take you," Sam offered. Talia neither acknowledged him nor made eye contact; instead, she busied herself picking up the fabric scraps and straight pins Riley had spread over the kitchen counter. She couldn't think of a single question to ask Sam that wouldn't sound too forward or like she was prying. She didn't want to be too inelegant, as Aunt Miriam would have put it. She caught herself smiling at the possibility of just how amusing it would sound to start with, *So I hear you're single?*

Fortunately, Sam broke the awkward silence for her a moment later. "This is a great little neighborhood, isn't it? Everyone has been so friendly and welcoming."

"How do you like the house?" Talia said, hoping to deflect from the fact that she herself had not made any effort to welcome them. She thought about mentioning how often she'd visited there when Cindy and Bob had been her neighbors. How the place had been almost a second home for her and Riley before the Reeds had moved. That would be sharing too much—far too inelegant.

She fell silent, not really hearing his answer and weighing what she might say next in the way of small talk. She didn't really want to ask questions that she already knew the answers to. What had brought him to the area? Where was Brandon going to school? Why wasn't the child's mother in the picture? Mrs. Kravitz had already filled Talia in on all the details when she had picked Riley up from her home, the night Aunt Miriam had been in the ICU and Mrs. Kravitz had been babysitting.

To pretend she didn't already know these details might seem polite—but Talia said nothing, either because she didn't want to seem too curious or to be at all dishonest since she already knew the answers. And so she settled for silence as she stood barefoot, holding the pendant on her necklace up to her lips, in front of the tall stranger in her kitchen. Sam must have sensed her unease. He rose slowly to his feet, pushing the stool he had been straddling back under the kitchen counter.

"Well, we should be heading home. We just wanted to stop in and share the wealth from the orchard."

"It's nice meeting you, and thanks again for the oranges," Talia offered, keeping her arms tightly folded over her chest to avoid another handshaking faux pas. She called upstairs for Riley and Brandon to come down. Funny, she thought, the action seemed so familiar, like déjà vu, as if she had gone through the same motions a hundred other times.

A few minutes later, she and Riley closed the front door behind Sam and Brandon—after she had promised the children they could play together again soon.

The house felt oddly empty.

CHAPTER 16

THE ORPHAN WIDOW

I t was October 22, 1997.

Two years ago to the day, Talia was visited by the fire department chaplain and Chief Graham on what would become the worst day of her life. She deliberately made no mention of the anniversary to Riley, knowing her daughter was too young to piece together the day's significance, and dropped her off at school as though it were any other day.

Talia would call Rose later. She knew some of the firefighters from the department would be calling to check on her throughout the day too. The previous year, some of their families had gone so far as to send flowers and cards. It was amazing to witness the kindness of strangers who came together after or during a time of crisis, behaving like an extended family.

On days like this, it was hard for her not to think of her mother's death too. Talia wondered what kind of woman Shira had been. She could only imagine her young mother's distress, trying to protect two small daughters from the ugly realities of domestic violence. Aunt Miriam had been close to forty when her younger sister died at twenty-three. Twenty-three was so young. Talia had been quite naive at that age. She hadn't known a thing about love and had been in no way ready to start a family. How had her mother managed to love the monster, and why had she had children with him?

Talia wanted to believe her mother must have been a loving and for-giving person, and perhaps she'd given her husband too many chances to straighten himself out and appreciate the gift his little family was. If Grandad had known about his youngest daughter's marital troubles, he would have been there for her, Talia was sure. There was no doubt he had loved Shira dearly and would have supported her and tried to keep her safe, despite the choices she'd made.

Her memories of her grandfather, as vague and limited as they were, were full of love. If nothing else, they held for Talia a tiny glimpse of the person her mother might have been. Her maternal grandmother, Esther, died of a stroke before Naomi and Talia were born. Aunt Miriam hadn't mentioned her much. Talia hoped, for her grandfather's sake, that she had been a kind and loving woman and not at all like Aunt Miriam.

Talia stopped by the cemetery early that afternoon, where they had laid Russel to rest. What was left of Russel, anyway. What hadn't gone up in smoke to join the ether, swept away by the Santa Ana winds forever.

The sky was cornflower blue, and the rolling, manicured lawns of the cemetery were a deep-green splendor. She stood in the shade of a tall river birch, listening to its tiny leaves rustling in the breeze above her. Sunlight flickered through the patchwork of shadows on Russel's granite headstone. She had anticipated the day would make her revisit unbearable pain, but she felt none of the overwhelming sadness that had incapacitated her on the first anniversary of his death. Instead, she felt only a familiar ache, a distant echo of the sorrow that had been too unbearable to carry indefinitely.

She lowered herself to the ground and sat cross-legged on the freshly mown grass, the warmth of the sun on her back. She felt profoundly alone. Russ wasn't here; he really was gone forever. He had vanished like a wish never fulfilled—or worse, like a half-forgotten dream.

As a child, Talia always told herself the death of her mother had made her stronger. She would tell herself the loss had been a test, a trial to make her resilient, and that being an orphan had forged her into the fighter she had become. But when it came to the death of her husband, she'd felt nothing like a fighter. She didn't feel in the least bit resilient at all.

Losing Russ had only made her angry.

It felt so unjust that she had suffered two catastrophic losses. Who deserved such a cruel hand dealt from the universe? She had tried to reframe this self-pity, to find something positive, but it had not been easy, especially when she reminded herself of how much Russ had loved her and the happiness he had brought to her life. She chided herself for not being able to feel worthy of Russ's love now that he was dead. By filling her heart with resentment, she was spoiling what had once been so beautiful.

Sitting in the warmth of the sun, she closed her eyes and listened to the chirping of the birds and the drone of a far-off lawn mower.

Life was calling. It waited for no one.

She dreaded another year without Russ, but she would have to be strong for Riley. Talia realized the strength she needed would have to come from a part of her she had forgotten, a part of her that was separate from being the child of her mother and the mother of her child. A part that had already triumphed and survived, despite her anger. Only by letting go of regret could she embrace the future and do what Russ had asked of her in her dream: to step into the world of the living again.

There was no other choice, really. If she continued to hang on to what had passed, wouldn't she be making an orphan out of Riley?

Talia had to pull herself together and get on with life. Riley deserved better — and maybe she did too.

CHAPTER 17

PROGRESS

Talia met with Dr. Cohn again on Friday that week, and then regularly in the following weeks. In their third session together, she talked more about Riley and her efforts to be a good parent, move on in life, become less isolated, and start making more friends outside of her current circle. As she went on, she listened to herself as if hearing her own thoughts for the first time.

As usual, Dr. Cohn listened quietly, her face revealing nothing.

As they continued to meet, Talia sometimes felt Dr. Cohn was letting her carry on long enough to weave a web of contradictions and prove herself a fraud, but it never came to that. Rather, Talia's words began to conjure a convincing image of herself as a resourceful and resilient survivor, one who would persist despite catastrophe.

After a while, it became clear to Talia that the more she was willing to reveal her fears, the more cogent she sounded. In her own estimation, she was gaining a little ground on the path to becoming a person with healthy coping strategies. In fact, she'd even begun to sleep better at night, which did more for her daily sense of optimism than she'd ever imagined.

As the weeks passed, Talia began to measure her emotional progress by the hours of Dr. Cohn's silence. It seemed the ice was gradually melting and that this was a good thing. It must have been, because Talia began to trust that, for once, the melting of the ice did not foreshadow a coming flood.

AN UNCEREMONIOUS PARTING

Talia had chosen cremation for her aunt's remains. She planned to scatter her ashes on a Sunday in mid-November. John agreed to take Riley and his two daughters to the movies, allowing Naomi and Talia the afternoon to themselves.

Talia had planned quite a production. She'd chartered a fifty-four-foot sailboat to take them from Ventura Harbor out to sea so that they could legally dispose of Aunt Miriam's remains. Naomi had not been enthusiastic about the idea but had agreed once Talia explained there would be champagne involved and that the trip could be a sightseeing adventure. Coincidentally, it was migration season for gray whales—the giant creatures undertaking a five-thousand-mile journey from the Arctic to their breeding grounds off the coast of Baja, California.

Talia counted herself lucky to have secured a sailboat during the height of the season. Since they would require the vessel for only around two hours, it was both affordable for her and convenient for the busy charter service.

Aunt Miriam had lived on both sides of the Pacific, so the location seemed a fitting choice to spread her ashes. The very simple and private service Talia had planned was more for herself and Naomi than for their aunt. They would follow the brief outing with a champagne toast to new beginnings and an early dinner somewhere on the boardwalk.

That Sunday in mid-November arrived unexpectedly quickly, and before Talia knew it, she was on a sailboat with Naomi on a crisp, clear afternoon.

As the boat motored out past the breakwater, they passed several fishing and whale-watching vessels that were going back to the harbor. The wind speed was about ten knots, and there were some scattered whitecaps. The crew hoisted the mainsail, and they were soon flying downwind, with few maneuvers necessary to maintain their course.

The going was swift and only slightly choppy, which relieved Naomi. Talia sat with her sister in the cockpit while Gene, the captain, was at the helm. He was an older gentleman with sky-blue eyes and a full head of curly white hair. His first mate was his granddaughter, a young woman named Kerstin, who handled the rigging and sails as though she had done it a thousand times. She made her way around the boat with astonishing agility, despite the slant of the deck and the speed of the vessel. When she later joined them in the cockpit and took the helm, she explained they were legally required to be at least three nautical miles offshore to scatter ashes. She pointed out and named each of the Channel Islands visible in the distance, as well as the ones nearby, Anacapa and Santa Cruz, where Talia remembered hiking once with the girls on her college cross-country team.

A few minutes later, Kerstin announced they were sailing over one of five deep trenches along the California coastline that had been caused by sliding tectonic plates. The waters in this area of the Pacific were surprisingly cold and exceptionally deep. This detail seemed to raise Naomi's spirits when she considered Aunt Miriam's final resting place, but she had to admit, she wasn't entirely comfortable knowing what was under the water beneath them. Neither was Talia. The two of them held on to the straps of their life jackets, bracing against the chilly ocean spray.

Whitecaps popped up here and there in the channel, and an occasional swell lifted them gently as the vessel steadily cut its way out to sea. The mainsail, fully deployed, provided some shade—respite from the glaring afternoon sun—but no reprieve from the bitterness of the wind.

When they had reached the necessary distance from the mainland and then pressed on a little farther just for fun, Captain Gene took the helm again, and Kerstin dropped the mainsail. The crew then quietly retreated to the cabin below, allowing Talia and Naomi their privacy. Talia leaned over the vessel's guardrail, looking out at the vast expanse of the Pacific. The water was truly navy blue, almost black.

Naomi and Talia made their way up to the bow, holding on to whatever they could to maintain balance as the boat bobbed on the rolling swells. Naomi had always suffered from motion sickness, and Talia was expecting she would start complaining about the choppiness of the seas any moment now. *Maybe Naomi is more focused on the gravity of the occasion than I realized,* Talia thought. Talia felt it was necessary to find something kind to say about Aunt Miriam now that they were about to part ways permanently. Naomi, of course, had difficulty thinking of anything charitable. Talia admitted to herself that she was finding it difficult too. But Miriam had been their mother's sister, and so it felt right to honor her passing in some formal way. They stood side by side and looked out over the deep ocean, feeling the boat rocking gently like a giant swing. The water slapping the bow cut the silence.

"Life is short," Talia finally said, searching for something meaningful. "We should live each day with the intention of being good and kind souls so that we make others' lives easier. Let us bring joy into this world and share it willingly. Let us find peace in our hearts and spread that peace to those around us. Let us also be generous with our love, with our knowledge, and with our time. We should do these things because it is right and because it will make our lives more meaningful."

The brief oration was all Talia could muster. She realized the irony, though. She had just made a list of things Aunt Miriam had not done during her time on Earth.

Naomi made no attempt to add to the eulogy. She stared out to the horizon. Maybe she was feeling a little seasick, after all. The color had drained from her cheeks. Or perhaps her words, Talia thought, were striking a chord with Naomi. She felt compelled to go on.

"I suggest we make a pact to scatter, along with Aunt Miriam's ashes, all our resentments for the way she treated us as children and all our sorrows and regrets about the loveless existence she imposed on us when we were vulnerable orphans. Such a gesture on our part would likely be liberating."

These words will stir something in Naomi, she thought, but when Naomi turned to face Talia and lowered her sunglasses, she was rolling her eyes in exasperation.

"Is this a case of 'please, take my advice—I don't need it,' Talia?" She laughed then, though it was not a joyful laugh. Talia felt ridiculous. Her sister had reason to be angry, she admitted, but she'd hoped, for Naomi's sake, that she would see it was time to move on—time to let go of the resentment she was still holding on to.

Naomi grasped the boat's lifelines with both hands and leaned her head overboard.

Talia thought she was about to be sick, but her sister chuckled wickedly and added her own touch to the eulogy. "I'm terribly sorry, little fishes, and big fishes, too, but we're about to contaminate your environment with the most toxic of agents!"

Talia didn't see the humor. It was clearly best if she relinquished her hope that the day would be cathartic for her sister and focused instead on whatever catharsis she could bring for herself. Even if she didn't have quite as much of a reason to hate Aunt Miriam, there was still plenty of baggage weighing her down.

"It's good riddance and a fine farewell to misery," Naomi added. She wasn't finished. "Let me also remind you, little sister," she said, turning to Talia and looking down at her. "It's time for you to move on with life! Time for your own new chapter. Stop giving advice and start taking some of it for yourself."

Talia should have known better. Naomi always wanted the last word. Part of her wanted to tell Naomi that she'd been doing just that recently—that she was in therapy; occasionally chatting with her neighbor Sam; and now on a boat in the Pacific, parting ways impartially with the main nemesis from their past. Naomi's childhood might've been objectively rockier than Talia's, but Talia's last two years had been equally challenging.

The last thing she wanted was to be like Naomi, stuck like a fly in the amber of the past, forever resenting what had happened and lamenting what could've been. It was one thing to mourn, but it was something else altogether to simply refuse to heal.

But now wasn't the time for that. It was time to defuse the situation.

She made her way back to the stern of the boat, holding on to the rigging here and there to steady herself, and climbed into the cockpit to retrieve from her backpack the brass urn containing their aunt's ashes. She tucked it under her arm, leaving one hand free to hold on to the boat as she returned to Naomi on the bow.

She positioned herself strategically downwind, right against the lifelines. Both she and Naomi peered into the deep beyond as if it were the face of an eternal abyss. Steadying herself while the boat bobbed, Talia held the heavy urn firmly with both hands and put it between her knees, bracing as Naomi tried to unscrew the tightly sealed lid. She seemed to be having trouble. Talia could see her sister was using all her force as she gripped the urn tighter. The joint maneuver on a bobbing sailboat required more agility than they had anticipated, and they began to stagger around like drunken sailors wrestling over a keg of ale. The comedy of it broke the tension between them, and they were soon giggling. When the lid finally gave way, they both shrieked. Talia nearly tipped the contents onto the deck, and Naomi almost went overboard.

When they had composed themselves, Talia got on with it. Just as she was leaning over the guardrail to pour Aunt Miriam's ashes into the midnight-blue Pacific Ocean, the waters near the boat heaved and parted in a strange, audible release that was both startling and awe-inspiring. A huge spout of water shot high into the air. A second later, another spout, and then a third.

The sisters had barely registered the odd occurrences when a massive gray whale breached within twenty feet of the sailboat. The spectacularly immense creature launched itself out of the water, higher than Naomi and Talia would have thought possible. It hung in midair for a split second and returned to the water with a thunderous crash, displacing a massive amount of water that then washed over the deck.

They were caught off guard when a great icy curtain of water fell over their heads, like an unholy baptism, soaking them thoroughly.

Naomi shrieked with surprise and scrambled to maintain her balance on the deck, which was now treacherously slippery. Talia was flying from one side of the bow to the other. A moment later, the boat rocked wildly in the other direction, sending Naomi scrambling for the lifelines while Talia did her best to avoid going overboard headfirst. She had lost her grasp on the urn, which dropped onto the deck like a cannonball and rolled unceremoniously overboard.

It disappeared into the blue nothingness with the haste of an unchained anchor.

Talia gasped in disbelief.

Naomi held fast to the rigging, the boat swaying wildly for several seconds, as Talia did her best to get back on her feet. Her sandals had disappeared, and the deck was now a river of salt water. Naomi's dress, soaked through, clung to her shivering thighs, and her hair, like a mop of seaweed, dripped salty brine into her eyes. Talia had to have looked just as bad, based on the way Naomi was staring at her.

Kerstin and Captain Gene clambered back on deck and found Naomi and Talia sitting on the bow, laughing hysterically.

When Naomi caught her breath after a long-winded fit of laughter, she began to cry.

Her eye shadow formed long dark streaks that ran down her salty cheeks and onto her bright-orange life jacket. The dismay on the faces of the crew made Talia laugh even harder, though she wasn't sure if she was laughing out of amusement or relief that she was still on board. What an uproarious, undignified sight she and Naomi must have been.

On the way back to the harbor, Naomi sat in the cockpit, wrapped in Talia's windbreaker, with her knees pulled up under her chin, her hair in a long soggy braid over her shoulder.

Talia regretted not getting any photos of the whales they had encountered. *Too bad Riley missed all the excitement,* she thought as she sat shivering under the now-damp towels Kerstin had wrapped around her earlier. Nothing that afternoon had gone quite as she had hoped. Her sandals were probably at the bottom of a Pacific trench, along with Aunt Miriam's urn. As soaked as Naomi and Talia were, there would be no going out to dinner and no champagne toast. Talia wondered if she could convince Naomi to settle for a hot chocolate in front of the fireplace at home. No doubt it would have to be *spiked* hot chocolate to do the trick.

CHAPTER 19

CHOICES

On the Monday after Thanksgiving, Talia received a large manila envelope with a string of familiar-looking green and white Australian postage stamps on its top right-hand corner. On the back was a stick-on label that revealed the origins of the package: *Law Offices of Heslop, Harvey, and Bergelsohn, Brisbane, Australia.*

She was saddened to see that the sender was Ari Bergelsohn and not his grandfather, Bernard. She was immediately concerned that the older Mr. Bergelsohn might have succumbed to cancer in the weeks since they had first chatted on the phone. She went so far as to pick up her letter opener before she decided Naomi should be present for the opening of the mystery package, which Mr. Bergelsohn had promised would hold something of great interest to them. She called her sister, and Naomi agreed to come to dinner that night.

Talia took Toby with her to pick up Riley from school that afternoon. Riley hadn't been out on the playground as she normally would have been when Talia arrived on campus. It had been raining on and off all day, and when she pulled into the school parking lot, she was alerted by the school nurse that Riley was waiting for her in the principal's office after an unfortunate incident on the playground.

The look the nurse gave her as she unlocked her minivan in the parking spot next to Talia's truck was not one of concern but rather one of disapproval, and this was somehow reassuring to Talia that Riley was not injured in any way but more likely the accused perpetrator in the aforementioned playground incident. And her assumption—supported by the fact that the nurse seemed to be abandoning her post—proved Talia correct. And so it was that Talia spent the next half hour having a heart-to-heart with Ms. Curtis, the school principal, about Riley's behavior.

On the way home, Talia decided to make a detour to Riley's favorite park so that they could talk about what had happened at school and enjoy a brief break in the weather. It seemed obvious that the child needed to unleash a little energy.

As Talia's truck rocked into the muddy, pothole-ridden parking lot at the playground—deserted that day, no doubt given the unfavorable weather—she looked over at Riley, who, along with Toby, sat poised to spring from the vehicle as soon as they came to a stop.

"Hey, sweetie, I'm going to let Toby out so that he can run around a bit, but before you and I get out, do you want to tell me what happened at recess today with the twins?" Everyone knew who the twins were. The Smedsrud boys, first graders at Riley's school, were a full head taller than most kids in their class. They were the only children of a celebrity couple in town and had earned themselves a reputation as playground bullies. Talia was anxious to know Riley's side of the story. She'd already had an earful from Ms. Curtis.

"I *had* to bite them, Momma," Riley said, looking up at her mother, brows knit, lips angling down in an unhappy face. "They wouldn't let me out of the playhouse, and you said never to let anyone bully me. I tried climbing out the window to get away from them, but they pulled my legs back, and I fell on my elbow."

Riley's lip quivered, and Talia saw red as she pictured the scene. Like Talia, Riley was petite—scrappy, yes, but petite. She grabbed her daughter's arm, pulled up her sleeve, and examined her elbow. There was a small red bump visible, but the skin had not been broken, and Riley clearly did not appear to be in any pain. Nonetheless, Talia was furious that the playground monitors hadn't been supervising more closely and that Ms. Curtis had blamed the entire incident on Riley alone.

"Sounds like you did the right thing to take care of yourself. I'm glad you didn't get hurt worse." Talia bit her lip, doing her best to keep her temper in check. She put both hands on the steering wheel and gripped hard. "I think I'll give the twins' momma a call when we get home and let her know her boys are in for more of the same if they don't steer clear of you and quit bullying. I'm sorry that happened to you, but it sounds like you handled it."

Riley suddenly beamed from ear to ear as she tugged on the door handle inside the truck cab, indicating the conversation was over.

The wind had changed direction in the prior week, bringing with it the chill of an early winter. Talia and Riley zipped up their jackets before getting out of the truck. It had rained most of the previous week, which had kept them indoors over Thanksgiving weekend. The ground under the trees in the park was soggy. Small white clouds trailed large gray ones above the mountain range to the west that separated the valley from the Pacific Ocean.

Toby was already on a mission to find a stick for someone to throw for him. Talia chased her daughter over the open field across from the park's playground equipment. Riley was fast as she darted between the shrubs and rosebushes that bordered the field. She wondered if one day Riley might enjoy long-distance running too. If she might run with Talia to the top of the mountain, where they could sit, take in the view, and share the serenity of the valley from on high.

Maybe not, Talia decided. Riley was on her own path in life. There was no need for her to follow anyone else's lead. She was already making her own brave choices.

Choices.

Nineteen-year-old Talia's college roommate, Stephanie—a less-than-benevolent creature whose favorite pastime had been making disparaging remarks about what she called Talia's thrift-shop wardrobe—had quit school without explanation and moved back to the East Coast. Actually, Talia had no idea where she had moved. She'd only guessed because that's where Stephanie had lived before coming to college in California. Either way, Stephanie hadn't taken the time to inform Talia of her plans. All Talia knew was that her Gucci-flaunting, thrift-shop-hating roommate had vanished in the middle of the quarter without paying her share of the rent. The only good thing she could say about Stephanie was that she had turned her on to one of her favorite electives. In the prior quarter of classes, Stephanie had raved so much about her music appreciation class—and the amazing instructor who taught it—that Talia had been persuaded to sign up for the class the following quarter to see what all the fuss was about. Of course, it hadn't been a smart idea, as she already had a hectic track and cross-country schedule and a heavy course load in social studies.

Stephanie hadn't been wrong about the class, though; it was one of the best courses Talia had ever taken. But other than their shared love of the subject—and an unhealthy infatuation with its instructor, Professor G.—she and Stephanie couldn't agree on anything. Talia understood that nothing in the way of housing in the general vicinity of UCLA was affordable for a single student trying to get by on a modest athletic scholarship. Her only hope to avoid falling behind on the rent was to find a new roommate immediately—not a likely prospect.

Professor Carlo Giovanucci, Talia's music appreciation instructor, was a handsome Italian American in his late forties with wavy auburn hair, the eyes of an angel, and a smile that could melt an iceberg. For the first two weeks of the quarter, Talia sat in the front row of the lecture hall, where she did her best to impress Professor G. with her enthusiastic responses to his questions. The first time his amazing dark eyes settled on her, she was lost. No one had ever looked at her that way before.

Professor G. talked passionately about the classics as he played cuts of beautiful music for his students—his hands waving wildly in the air as if he himself were the conductor. His eyes, with their full, thick lashes, seemed to focus on otherworldly landscapes Talia could only imagine. The superb music he shared touched her soul and stirred something in her she hadn't known existed. She discovered a love for the energy of Vivaldi's *Four Seasons*, an appreciation for the drama of Bach's cello suites, and a true sense of rapture when listening to Mozart's *Requiem*. The realization that these composers had all made the world a more beautiful place with their masterworks rekindled Talia's faith in humankind and moved her on a spiritual level—something she hadn't experienced in years.

Who could question the assertion that music was the transcendent language of the gods after hearing *Miserere mei, Deus* by Allegri? Although something inside of Talia bubbled up with joy during Professor G.'s lectures, she was not alone in this sentiment. In fact, Talia was sure there wasn't a girl on campus who hadn't heard about the lecturer.

She knew she was no competition for the other Los Angeles coeds in her class who were also swooning over Professor G. Just like Stephanie, they dressed to the nines every day, wore gallons of makeup, and carried designer purses. Each of them could, no doubt, also discuss opera and theater cogently and perhaps even in Italian. But Talia had always enjoyed a challenge. She was not deterred, and her efforts to gain Professor G.'s attention employed all the subtlety of a French horn solo.

The professor had a habit of pacing the floor of the lecture hall like a man possessed. He'd cross to the far side of the room, where he would stop and stare out the window as he lectured. Talia envisioned him away from the confines of the classroom. She saw the two of them walking hand in hand through a park, Talia in a silk frock with a floppy straw hat, with the sun at their backs and the soft grass between their toes.

She should have known from the beginning the attraction was ill-conceived and destined to end badly. First, Professor G. was married. Second, Talia didn't own a straw hat, nor had she ever, in her entire life, worn a silk frock. She'd never been big on dresses, and silk seemed out of her league. Shorts, sweatshirts, one pair of old blue jeans, and two pairs of running shoes was the sum of Talia's college wardrobe.

But she had to hand it to herself. Neither her limited wardrobe nor her cultural impoverishment precluded her from successfully competing for Professor G.'s attention. Talia was certain he had noticed her.

Professor G., or Carlo, as Talia began calling him in her daydreams, was all she could think about. At night, she had trouble sleeping. Thoughts of drowning in the fragrance of his manly cologne were all-consuming.

When the inevitable did occur and they became closer than they should have, the affair was passionate and short-lived. Oddly, there were no trips to concert halls to see the Los Angeles Philharmonic with Carlo, nor walks in the park with the grass between their toes—only clandestine meetings in dimly lit nooks around campus. Places that did not leave Talia feeling good about herself. Still, despite her dismay at her own conduct, nothing deterred her from her pursuit, not even the unwelcome realization that Professor G.'s

manly cologne was only a cover for the alcohol on his breath. Talia had simply slipped away under the man's spell, and now she recognized nothing
of herself.

She was finally the one to end it. Though to her own discredit, Talia
didn't end it out of remorse for loving a married man, nor out of shame for
the way she had pursued him at the cost of her own self-respect. Not even
common sense or their twenty-five-year age difference had compelled her to
walk away. As it turned out, Professor G.'s inability to distract himself from
the advances of other foolish young women had been the final deal-breaker.
Talia had ended it for no reason other than plain old-fashioned jealousy after
she found Carlo with another of her classmates one afternoon.

After she'd broken it off, Carlo's viselike grip on Talia only tightened.
Despite his blatant philandering and obvious character flaws, he had a hold
on Talia that felt deeply personal. The thought of him looking at anyone else
the way he had looked at her was soul-grating. The fact that he was able to
move on to the next girl so quickly left Talia feeling worthless and used, even
if she had foolishly invited his attention. She wasn't mature enough to realize
how disparate the power balance in their relationship had been or how lucky
she was to have escaped him. All she knew was that, more than anything on
the face of the planet, she wanted him back. Sitting through his lectures was
torture—even from where she'd cower at the back of the hall, doing her best
to stay out of sight. But it was during one of those times when she'd suddenly
realized that Gucci-loving Stephanie might also have fallen prey to Professor
G.'s gypsy magic. Why else had she left school so hastily and clandestinely
right after taking his class?

That unwelcome realization was just the beginning of Talia's problems,
unfortunately.

She had become a victim of her own making, and something about the
situation felt so familiar. She was alone again. It was a confusing and awkward time in her life.

To make matters worse, her period was late, which was directly affecting
her ability to concentrate on her coursework. Talia could feel the shadows of
fate closing in on her, and it made her want to run. In fact, she *needed* to run.

At afternoon track practice, she started pushing herself mercilessly, to
the point of near collapse at the end of each interval on the track. Sometimes

her own ruthlessness scared her. Waves of dizziness swept over her after practice, leaving her without an appetite for dinner in the evenings.

She lay awake next to the phone for hours each night, hoping Carlo would call. He never did. But she couldn't find it in herself to resent him for his betrayal. It was easy to make excuses for him. Maybe he had a legitimate reason not to call. His life was busy and complicated, and he was still married. Talia hated herself for her inability to put him out of her mind.

On particularly restless nights, she would drift off to sleep in the early hours of the morning, only to awaken within an hour or two. Escape from the angst was impossible, which was the reason she began running in the darkened, deserted streets around campus in the cool predawn hours.

In the initial silence of those early mornings, Talia heard only the sound of her feet hitting the sidewalk. Like a metronome, her steps measured out her pursuit of something familiar in an otherwise disordered existence. As she coursed along the edge of campus, passing the manicured flower beds and tall iron gates of the larger private estates, the world would begin to wake up, and she would focus on her breathing and on counting her steps. What had she become? What had she done to herself?

Despite her despondency, there was something empowering about being awake before the rest of the world, before even the birds had arisen. These sojourns in the darkness gave Talia a respite from the chaos that consumed her days, her sense of isolation, and the uncertainty of what lay ahead.

When she wasn't running, her anxiety was compounded by the fact that she wasn't eating well. Within a week of ending things with Professor G., Talia became tormented by frequent migraines and stifling nausea. She was constantly woozy and had trouble lifting her backpack full of textbooks. She didn't know how she managed to maintain her hectic schedule, much less survive, in such a state of pure exhaustion. Perhaps, on some level, she was hoping not to survive.

Naomi remained distracted by her jobs and her errant boyfriend, so it was no surprise that Talia's cross-country coach was the first person to notice the changes in her.

Coach Martha was from Tennessee and a former track star herself. She was a kind woman with a southern accent who employed tireless diplomacy in her dealings with the fragile egos of the young athletes in her charge. At every track meet, it was plain to see in Coach Martha's eyes that running was in her blood. Talia would never forget the lessons she taught her about perseverance and self-respect.

Shortly after she'd broken off the affair with Professor G., Talia began to suspect she was pregnant. The complexities of her situation were daunting—not only on the level of what a pregnancy would mean for her immediate future but also on a far deeper level. She was ill-prepared to take care of anyone, even herself, it seemed. Her predicament shocked her. Had she really fallen prey to the same quandary as her mother and Naomi? How could she have been so careless?

An unexpected pregnancy had bound her young mother to an abusive monster, and that choice had purportedly taken her life. And Naomi had destroyed her adolescence with a reckless choice, one that had left life-long scars.

Talia knew no one shared the blame for her predicament. She should have known better. Had there not been enough warnings? Enough sacrifices? She saw herself as the last remaining piece on the board in a cruel game of chess the women of her family were losing. She resented it. If she were answerable to only herself, her plight would have been more tolerable, but the situation was more complex than that. Her mother had been forced to swallow the bitter pill of propriety, and her sister had been spoon-fed the same by the Australian health-care system. They had each sacrificed so much, without having had a real choice in the matter, and their suffering had issued a warning to Talia—an unspoken edict that she should learn from their mistakes and steer clear of the pitfalls they had pointed out along the way. But Talia had failed to heed their warning, and now she would pay a dearer price.

Ending her pregnancy—taking the life of her unborn child—would cost Talia her soul. At least, that's what her Catholic upbringing had taught her. The decision would send her to hell, no question about it, and yet that still wasn't enough to change her mind.

She chose not to reach out for help, instead reaching deeper within herself to carry out her terrible plan in secret, just as she was carrying her pregnancy in secret. Talia made an appointment at a family planning clinic in Venice Beach, a small community far enough away from campus to make it unlikely she would encounter anyone she knew and close enough to her apartment to rapidly execute her plan before she could change her mind. The clinic would see her the following week; in the meantime, Talia ran.

She skipped her afternoon classes to run the four-mile loop around the north end of campus every day. It wasn't an accident that she passed the chapel at Marymount—a private Catholic high school for girls on the edge of the UCLA campus—every day at noon. More than once, she'd felt compelled to enter the chapel, throw herself on the altar, and beg God's forgiveness for her moral stumbling with Professor G. and her sinister plan to end her pregnancy. She'd hoped beyond all hope that a priest or nun would emerge from the doors atop the marble stairway by the chapel and, knowing her dilemma through some divine means, implore her to abandon her path to damnation. But such a reprieve did not come. The decision was Talia's and Talia's alone.

A miscarriage would have been her salvation, an act of God's will, letting her off the hook. But it seemed the life inside her had a way of clinging to this world undeterred. No amount of hope, recklessly fast running, or wishful thinking could coax it out of her body.

She was glad her appointment at the clinic was just around the corner. No one, not even Talia, could keep a mortal sin a secret forever.

The night before her appointment, she sat under the glaring stadium lights and watched the men's team finish their hurdle sprints on the track. Talia was weak and very tired. She hadn't weighed herself in a while, but even her smallest bargain-basement shorts hung loosely on her. She was Snake Hips again, and she felt all the bad feelings that went with those words, all the isolation and shame. When Coach Martha sat down next to her on the bleachers, Talia felt herself snap to attention. Despite being a large woman, Coach moved silently. When she placed her hand on Talia's shoulder in a manner that told her she knew, Talia's heart sank.

Maybe Coach was in on the faculty gossip circuit and had heard about Talia's affair with Professor G., or maybe Talia was just that transparent. Whatever her means, it was clear that Coach could read the situation. Talia's cheeks flushed.

Coach Martha crossed her arms over her chest and leaned back on the row of seats behind them.

"See those hurdles out there on the track, missy?" she asked, nodding in the direction of the field. Talia didn't dare look at her. They both knew where the conversation was going. "I put those hurdles out there to make my run-ners strong and agile." She was quiet for a moment before adding, "The trick is to get the height exactly right. They gotta be high enough that you really must stretch to get over them but just low enough that you can achieve suc-cess without getting hurt."

Talia kept her eyes on her feet. Her dusty running shoes looked blurry through a growing pool of tears, and her throat felt too tight to allow words to escape.

"Some of the tall hurdles you've put in your own lane," Coach went on carefully, "are going to do nothing but bring you down, Talia."

Talia's stomach dropped. *Oh God!*

"Now the good Lord knows what you're fixin' to do, but you better think it through. I know you're a fighter, and that's good. But keep in mind, missy, life's no sprint. You might want to set a different pace for yourself if you plan on finishing this race."

That night, Talia cried herself to sleep. She cried for her mother and for Naomi and for the baby she could not allow to be born. She cried for the kind words and concern from Coach Martha, who'd never had the chance to carry a child of her own. But all her tears, like all her running, could not spare Talia from her fate—which she saw as her responsibility, her duty, and her sentence. Her appointment was just hours away, and like a giant spiderweb, it waited to ensnare her soul.

The lobby of the clinic in Venice was packed. Apparently, affordable family planning was in high demand in that neck of the woods. She cau-tiously surveyed the other women who, like her, were waiting to see the doc-tor—though perhaps not for the same reason that she had come. On the far side of the room, there were some tough-looking girls gathered around one of their friends, who appeared to have a passion for big hair, pencil-drawn eyebrows, and according to one of her tattoos, some dude named Sergio.

The group's mood was remarkably jovial; they seemed to be gathered for a celebration of sorts. There were two or three older women in the wait-ing room, perhaps wives and experienced matriarchs reluctant to give moth-erhood another go-around or perhaps dealing with some other life-altering worries. To Talia's horror, almost everyone in the room had noticed her—not because she deserved any more attention than the next woman facing a difficult choice or a concerning diagnosis but because she was sobbing like a child. A tall, slender girl with beautiful dark hair tied in dozens of long braids broke away from her friend in the corner.

"Is this your first time?" she asked.

Talia was too shocked to answer. She could not imagine getting herself into such a dire situation more than once. After all, she only had one soul to damn. She simply nodded and blew her nose into the tissues she'd been handed. The girl placed a comforting hand on Talia's back.

"Oh my gosh, girl. You're nothin' but skin and bones," she said.

The remark cut deeply. Talia could hear Uncle Gus's words: "Men are not liking bonz; only dogz are liking bonz."

Talia did her best to compose herself. She tried to slow her breathing, though she found it remarkably difficult. A brightly colored sign on the wall proclaimed CHOICE IS YOUR RIGHT. Another read WOMEN HAVE A RIGHT TO CONTROL THEIR BODIES. She found herself lamenting that she now seemed unable to control anything at all.

When it was Talia's turn to be seen, the nurse sent her into the bathroom to collect a urine sample. She waited for the results of her pregnancy test on the edge of her seat in the lobby, her damp fists clenched in her lap. When she was finally called in to see the doctor, she was almost too weak with anxiety to stand. Her legs felt like jelly as she propelled herself—through sheer determination—like a lamb to the slaughter, into the exam room.

A short, obese man with no discernable neck came out from behind the cubicle drapes and introduced himself as Dr. Daniels. Talia felt an overwhelming sense of pity for him. She might have been on the precipice of damning herself, but this man was a serial offender. As soon as that thought had formed, it was replaced by another. She realized Dr. Daniels and others like him were a lifeline for many girls and women who, in the battle to maintain control of their bodies and lives, might otherwise die from a hemorrhage or sepsis or worse—or might be obliged to bear a torture inflicted upon them by violation or subjugation.

In a sudden epiphany, Talia understood there was no comfortably polarized position she could take regarding a woman's right to choose. The duality of an abortion doctor's work existed in the same fragile balance life and death themselves did. The life-taker was the life-giver, and the life-giver was the life-taker. This was a plain and undeniable truth. Life and death were as married as day and night.

Talia had imagined the consultation with Dr. Daniels would be an uncomfortable one, but his first question took her by surprise. "Ms. Altman," he began, "are you a runner or a gymnast?"

Talia balked, utterly taken aback by his ability to make small talk in such grave circumstances, but the man seemed not to notice her dismay. "I . . . I'm a runner."

The doctor glanced at his clipboard with her paperwork. "Have you lost weight recently?"

She officially began to doubt her reading of the situation. "Uh . . . I have no idea. Well, probably," she stammered.

"It's quite clear that you're training far too intensely." Dr. Daniels studied her then, a look of concern clouding his face. "You cannot expect to have a normal menstrual cycle unless you gain at least ten to fifteen pounds. Your body weight is dangerously low, young lady."

Talia stared back at him, mouth gaping like a fish. "What?"

Dr. Daniels followed this gentle reprimand with a life-changing statement: "You're not pregnant, Ms. Altman. You're merely experiencing a problem quite common among female athletes with low body fat." After a long pause to allow Talia to quiet her sobs of relief, he added that there was almost no chance of her becoming pregnant in her current physical state.

On her way out of the clinic, the nurse at the front desk handed Talia the business card of a therapist who specialized in anorexia and other eating disorders. Talia snatched it gleefully and bolted to the exit, her strength suddenly and miraculously renewed.

As for Professor G., Talia saw him only once after her pregnancy scare, years later, after she had finished graduate school. Despite his shocking appearance, she would have recognized those eyes anywhere. He was standing on a sidewalk in downtown Los Angeles, outside the Natural History Museum, where she had accompanied a group of foster children on a summer field trip. Talia's eyes settled on him as she stepped off the bus and onto the searing sidewalk. Fortunately, she saw no spark of recognition in his gaze. She wondered how long he had been living on the streets.

Carlo was unkempt and shabbily dressed. His mop of once-auburn hair, now completely white, blended seamlessly into the unshaven beard on his sun-scorched face. He could not have been more than sixty years old, if Talia's math was correct. Her heart sank at the sight of him. A lifetime of excessive drinking and poor choices had taken their toll. This once-privileged man had indulged himself to the point of undoing and, no doubt, had left a trail of heartache in his wake. Talia's sense of anguish upon seeing his condition was almost immediately replaced with a surge of regret over the grief she had caused herself in his company.

Without making eye contact again, she handed the man a five-dollar bill and hurried the children up the stairs to the museum entrance.

CHAPTER 20

RICHES OF THE ROBBED

Talia tossed another log on the fire while Naomi slipped back into the kitchen to pour herself some more wine. Riley had been tucked into bed thirty minutes earlier, after the three of them had finished a hearty dinner of vegetable stew and homemade whole-wheat bread—winter food, Talia was prone to calling it, though she arguably loved it year-round.

On the coffee table separating the couch from the fireplace was the manila envelope from Mr. Bergelsohn's office.

Talia dusted off her hands, warming herself by the fire. It had started to rain again that evening—a biting, cold downpour. Toby was happily warming himself next to her, sprawled out on the rug at her feet. His snoring was soothing and hypnotic above the sound of the wind and pelting rain on the glass patio doors.

When Naomi returned with her wine, she wordlessly handed Talia a pair of scissors, brows raised in a guarded expression of anticipation, as though to say, *I'm ready whenever you are.*

"Well, here goes," Talia said as her scissors sliced through the edge of the large manila envelope.

Mr. Bergelsohn had not said exactly what it was he was sending, only that Talia and Naomi would find it interesting. She wondered now whether she was expecting too much. What if she'd built this whole thing up to be something it wasn't? Maybe she should have warned him that it was not in Naomi's nature to take disappointment well.

Out of the envelope fell several folded pieces of paper, including a personal note from Ari clipped to an old newspaper page. Naomi reached for one of the scattered documents, but Talia swatted her hand away. "Patience, sister. All in good time," she teased.

Talia's eyes skimmed over Ari's handwritten note. "He sends his condolences for the death of Aunt Miriam." Naomi sighed impatiently. "And he hopes we're well. Oh boy. It seems that just as I feared, Mr. Bergelsohn—Ari's grandfather—did indeed pass away since we last spoke. What a shame." She glanced up with disappointment at Naomi, who answered only by loudly sipping her wine.

Talia cleared her throat and continued, "Ari says his grandfather had been a close friend to Grandad, and he had been honored to handle his affairs for all these years." Talia stopped reading, giving her sister a pointed look. "All these years?"

"What?" Naomi inquired, balking. "What does that mean? Grandad died thirty years ago. What sort of affairs could Mr. Bergelsohn's firm have been handling for him? I hope they haven't sent us a bill."

Talia shook her head, at a loss. She read on, revealing that—according to Ari's letter—"Grandad had had a decades-long monopoly on sorghum production in Queensland. In his later years, blah, blah, blah, he had invested a handsome portion of his profits in prime real estate around Brisbane. Under Mr. Bergelsohn's management, many of these properties remained a part of Grandad's estate for years after his death."

Talia stopped, picked up her wine from the coffee table, took a sip, and held the glass to her chest as she went on. "Listen to this," she said. "According to the terms of the trusts Grandad had set up, which, by the way, Ari says, 'were some of the first family trusts ever set up in Australia,' Grandad's real estate assets were to be liquidated upon the occurrence of certain events stipulated in his will."

Naomi put her wineglass down, cupped one hand over her mouth, and fixed her eyes on her sister. Talia followed her lead and placed her own glass down. She folded Ari's note up again, slipped it back into the manila envelope, and reached for one of the other two documents that had accompanied

Ari's memo. She did nothing this time to stop Naomi from reaching for the other document, which her sister rolled into a tube and batted against her open palm nervously as Talia scanned the first.

The record Talia held was a certified copy of her grandfather's will, dated May 16, 1968, almost a year before his death, according to the yellow sticky note Ari had attached to it. Talia read it to herself in a hurried whisper and then out loud to Naomi. "Okay, this is crazy. Listen up. Grandad's liquid assets were divided equally into two trust funds, one for you and one for me, though I'm listed as Natalia, obviously, not Talia. According to this, Grandad left nothing to anyone else. In fact—*get this*—the document explicitly states his 'only surviving daughter, Miriam, is expressly prohibited from entitlement to any of his assets, under any circumstances.'"

Talia sat with a slack jaw, watching Naomi process what she had just shared.

"Well, I always knew Grandad was a smart cookie." Naomi smirked. "Obviously, he knew a bad apple when he saw one. Good going, Grand!"

"What I think this means," Talia said almost breathlessly, "is that the only way Aunt Miriam could ever see any of Grandad's fortune was if she got at it through us. That explains so much, doesn't it?"

"Not a surprise to me," Naomi added with an *I told you so* look. "And that's exactly what she did. She hid us away in that godforsaken orphanage until he was dead, and then, when his will was read—and she realized we were the only heirs—she went after our trust funds. What an evil witch."

"Well, that's one way to look at it," Talia said, "and I'm sure you're right, but the flip side is that Grandad knew by writing the will the way he did—after we disappeared—Aunt Miriam would *have* to locate us to see a single penny of his wealth. He was even smarter than you think, Naomi! He basically tricked her into bringing us home."

Talia and Naomi sat with that fact for a moment, both soaking it in. "Well, maybe the plan was smart," Talia finally said, "but I bet Grandad would have hated how it all turned out. How we were just bait in a trap for Aunt Miriam and how his money bound us to her and her craziness for all those years. And in the end, after she'd gotten her hands on his fortune, to have Uncle Gus steal it from her. He got every cent that she didn't have tied up in that house

in Brisbane. Thank God she still had that investment—the house, I mean—or
there would have been nothing left at all."

"You mean Gus stole it from *us*!" Naomi snorted. "He didn't steal it from
her, Talia. He stole it from *us*—and God didn't have anything to do with it!"
Naomi set her dark eyes on Talia as if she, too, were somehow involved in
the conspiracy.

Outside, the rain pelted the glass patio doors mercilessly, and the wind
whipped the shutters as if threatening to tear them from the house. A cold-
ness settled in Talia's spine. She shifted herself, turning her back to the fireplace, kneeling next to the coffee table. "Grandad wouldn't have wanted us
to suffer the way we did with her. Maybe he should have just donated it all
to charity and spared us." Talia reached across the coffee table and relieved
Naomi of the second document she had been compulsively rolling into a
tight tube. Naomi moved herself off the couch and knelt on the floor by the
fireplace, hovering over Talia's shoulder as she began to read the document
titled "Addendum."

"So the date on this addendum—and I'm guessing it's an addendum to
Grandad's will—is February 11, 1969. So let's see, that's . . . what?"

"Three months before his death?" Naomi jumped in, suddenly seeming
far more perceptive than she might have been after two glasses of wine.

Talia read on, hardly believing what she was seeing. She stopped mid-
sentence, placing a hand over her mouth. "Oh my God! *He didn't!*" She
dropped the document to her lap. Naomi, now appearing beside herself with
suspense, snatched the page from her sister. A moment later, they were both
laughing out loud.

Naomi came back into the living room from the kitchen, carrying the
half-empty wine bottle. She filled her glass and settled back onto the couch.
Talia hadn't moved from her spot on the floor in front of the fireplace. She
seemed to still be in shock. She was reading the addendum to her grandfather's will for the third time.

"So let's see if we've got this straight, Talli," Naomi said, grinning from
ear to ear. "The money Grandad put into our trust funds was less than one-
tenth of his accumulated wealth in 1969. He must have figured that would be
enough to see us raised and educated. The rest of his assets remained tied up

in real estate, and they were to be liquidated upon only one condition. And that condition was the death of his daughter Miriam?"

"Right," Talia answered matter-of-factly. "And God knows what those assets are worth today," she added, shaking her head in disbelief.

The embers in the fireplace crackled loudly, causing Toby, who was lying between Talia and the fireplace, to jump suddenly and then, as if he were embarrassed by his overreaction, pretend to just be stretching lazily.

Talia and Naomi both laughed at the dog's attempt to recover his dignity, but there was no doubt they were really laughing at much more.

"You know, it's not just the absurd amount of money that has transformed how I feel. Don't get me wrong, I'm ecstatic about how this will change our lives and our girls' lives. It's knowing that Grandad was always there for us. That he had a plan to take care of us all along. It's astounding. We've always had such bad luck. And now this!" Talia's eyes teared up briefly.

"The bad luck we had was mostly Miriam, Talia. She was pure evil. Grandad was a kind, loving man; I remember him more than you possibly could. He didn't have a mean bone in his body. There was a reason he cut Miriam out of his will. And I'll bet it was a damn good reason. Everything we ever suspected about her will prove true—you'll see. We'll find out what went on back then. We'll get to the bottom of all this."

"I'm sure there's an explanation somewhere," Talia said, but her voice, like her gaze, drifted off in bewilderment. "What was always so confusing about Aunt Miriam was how much she seemed to hate our mother. That never made sense to me. Why hate your little sister? Yes, I could see being a little resentful when a new baby comes along and you've been the only child for so long, but hate? I just don't get it. And then the way she treated us—she was always so unnecessarily cold."

"Not cold, Talia. Cruel and calculating and punishing. I'm not sure how someone maintains that amount of resentment for so many years. It seems unnatural."

Talia watched Naomi's dark eyes cloud over with anger. She realized that in some ways, Naomi could have been describing herself. There were times she seemed so much like Aunt Miriam. Talia wondered if her sister would ever recognize that in herself. Or was she wrong about Naomi? Was Naomi's reaction just a reflex, a default mode, programmed after so many years of exposure to Aunt Miriam's toxic behavior? She couldn't be sure, but she didn't want to see Naomi waste the rest of her life on resentments— keeping score of both real and perceived insults as Aunt Miriam had done all her life. Not now—not when a reversal of life circumstances could free both Talia and Naomi from the cageless prison they had both inhabited since leaving Saint Mary's.

As if on cue, Naomi switched gears. A little sparkle returned to her eye as she emptied her wineglass and launched into a story about how Grandad had been with them when they were just small girls. How he would send them on scavenger hunts to find the presents he had hidden for them around the farm and how he would make them laugh with his magic tricks.

"I don't know if you remember, but he would sit us on his knees, take his big old farmer's hat off, say a magic spell over it, and then these pink and white peppermints would somehow magically fall into our hands." Naomi laughed. "He absolutely adored you, Talia. I might have been his butterfly in winter, but you were his favorite. Little bright eyes, he called you."

Talia smiled, nodding slowly. She vaguely recalled her grandfather and the magic hat trick—or was she just remembering things the way Naomi had told them? She had heard the stories so many times. It was hard to tell what the truth was anymore, but what Talia did know was that it was good to see Naomi recalling something happy from their childhood for once.

It seemed Grandad's handling of Aunt Miriam had been his ultimate magic trick, and it was a masterpiece, according to Naomi. Though Talia couldn't help but feel there had to be something more to the story—something about their aunt they hadn't yet grasped. She was more interested in understanding Miriam's behavior than simply vilifying it. She knew enough now as an adult, and as a social worker, that Miriam's conduct may have indicated some sort of mental health problem—some type of pathology, perhaps reflective of a childhood scarred by trauma.

Naomi held her glass up to make a toast as Talia got to work jotting down questions to ask Ari. She would call him in a day or two when she was sure they had thought of everything they would want to discuss with him. Naomi insisted they would need an attorney in California to manage any transactions that might be necessary while Ari's firm handled things on the other side of the Pacific. Maybe they would even be required to make a trip to Australia, Naomi mused.

When she was satisfied that they had thought of every question to ask Ari, Talia braved the weather on the back porch to bring in a little more firewood from under a tarp. Naomi telephoned her girls—apparently, neither of them had moved out of her home and in with John, as they had threatened—to make sure they had done their homework and to let them know she wouldn't be home until late. She had a wonderful surprise to share with them in the morning, she promised, but only if they both went to bed on time.

There was no hurry for Naomi to head home, Talia insisted. The rain and wind had not let up all evening, and the roads would be awful. Besides, Naomi had had her share of wine. She probably should have been considering spending the night in Talia's guest room. But Talia knew better than to think she could police Naomi. She could get away with playing weather forecaster, though.

"The weather should clear by midnight," Talia said, eying the clock above the fireplace. "I wouldn't brave the roads till then."

Naomi sat crossed-legged with her back to the fireplace, chatting happily about her memories of Grandad and the amazing turn of events that had just taken place. Talia had traded places with her and was now on the couch. All she could think about was Russ not being alive to share in her reversal of fortune. It just didn't seem fair.

It was ten o'clock when Talia put on a pot of coffee to clear her head. There was no need to even pretend she might get any sleep that night. She poured them both a big mug, then secured the documents Ari had sent her in the locked drawer of her office desk, handling them as if they were precious parchments of historical significance.

It was then that she noticed the newspaper clipping attached to Ari's handwritten memo. Earlier, she had assumed it was an article detailing her grandfather's status as an agricultural baron and real estate magnate in Australia. As she unfolded the clipping, the headline caught her off guard. She hurried back to the living room and positioned herself on the corner of the couch, under a lamp. Naomi leaned over her shoulder impatiently, trying to read along with her.

The article was from the *Courier-Mail*, dated November 30, 1964. The headline read "No Sign of Missing Girls Following Mother's Brutal Murder in Brisbane Hotel."

> Authorities continue to search for two missing girls, ages three and five, following the slaying of their mother, twenty-three-year-old Shira Emerson (née Altman) late Friday afternoon in a Brisbane hotel room. The woman's body was discovered by local police after a phone call reporting the sound of gunfire. The girls are believed to be in the company of their father, Jacob Emerson, who is wanted in connection with the brutal crime. Emerson, a US serviceman, is currently absent without leave from the US Consulate General in Sydney, where the family resides. Emerson, a Vietnam veteran, has a history of domestic violence and is considered armed and dangerous. Investigators believe a service revolver may have been used in the crime. It is unknown why the slain woman was in Brisbane. She reportedly checked into the hotel with her two small daughters earlier in the week. The hotel manager, Mr. Green, stated that he had not seen the children since Wednesday after an unidentified middle-aged woman had visited Emerson. Contact local authorities if you have any knowledge regarding the whereabouts of the missing girls. A substantial reward for any information is offered by the children's grandfather, Josif Altman of Brisbane.

Talia's eyes roved the page, finding a picture of her mother. It was the first she'd ever seen, the first she'd ever found to exist—and despite Talia's long-held belief that she could not remember how her mother, Shira Altman, looked, the woman in the black-and-white clipping looked *exactly* the way Talia now remembered her.

Her throat burned; her nose tingled as though she might start crying at any minute. Naomi stood at her side, dead silent. The paper shivered in Talia's hands, prompting Naomi to reach for it and set it down on the table beside them—and for a few silent seconds, they just stared at each other.

Talia eyed her sister with concern. Naomi seemed temporarily paralyzed on seeing the image of the woman she was more likely to have remembered than Talia.

Self-invented images of twenty-three-year-old Shira lying sprawled on a hotel room's dirty floor, her body glossed in a wet lacquer of her own blood, bombarded Talia's thoughts. Twenty-three was so young to meet with such an awful death. How terrified she must have been. What had prompted their father, the monster, to pull a gun on her? Did they ever find him, prosecute him?

Talia looked over at her sister, who was crying quietly. She reached up, placing both her hands on Naomi's quivering shoulders and squeezing. "I see now why they never told us."

"As girls, perhaps," Naomi countered, swallowing hard. "But as grown adults, we deserved to know what happened. Part of me is angry at Gran Marie and Grandpa Joe. Didn't they think we should have known?"

"Maybe this explains why we hardly ever heard them talk about him." Talia fell silent for a moment, reflecting on how her father's name had been mentioned by their grandparents only in hushed tones and whispers—the way one spoke of the dead. Talia remembered Gran Marie saying, "Jacob had changed after his time in Vietnam"—and maybe he had, but that was no excuse for domestic violence or murder. *Was it?* No, it wasn't an excuse, but it might have been an explanation, given what Talia, as a social worker, had learned about the effects of PTSD.

She and Naomi sat on the couch in front of the dying fire, Naomi with a handful of soggy tissues.

"Why do you never cry anymore, Talia?" Naomi practically spit—as if the words were bitter, as if she resented the burden of her own tears.

"I just can't cry anymore, Naomi," Talia said quietly, almost apologetically. "Ever since Russ, I . . . I figure if my eyes are dry, it's a sign to myself that I'm doing okay."

Naomi only gave her a sideways glance. It seemed she didn't understand.

Talia felt a familiar apprehension permeating the sanctity of her home—like the return of the dread she had experienced in the days following Russ's horrific death.

"Well, so much for our cause for celebration earlier tonight," Naomi said flatly, staring off into oblivion the way that she did whenever she thought of their past. "One step forward, two steps back."

"I feel haunted," Talia added numbly. "Jinxed!"

"We both are," Naomi cut in. "We're damaged goods, Talli. We've had a hell of a time of it. And it only got worse after *you know who* took us out of Saint Mary's." Naomi's speech was nasal, her swollen nose and lips still reflecting the outlet of her sorrow.

"But there's so much we still don't know," Talia said, looking down at the cup of coffee she hadn't touched. "For example, how did no one know where we were all that time we were at the orphanage? And how did Aunt Miriam get away with dumping us there and then showing up five years later, professing to have found us by using a private detective?" Talia shook her head in confusion.

"Yeah, you have to wonder what story she gave the officials at Saint Mary's," Naomi said, pulling her legs up underneath herself on the couch and clutching a throw pillow to her chest. After a moment of silence, Naomi added, "She had to be in cahoots with someone. Think about it, Talli. She couldn't have pulled off such a scam without help from someone at the orphanage, someone on the inside who was willing to go along with the deception. Perhaps for the promise of a large donation to the orphanage or a payoff at some point. That old crow at Saint Mary's—what was her name? The horrid little woman with the Coke-bottle glasses?"

"Kookaburra, not crow," Talia added flatly, not bothering to look up.

"Right! Kookaburra." Naomi nodded slowly.

"Sister Mary Ignatius."

"Yeah, she was a malevolent witch. I wouldn't put it past her," Naomi said.

"Remember how she tried her best to talk those weird people out of adopting me? The strange couple?" Talia asked suddenly, recalling the incident. Naomi gave her sister a blank stare. "You know? *The couple!* The man with the missing front teeth—the one who looked like a giant baby. He gave me the creeps. Actually, they *both* gave me the creeps."

"No, I don't remember that. I hardly remember anything from that hellhole except the horrible food and that disgusting smelly crap we had to plaster on our chapped hands and lips before bedtime. That stuff that used to make you throw up."

"What I mean is, weren't we missed by other family members and friends? Kids don't just disappear."

"Oh yes, they do, Talia. You should know that in your line of work. Kids disappear all the time. But to answer your question—yes, someone else besides Grandad missed us," Naomi said, eying Talia over the rim of her coffee cup, her dark eyes energized with conviction.

"Who do you mean? The Emersons?"

"No, not the Emersons." Naomi scoffed. "I think they were totally in the dark—not to mention they were a continent away. I mean M—whoever that was. The person who sent us the mystery birthday presents every year when we lived with Aunt Miriam."

"Yeah, I have to say, it's weird that they started arriving only after we left Saint Mary's and then—"

"They stopped when we moved to the US," Naomi jumped in. "Whoever was sending those gifts obviously lost track of us once Miriam moved us to the US. And I can't help but wonder if that's the real reason she moved us across the Pacific in the first place. Remember the way she used to react to those gifts every year on our birthday? I'll bet they were coming from someone she knew. Someone who was sending a message—letting her know that they were keeping tabs on us. You know, a warning shot: *Don't disappear those girls again. I'm onto you, Miriam, and I'm watching you.*"

"God, that's twisted, Naomi. How the hell do you come up with this stuff?" Talia scoffed. But in truth, she had to admit that Naomi might be onto something.

CHAPTER 21

CONFRONTATIONS

Talia should have canceled her appointment that Monday morning. She didn't have the energy for therapy, and her meetings with Dr. Cohn were starting to wear on her. Only a sense of routine had compelled her to show up, and so she'd made her way over to the office after dropping Riley at school.

After they'd settled in and begun the session, Dr. Cohn surprised her with an uncharacteristic suggestion. She had never given Talia direct advice before. Though it was framed as a question, Talia saw it for what it was—a recommendation.

"Talia, what do you think about expanding your social circle?"

Talia leaned back in her chair and folded her arms across her belly. Either Dr. Cohn had never been taught Body Language 101, or she was choosing outright to ignore Talia's opposition to the topic. She had already voiced a desire to expand her social network, but she knew *exactly* what Dr. Cohn's question really meant. That she should consider dating and perhaps find a new partner. While it was true that social support was generally a good idea, Talia just didn't have the enthusiasm for dating. Perhaps she'd grown accustomed to the isolation. There *was* something comforting about not having to meet anyone's expectations. Was that it? Was she just too lazy to put in the effort? Something Naomi had said to her—on the night they'd found the newspaper article about their mother's murder—suddenly popped into her head. "We're damaged goods, Talli." Naomi had been right, of course, and if nothing else, Talia had to acknowledge she was just not healthy enough to be in a relationship right now.

She stared at Dr. Cohn's petite form perched across from her in her great big office chair, wondering what her social situation looked like. Wasn't everyone struggling to some extent with relationships?

Talia hadn't seen any sign of Dr. Saul Cohn in all the time she had been coming to their shared offices. Were they still partners, or had there been a falling out? Perhaps a divorce? She wondered if Saul wouldn't have been a more agreeable therapist for her than Eleanor Cohn. Well, maybe it was a moot point. They were nearing the end of her allotted eighteen visits, anyway. Did she even *need* counseling anymore? Most of the conclusions she had come to about issues she'd raised with Dr. Cohn—issues she felt were now resolved—she had arrived at on her own. She slept better some nights now, and the sleepwalking incidents were few and far between over the last several weeks. Even though she had never mentioned them to Dr. Cohn, Talia supposed they had subsided just because she was feeling less stressed about parenting Riley on her own, and she wasn't obliged anymore to visit Aunt Miriam in a nursing home every week. Yes, things had eased up a little, she had to admit.

But she still hadn't mentioned her childhood traumas or the murder of her mother to Dr. Cohn. That was sacred territory, not to be explored with anyone and certainly not to be exploited, which was exactly what would happen if she were to bring it up in a session, she was sure. *Lots of mileage to be had from those subjects, no doubt.* She could only imagine the rabbit holes they could go down.

She and Naomi were still reeling from the impersonal way they had learned the details of their mother's brutal murder. In their conference phone call with Ari yesterday, he had apologized for the raw presentation of the facts and regretted that he was unable to provide any additional information about the tragedy.

"No one in the office had any idea the two of you didn't know the details surrounding your mother's death," he had said. "Of course, with my grandfather now gone, I have no idea why he might have kept the newspaper article alongside the copies of your grandfather's will. I can only assume that he had kept it to chronicle his efforts to locate you during those years you were both apparently missing." Talia had had trouble concentrating on Ari's apology. She'd been distracted by his accent—how familiar it was—and how it pulled her back to her time as a young girl in Australia. During her lapse in attention, Naomi had taken over the conversation with Ari on the conference call. She'd asked him how she might find out more information about the events surrounding their mother's murder.

"Why don't you contact the newspapers here in Brisbane?" he'd offered, and Naomi had jumped on it immediately, hurriedly scratching down the names of the newspapers Ari was rattling off.

And within hours, Naomi was on a mission. Totally obsessed, as far as Talia could tell. She contacted an archivist at the *Courier-Mail*, who promised to search through the paper's microfiche library for any additional articles about their mother's murder and the girls' disappearance.

Dr. Cohn cleared her throat, and Talia's attention snapped back to the room.

Talia reluctantly made eye contact, realizing she still hadn't answered her last question about dating. "Dr. Cohn, as I have stated on several occasions now, my primary mission in life is to be Riley's parent. I consider this my only real responsibility," she said flatly. "There is little point in complicating matters by bringing a romantic interest into the picture. Not to mention I have absolutely no need for a man in my life, nor any desire for romance. I would think you would find it healthy that I don't need validation from a man to feel fulfilled."

Dr. Cohn's eyes didn't show the slightest flicker of annoyance or surprise at Talia's rebuttal. It seemed that only Talia was angry. She found herself questioning Dr. Cohn's motives. What did she think—Talia could just pull any guy off the street, and he would fill Russel's shoes? He would somehow make her whole again? The more she considered it, the more intensely her anger boiled. Now that she thought about it, she found Dr. Cohn's focus of interest not only frivolous but also aggravating—infuriating, even.

A helpless-woman mentality had always been loathsome to Talia. She admired strong women—women who were not afraid to take a stand and not afraid to face the challenges of life alone, like Russ's mom, Rose. She was running her own ship, and as far as she could see, there was no room for additional personnel. Was Dr. Cohn suggesting Talia was not enough for Riley? Talia occasionally had her doubts about her abilities as a parent, but that was not for Dr. Cohn to question. She hadn't exactly had any role models in life, had she? She was doing just fine.

Nothing unsettled Talia more than Dr. Cohn's silence. She felt she was being managed. No, it was worse than that. It felt as though she was being manipulated. The counselor's lack of response seemed to imply the question itself had been sufficient to expose Talia's fears, and therefore no discussion was necessary. Were these silences meant to be Talia's cue to just admit to Dr. Cohn the things she was reluctant to admit to herself?

If she were being honest, ever since Russ's death, she had once or twice entertained thoughts of other men. But Talia was in no hurry to replace him with someone who could never measure up. Besides, she was too busy to date. Aside from her volunteer work, the demands of running a household and raising her daughter alone were consuming enough for any mortal.

Her anger dissipated slowly in the minutes of silence that followed. She felt reason gradually seeping in. "My heart wouldn't be in it, Dr. Cohn," she elaborated. "I just don't have any interest in dating, to be honest. That should be understandable."

Dr. Cohn nodded in what appeared to be capitulation. "I do understand," she said. "I only want to know if it's a thing that you're open to and, if not, why that may be."

Talia stayed quiet for a few breaths, rubbing the pendant on her necklace between her fingers.

Dr. Cohn added, "On a positive note, I'm very pleased with your progress."

Talia's brows raised. She wasn't sure what to say.

"What you're doing is difficult, Talia," Dr. Cohn went on. "Being a single parent is not only challenging but also limiting. I'm not saying you could do better. I think you are doing a fine job, but don't be afraid to accept help. Be open to that. No one can tell you when it's time to move on, but it has been two years now."

As if I need reminding, Talia thought. If no one could tell her when it was time to move on, why was Dr. Cohn doing just that? Talia felt herself flush with frustration. No, it wasn't frustration. It was yet another burst of raw anger.

"Is there a magical point in time when my grief will suddenly disappear?" She did her best to temper her tone but fell short. "I am fully aware that Riley doesn't have a father. Her father is dead. I haven't chosen this. I'm simply trying to live with it."

Again, Dr. Cohn showed no reaction to Talia's sarcastic outburst. She stared silently at her. Any sort of visceral response from Dr. Cohn would have been infinitely more satisfying. Talia had begun to suspect the woman was incapable of showing emotion. She was an enigma. An enigma to be admired, maybe, at least on some level. For instance, it was admirable how proficient she was at being completely and totally detached from the world around her. How Talia wished to be as detached as Dr. Cohn seemed to be. She was working on it. Detachment wasn't easy for her, especially as the session that day had been more distressing than she had expected. Suddenly she realized how badly she had reacted to everything that day and regretted it immediately.

Certain things set her off. A small voice reminded her it would be wise to consider any valid points Dr. Cohn might have been raising. But a louder, angrier voice was winning. *Why the hell am I so angry? She's only trying to help.* And then it hit her—the truth. The truth that Talia had been doing her best to deny for two years. She was furious at Russ. Not just heartbroken, wrecked, and forever changed but absolutely *furious*. Russ had let her down. Of all the people she had ever loved, of all the people she had ever dared to trust, why had he been so careless? Russ had made a victim out of her and, worse, a victim out of their beautiful, innocent little daughter. She felt like she had a grenade in her chest, and it was about to go off.

Talia left Dr. Cohn's office that morning blinking back tears of rage, driving home from therapy like a kamikaze pilot, feeling crushed and hopeless.

When her old truck squealed into the driveway, Sam was across the street, loading his kayak onto the roof of his Jeep. His smile was a white flash of delight against his tanned face. Talia barely acknowledged him, returning his grin with a vague hand gesture that probably looked more like she was swatting a fly than offering a greeting. As soon as the back end of her vehicle cleared the threshold of her garage, she lowered the garage door.

Though they lived directly across the street from one another, Talia and Sam did not bump into each other often. On the few occasions Brandon had come over to play with Riley, Talia had kept small talk with Sam to a minimum. She didn't want to be too warm toward him, she'd decided, and that was especially due to Kim and Pamela's original encouragement of their dating. Perhaps that was still Sam's goal—but if it was, he'd kept his motives covert. Besides, there was no hurry to make him her friend, even if the children did play well together. Brandon was a sweet, bright boy, and Riley loved his company. That was good enough for Talia.

Everything Talia knew about Sam she had learned from her other neighbors—especially old Mrs. Kravitz, who was skilled at pressing people for details. According to her reputable report, Sam owned a chain of sporting goods stores in the Valley and had done well for himself over the years. His former partner, Brandon's mother, had recently relocated to Chicago. She was an anchorwoman at the NBC affiliate there. Talia wondered how Brandon's mother had been persuaded to move across the country without taking her child. As a social worker, Talia had seen women live in intolerable conditions to provide for their children. She had seen women who had sold their bodies and their souls to feed their kids. Long before she had her daughter, she'd known how strong a mother's love could be. She wondered if Brandon shared Riley's pain from the loss of a parent. She knew how important those bonds were. Her few memories of her own mother's love had sustained her for all the years she had spent with Aunt Miriam, who had never so much as held her hand or kissed her cheek.

The doorbell rang a few moments later, and Talia knew instantly it was Sam. And to make things worse, she knew Sam had seen her pull into the garage. She had no choice but to answer the door.

"Yes?" she snapped as she nearly pulled the door off its hinges. Sam's smile vanished as if a wave had just washed away his sandcastle in one sweep. He seemed genuinely speechless at the reception, and the look on his face made Talia feel both heady and humiliated all at once.

"I . . . I'm sorry to bother you," he stammered, taking a step back, as if the welcome mat on the front porch had suddenly burst into flames. He had probably been expecting a hearty welcome, Talia reckoned. He was no doubt accustomed to women who fell all over themselves trying to please him.

"I just wanted to warn you that there was a mountain lion sighted on the trails this morning." *Is his face turning red?* She felt like a jerk. "I didn't know if you'd heard, and I know you like to run out on the trails, so I thought you should be aware."

Now she felt awful. But how to backtrack? It was too late to apologize. Talia badly needed her run that day, obviously. She felt as if her sanity hinged on it. Not even reports of a homicidal maniac roving the trails with a chain saw could stop her from taking her customary jaunt through the hills. She regretted her reaction to Sam and considered offering some piece of information that might explain her lack of civility, but Sam's news had done little to lift her mood. Before she could stop herself, her lips were moving again. Apparently, she was going all in on total bitch mode.

"Well, thanks for the warning, Ranger. I'll be sure not to call out 'here, kitty kitty' while I'm out there," Talia said, letting the door between them swing closed.

That evening, after her trail run—which had been feline-free and perfectly routine—Talia took Riley out for dinner and a walk around the fountain at the Village, an outdoor mall just a few miles from home. She was feeling a lot better after getting out for some fresh air and had begun to regret her earlier hostility toward her well-intentioned neighbor.

Conflict always ate her alive, and Talia was growing more aware, with every passing hour, of just how rude she had been to Sam. He had only wanted to warn her. It wasn't like he was Dr. Cohn's accomplice and stopped by to ask her on a date. She really appreciated his concern. Actually, she found it sweet. Why had she been so aggressive? What the hell was wrong with her?

The news of the mountain lion had left Talia a little uneasy. A few years back, one of the women she ran with, Kim, had lost a running friend to a mountain lion attack in Northern California. The fear of a similar fate had crossed Talia's mind when she was out on the trails alone. She also knew this was an unreasonable fear—mountain lions were reclusive creatures and avoided humans whenever possible. Humans were not their preferred prey, and when they attacked someone, it was usually under rare and extenuating circumstances. She also knew—as most trail runners did—that for every time she'd seen a big cat, there were probably a hundred times one of the reclusive creatures had seen her and she'd been oblivious to it.

She was always keenly attuned to her environment while running. She listened carefully and observed what was going on around her. Sometimes she made a game of identifying animal tracks in the soft earth of the trails. Coyote and rabbit were most common in their area, but she had also seen deer and bobcat tracks. Only a few times, in all her years of trail running, had Talia seen a mountain lion's prints. They were the size of her fist or larger, and they fell in a nearly straight line, one behind the other—the signature pattern betraying the supple-shouldered walk of a great cat.

The sight of fresh mountain lion tracks usually made Talia switch to running on the road for a few days, but she always returned to the tranquility of the mountains and the rocky trails that wound themselves through the peaceful, shaded valley near her home. The psychological benefits of trail running clearly outweighed any fear she had of encountering predators. Truth be told, she had experienced a few bizarre confrontations with people when she was running alone in the mountains, and humans caused her far more anxiety than any wildlife she might have chanced upon. She had once been stalked by a naked man who had waited for her behind a tree on a particularly steep section of a single-track trail.

Talia sat on a park bench, watching Riley play around the fountain, when she was suddenly reminded of that bizarre and disturbing experience. As she'd approached the narrow section of the trail, her eyes had been completely focused on the rocky, almost vertical path ahead of her. The naked man leaped out at her from behind a large oak. Talia was vulnerable and had only a slim margin of space to escape him. She was flanked by a high embankment on one side and a significant drop-off on the other. The man did not attempt to grab or restrain her in any way. He simply stood, three feet in front of her, totally naked. Perhaps he'd been hoping to impress her or shock her with his nudity. Maybe he had been expecting some other reaction.

She felt her cheeks flush at the mere memory of the incident. She'd made no attempt to understand the man's intentions. Who could know what he was thinking? Naomi had later explained he was probably just an exhibitionist, which sounded likely. Talia was sure, though, that the man had been lying in wait for her, and this realization was nothing short of enraging.

Thankfully, her instincts were both quick and primal when he jumped out at her. She launched into a litany of choice expletives and insults, including graphic threats of bodily harm. Without missing a step, she pushed past the man and continued running at full speed up the trail. Though she soon realized there was only one way for her to get out of the situation. The trail she'd been on went farther up the mountain, to areas far more remote than where she was. To make things worse, she'd be hemmed in by steep canyons. If she stayed on her current route, her next opportunity to exit the wilderness wouldn't come for another twelve miles or so. It was a hot summer day, and she wasn't carrying any water. She hadn't planned to run for that long.

At the time, Riley had been in a half-day program at a local preschool, and Talia needed to pick her up within the hour. She had no choice: to get back in time for Riley, she would have to turn around and head back down the trail, past the naked man. She kept running for a while, considering her predicament, until she happened upon a fallen tree branch. The limb was about the size of a baseball bat. She picked it up with both hands, turned around, and headed back down the trail with determination. While she ran, she loudly proclaimed what she and her very big stick were about to do to the naked man.

When the man saw her returning at a full gallop with her newly acquired club, he grabbed his discarded clothing with one hand and scampered up the steep, rugged hillside above the trail, pulling himself up with his free hand. His vulnerable undercarriage was fully exposed in his hasty retreat.

Talia would not have struck him with her weapon or pursued him. Her aim was to scare him off and, of course, to protect herself. Mother Nature had her own revenge in mind, however. Talia could see the man was heading into a large overgrowth of waist-high poison oak. As she watched him retreat steadily uphill, fear replaced her anger. She'd bolted back down the trail at full speed in more of a controlled fall than a run, and when her trembling legs reached home, she called the police immediately. Then she'd stopped by the local station to file a report on her way home from picking up Riley. She never saw the man out on the trails again, but she thought she might have recognized him in town, months later, as she'd strolled by with Riley on their way to get shaved ice. He was dining on the patio at the fancy Italian restaurant, right next to the fountain where Talia now sat on a park bench and where Riley played. He was seated at a table with a woman and two small children. She wasn't certain it was him, however, because the only vision of the man she could conjure did not include his face.

After her unsettling encounter with the naked man, Talia had taken to carrying pepper spray on her runs, but when the canister expired, she hadn't bothered to replace it. Her running friends had also reported occasional strange encounters out in the hills, but for the most part, very few people braved the remote mountain trails. Most folks, it turned out, didn't appreciate the wilderness quite the way runners did—which was a relief to them all.

Talia shook off the memory and gathered Riley. Together, they walked through the Village on their way to get dessert near the center of the mall. The winter days were short and cool, but Riley never needed an excuse to enjoy shaved ice, no matter the time of year.

Riley was just finishing her blueberry-flavored cone when they passed a sporting goods store. Seeing as Talia had been thinking about safety on the trails, she decided to pick up some pepper spray as an added precaution for her next solo run. As she reached the counter to pay for a bright-yellow canister of spray, she heard a familiar voice. Sam was coming out of the back office, behind the counter. He was joking around with someone. Talia felt herself shrink, only to fail in her endeavor to disappear altogether.

If she'd only been civil earlier, this wouldn't have to be such an awkward encounter.

To make everything worse, Sam's booming laugh could warm any heart. Talia cussed at herself, realizing she'd unwittingly walked into one of his stores. It was difficult to hide her embarrassment when Sam made direct eye contact with her. His smile came too easily. Was it possible he was gloating at her embarrassment? She turned to leave, praying he hadn't recognized her, but he quickly swept Riley off her feet and tossed her playfully into the air. The child squealed with delight and grabbed Sam's rugged face with her sticky, wet hands. He held them jokingly, pretending to gobble them up.

"Those taste like blueberry," he said, making hungry monster noises. Without skipping a beat, Riley asked where Brandon was. Sam pointed to the office. "He's back there, coloring the pages in my calendar. Go see if you can help him."

Riley dashed off to the office before Talia could protest.

They looked at each other for a split second, and Talia couldn't hold it back any longer. The truth tumbled out of her almost autonomously. "God, I'm so embarrassed. I really don't know what came over me today. To be honest, I was having a terrible morning, and you just happened to be in the wrong place at the wrong time. I don't usually behave that way."

"That's okay," Sam said, his smile fading. "I heard you've had a rough time of it."

"I'm sorry. Please accept my apology."

"I'll forgive you if you'll agree to go kayaking with me once the weather warms up a little."

Great, Talia thought. She'd walked right into that one. It sounded like fun, though, and it wasn't like he was asking her out for a romantic dinner. Kayaking would be harmless enough, right? And she could bring Riley. It'd be a fun experience.

"Sure," Talia managed, trying not to look put out. "That'd be fine."

Besides, warmer weather was several months away, and there would be time to make excuses if she needed to. She wondered what Dr. Cohn would say if she could see her now. She would either be surprised by Talia's capitulation or pleased with her hasty progress.

Sam insisted the pepper spray was a gift, and he threw in a couple of canisters for Talia's running partners. Once Talia was able to pry Riley away from Brandon and his crayons, Sam walked them to the parking lot. She fully expected him to ask her where she had parked her broom—but as she had already begun to learn, he was not as predictable as she had assumed.

"She's a beauty," he said, patting the hood of Talia's almost-antique Ford truck as if it were a prize heifer and he were a proud farmer.

"Yeah, she is," Talia agreed, feigning appreciation for the old rust bucket. She hoisted Riley into her car seat and fastened her seat belt. Riley waved goodbye to Sam as they pulled out of the parking lot. Talia watched him standing under the streetlight through her rearview mirror.

"He sure is tall, Momma," Riley said with a smile, her mouth still encircled by blue stains.

"He sure is," Talia answered softly. "Think he's nice?"

"Do you think he's nice, Momma? I think Brandon's nice. He's my best friend now."

"Yes, he seems to be a nice friend, and I'm happy about that. Having friends is important." Talia realized she was offering that affirmation to herself as well as to Riley. A few moments passed. The silence was filled by the sound of the engine's loud roar, and just as Talia's mind began to wander to other things, she heard Riley quietly ask, "Is Brandon's mom in heaven?"

It was a change from the questions Riley usually asked about Russ. Talia was touched by Riley's concern. She was a thoughtful child. Dr. Cohn had assured Talia it was normal for many children of Riley's age, not just those who had lost a parent, to begin asking questions about death.

"I think you should ask Brandon where his mom is," Talia replied, figuring that was the safest answer she could give for the moment. "But remember that if he doesn't want to talk about it, that's okay. We don't want to make him uncomfortable, all right?"

"Okay, Momma." A few beats of silence passed again before she added, "Is Miriam in heaven?"

"Miriam?" Talia balked, taken aback. Riley had never met the woman, but clearly, she'd overheard the many conversations Talia and Naomi had about her lately. Riley surprised her sometimes. The girl picked up on everything. "What do you mean, honey?"

"She died like Dadda, right?"

"Oh, sweets," Talia said, looking to Riley in the passenger seat. "Aunt Miriam was really old and sick—and she'd been unwell for a long time. She died of a stroke." Talia wasn't sure how to temper her answer for a five-year-old's comprehension level. She wanted to be informative but not too alarming, so she chose her words carefully.

"Is a stroke just like smoke, Momma?" Riley's eyebrows arched in question. "Just like Daddy?"

"I . . . *Riley* . . ."

"He was too close to the smoke from the fire, right?"

"Oh, love." Talia's nose tingled with the threat of tears. Thankfully, they pulled into the driveway at that moment, and she was able to turn off the engine and give her full attention to Riley. "You don't need to worry about things like that. You're too young to concern yourself with how people die."

Talia reached over, freed Riley's seat belt, and pulled her daughter onto her lap, holding her to her chest and rocking her. Riley giggled out loud and pushed her mother away, looking at her quizzically.

"Momma, it's all just part of nature," she said matter-of-factly, grabbing her mother's face with both of her hands as if it were she who was now lecturing a child. "Miss Austin at school says all things must die sometime. It's just part of nature. Sometimes grandparents must go to heaven—or pets. Even pretty flowers die. And when sharks are hungry, they have to eat fish, and if there's no fish, then they have to eat us. So you see, Momma, we all die."

Talia couldn't help but laugh at that last one. She hugged her daughter tight, kissed the top of her head, and silently rejoiced in the magic of her innocence.

CHAPTER 22

SECRETS

Talia and Naomi had decided to sell all but one of their grandfather's properties. Gina Panteletes, the attorney Naomi had hired to take care of things stateside, said she had found Mr. Bergelsohn's firm in Australia to be immensely helpful over the past few weeks. With a few late-night phone calls and a string of faxes, Gina and Ari had sorted out most of the details of the necessary financial transactions involved in the management and transfer of Talia and Naomi's grandfather's estate.

Gina reached for the crystal pitcher on her desk. The silver buttons on her silk sleeves glistened in the afternoon sun streaming through the floor-to-ceiling windows in the Santa Monica high-rise office building. She refilled her water glass after topping off Talia's. Naomi waved her hand to decline.

"It seems your mother's family in Australia was quite successful all the way back to just after the Second World War," Gina said as she slid a dossier across the glossy surface of her mahogany desk toward Talia and Naomi. "If you'll turn to page six, you'll see the details on the property in question. The Warwick Grain Farm is apparently quite a spectacular three-hundred-fifty-hectare estate—in US terms, that's almost a thousand acres, so we're talking about a pretty sizable parcel of land—in Queensland. The property has been leased to a family friend of your grandfather's, a Mr. Simonson, who apparently has been the tenant there since the late 1960s."

Talia thumbed through the document, perusing the color photographs and aerial maps of the property in Warwick, hoping for any spark of recognition, anything at all that looked familiar. But so far, she was coming up empty. Naomi sat back in her leather chair, legs crossed, sunglasses still on but clearly laser-focused on Gina's presentation.

"From what I gather from Ari in the Aussie office," Gina went on, "Mr. Simonson's father, Karl, was very close to your grandfather. It seems they were acquainted back in the old country. He had worked for your grandparents in one capacity or another for most of his life." Gina leaned forward in her chair, elbows on her desk, rolling a mother-of-pearl-encrusted pen between her hands as she went on. "Sounds like a long history between the two families. They apparently emigrated from Vienna to Australia together in 1939."

Talia raised her brows in curiosity. She was fascinated to hear some of her family history. She'd had no idea they had an Austrian connection. Aunt Miriam had not talked about her past life in any detail.

"So the Mr. Simonson now residing on the Warwick farm—on *our* farm—is not the same Mr. Simonson who emigrated from Austria with Grandad, right?" Naomi slid her sunglasses up to the top of her head.

"Correct. The Mr. Simonson who now oversees the farm would be your grandfather's friend Karl's son. Let me see." Gina rifled through a file sitting in a documents tray on the table behind her desk. "The current tenant is a Mr. Moshe Simonson. He was born in 1923, so today in 1997, he's seventy-four years old—sounds like he's running things with a couple of his sons."

Talia gave Naomi a quizzical look. Naomi kept a poker face, but they were thinking the same thing. If their families had been that close, could this man, this Mr. Simonson, shed some light on the mysteries of their past? They both knew now wasn't the time—nor was that topic something to be raised with Gina.

"So will it be possible to have Mr. Simonson and his family stay on? I don't think we'll want to do anything to disrupt his long-standing agreement with our grandfather's estate, let alone interfere with his home if they've been living there and managing the property all these years." Talia knew she was making the suggestion single-handedly; she couldn't help but notice Naomi shifting uneasily in her seat next to her, as if she wasn't at all keen to simply continue the status quo without knowing the first thing about Mr. Simonson.

"Agreed." Gina was quick to endorse Talia's suggestion. She had clearly already considered this option as the best course of action. "It appears there's a sizable staff working on the farm that the Simonson family has been over-seeing for years. I think it best not to disrupt anything that seems to have been working well for so long. We can always change things—if you're so inclined—after we explore the details of the company's books."

"Surely there are tax implications we'll want to explore," Naomi added, still not settled on the notion that she and Talia now had an enterprise and employees to be concerned with.

"Absolutely. There will be tax implications to consider," Gina agreed. "And that's why you have us. That's the job of this firm, and you can both rest assured we will do our homework."

Naomi seemed to relax at this, but Talia was already doing the arithmetic in her head. Gina's law firm was obviously high-end. She took in the office again, sweeping her eyes over the plush Oriental rugs and the overhead chandelier. *Where oh where did Naomi find Gina?*

"As far as all the other properties, for those in downtown Brisbane that you wish to liquidate, I suggest we explore the real estate market, and then, when and if sales go through, we'll time monetary transfers for when the exchange rates are most favorable."

Gina seemed to have things well in hand. Talia relaxed a little. After all, she really didn't want to bother with the ins and outs of every transaction. She supposed that peace of mind had a price. She also reminded herself that money worries should become a thing of the past now. If she was totally honest, she had already troubled herself about what she would do with all that wealth. How had she managed to find a dark cloud in such an open blue sky? The Altman estate would be enough to keep both her and Naomi's fam-ily comfortable for the rest of their lives. For one thing, she could pay off the bills that had lingered since Russel's death. Her truck was well past its prime, and like her vehicle, the house had begun to show its age. New win-dows and paint were long overdue. The freedom she'd now have financially was a dream come true. More than that, it was a prayer answered. Of course, she had already decided that a portion of her inheritance would go to charity, including the women's shelter where she volunteered and other centers around Los Angeles. Perhaps she would even set up a nonprofit in the name of her late mother for victims of domestic violence.

After picking up the mail for the first time in almost a week, Talia sat at her desk, going through some bills. She came across a manila envelope from Ari's grandfather—the now-deceased Mr. Bergelsohn. The postmark was from the previous November. The package had apparently been lost in the mail for some time. It looked a little worse for wear, its corners tattered and bent.

She tore open its ragged edge and tipped out its contents. A small yellow envelope slipped out of the larger envelope and onto the pile of bills in front of her. It was an old, fragile-looking piece of personal stationery, like a love note that had been tucked away in an attic, only to surface a generation or more later. The seal on the back of the letter belonged to her grandfather, Josif Altman, and it listed his old Warwick address. Talia opened the letter carefully, not wanting to damage this physical link to her past—a link that had transcended time. Inside was a note, written by hand with a black fountain pen on fine-quality onionskin paper. In big sweeping letters, Grandad spoke to Talia and Naomi across the decades.

To my dears, Naomi and Natalia,

God willing, you have finally been found. We have never stopped searching for you. I have prayed every day for your safe return. If you are reading this letter, I have already passed from this world, but my promise to you both, as the daughters of our beloved Shira, is that you will have the bright future your mother was denied.

Forever your loving grandad,
Josif Altman

Also inside the yellow envelope were three smaller pieces of heavy linen paper, each folded in half, and a small object wrapped in tissue paper. Talia gently opened one of the folded pieces of heavier paper, being cautious not to damage it. It was a badly faded copy of Naomi's birth certificate from 1959. She studied the names of her parents, listed at the bottom of the document. She ran her thumb gently over the cursive lines of her mother's pale signature, a beautiful hand in fountain pen—the indigo ink now faded to a soft periwinkle. As she had expected, Talia's own birth certificate was also enclosed. She checked the date on it.

She and Naomi had indeed been born on the same date in October, two years apart.

She felt some relief upon confirming the coincidence of their shared birthday as fact and not just an invention of Aunt Miriam for the sake of her own convenience. The third document in the envelope was also a birth certificate. It belonged to Talia's mother, Shira Altman. Talia held it for a moment, studying the date and feeling grateful it had been included with the others. It felt like a precious link to her mother.

The paper was worn on its folds, as though it had been handled and folded many times over the years. The date of Shira's birth was listed as April 11, 1941. Talia had never known her own mother's birthday, which struck her suddenly as profoundly sad. How could she bear faithful witness to her mother's life if she hadn't even known her birthday?

And then it happened. Something caught her eye. At first, Talia thought there had been a clerical error of some kind. The space above "name of father" was blank. The space above "name of mother" bore Miriam Altman's name. Talia's eyes widened. *That couldn't be right.* Maybe her grandmother and Aunt Miriam had the same first name, but she knew that wasn't the case. In all their previous correspondence, Ari and Mr. Bergelsohn had referred to the girls' long-deceased grandmother as Esther Altman.

Aunt Miriam had been Shira's *mother*, not her older sister.

The reality changed absolutely everything Talia had thought of her aunt—who she now came to realize was actually her grandmother. Miriam had been only a fifteen-year-old child herself when she gave birth to the daughter her family would pass off as her younger sister—the younger sister who would later replace Miriam as the sole heir to the family fortune.

Talia's hands were shaking. How in the world would Naomi react to this news? The thought scared her.

Her mind raced as she unfurled the small object wrapped in tissue paper. It was a gold locket the size of a nickel. On its front was a Star of David, and her mother's name, Shira, was engraved on its back. Talia recognized the symbol on the locket as one of religious significance, but it lacked context. What did it mean?

A pinhead-size button on the side of the locket required a little encouragement, but Talia was eventually able to depress it using the end of a paper clip. The locket popped open softly. Two tiny oval black-and-white photographs were inside, each of a small child. One of the children bore a striking resemblance to Naomi. Talia had never seen any photographs of herself or her sister taken before they were eight and ten years old and had left Saint Mary's orphanage. They had school photographs from that age on but none from before.

Talia knew immediately the child in the other photograph had to be her.

Over the next few days, she came up with more questions than answers about her family's history. She wondered if she knew anything at all about the woman who had passed herself off as their aunt for so many years. And now, more than ever, she wanted to know about her mother's life.

She was captivated by the engraved locket and the photos of her and Naomi. More intriguing still was the question of why her mother had possessed something with a Jewish symbol in the first place. It crossed Talia's mind their mother might have converted to Judaism when she'd married their father, but Talia had never had any inkling of anyone in the Emerson family being Jewish. As far as she knew, Grandpa Joe and Gran Marie and their extended family were Christian. But she had never had a reason to discuss religion with the Emersons, so it was possible she was wrong about that detail.

There was a lot to figure out. The more Talia learned about her mother's family, the more questions arose. What seemed probable to her was that Miriam, being an underage mother, must have agreed to have her parents raise Shira as their child. It would have been more socially acceptable at the time. Talia could understand this. When she was a nineteen-year-old college student in 1980s Los Angeles, she had been terrified of becoming an unwed mother—and the stakes for an unwed teenager in 1950s Brisbane would have been considerably higher.

It also was likely Miriam had been given no choice in the matter.

In any case, it would have been a difficult situation for the family and especially traumatic for young Miriam. This revelation complicated things, Talia admitted to herself. Perhaps it was time to see Miriam in a whole new light.

So many things the woman had done and said to Naomi and her over the years suddenly took on new meaning. It was clear now why she had been so outraged by Naomi's teen pregnancy. It must have been an unbearable reminder of her own troubled youth and would have rekindled sad memories of everything that had happened to her own daughter, Shira. Talia was sure Miriam would have loathed that her child pay for the disastrous choices she'd made in life—and to then see Naomi repeat them would've been devastating. Miriam had told Talia and Naomi many times that their mother's foolish decisions had resulted not only in an unplanned pregnancy but also in an undesired marriage to a man who proved to be cruel and abusive.

Any mother would have suffered greatly watching her daughter's life unravel in that way. The possibility made Talia wonder if Miriam's decision to hide her and Naomi at Saint Mary's had perhaps been for their own safety. Had it been a way for Miriam to assure the girls' murderous father would never find them, even if it had meant Grandad was also in the dark? Had it been for their own good all along? It would take a little more detective work on Talia's part. Some fact-checking would be necessary before she could render any judgment. And she would need more clarity before she shared her findings and suspicions with her sister. Naomi had an innate penchant for tragedy and drama. There was no need to carelessly fuel those fires of doubt and confusion about their family history.

Sifting through old memories and looking for hidden meanings in the things Miriam had said over the years became an obsession. Talia didn't know how Miriam had kept her secret for so long, but she knew such a secret would surely have taken its toll. She recalled the way Miriam had looked at her on that last day she had visited her at Hillcrest Manor—when Talia had held a glass of water to her lips and she could have sworn she'd seen tears in the old woman's eyes. Why had Miriam been so obviously distressed at

Bernard Bergelsohn's call from Australia that afternoon? What truth did she think he might reveal to Talia, and had that incident so upset her that she'd had another stroke—the stroke that had ultimately taken her life?

CHAPTER 23

REVELATIONS

hile running through the foothills between her home and the Pacific Ocean, Talia reflected on the victims that history had made of the women in her family. Miriam's life could not have been easy. What circumstances could have led to her becoming pregnant at only fifteen? Had it been a case of young love, or had she been someone's victim?

Talia also wondered whether Shira had known the truth about Miriam's identity and whether the two of them had ever been close. There was no one in the family left to ask; they were all gone now. If Talia entertained any questions about Miriam and Shira's lives, she would have to arrive at her own conclusions. She wondered if she would find peace in knowing more about them or if that family history was a book best left on the shelf.

Talia stopped running for a moment to retie her shoelaces before heading up the last big hill leading out of the canyon. It was a warm spring morning, and the sun beat down on the dusty trail with an intensity usually reserved for midsummer. She had not had a good night's sleep in over a week, and a weariness hung heavily over her. She turned and backtracked a few steps to the shade of a giant sycamore and sat on a small rock next to an old fire hydrant, letting the sweat drip off her face and arms. The spot was a routine stop for her on any run in the canyon. It conveniently provided fresh water via the tap on the side of the fire hydrant. Talia turned its squeaking handle and drank thirstily from its cold, sputtering flow.

It was remarkable to think that she had spent the bulk of her youth resenting Miriam because she wasn't her mother and because she had taken them away from Grandad. But wasn't it Miriam who had found the Emersons, the only family they now had left? And hadn't she also brought them to the States, where she and Naomi had both thrived?

Talia washed her face with the cool, flowing water from the hydrant, letting the stream run over the back of her head and soak through her hair. Then she cranked the faucet closed again and wrung the excess water out of her ponytail.

She pushed herself off the rock and made her way steadily up the last long hill out of the canyon. Her shadow, like a silent running partner, bounced off the hillside next to her as it had on so many days. As always, they paced each other to the crest of the canyon and down the undulating trail toward home.

That evening, after Riley was tucked in for the night, Talia retrieved the two large boxes of Miriam's belongings from the corner in the garage, where they had been stacked atop one another since she had picked them up from Hilltop Manor the previous fall.

This is going to be interesting, she thought, feeling like a sleuth. She poured herself a glass of wine, filled a small bowl with salted cashews, and settled in for some intense perusing.

The cardboard folds on the first of the two boxes were loosely overlapped, making for easy access. The box contained items of daily use: reading glasses, a small satin purse with a string of pearls tucked inside, nightgowns, bed jackets, and a ceramic pot holding a silk flower arrangement. After surveying all the box's contents, Talia removed the string of pearls from the satin pouch and set them on the kitchen counter. Perhaps they belonged to another patient at Hillcrest and had simply been mixed up with Miriam's belongings. Miriam hadn't worn jewelry in years. When she had, she had always favored rubies, and Talia had long ago secured those in her safe-deposit box at the bank when she had first moved Miriam from Seattle to California. The string of pearls did look somehow familiar, though. *Are they real?* They looked real. The gold-colored clasp looked expensive. Naomi would undoubtedly know if they were the real McCoy. Talia set the first box of Miriam's belongings on the floor, where Toby gave it a sniff or two before settling down at her feet.

She dragged the second box over to her—this one was heavy and securely sealed—and used a pair of kitchen scissors to cut through the thick strips of packing tape. The box had been sealed since Miriam lived in Seattle, long before her first stroke—perhaps even as far back as their move from Australia to the US. Whatever the contents, Miriam had evidently not wanted them to be easily accessed. There were four old hardcover books inside the box. Their worn bindings indicated years of use. A few old photo albums Talia was anxious to explore were sitting atop the books. A good-size candelabra sat unceremoniously on top of it all. It was wrapped loosely in a black-and-white cotton scarf with tassels on each end.

Talia lifted it out of the box. It was quite heavy, and surprisingly, it wasn't tarnished. It was gold-plated bronze, she guessed. She set it upright on the kitchen counter, admiring its design. It was old, maybe an antique or possibly a family heirloom. The candelabra could hold nine small candles, with the center candle a little higher than the others. Above the candelabra's base was a Star of David, just like Talia had seen on her mother's locket. She knew she had seen a similar object in Mrs. Kravitz's window during Hanukkah each year. It was a menorah, if she remembered correctly.

Suddenly it hit her.

Jesus! She felt the air leave her lungs in the same crushing involuntary manner that it had during Riley's birth. Talia's eyes flooded with tears; she blinked them back furiously. She could not determine whether they were tears of rage, tears of love, or tears of regret. All these emotions inundated her as she realized what the contents of the box meant—what they confirmed—what she *should* have always known.

Once Talia could speak without her voice breaking, she reached for the phone. She had wanted to call Naomi right away, but her fingers were tapping out another number on the keypad before she could stop herself.

"Mrs. Kravitz? It's Talia. I hope it's not too late to call."

Frieda Kravitz was a gem. She came right away in her baggy sweats and her house slippers, hurrying down the sidewalk from the home she shared with her husband, Abe, just four houses down the street. Talia and Toby were waiting at the front door for her when she arrived.

Talia had emptied the contents of Miriam's sealed box onto her coffee table. She and Mrs. Kravitz sat poring over the hardbound books that had been packed together under the menorah.

"So I'm assuming this text is Hebrew, then?" Talia said, passing what appeared to be an old diary to Frieda.

"It is indeed, *bubbale*." Mrs. Kravitz nodded as she opened the book from the rear cover and ran her finger over the faded ink symbols. She had always called both Talia and Riley by the Yiddish term of endearment *bubbale*.

"We always hoped we would find my aunt Miriam's diary," Talia said, realizing immediately that she had misspoken. But Mrs. Kravitz didn't need to know Miriam wasn't really Talia's aunt just yet. "My sister will be beside herself to know what stories these diaries and photo albums will tell us about our family's past. We're pretty much in the dark when it comes to my mother's side."

Mrs. Kravitz was silent for several minutes as she sat hunched on the couch under the light of a floor lamp, examining the pages of Hebrew script, her face somber, her typical jovial nature replaced with an expression betraying a darker sentiment Talia had never seen before in the woman.

Mrs. Kravitz looked up then, as if perceiving Talia in a whole new light. "My *bubbale*, this does appear to be a woman's diary, a book of fears and of dreams—no doubt meant to be private, but the name of the author is not Miriam. This book belonged to Shira."

"Jesus," Talia whispered into her cupped hands, suddenly recognizing the same beautiful handwriting in the diary as that which she had seen on the signature line of her own birth certificate.

"Well, Moses, anyway." Mrs. Kravitz smiled wanly, placing a hand on Talia's knee and shaking it in jest. "It seems I was right to think of you as family. You're one of us, *bubbale*."

Talia froze for a moment, taking the woman's words in. Why did she suddenly feel like perhaps she did belong somewhere after all? Throughout her whole life, she'd felt like an outsider, like someone who had lost her way.

Mrs. Kravitz stayed for over an hour, sifting through the books from Miriam's box with Talia—translating the Hebrew script for her and summarizing, as best she could, here and there a few of the diaries' entries. There were four books in all. Two of the diaries belonged to Shira and two to Shira's grandmother, Esther Altman.

"My little darlings," Mrs. Kravitz read on from the very last page of text in Shira's diary, "we must be on the move again. There is a danger in our midst, and I must keep you safe. One day you will understand, but for now, we must all just disappear."

Talia sat still, transfixed by Mrs. Kravitz's words. But then the woman fell mute, reading on in silence, her eyes sweeping the page hastily, an undiscernible expression overtaking her face. She closed the book then and placed a hand on Talia's shoulder. "For now, *bubbale*, let's put this one down. We can come back to it when you are ready. It's not going anywhere, and we have all the time in the world to get through it. It seems that your mother faced some really difficult decisions but that she loved you and your sister dearly."

Talia nodded in resignation. She didn't want to overextend her request for Frieda Kravitz's help. There would be time to explore the details of the past, and truth be told, she wasn't sure she was ready to know those all of those facts just yet.

Frieda picked up another of the journals, flipped through a few pages, and froze. "This one belonged to Esther. Your grandmother?"

Talia nodded. Even if she could not interpret the script, she could see the handwriting was different from that of her mother's—probably quill and black ink.

"Just a few words from this one, *bubbale*, and then we call it a night, okay?"

Talia's eyes found the clock above the fireplace. It was only 9:00 p.m., but she didn't want to be rude. Mrs. Kravitz had already helped her more than she could say. She sat back on the couch with a pillow in her lap, listening quietly, imagining the scenes described and the woman whose words she was hearing—the grandmother she had never known, Grandad's long-deceased wife, Esther.

"We are truly heartsick at what is happening here in Vienna with the annexation and with Chancellor Schuschnigg under house arrest," Mrs. Kravitz read on, noting the date of the diary entry was October 19, 1939. Tears filled Frieda's eyes, signaling some significance Talia could not yet discern. "The country has gone mad—*all* of Europe has gone mad. Imma and Abba have both passed since my brothers, Saul and Samuel, were taken in March, after the referendum on reunification with Germany was canceled. We can only guess at their fate, and Josif fears the Nazis will come for us next. Our shops and our synagogues are now reduced to nothing but ashes— there is nowhere safe for us. Karl and Alma Simonson have secured a way to leave Vienna with their boy, little Moshe, but Alma is taken ill, and Karl fears she cannot make the voyage. America is refusing to take refugees; can you believe we are to be refugees? Our only hope now rests with good friends. Karl has told Josif of a close colleague, Bernard Bergelsohn, who has made his way with his young family to the shores of Australia. We will try for asylum there, but moving around the city here to obtain documents, even going to the post office, is fraught with danger. Getting our papers will be difficult, Josif says. Getting across the border without them will be near impossible."

Mrs. Kravitz put the book down in her lap and reached for a tissue which she dabbed under her reading glasses. "This will be hard to hear, Talia. We will need to take our time. *I* will need to take my time." Frieda sat for a moment, seemingly catching her breath. "Most of my Ukrainian family was lost in the Holocaust. Your grandmother's diary reflects a very dark time in the world, and I must say, her words will be hard to read."

"Of course," Talia whispered, placing a hand on Frieda's shoulder. "Absolutely, Mrs. Kravitz. I had no idea about your family. We can take our time if you are willing to go on. No rush. You can let me know when we can meet again. When you are ready to read more. And of course, if it's too difficult, there must be professional interpreters I can turn to."

"No, no, my *bubbale*. I will help you. You will just need to be patient with me. It would be my privilege. But we will take our time. If you will trust me to take each of these books, one at a time, I will translate every page for you. You and your sister will know everything they can tell."

After Talia closed the front door behind Frieda Kravitz that evening, she collapsed onto the couch and called Naomi.

It took only twenty minutes for Naomi to show up. On the phone, she'd said she had received something unbelievable via fax from Australia that afternoon that she wanted to share, but Talia doubted Naomi's news would hold a candle to the bombshell she was about to drop regarding Miriam. By the time Naomi let herself in, Talia had already rehearsed what she'd say. She brought Naomi up to date quickly and efficiently—filling her in on the previously unshared details about their birth certificates and the mind-blowing news that Miriam had been not their aunt but their grandmother.

Naomi sat in stunned silence. Talia wasn't sure if she was in shock or fuming that she had been denied these details until now. Finally, Talia presented Naomi with the information she'd realized about their long-hidden identities and what Mrs. Kravitz had translated from the diaries. Naomi was overwhelmed by all the details. Talia was a little relieved to see that her sister seemed more shocked than angry. It was more than anyone could be expected to wrap their head around, she realized, feeling just a little guilty for dumping it on Naomi all at once.

"What better place to hide two Jewish heirs to their grandfather's fortune than in a Catholic orphanage," Naomi said as she wiped her eyes with a well-used tissue. "We were nothing more to Miriam than a long-term investment." Clearly, whatever revelation Naomi had promised over the phone earlier had been forgotten in the wake of Talia's news.

"Well, maybe we'll know more when Mrs. Kravitz finishes with the diary translations. Surely they'll shed some light on what really happened back then." Talia sat quietly for a moment, giving Naomi time to take it all in. "Honestly, Miriam's most egregious act was forcing us into Catholicism as children. What a betrayal of our culture and of her own heritage."

"It's clear now why she never once went to Mass with us," Naomi added. "Conniving witch."

"The truth was there, in plain sight, Naomi. We just never saw it because we never knew to look for it."

"We were small children, Talia." Naomi shot her sister a look of frustration. "Of course we never saw it. But you're right about one thing—what a betrayal."

"I honestly feel more dimwitted than duped on this one, Naomi. I mean, we had always known our family's name was Altman. As we got older, we might have put two and two together. True, Altman is a pretty common name—German, for sure—but it's also a Jewish name. Put that together with the fact that the first names of every relative in our maternal family are of Hebrew origin and—bingo!" Talia knew she was about to add insult to injury, but the words were tumbling out before she could weigh their impact. "Russ would have told us we had been standing on the back of a whale, fishing for minnows, as the Polynesian saying goes."

The insinuation was lost on Naomi, and Talia was reminded that her sister was incapable of putting reason over emotion.

"Oh God!" Naomi suddenly jumped up from the couch. "There's something I wanted to show you." She headed to the kitchen counter, where she had left her briefcase. Talia found herself, in that moment of silence, thinking about Russ and how he might have reacted to their news. How he would have also reacted with emotion, but—unlike Naomi—he would have found the silver lining in the storm clouds that had just unleashed themselves on her.

"Mommy's. I remember these, for sure. They're Mommy's." Naomi was waving something in her hand as she hurried in from the kitchen. "Where the hell did you get these?"

"What?"

"These pearls. They were Mommy's." Naomi, almost in tears, held up the string of pearls Talia had found in the first of Miriam's boxes and had left on her kitchen counter. "No doubt about it, I'd know these anywhere. See the little diamond-shaped clasp here with the tiny emerald? These are definitely Mommy's. She always wore these pearls."

A snippet of memory flashed in Talia's mind, like a half-forgotten dream. She remembered being on someone's lap as a small child, her fingers wrapped in a long string of pearls—the woman singing her a lullaby—a soft, rhyming song in a language she had never been able to recall. Now she knew. It was a Hebrew song, and the woman was her mother.

Naomi sat on the floor of Talia's living room with her mother's pearls around her neck, perusing the old black-and-white photos in the albums Talia had found among Miriam's belongings. The images revealed the faces of deceased relatives and family friends they had never known, as well as old reminders of places they may once have visited but had long since forgotten. Yet somehow, the images brought a sense of connection, rekindling a feeling of belonging they had been denied for all their lives.

In one album, there were several pictures of Miriam as a young girl in pretty lace dresses, some with her hair tied up in ribbons and others in which she wore wide-brimmed hats—no doubt to protect her pretty face from the scorching Australian summer sun. In one of the photos of Miriam as a young adult, she was accompanied by a handsome young man in a suit and tie, identified in the margin as Moshe Simonson. The couple looked about the same age, and Talia realized that Moshe was no doubt the same Mr. Simonson who was currently residing on Grandad's Warwick farm in Australia, the same little Moshe mentioned in her grandmother's diary—who had fled Vienna with his parents in 1939, narrowly escaping the horrors of the Holocaust.

"They look like they could've been more than just friends," Naomi noted. "Perhaps we should write to Mr. Simonson and see what he can tell us. He clearly knew Miriam well."

"To what end, Naomi?" Talia replied flatly. "These revelations are all quite exhausting—each one more taxing than the last. Is it really in our best interests to open another Pandora's box?"

Naomi didn't seem convinced. Her eyes still sparked with resentment for Miriam and a need to get to the bottom of all her deceit. "Honestly, Naomi, do we want to drag this Mr. Simonson through all this? Let alone rake up all the muck it could expose?"

Talia's entreaty was worth considering: If Mr. Simonson—Moshe—had been romantically involved with Miriam and was the father of her child, Shira, things could get even more complicated. It would mean Moshe was actually their grandfather. Was Moshe Simonson the mysterious M of their annual childhood birthday gifts? That possibility made more sense now than any alternative they had considered over the years.

After seeing their mother's birth certificate, Naomi and Talia were forced to accept that Miriam was their grandmother and this made Grandad their great-grandfather. This biological detail did not negate the love they had for each other or their family ties. Grandad had, after all, adopted and raised Shira as his own child, so Talia and Naomi were his grandchildren by adoption. Not that this had any bearing on the relationship, but it was messier than Talia would have liked.

"Oh my God, I've lost my mind tonight with all this excitement. How could I have forgotten? I wanted to show you this." Naomi locked her eyes on Talia as she dragged her briefcase off the couch and over to where they were sitting on the floor. She reached inside. "My contact, Suzanne, at the *Courier-Mail* in Brisbane, sent me this. It arrived in my office late this afternoon via fax," she said, pulling out a photocopy of an old newspaper article. She handed the article to Talia, who took it from her warily. What would the bad news be this time? The article was dated May 5, 1970.

Remains Positively Identified as US Serviceman Suspected in 1964 Murder Mystery.

Local authorities working in conjunction with the US Consulate General in Sydney have confirmed the skeletal remains found last month in an abandoned mine outside of Broken Hill, NSW, to be those of missing US serviceman Jacob Emerson. Emerson was suspected in the 1964 slaying of his twenty-three-year-old wife, Shira Emerson (née Altman), in Brisbane. The couple's two daughters, then ages three and five, disappeared around the time of the murder. Their abduction spurred a national search and fueled international fears that the children had suffered the worst. Investigators report Emerson's service pistol was located with his remains. The cause of death is presumed to be suicide.

In a bizarre turn of events surrounding the years-long mystery, Emerson's daughters were located at Saint Mary's Orphanage for Girls in Melbourne earlier this year by a private detective working for the family. The girls' grandfather, now deceased, had searched for the children since the murder of his daughter some five years earlier. After his passing, the girls' maternal aunt, Miriam Altman of Brisbane, took up the cause. The Mother Superior overseeing the orphanage where the girls were located was stunned by the news of their true identities and saddened by the ensuing scandal surrounding the organization's role in the matter. She told reporters the children had been surrendered in October 1964 by a woman claiming to be their mother. The woman, who used a fictitious name and address, alleged she was suffering from an incurable illness and could no longer care for the children. Saint Mary's maintains that the actions of the Sisters of the Immaculate Heart were solely to serve the children's best interests. Investigators believe the unidentified woman, who remains at large, may have been Emerson's accomplice. The children, who were found in good health earlier this year, are currently under the care of their aunt and uncle

in Brisbane. The family declined an interview request and asked for privacy
as they attempt to build a stable and loving home for the children.

"Explains volumes, doesn't it?" Naomi said, reclaiming the article from
Talia's limp hands.

"Well, it explains *some* things but not everything. What a nightmare this
is! You might just possibly have broken my mind, Naomi. I'm not sure I want
to know anything more about our family."

Talia sat for a moment, trying to process what this latest news meant,
how it fit with everything they had recently learned about their past. "The
good news is at least we don't have to worry about him showing up out of
the blue. I'm guessing he was probably suffering in some way from his time
in Vietnam. That would make sense, wouldn't it? You know, PTSD or something like that? He loses his mind and becomes abusive; one thing leads to
another and—"

"I'm not so sure you're right at all, Talia. I say Miriam set our mother
up—told her to flee Sydney. *Come to Brisbane, little sister, and I'll provide
a safe place for you and the girls, where he won't find you.* Then she calls
Jacob, the monster, tells him where to find our mother, takes the two of us,
friggin' dumps us at Saint Mary's, and boom, she's next in line for the family fortune."

"That's dark, Naomi. Really dark. You think Miriam was capable
of that?"

"Oh, I can make it darker." Naomi smirked. "Who's to say, after all, that
Miriam doesn't have Jacob meet her somewhere remote, with the promise of
passing his daughters off to him, and then she and Uncle Gus ambush him,
and he ends up conveniently dead. No one finds the body for years. When
they do, everyone thinks it's suicide. All the loose ends are neatly tied up.
Except Grandad has his suspicions. See, he knows Miriam better than anyone.
When Grandad dies, and his will is read naming us as the sole heirs, Miriam
employs a private detective who conveniently receives an anonymous tip that
we can be found at Saint Mary's orphanage. Voila! Miriam and Gus become
our devoted custodians. All very well and good, until one day, years later,
Gus double-crosses Miriam, takes every dime she has, and disappears."

Talia sat stunned, not sure if she was more disturbed by the possibility the version of events was correct or by Naomi's manic machinations.

"Didn't you ever wonder why Miriam never involved the police after Gus absconded with our trust funds? And why would our father go somewhere remote, like an abandoned mine, to kill himself? Makes zero sense, Talia! Suicide can be carried out anywhere."

"Jesus, Naomi. Your imagination is incredible. Do you really think Miriam—"

"Well, we'll see, won't we?" Naomi interrupted before Talia could offer a rational alternative. "When your Mrs. Kravitz finishes translating the diaries, we'll see where the facts fall. We'll see what the general consensus on Miriam's character was. Also, Moshe Simonson is still around. Maybe he can shed some light. I'll bet Miriam had a long history. No one becomes that evil overnight."

"And what justice can come from knowing the truth now, Naomi? Something terrible must have happened to Miriam to make her the way she was. Maybe the loss of her mother at a young age, maybe the teen pregnancy." Talia regretted the words immediately as she realized she had just described Naomi's life. In fact, arguably, she had just described her own life too. And neither one of them had turned out to be a sociopath.

After Naomi left that night, Talia lay awake in bed, trying to make peace with so much. There was nothing she could do about the death of her parents, any more than she could undo the loss of Russ. Perhaps one day, she would have the curiosity to pursue the truth about Miriam's intentions and actions. Were they really even relevant? In some ways, that pursuit seemed trivial, given what she had just learned from Mrs. Kravitz about her extended family and their trials during the Holocaust—fleeing the war in search of freedom and a better life. Wouldn't it be a shame to negate all those struggles—and ultimately their triumphs and good fortune—simply to focus on one bad apple?

Tying up the loose ends of Miriam's sordid history would require energy and curiosity—not to mention a stomach for unwelcome surprises. God forbid Talia were to find out that Gus had been Shira's father. The implications were terrifying. She was fresh out of stamina for the pursuit of facts. And since Naomi was planning to contact Mr. Simonson about a visit to the farm in Australia, Talia would leave the questions to her older sister.

After some consideration, Naomi had agreed that the topic was one best discussed in person with Moshe Simonson rather than through a lengthy letter or over the phone. Talia had been quick to agree with this approach, largely because a visit to Australia felt like only a remote possibility.

With each hour that passed, Talia's feelings about Miriam fell under the spell of Grandad's generosity, Mrs. Kravitz's kindness, and the sense that she and Naomi finally belonged somewhere.

She drifted off to sleep just as the morning sun was lighting up the new spring leaves on the birch trees in the backyard.

CHAPTER 24

THE RECKONING

T alia sat in the back row of a crowded meeting hall, next to the petite form of Regina Delgado Juarez. They were surrounded by dozens of other women, the soft murmur of their chatter filling the packed space. She had only met Regina the day before but already felt they had forged a bond.

When the police dropped Regina off at the women's shelter, Talia had immediately recognized the expression in the girl's eyes—she'd seen it many times before, sadly, throughout the last two years of her time spent volunteering. After being treated for her injuries, Regina had been transported from the emergency department at the county hospital to the shelter in Ventura. She appeared to be in her midteens, but no one was able to verify her age, and Regina said she did not know her date of birth. This was not particularly unusual among the seasonal farm workers who came from Mexico and Central America to California for the spring and summer.

When the policewoman helped her out of the cruiser, Regina had almost tripped over the hem of her torn skirt. Her right arm was strapped across her chest in a sling the same color as the blue hospital socks on her feet. Talia had initially mistaken the bruises on her legs for dirt, but the marks on the girl's face and neck were clear signs of a brutal and recent assault.

Officer Barns had told Talia that Regina's husband, Enrique, was under arrest, suspected of causing her injuries. Despite her condition, Regina refused to confirm whether Enrique was the person who had harmed her—which had been confirmation in and of itself, really. Denial of abuse by victims of domestic violence was not at all unusual, and Talia knew this well.

Shortly after Regina arrived at the shelter, Talia learned that she and Enrique were already known to the local police. In the prior week, their two-year-old son, Jessie, had fallen to his death from the third-story window of the apartment the couple shared with two other migrant families. Social services and the public health nurse had been visiting the home regularly in the days following the incident. The circumstances of the child's death were under investigation—and to make matters worse, neither Regina nor Enrique was cooperating with the investigation or coping well with the tragedy. Another police officer, who had come to the shelter to take a statement from Regina, had told Talia it would be at least another twenty-four hours before they received the coroner's report on Jessie's autopsy. She suspected the pending investigation of the tragic death of Regina's baby was the only reason immigration authorities had not yet deported her.

The crowded meeting hall hummed with chatter as it always did before the program started. Regina was doing her best to sit still on the chair next to Talia. She wore an oversize, donated red-and-white dress and a pair of old slip-on shoes that hung loosely from her swinging feet. Her right arm remained in its bright-blue sling like the clipped wing of a colorful bird. Regina kept her head down in what Talia suspected was an effort to hide her battered face and avoid any conversation. The girl's English was as limited as Talia's Spanish, and so their communication was rudimentary and dependent on universal hand signals and gesticulations when their assigned translator, Lupe, wasn't around.

The facilitator of the monthly tri-county women's bereavement support group announced they were about to get underway. Talia surveyed the room of solemn faces.

This was the second time she'd been asked by the shelter's director to take one of the residents to a meeting of this group. Without Lupe's help with translation, Regina wasn't going to understand more than a few words of the proceedings during the main presentations, but there would be a small break-out group for those who spoke Spanish after the meeting, Talia suspected.

Talia looked around the room for the translator and saw her greeting a colleague in the entryway.

"Lupe!" she said with a wave, garnering the woman's attention. Lupe smiled and beelined toward where Talia and Regina were seated. Though Talia doubted Regina would be comfortable speaking up, Lupe would help her if she wanted to share any thoughts with the group, so at least the option was there.

The support group meeting was held at the same four-star hotel on the rugged coastline between Ventura and Santa Barbara Counties every month. Community leaders, clergy members, and social services professionals had come from Ventura, Santa Barbara, and Los Angeles Counties to share in the work of grief counseling and offer support to the community of women who had lost family members—especially those who had lost children. The meeting usually included a formal presentation by one or two professionals, and then time was provided for attendees to share their experiences of loss and messages of hope and healing.

Today the meeting hall was at capacity.

The low hum of voices in the audience faded quickly as the facilitator began her opening remarks. Talia decided to look for a spot out of the way of the crowd, where she could lean against a wall or sit cross-legged on the carpeted floor.

From her position near one of the rear exits, Talia could see the stage. She surveyed the crowd of mothers and daughters, wives and widows, of all sizes, ages, and shapes. The universe's selection of victims seemed random—the only thing the attendees all had in common was their shared sisterhood of grief. Some of the women possessed the resigned expressions of those whose pain was distant enough to allow them to relate their stories more objectively. Those were the women who would share messages of resolve and words of comfort for others who were less able to control their quivering voices or tears.

Talia listened intently to their accounts, trying to apply a degree of clinical detachment. But ever since her own world had been turned upside down, clinical detachment had eluded her.

The stories of women who had lost children were the most difficult for Talia to listen to. The pain of losing a child was unfathomable to her. She checked her watch and imagined what Riley was doing at that very moment in kindergarten. She glanced to the back of the hall, where Regina and Lupe were seated side by side; Lupe leaned over and whispered something into the girl's ear. Regina wiped her nose with a fistful of crumpled tissues. Her expression was pained. Grief needed little translation.

The heavy velvet drapes in the meeting hall had been drawn closed across the west-facing windows, blocking out the beauty of the Pacific Ocean that lay below. The effect was one of oppressive closeness in an already over-crowded room. Talia's sudden hunger for fresh air could not be ignored. She rose quietly from her seated position on the floor and slipped through the closest exit.

Out in the hallway, she took a long, cool drink from the water fountain and leaned against the nearby windows, looking out at the vast expanse of the Pacific Ocean. She surveyed the beautiful view from the enormous pic-ture windows. The rolling coastline was covered in a swath of tiny yellow wild mustard flowers. Beneath the hillside on which the hotel was built, an embankment plummeted into the cold Pacific. It was a clear, windy day, and Talia could see the coastline wrapping around Santa Barbara and pointing toward the Channel Islands. The cobalt-blue water was speckled with white-caps. The dark silhouette of an ocean frigate inched along the distant horizon.

Talia did her best to put her anxiety aside. With a little luck, the winds would pick up, and it would be too dangerous to go out on the kayak with Sam the next morning. Much to her chagrin, rather than forgetting all about the proposal he'd made in his sporting goods store months earlier, he'd stopped by her house over the weekend to formally invite her to join him. And naturally, she'd failed to cobble together an excuse valid enough to get out of it, especially with the weather being unusually warm for that time of year. Was that the root of her anxiety? Going kayaking the following morning with Sam? Going anywhere with another man?

Upon her return to the meeting hall a few minutes later, Talia heard a familiar voice at the microphone. Though she hadn't been expecting to run into Dr. Cohn, she was not surprised to see her in this setting. Perhaps she was an event organizer or a facilitator. A moment later, it became painfully clear Dr. Cohn was not a facilitator but a participant, sharing her grief at the podium. Talia then understood why she had never seen Dr. Saul Cohn at their shared offices.

Contrary to what Talia had assumed, Saul Cohn had been Dr. Cohn's thirty-year-old son, not her husband. A self-inflicted gunshot had ended his life eight months earlier. Talia's heart was in her throat when she heard this. Dr. Cohn's revelation was both disorienting and humbling. The woman spoke slowly and deliberately, the drifting sound of her voice lingering unnaturally in the warm, stuffy air of the hall. Her usual cool countenance had been replaced by deep, unchecked anguish.

It was viscerally disturbing to Talia, given their therapeutic relationship. Dr. Cohn was a professional who, in Talia's view, was devolving helplessly, her dignity draining away from her as she unraveled in front of the audience.

It dawned on Talia that when she'd begun seeing Dr. Cohn, the doctor had been trying to manage the immediate aftermath of her son's suicide. There had been times when Dr. Cohn had seemed distracted during their sessions, but Talia could never have imagined the reason for her lapses in attention. Of course, she couldn't have been expected to know those things.

Reflecting on the indifference, if not the contempt, she had shown Dr. Cohn during their last few visits made Talia feel awkward and incredibly guilty. After all, Talia was a trained social worker with years of experience in professional intervention. But she had not exercised her professionalism during her visits with Dr. Cohn, nor had she expressed a modicum of curiosity about the woman. Instead, she had opted for blind, childish, self-centered obstinacy.

"I don't know how I overlooked the cues that he was going through some tough times," Dr. Cohn continued at the podium. Her tone revealed the torment and self-loathing of a woman who, despite her years of experience and professional insights, had been helpless to save her own son. "I'm ashamed to say I was entirely oblivious to his difficulties." Dr. Cohn halted for a moment—the room frozen in silence—and then added tearfully, "I thought we were close. I was sure he knew he could come to me for anything." She paused again, attempting to compose herself. Perhaps, in a sudden recollection of her professional role, she intended to share some nugget of wisdom with the audience. "Denial is a strange and insidious lack of consciousness that robs us of our judgment. I was truly, utterly oblivious to Saul's level of despair. If this could happen to me, a trained professional with years of experience, it could happen to any of us. Check in with each other; make sure those close to you are coping. Even if they look like they're managing, be vigilant."

Dr. Cohn's voice cracked a little, and the collective murmur in the hall surged in sympathy. Her words of advice to the audience belied her inability to separate her professional role from her personal pain. The woman sighed deeply, her shoulders sagging, as if under a tremendous weight. Her lips quivered. The tension in the hall was excruciating. Talia thought about quietly sneaking out again, but her feet felt riveted to the floor.

"I failed him. I failed him catastrophically," Eleanor went on, almost whispering. She wiped her nose with her sleeve as if she were an injured child and not a professional woman addressing an enraptured audience. A bewildered silence, raw and palpable, replaced the soft musings of sympathy in the hall. Every eye was on her. A few folks squirmed uncomfortably in their seats, and others blew their noses or sniffled loudly. A woman in the front row rose from her seat and handed Dr. Cohn a box of tissues. After slowly pulling a handful of them out of the box, one by one, Dr. Cohn cleared her throat. Her tears remained a constant stream, and she dabbed futilely around her precariously perched spectacles, trying to divert the flow. Talia watched her in stunned silence. The woman's face had become utterly unfamiliar, distorted by grief.

As Talia witnessed Dr. Cohn coming undone, a strange sense of accountability was building in her—a feeling of being guilty by association, maybe. She probably knew Dr. Cohn better than most people in the room did, but that didn't make Talia responsible for her pain or her words. Yet she felt culpable.

She ached to go to the stage and place her arms around Dr. Cohn—less to comfort her than to silence her. To make her stop sharing her unbearable pain. As if reading Talia's mind, Dr. Cohn locked eyes with her from across the hall. Talia held her gaze, signaling her silent solidarity with the woman, though the role reversal was agonizing.

The horror only intensified as Dr. Cohn went on, veering further into the distressing details of what occurred after her son's suicide. She told the audience how she had been the one to find him, how Saul had been slumped over his desk late one afternoon when she'd returned to their offices after running an errand. Life had drained out of him, onto the carpet at her feet. When she'd tried to breathe breath back into him, his lips were still warm.

Talia's sympathy for Dr. Cohn grew in equal measure to her guilt over the way she'd treated her. She couldn't help but picture a woman of Dr. Cohn's petite stature attempting to lower her adult son to the floor and frantically resuscitate him while she waited for the ambulance to arrive.

The growing tightness in Talia's chest could not be reasoned with. She felt as if she had swallowed a hand grenade.

Suddenly the vision of her own mother lying on a hotel floor covered in blood, a string of pearls wrapped around her neck, then a vision of the father she couldn't remember—the soldier she had seen in the picture above the Emersons' fireplace—lying in an old abandoned mine for years, with a bullet in his head—came into focus.

At that moment, a brutal truth dawned on Talia.

She realized her struggle to rise above her grief and over the tragedies in her life—losing Russ, losing her parents, losing her identity for so many years—was pointless. Here was proof in plain sight: the counselor who was supposed to be saving her from drowning in self-pity was instead beckoning to Talia from her own wreckage beneath the waves.

Out of the corner of her eye, Talia caught a glimpse of Regina. The girl had slipped off her shoes and was rocking herself in her chair, her right arm in its sling, the other wrapped around her folded knees, her bare feet on the seat of her chair. She looked like a small child. Perhaps that was because she wasn't much older than a child. Talia imagined the depths of her grief after losing her baby. It must have been incredibly difficult, at her age, to be in so much distress and in a foreign place where she didn't even speak the language.

A glance around the room suggested that everybody present was experiencing similar levels of distress and anguish. It was everywhere, inescapable. The crushing gravity of it all rose with every passing second, reaching levels of suffocating tangibility. Suddenly Talia couldn't focus on what Dr. Cohn was saying anymore. All she could think about was how she'd become so overwhelmed and physically drained.

Lacking the strength to make her way to an exit, she lowered herself back down to the carpeted floor, crossed her legs in front of her, and leaned her head against the wall behind her. The biting realization that she could no longer avoid the inevitable was growing. That grenade she'd felt in her chest on so many occasions was really going to go off this time. She closed her eyes, squeezing them tightly, trying to ward off the reckoning she knew was well past due.

And then she finally cracked.

Not like an oak being split in two by a lightning bolt. Instead, like the slow splintering of fine crystal—coming apart in a thousand tiny fissures, releasing what had been held back for so long. The corners of her mouth twitched and twisted violently, as if she were possessed by something malevolent. An involuntary quivering began in her chin and rippled across her face in unchecked spasms.

Once the tempest of emotion had begun, it was unstoppable. Years of bottled-up fury and sorrow ripped its way out of her eyes in a ferocious torrent. She simply sat where she was, sobbing desperately into her clenched fists, oblivious to any sense of comportment and her surroundings.

Time stopped.

Talia didn't know how long she sat there, sobbing like a child. A soft hand on her shoulder eventually brought her back to the room. She looked up and saw the bruised face of Regina Delgado Juarez looking down at her, tears of concern in the girl's eyes. In a gesture that transcended culture and language and circumstance, Regina dropped to her knees, wrapping her arm around Talia. Together, they poured out their grief. The display of empathy from someone whose need was greater than her own was Talia's final leveling. She truly let go. Any effort to retain a secure mooring in the crazy storm that was her life—Talia let it all go.

Dr. Cohn had just shown the entire hall how grief should be managed.

Grief was not meant to be repressed or buried with the dead. Grief was meant to be totally and wholly embraced. It was to be worn courageously, like a medal of honor, hard-won through fearless and enduring love. This truth sat heavily with Talia as she reflected on how she had handled losing Russ. Her stubborn refusal to shed tears or acknowledge her pain over losing the man she had loved so much had cost her dearly. Putting reason over emotion had robbed her of the gift that only grieving could give her—the riches that remained in the shadow of true and enduring love.

The universe's selection of victims was indeed random. Each one of the women in the hall had experienced a tragic and uniquely painful loss, yet they were all connected—like a string of paper hearts—by a common thread. That thread was love. It was not possible to experience grief if you had not first loved. But Talia, in her efforts to spare herself, had made a ghost of grief. It was no wonder, then, that she had been haunted for so many years.

She realized now that she had done this all her life—exorcised her grief through measures of anger or self-loathing—instead of embracing grief for what it truly was: love's translation of immeasurable loss.

CHAPTER 25

TALIA'S WAKE

T alia sat in the parking lot of Riley's school, holding a paper cup of melting ice to her forehead. It was all she had left of the cold drink she had grabbed from a fast-food joint on the way to pick up Riley. Lupe had been gracious enough to drive Regina back to the shelter after the grief counseling meeting.

Talia checked her face in the rearview mirror again. Her eyelids were still puffy, and her very red nose was in critical need of powder. She regretted her shortsightedness in never having owned any face powder—or any makeup at all, for that matter. She didn't want Riley seeing her like that. The child was too sharp—she never missed a thing—and knowing her mother was upset would worry her.

Talia blew her nose on a soggy napkin and put her sunglasses back on. She practiced smiling in the rearview mirror a few times and then again while she took her time walking up the stairs to the main entrance of Sierra Vista Elementary School.

She thought about what she had learned regarding Dr. Cohn that morning. In the months she'd been meeting with her, Talia had decided she and Dr. Cohn were about as good of a match as an overextended credit card and a department store sale. She had seen their therapeutic relationship as a necessary evil. One that had the potential to be quite painful. If Talia were to share her complicated feelings about Russ's death and what had really happened to him that night up on Sycamore Ridge, she might open wounds that would never heal.

Before today, she had taken Dr. Cohn for the kind of woman who thrived on detachment and who had been untouched by suffering—and Talia had wanted to be just like her in that regard. She'd wanted to spare herself the pain of self-recrimination for the guilt she was carrying about how Russ had died. But now she understood there was no high ground, no shelter from grief. Dr. Cohn did not possess a road map to painless self-preservation; she was struggling to endure the double-edged sword of love, just like Talia and all those other women at the meeting who had suffered losses.

As she reached the main entrance of Riley's school, the loud drill of the bell announced the day was over. The classroom doors across the courtyard swung open, and a colorful flood of children streamed onto the playground, their shrieks of joy only amplifying the depths of Talia's melancholy. She felt her chin quiver—realizing with chagrin that she was now officially a crier— as she scanned the playground for Riley's bright face. The child tackled her from behind with a shrill giggle and a tight hug.

Later that afternoon, Talia sat on the floor of her living room with her sister.

Naomi had been uncharacteristically quick to return Talia's phone call and had shown up an hour later with a huge bag of Chinese takeout and a large bottle of ice-cold Thai beer. Naomi did most of the eating and, for once, Talia did most of the drinking.

In the backyard, Riley and Elizabeth, Naomi's youngest daughter, were throwing a ball for Toby.

Naomi wasn't interested in Talia's admission that she had finally broken her two-year-long no-cry streak. Talia doubted Naomi was capable of comprehending such a colossal accomplishment in the first place. While she found Naomi's indifference slightly wounding, Talia had to recognize that she herself had once admired a perceived detachment in Dr. Cohn. Everybody had their own unique relationship with grief, and she acknowledged that Naomi's was probably a complicated one.

"You know, Talia, you're going to have to get on with life. Big deal—you friggin' cried! Jesus, it's not the end of the damn world. I don't know why you've always had to play these stupid competitive games with yourself. Nobody else cares if you carry the weight of the world on your shoulders and never show any signs of cracking. You are human, you know."

Talia gave her sister a long, cold stare, though she doubted anyone could take her seriously while her nose was as red as a clown's. Hell, Talia knew she needed to move on. She *was* moving on, but it had been a rough day. Couldn't Naomi see that?

"You should take a vacation. Get away for a while. Leave Riley with us and take a trip by yourself. You need a break, and we both know you can afford one now."

Talia rolled her eyes; she had never considered taking a vacation without Riley. It was out of the question. She filled her glass again from the tall bottle of beer and sat quietly, using her chopsticks to pick the pineapple chunks out of her fried rice, pretending to ignore her sister. She briefly considered telling Naomi she had been going to counseling, that she was over it now and had every intention of moving on, but before she could weigh the odds of such an admission, Naomi was driving her point again. "What about going somewhere tropical, reading a good book, and just finding some peace? Maybe even meeting a handsome new man?"

Talia took another swig of beer, this time straight from the bottle. If she told Naomi she'd even been considering dating again, it would somehow feel like disloyalty to Russ. On the two occasions she'd mentioned Sam to Naomi, her sister had shown more than a little interest in learning more about him, especially after she'd seen him working in his front yard in a pair of shorts and a sweaty T-shirt.

"I'll think about it," Talia replied flatly, clearly not contemplating a tropical vacation. Naomi shot her a dubious glance while rescuing the bottle of beer from her sister's clutches.

Just then, Riley poked her head in from the back door, breathing hard from running around the yard with Elizabeth and Toby. Her face was beaming.

"Momma, can Lizbeth sleep over again tonight? Please, please, please?"

"You'll have to ask Aunty Naomi," Talia said, standing to clear the leftovers from the coffee table.

"I've got a better idea," Naomi said as she wrestled the bag of fortune cookies away from Talia. "There's no school tomorrow. Why don't you come home with us? You two can sleep in Elizabeth's new bunk beds tonight. I'm sure she won't mind if you take the top, right, Lizzie?"

"Yeah!" the girls cheered together.

"Can I, Momma? Please?"

"Why not? I'm smart enough to know when I'm outnumbered."

Naomi opened a fortune cookie and gave her sister a sly look as she popped it into her mouth. "That way, your mom doesn't have any excuses for tomorrow morning. She'll have to keep her plans to go kayaking with the very handsome and charming neighbor man."

"Ugh," Talia groaned. She had forgotten all about the kayaking plans. There was probably no way out of it this late in the game. "Smooth," she said, snatching a fortune cookie from her sister. "You're a real sweetheart."

Naomi answered with only a wicked chuckle.

CHAPTER 26

EULOGY

Talia stood with Toby at the bottom of the driveway, watching Naomi and the girls pull away in Naomi's brand-new Mercedes convertible. She had replaced her one-year-old BMW the same week she and Talia had received the first bank transfers from their grandfather's estate in Australia. Riley waved, grinning fiercely from her car seat behind her cousin. She'd lost a front tooth in the previous week, and Talia couldn't help but laugh at the sight of her sweet, gap-toothed smile and the pure joy on her face.

The evening was cool and still. The sun had just dipped behind the mountains, and the wispy web of clouds in the western sky hung like a sheet of pastel chiffon above the Santa Monica Mountains. On the hill behind her house, a massive oak stood proudly, its dark silhouette in stark contrast to the glowing full moon snared in its crooked arms.

Talia walked with purpose, and Toby swung his tail as he followed her past the houses on their quiet street to the trailhead, where the forest waited in the long, cool shadows. The gallon-size jug of water at her side bumped into her leg with every step, and she shifted it from hand to hand as she usually did on her way up the steep, rocky incline. Toby scrambled ahead and waited for her at the top of the trail; he knew where they were going—not through any sixth sense but because Riley was not with them, and Talia was carrying the gallon of water. Talia would not bring her daughter to this place, not yet.

She crested the hill and followed the narrow trail as it curved to the left and dipped into a small gully that had been dry since the previous winter's storms. Natural limestone stairs wound around the dry banks and under the canopy of oaks, near a plateau where she'd rolled a small rock to sit on when she came this way. Talia unscrewed the top of the water jug and set it down heavily at her feet, her aching fingers glad to be free of the punishing weight. The white oak sapling at her feet looked frail and thirsty. It was only slightly taller than a switch, and now it sported five small round-edged leaves. The infant tree struggled to hold up its arms and be noticed, hoping to be counted one day among its giant brothers lining the deeper creases of the valley.

Talia had planted it there the year after the fire, on Russ's birthday. She had been coming to water it once a week during the dry months. It was tall enough now that she could remove the cage of chicken wire protecting it from wildlife. There had been no substantial rain since late spring, and the earth at the base of the sapling swallowed the water greedily. With the tips of her fingers, Talia packed the soil around the small trunk. She piled a few more stones around it, hoping to secure the sapling's roots a little more firmly to the earth until it could forge a stronger hold of its own.

She sat for a while in the twilight, studying the little tree with its shiny leaves and thinking about Russel and how much her life had changed since he'd left. He had loved her more than she had ever deserved, she thought. She hadn't known how he'd found the patience to always show her kindness, even when she was being unreasonable, but he always had. He'd been naturally skilled in finding the right words to soothe her anxieties without ever making her feel needy or weak.

While she'd often wondered if he had lacked the ability to discern how infrequently she'd deserved his love, Talia was always grateful to him for giving it to her so freely. And there was no question Russ had loved their daughter more than life itself. Riley was lucky to have had such a caring and playful father. He was unlike any dad Talia had encountered in her own childhood, and she had never taken Russ's parenting abilities for granted. He'd loved reading to Riley and exploring the wonders of nature with her. The two had shared a passion for all creatures, including snakes, lizards, and frogs. Unfortunately, Riley had also developed a love of horses. This love, however, was not learned from Russ but from her mother.

The first time Talia had taken Riley to visit a herd of mares corralled at Sycamore Ridge, the child had been immediately entranced by the gentle giants. She'd insisted they return as often as possible. Since the equestrian center was only a thirty-minute drive from home, Talia had made it a weekly adventure. It wasn't long before Riley had a favorite horse at the corral: a large gray mare named Mia, who was the alpha female of the herd. Mia was a spirited beast; she kept the other horses in check but also mothered the herd. The mare was always calm and patient with humans, exceptionally so with Riley, even when the child failed to show any caution around the huge creatures or when she insisted on introducing Nay-Nay, her stuffed toy horse, to each member of the herd. It was Riley's idea to ask Russ to join them on one of their weekly visits to feed the mares. She and Talia usually brought chopped apples and celery greens for the horses.

When Talia heard Russ's three-man engine company had been overrun by smoke and flames during the brushfire on Sycamore Ridge, she guessed what Russ had been doing up there. When she finally gained access to the department's report on the incident, her suspicions would be confirmed.

The Santa Ana winds were whipping the flames from the eastern grass-lands toward the coastline with fury that night. The combination of flying embers and raging winds had resulted in several spot fires being ignited throughout the area. There was a confluence of active burns threatening a massive area south of town, stretching from the 101 all the way out to the coast, eight miles to the west. The raging wildfire generated additional winds and fire whirls, tornadic formations of intense heat that sprang up in proximity to the main fire, exacerbating the spread of the firestorm.

Resources were stretched thin that night, and the battle was on to save property and lives in the dry areas between the foothills and the coast. By midnight, several homesteads on the high ridges overlooking the valley to the west had already been lost, despite aggressive suppression efforts. The fire was spreading quickly, and there had been little time for a proper evacuation. In some areas, there was only one way out of the hills, and typically, these mountainous routes included steep, winding, narrow canyon roads. Traveling along these corridors could be dangerous under the best of circumstances, but an emergency evacuation in the dead of night compounded the risks. The fire was completely uncontained, and Russ would have known that, despite residential evacuations, there had been no time to round up or evacuate livestock in the canyon. The horses at the equestrian center up on Sycamore Ridge would have been trapped, with no chance of escape.

At 1:33 a.m., fire command dispatchers reported Sycamore Ridge Equestrian Complex was downwind from, and directly in the path of, the oncoming firestorm.

Despite her persistent inquiries over the following year, Talia would find no evidence Russ had sought permission from fire command to head in the direction of the equestrian center, nor had he been ordered to do so. This would prove to be the lynchpin of the ensuing investigation into the incident.

The report from Russ's engine driver, Tony Castaldo, a seven-year veteran of the department, indicated that at 1:40 a.m., Russ and his crew had taken the initiative to head up the gravel road to the equestrian center, six miles from the campground where they were stationed.

When they arrived, Russ and his crew estimated it would be less than five minutes before the entire ridge was overrun by the approaching firestorm. Fire knockdown would be impossible. There was absolutely no time to spare. The air was thick with smoke despite the howling wind coming over the ridge from the east. Transporting panicked horses under these circumstances would have been impossible, even if a trailer had been available. The closest structures to the corral, an enclosed riding arena and an old barn, were engulfed in flames within seconds of the engine company's arrival. Despite the proximity of a functioning hydrant, Castaldo reported, fire-suppression efforts with a three-man crew would have been futile.

The men didn't know if any horses were in the barn, but it was already too late to reach them. The nearby open corral, with its large lean-to, housed seven mares. The horses were panicking and tearing around the interior of the corral in a circular stampede. Russ ordered his driver, Castaldo, to turn the engine around on the narrow lane between the corral and a stand of oaks. He was to be prepared for immediate evacuation back down the canyon when Russ returned. Russel then exited the fire engine, taking with him a pair of bolt cutters. He was wearing standard protective gear but did not take the time to put on his air pack or breathing apparatus. He told his crew he would be gone for less than a minute—he intended only to unlock the gate of the corral and give the horses a chance to escape. The third man on the crew,

Mike Peet, a rookie, reported Russ made a dash toward the north-facing corral gate as Castaldo turned the engine around.

Russ disappeared into the night, his flashlight sweeping wildly through thick ash and showers of glowing embers. Approximately a minute later, several horses were seen charging out of the arena, away from the oncoming flames and down toward the coastline. Russel did not return, however, nor did he respond to radio calls. Despite the growing wall of rapidly approaching flames and the high winds, the two remaining crewmen put on their breathing apparatuses and went in search of their engineer. The fence railing surrounding the corral was in flames and melting in front of their eyes. The conflagration raging in the barn had sparked a crown fire in the adjacent stand of oaks, above the heads of the two remaining crewmembers.

Through the smoke and ash, the engine driver and the rookie fireman spotted Russ at the far end of the corral. He was attempting to free a large gray mare. The animal had become ensnared in the wire fencing when she'd tried to escape the corral through a second gate. She was on her side, thrashing about, with her back legs entangled in the wire. Before the men could make their way to their engineer, a giant fire whirl formed in the middle of the corral, separating Russ from his crew. Castaldo reported the tornadic flame was more than forty feet tall and at least ten feet wide. He and the rookie were overcome by the tremendous heat of the fire whirl, the temperature of which likely exceeded two thousand degrees. Russ and the trapped mare were directly in the path of the twister; a rescue would have been impossible. Without his breathing apparatus, Russ had no chance of surviving the gases and high temperatures of the twister. The remaining two crewmembers, now in grave danger, barely made it back to the engine before the entire stand of oaks was incinerated.

On the morning of October 22, 1995, at 2:03 a.m., Los Angeles Fire Department engineer Russel James Brighton, a ten-year veteran of the department, was not responding to repeated radio calls. His retreating crew, outflanked on both sides of the narrow road by flames, only just made it out of the canyon as the entire mountainside behind them was overrun by flames.

The following morning, seven exhausted horses, including a large gray mare, were found on a beach in Malibu.

Russ's last act was one of unselfish love for his daughter and wife. Talia respected him for his brave and noble intentions, but she bitterly resented the choices he'd made that night. He had been their hero, but his heroic act had affected their lives in ways Riley and Talia had yet to fully comprehend.

She knew she couldn't change what had happened. Russ had taken a chance, and it had cost him everything. It had cost them all.

At times Talia had found herself outright angry at Russ for his actions, but those spells were usually short-lived. She was also angry at herself. There had been a thousand times she had regretted ever taking Riley up to Sycamore Ridge to visit the horses. Over time, though, she had learned not to dwell on this pointless obsession. She and Riley were lucky to have had such a kind and principled man in their lives, even for the brief time they shared with him. It was Talia's responsibility now to make sure neither she nor Riley focused on their loss or what could have been. They needed to cherish the memories they had.

After seeing Dr. Cohn's raw pain revealed in the bereavement support group, Talia understood love and grief were simply two sides of the same coin.

Life was complicated, and sometimes it even seemed unbearable. But the minute Talia thought she could not endure a moment more of suffering, she realized she had already proven she could. She was immensely capable of withstanding the insufferable. For those who chose to live a life devoid of love, there were fewer risks and arguably less suffering. This was perhaps how Miriam had chosen to live her life, without the courage to love. And who could know where the turning point had been for her? Her early years had been challenging. Perhaps she had been innocent and trusting once. No one's path was ever easy or without consequence.

In time, thoughts of Miriam were swept away like smoke in the wind. In the end, Talia's letting go of her did not come from resentment, or even from forgiveness, but from a cool and clear-minded choice to focus on what had already been sacrificed and the bright future that lay ahead for her and Riley.

That night, Talia had a dream. In many ways, it felt like so much more than that, though. And perhaps it was. Perhaps it was a vision—a vivid and compelling vision—that left her both bewildered by and resigned to the predicament that lay ahead for her.

She was alone in a canoe at nightfall, gliding on the glassy surface of a waterway in a steep-walled canyon. Night was closing in, and the darkness of the canal was silent as she drifted along. Embedded high in the canyon's cliffs were dozens of ancient, abandoned dwellings carved from the rock face. Their dark doorways beckoned to her, but the canoe drifted steadily along on its predestined course. As the boat rounded a bend, the canyon fell away, and the land stretched out in flat pastures on either side of what was now a slow-moving stream. The full moon hung heavily over the horizon, its soft light illuminating an orchard on the bank. Instead of fruit trees, the orchard was populated by rows of headless mannequins, all dressed in elaborate ivory-colored wedding gowns, that stretched as far as the eye could see. Talia reached her hand down into the stream, trying to slow the canoe so that she might look at the puzzling scene awhile longer, but the boat held its course, and she was compelled to withdraw her hand from the water, which was as thick and warm as a river of blood.

Dr. Cohn would have had a field day with the dream. Talia wouldn't mention it to her. She doubted they would be seeing each other again. Relationships sometimes run their course and then simply peter out. Besides, her eighteen sessions were up, and she could think of no reason to continue her visits. Talia did not want a professional interpretation of her surreal dream.

When she was quiet, she could hear the soft musings of her own consciousness, like gentle wind chimes calling her to the truth. She knew she would have to heed the wisdom of this tender voice. The truth came from somewhere unconstrained by doubt and imagination. It was clear, just, and undeniable.

Somehow Talia could answer her own questions with clarity beyond her understanding. The waterway in her dream represented the river of tears she had finally released. The vacant dwellings in the cliff symbolized the abandonments in her past. The headless mannequins in their ivory wedding gowns were the embodiment of her irrational fear of commitment in relationships. The darkness of the night reflected her apprehension of death and what lay beyond, and the bright, full moon represented her own consciousness, illuminating these truths so that she could better navigate the river of life.

No, there was no need for professional help on this one. *When all is said and done in life,* Talia told herself, *everyone is really on their own.* No one else can chart a course of action or make decisions about someone else's future. We must come to know ourselves, and if we are to truly love anyone, we must first come to love ourselves. This takes great courage, but we owe ourselves that much.

EPILOGUE

Sam's kayak bounced over the surface of the waves, making small clapping sounds as they paddled away from the shore. The water of the Pacific was a deep shade of indigo and bitingly cold. Along the horizon, the sky was azure and cloudless, and the ocean spread out in a vast, flat spectacle, with only an occasional swell to break the straight line of the horizon. Morning sunlight bounced off the water in eye-piercing, quicksilver streaks. Despite what she'd hoped, Sam had not forgotten Talia had agreed to join him that morning for an excursion. Since he had picked her up, she had made every effort to avoid direct eye contact, but she was otherwise doing her best to be genial.

"Follow my lead," he called. Talia watched Sam's broad back as he swung his paddle from side to side, stroking the water effortlessly. His bare shoulders were tan and surprisingly muscular, with a youthful smattering of freckles that peeped out from under his life jacket. "What you want to do is stay in sync with me. Watch my stroke and do your best to follow. I should really be sitting behind you, but I figured this would be easier for me to show you what you should be doing. We can trade off later, if you like. Right now, you should be concentrating on steering like I showed you earlier. That's your job today."

Wonderful, she thought. They could end up in Hawaii before the trip was over.

"Aye aye, Captain," she muttered. They had only been out on the water a few minutes, but already Talia's arms were aching from the effort. She looked over her shoulder to the shoreline, wondering how cold the swim back to land would be and whether the tide would be kind enough to do the work for her if she were to go overboard.

"Well, this *is* fun, but it's also a bit of work, especially if you don't know what you're doing." Talia laughed, doing her best to sound cheerful despite her paddle colliding awkwardly with Sam's.

Was she making it obvious she wasn't comfortable in the situation?

Sam chuckled, a deep, manly murmur—rich like warm syrup running over a stack of pancakes. He apparently had enough confidence in himself for both of them.

"It's like anything else—you can learn how if you really want to." He was quiet for a moment before adding, "If there were a way to paddle this thing using those runner's legs of yours, we'd be passing the Channel Islands by now."

Talia wondered when Sam had had a chance to observe her runner's legs. She shifted her feet self-consciously in the small puddle of overflow water in the bottom of the kayak and put her paddle to work. When she'd thought she was seeing Russ in the woods near home, had it simply been Sam? Sam and Russ were about the same height, she realized now.

"Not so fast, Pocahontas. You gotta let me take the lead." Sam was laughing again.

Talia felt silly and awkward. She was glad he was facing away from her and couldn't see the flush on her cheeks.

They were almost half a mile out when a pod of dolphins swept by them, their dorsal fins cresting the delicate waves of the water and dipping playfully back under. Their beautiful, sleek forms slipped in and out of the swells but stayed notably close, as though just as curious about Talia and Sam.

In her excitement at seeing them, Talia leaned across Sam's shoulder and almost sent them both overboard. "Steady, mate," he said, reaching around and grabbing her arm. His hand was strong and reassuring, even through his paddling glove, and it steadied them both.

Talia leaned back in her seat, waiting for the boat to stop rocking. Her heart was pounding. Sam turned the kayak with one sweeping J-stroke, and they watched the pod distance themselves from their small craft.

When they were ready to move on again, Talia put her paddle back to work, trying to follow Sam's lead. They pulled together, powering their way over the swells and toward the endless horizon. Talia's gut was tight—a mixture of excitement and unease—as they surged ahead, farther and farther from shore. The rhythmic stroking of their paddles drew them away from comfort and familiarity and toward the vast unknown. The motion was fluid, musical, and exhilarating. Spray from Sam's paddle splashed Talia's face, showering her in a chilling cascade that made her gasp and then laugh out loud. The more he apologized, the funnier it seemed to her. The boat rocked with their laughter.

Finally, Talia settled down, bracing the boat against the swells with her paddle lowered, the way Sam was showing her.

Her throat tightened with the realization of how few times she had laughed out loud in the last two years. She felt her eyes filling with tears. Though she tried to blink them back, they spilled over silently and rolled down her cheeks, mixing with the cool salt water on her face. She tried to clear her mind of all that had transpired in the past few weeks and focus on the task at hand. Wiping her nose on her wet forearm, she settled back into the paddling before Sam could notice her hesitation. Within minutes, the motion had become familiar and comfortable. She began to count in her mind, just like she did on her trail runs. *One, two, three, four; one, two, three . . .*

She pushed past her regret and her annoying tears, plowing through the water with strong strokes, thinking only of swallowing the sea air in long, slow breaths. Sam responded to her surge of energy with powerful, graceful paddling. Even to Talia's untrained eye, his precision and skill were commanding. He drew Talia along with him, compelling her to follow his every move. They were one with the ocean, with all its power and serenity, and they pulled together with the strength of wild horses as they swept their way toward the horizon.

Talia's heart soared, and she felt renewed. Everything fell away except the sound of their paddles breaking the water and the warmth of the sun on her shoulders. *One, two, three, four.* They continued this way for what seemed an eternity. She didn't tire or weaken, only wanting what lay ahead.

After a while, they rested, gazing out at the thin blue line separating the sea from the sky. Talia could not say how long they lingered there, taking in the enormity of their surroundings. Time seemed immeasurable in that vast blue world where their tiny craft bobbed. Her misgivings faded away like distant memories of half-forgotten dreams, leaving her with an appreciation for the extraordinary completeness of the present moment.

Sam was quiet, too, perhaps preferring to forgo the mediocrity of language while in the bosom of that cerulean sanctuary. He eventually turned them toward the mountains, and they headed back to the distant, pale beach.

Talia closed her eyes for a moment, resting her paddle across her knees, and listened to the mesmerizingly soft effort of Sam's breath and the gentle lapping of water against the hull. She turned her face to the sun and tried to retain the essence of that moment—to capture a memory she might need to conjure in the future to dispel fear or sorrow.

Her closed eyes filled with tears, but she made no attempt to stem their flow. Out in the light, where there were no shadows to hide behind, a simple truth came to her: life, with all its pain and all its glory, was to be seized with both hands, *just like this*, one exquisite and fleeting moment at a time.

END

www.ingramcontent.com/pod-product-compliance
Lightning Source LLC
Chambersburg PA
CBHW020124120726
47903CB00007B/2087